TEENAGE GIRLS CAN BE DEMONS

HAILEY PIPER

TITAN BOOKS

Teenage Girls Can Be Demons
Print edition ISBN: 9781835411469
E-book edition ISBN: 9781835411476

Published by Titan Books
A division of Titan Publishing Group Ltd
144 Southwark Street, London SE1 0UP
www.titanbooks.com

First edition: September 2025
10 9 8 7 6 5 4 3 2 1

This is a work of fiction. All of the characters, organizations, and events portrayed in this novel are either products of the author's imagination or are used fictitiously. Any resemblance to actual persons, living or dead (except for satirical purposes), is entirely coincidental.

© Hailey Piper 2025
Hailey Piper asserts the moral right to be identified as the author of this work.

No part of this publication may be reproduced, stored in a retrieval system, or transmitted, in any form or by any means without the prior written permission of the publisher, nor be otherwise circulated in any form of binding or cover other than that in which it is published and without a similar condition being imposed on the subsequent purchaser.

A CIP catalogue record for this title is available from the British Library.

EU RP (for authorities only)
eucomply OÜ, Pärnu mnt. 139b-14, 11317 Tallinn, Estonia
hello@eucompliancepartner.com, +3375690241

Printed and bound by CPI (UK) Ltd, Croydon, CR0 4YY.

"*Teenage Girls Can Be Demons* is Hailey Piper at her best. In a publishing world where the novel reigns supreme, here a collection is the only way to really get to know the multiplicity of Piper's work. Harrowing, scary, and raw, most often all in the same story, with topics that range from the surreal, to the nostalgic, to the all-too-real. Terrific."

ADAM CESARE, Bram Stoker Award®-winning, *USA Today* bestselling author of *Clown in a Cornfield* and *Influencer*

"Nobody writes grounded cosmic horror like Hailey Piper. That might seem like a contradiction in terms, but read these thirteen wild—and wildly different—tales and get a taste of just how Piper can twist you into otherworldly shapes while still reminding you of your essential, heartbreaking humanity."

NAT CASSIDY, bestselling author of *When the Wolf Comes Home* and *Mary*

"Powerful, wickedly clever, and deeply intimate, Hailey Piper delivers a searing and entertaining anthology that speaks to the female rage of becoming. Delightfully and thoughtfully drawn."

DAWN KURTAGICH, bestselling author of *The Thorns*

"*Teenage Girls Can Be Demons* is sure to be a standout collection in 2025. Check out this fabulous and fearsome book as soon as you can."

GWENDOLYN KISTE, Three-time Bram Stoker Award®-winning author of *The Rust Maidens* and *The Haunting of Velkwood*

"With a delicious focus on rage and transformation, Hailey Piper's second collection offers up tales that are as bold as they are beautiful. Piper's ability to dive into the gooey substance that makes humans both fascinating and horrifying is such a marvelous strength. A demonically good time that you don't want to miss!"

SARA TANTLINGER, Bram Stoker Award®-winning author of *The Devil's Dreamland*

*Also by Hailey Piper
and available from Titan Books*

A LIGHT MOST HATEFUL
ALL THE HEARTS YOU EAT

CONTENTS

Why We Keep Exploding	*1*
Unkindly Girls	*15*
The Long Flesh of the Law	*29*
Thagomizer	*51*
Without a Face	*63*
Last Leaf of an Ursine Tree	*75*
Hopscotch for Keeps	*85*
Magical Girls Child Crusader Squad	*95*
Autotomy	*121*
The Turning	*135*
We Who Hold the Median	*149*
The Many Sins of Clara Greenstone	*161*
Benny Rose the Cannibal King	*195*

TEENAGE GIRLS CAN BE DEMONS

"Maybe I was never a child. Maybe I'm tendons
and ligaments wrapped in gauze. Maybe this is
all something else and none of this matters?"
—*Cynthia Pelayo,* Crime Scene

"Everyone expects you to just be happy.
Everyone acts like it's over, but it doesn't feel
that way. Everyone wants to sweep it under
the rug as if it never happened. But it's still
happening. I... I'm angry. I'm so very angry."
—*Ally Malinenko,* This Appearing House

WHY WE KEEP EXPLODING

Just a joke

The first girl explodes on the final evening of orientation weekend.

Allison Greer, Sutton University freshman, joins us in the dining hall, where all levels of college kids pack the inside, clacking dishes and loud voices bounding off every surface. Beneath that cacophony, no freshman would fear silence.

The boys who join us at our table are upperclassmen. They forego hoodies and torn jeans for stiff button-downs and slacks, like they have job interviews scheduled after dinner. Juniors? I can't say for sure.

The tallest, a blond boy with razor-straight teeth and a narrow face, sits across from Allison. I can't make out their conversation through the noise, but he points repeatedly to a cup of yellow liquid, likely beer, and then taps a penny on the tabletop, and I understand this is some kind of challenge.

She tells him she doesn't like games. When he doesn't let up, she curses him and throws her glass of fountain soda into his face.

I stare, awestruck, while Tall-Boy sputters. Shaking my head always felt like drawing too much attention, let alone cursing and splashing. I dread the glint in others' eyes, how I'll turn from *human* to *thing* in the flick of an internal switch the moment they realize I'm different. Vocal training hasn't come as easily to me as other girls still recovering from early testosterone infection. Some self-teach or find others to teach them. A few like their voices and insist everyone else had better deal with it.

I should be grateful that silence is my friend, that others don't clock me at a glance and figure out how I'm different from other girls. Lucky little Laurie started estro at fourteen.

Most days, I keep strict posture and bite my tongue. I would never throw soda into anyone's face. Had Tall-Boy challenged me instead of Allison, I would have agreed to whatever game he wanted. Boys like him twist sorcery on their tongues. They insist you play with them, and I'm easily witched.

Allison is my heroine for a few brief moments. She turns to stride from the table, a victorious warrior abandoning a corpse-choked battlefield. Carbonized droplets skitter down Tall-Boy's face while his friends laugh at him.

But then he weaves sorcery. "Chill, sweetie," he says, wiping a paper napkin down his face.

She turns to snap at him, dark hair coiling: "Chill yourself, asshole. Goodbye."

He leans over the table, and I see the witchcraft swirl in his piercing eyes. "Somebody has an attitude problem," he says. "It was just a joke."

Allison's lip curls back, but she hesitates. Her gaze darts back and forth, uncertain, sizing up witnesses and how they might judge her reaction. Was she the kind of girl who couldn't take a joke? She had to get her words just right or else see the dining hall condemn her a stuck-up killjoy for all time.

"Try—" she starts, fighting tooth and nail to get the words out. "Try. Being. Funny."

Tall-Boy turns on his *debate me* voice. "Humor's subjective," he says, smooth and smarmy. "Asking me to adjust for you when we barely know each other, that's completely irrational." His eyes stab through her, reading when she'll try to speak again. He doesn't let her. "Just a joke," he repeats, this time coated in slime.

Allison's lips fight her face to make words. I don't know what she would say if she could speak. I would like to.

Instead, the silence clamps over Allison's paling complexion, her dark hair shimmering with milky starlight. She clutches her gut, as if the unspoken words now burn her belly. Her legs stagger back from the table.

Tall-Boy and his friends lean in, like they know what's about to happen. Sorcerers must have that power.

Allison's skin ripples. Every muscle twitches. If there's a sound building toward what's about to happen, I can't hear it beneath the dining hall din, Allison rendered silent. I read words in her face, the ones that have done this. Just a joke. Attitude problem. Irrational.

And then she has no face. Her body flashes out, a sudden supernova of white light and viscera. I cover my eyes, but the boys keep looking, their heat oozing over the table, dwarfing Allison's cold, starlit explosion.

She doesn't even scream.

When I finally uncover my eyes, there's nothing left of Allison. The white-light explosion has burned away her every cell. She's erased, the boys having silenced her forever.

I'm not the only one looking—the place where she stood has the entire dining hall's attention except for Tall-Boy and his friends. They're looking around, making sure this explosion has been seen and understood.

They meant to make an example of her, and they have.

They leave us then, point made. We freshman girls sit quietly, out of respect for our deceased hallmate. The moment of silence stretches to dinner's end. Back in the dorms, someone is sobbing.

Not me. I've seen quiet horror. In high school, boys used to silence with fists and boots; here they use words. This is the way of college.

Have my hallmates absorbed the lesson?

Quiet girls don't get clocked. We aren't made examples.

Quiet girls don't explode.

Emotional

I watch the chattier freshman girls when crossing the quad or getting coffee at the open-air campus center—the ones who haven't learned.

One of Tall-Boy's friends reminds me that silence is a blessing. He circles the chatty girls, a shark sizing up swimmers, and intrudes with his *debate me* voice, egging the girls to engage him on human rights or politics or some superhero movie. Given time, one will speak, and then he mocks, and interrupts, and chastises. He puts her in her place. When she's upset, he calls her "emotional," and it's a silencing nail hammered through her tongue. She's learning terror, one syllable at a time.

Unspoken words can't escape. I watch her swallow them, and they stew in her guts like trapped gas in a mine. The more she tries to talk, the worse the pressure. It's slow for some girls, quick for others. Sometimes, when crossing campus, I hear a distant eruption, and I know we've lost another.

Survival requires silence. This is the way of college.

When do the boys turn from freshmen to sorcerers?

Who teaches them the silence spell-words?

Why don't they warn us before it's too late?

Allison wouldn't have come here had she known what Tall-Boy's tongue would do to her. She wasn't the type to be silent.

Except getting a rise from her was Tall-Boy's game. She didn't know better—how could any of us? Freshmen mouths might spit fire, but we know nothing of spell-words.

Our fingers are smarter. On the way out of the dining hall one evening, I steal a knife.

Irrational

Alone in the dormitory shower, I slide the knife down my upper arm and cut a small letter into my skin—A. The shape is ragged; the blade could be sharper. I tell myself that this is how I'll remember Allison when we took no selfies together; there is no body, no candlelight vigil.

We're afraid our gathering at campus center will lure the boys. They would hear our sneakers squeaking across cobblestone and be drawn like sharks to blood in the water.

I want the second letter to be L, and then L-I-S-O-N, but I'm no longer certain Allison had two L's. Instead of overthinking it, I let the blade take over.

Knives have always made sense to me. Hormone therapy has treated my features down to a cellular level, but deeper than that, our flesh holds bad habits holy. I thought I quit cutting myself in middle school, but a smoker smokes when the chips are down, and a cutter cuts. Transition during high school only pressed the pause button.

Still, I haven't been trapped in that *what am I?* body for years. Things have changed, even the cutting.

When I glance at the knife's work, I find the A is not the beginning, but the center. Before it, I've carved J-U-S-T. After, I've carved a J. I finish what the knife began and carve O-K-E myself.

I carve further spell-words. It's nothing like my old cutting: every bleeding stroke less about dulling psychological pain, and more about creating protective sigils. Silence spells will find themselves carved in my skin and scurry back to their masters. The boys can't witch me with words I've bled.

That's the theory, anyway.

Smile

There's a trick to keeping boys from telling you to smile. Most girls ignore or retort, but "smile" here is another silence spell. No comebacks, only combustion.

The trick is to always smile. The worst these boys can say is "Smile bigger" or "Show some teeth," but they never do. No matter how rancid I feel inside, my cheeks tug the corners of my lips. The expression is reflex now; no need to think, no effort needed.

I probably smile in my sleep.

Maybe it's that façade of cheery disposition that draws this boy to me as I cross campus center. He has a wolfish face, jaw hugged by scruffy dark hair, but his eyes look wide and unassuming, almost innocent. Their pretty gaze doesn't fit his lupine form, two damp orbs stolen from some gentle giant.

His voice is likewise sweet. "This sounds weird, and it's okay if you don't want to talk to me, but I just—sorry, I'm not good at this. Hello."

When I wave at him, he smiles, and my lips tug a little tighter from my teeth.

"You got a name?" he asks.

An invitation to speak, not like Tall-Boy's prodding. I tell Wolf-Boy my name, keeping my tone neutral, and I never stop smiling no matter the syllables. Keeping my voice tender to temper his. Sweet as he might seem, he's still a boy at Sutton University. I cannot trust him.

He's flummoxed though, makes sure to say my name as many times as can fit in his sentences, like it might flit away if he doesn't catch it. He chats at me until we reach the edge of the dorms, when a growl cuts through my body.

I slide a concerned hand over my middle. Does this count as breaking my silence? Will Wolf-Boy cast a spell?

"That's adorable." One arm folds around my elbow, and he leads me from the dorms. "Let's grab dinner. My stomach's rumbling too."

I let him escort me toward the dining hall, my face smiling to mirror his, but I scowl inside. That growl wasn't my churning stomach.

It felt like my skin.

Calm down

Outside the dining hall entrance, I excuse myself to the ladies' room. Wolf-Boy doesn't roll his eyes or chastise. Maybe the bar is too low at Sutton University, in this world, but his lack of impatience feels like hope.

I slip into a stall and pull up my shirt. I've carved letters beneath the short side of my ribcage, as if I-R-R-A-T-I-O-N-A-L can pretend that hormone treatment grows the absent strip of bone. Around the letters, skin ripples, a pond disturbed by thrashing fish.

Like Allison's skin before the end.

Maybe college just does this to girls, tells our skin to run away, fast as it can.

Or has carving the spell-word into my flesh stuck the sorcery inside? The words manifest, but unlike for other girls, my skin's set to unravel, muscle sloughing from bone. Different girls might self-destruct in different kinds of ways.

Not an explosion, but a meltdown. How long until the sorcery kills me?

If I'm dying, I don't want to die alone, and since there's no one else in the ladies' room, I find Wolf-Boy in the dining hall. I'm not sure if he's genuinely interested in me or if he's playing games like Tall-Boy. If I step away, tell Wolf-Boy, *Goodbye*, in Allison's fiery tone, will he toss a spell-word or let me go?

Worse, if I like him, will he want me to speak more? Boys can be harsh. Sometimes I envy the girls who like other girls. I used to radiate the sun, but hormones cooled my blood. The only girl I ever dated had hands and feet as cold as mine, lizards attached to our limbs. Boys are furnaces, and I crave the warmth.

Sometimes attraction is that simple.

We eat slowly, and I let him do the talking. Never spell-words, always gentle. He urges a few words from me here and there, but they're scaffolding through which he builds his side of the conversation.

"Where are you from?" he asks.

"West," I say, tender yet neutral, still smiling while I chew.

He has no opinions about that, and asks, "What's your major?"

"English."

He has opinions there, my answer prompting his every thought on literature classes, majors, and degrees. On the surface, I hear his critique. Deeper, I wonder if an onslaught of opinion is another means to silence me, a complex string of pieces that form a spell. Should I be terrified? My skin growls, but the dining hall din smothers the sound.

Even my body is silenced, but that's better than exploding.

When will the meltdown take me? Do Wolf-Boy and I have time for kissing and touching first? He's barely an acquaintance, but if I lead him to my dorm room, he'll follow. Will a nod be my consent for more? He'll have to notice the spell-words carved into my skin. I might even drag him into the meltdown. And shouldn't I mention how I'm different from other girls? My last boyfriend knew before he asked me out. Will Wolf-Boy still see that I'm human, or will I become a thing?

When it comes to girls, sometimes boys see little difference. Even the ones with sweet eyes.

As we leave the dining hall, his arm once again hooked around mine, I realize we're not going to find out how he sees me. Campus is no place for closeness or honesty. Another freshman girl whose name I'll never learn cowers at the edge of the dorms, caught in Tall-Boy's shadow. His friends linger close. Girls keep their distance, weaving around the scene or watching from doorways.

Wolf-Boy strides toward the cluster, a solitary angel who might make a difference in this undergrad hell. A familiar itch crosses my skin, the kind when you want to drag a boy by his jacket into your bedroom and then tear away that jacket and everything else.

The nameless freshman girl turns to speak to him, probably to plead. Her face is scrunched, desperate.

Wolf-Boy holds up an open palm. "Calm down," he says. "What's the trouble?"

Desire's itch washes off my skin, and the growling ripple returns. Tall-Boy and his friends lean in, expectant, but Wolf-Boy stares oblivious. My sweet wolf has no idea he's spoken another silencing spell.

I can't watch. Without waiting for him, I skirt around the crowd and run for my dorm's front doors. He doesn't mean to cast spells, but he can't help it. They are the words he knows. How long until he slings them my way? I catch the girl out of the corner of my eye, wrapping her arms around her torso as if trying to hold herself together. She's already reached her limit from Tall-Boy. Wolf-Boy's pressure is too much. She's done.

As I rush inside my dorm hall, I hear her explode.

Neurotic

My skin twitches harder each day. Wolf-Boy watched me run, and now he haunts my dorm hall. "Laurie, you there?" he calls, but I never answer. He might tell me to calm down, and I won't risk it.

No one guides him to my door. We girls are frightened, and the boys down the hall don't know my name. Those immune won't answer him—the musician who speaks more Mandarin than English, the history major with hearing aids, the non-binary students scattered between binary hall designations. They can't share their safety.

Not that I blame them; I can't share my knife.

And I can't quit cutting. My skin growls non-stop, every pore a mouth caught mid-snarl. Beneath the shower's spattering rain, I try to relieve word-driven pressure, but whispers aren't enough. Something inside me wants to roar.

Only carving settles my skin. I imagine spell-words Wolf-Boy might lace on to his opinions were we to peel each other's clothes off and bare my cutting. R-I-D-I-C-U-L-O-U-S. N-E-U-R-O-T-I-C. T-O-O and then M-U-C-H. I empathize with tattoo lovers—I'm running out of spare skin.

Still, no meat sloughs off. If I've averted the meltdown, will I still explode? Too many theories swirl inside—maybe I'm too different from the other girls. Maybe surviving attempted self-destruction years ago has helped me build antibodies. Maybe the carvings do their job so that Tall-Boy and friends can't destroy me. Maybe I haven't given them a reason.

And Wolf-Boy? In a darkened room, he might not notice my carvings. He might not care how I'm different. If my fingertips coax him to growl like a wolf, he might not hear my skin do the same.

But Wolf-Boy, Tall-Boy—they're of one nature. The boys pronounce themselves individuals for conflicting views on ethics, culture, and history, but they're each sharks in the same ocean. Tall-Boy the Cruel, but he's just joking. Wolf-Boy the Cruel, but *calm down* because he doesn't mean it. Surely the others have spiced up their cruelty to help live with themselves.

Excuses, excuses.

Our upperclassmen know when to be silent and when to speak —when spoken to. Those of us who survive our freshman year will grow into sophomores if we learn the same, a mandatory class we obliviously enrolled in upon orientation. Sutton University's spell-word crucible will destroy the rest.

In the end, we girls will likewise be of one nature. I won't be a different kind of girl anymore. Isn't that the dream?

As my skin ripples, filled with wolves and leopards and every growling angry beast that's ever walked this world, I wonder—if that's the dream, then what's the nightmare?

And the boys? What's *their* nightmare?

Attitude problem

Weeks have passed since Allison's death, but I finally muster a candlelight vigil for her. For all the girls who've exploded. I pass notes through the freshman dorm, meant for the girls, but others will find them, too. They'll spread the word.

The lure.

We gather after sunset at campus center to raise candles. This moment of silence might have stretched until midnight, but I hear Tall-Boy's snide voice at the crowd's edge. He's playing the shark, testing us for weaknesses. Sizing up who to bite.

I don't understand why he does it. Probing the freshman population for what he considers girlfriend material? A lackluster comedian hunting an audience for when he's *just joking*? Does he like to watch us brim with starlight and suffer explosions?

Or does he do it because he can?

I muscle through the vigil's crowd and find he's not alone. His cluster of friends traipse behind him in matching button-downs, eyes on their leader. I storm between him and the other girls, my candlestick spattering on cobblestone. Skin and mouth growl together as I hurl insults, telling him exactly what I think of Tall-Boy's unjust jokes, creepy grin, and shark-like face.

He smirks at first, but his confident mask crumbles when his friends snicker. Spell-words spit off his lips, sprinkle my face.

I shout an onslaught of opinions to rival Wolf-Boy's. Every word's emotional, my voice clumsy, my skin snarling, and I'm not sorry for it, and I can't stop. I won't stop. That's why Tall-Boy, tongue flustered, finally storms forward and shoves my shoulders.

I crash onto the cobblestones. My skin quits growling, the pain welcome, and I can't help the cracking shout that shoots up my throat. It is an old voice I keep meaning to leave behind.

The glint shifts in Tall-Boy's eyes. "Oh," he says, piercing gaze at last seeing me. Clocking me. His barracuda smile returns.

The moment stretches in pregnant silence. I've turned from *human* to *thing* in his eyes, but I don't mind because that's how he sees every girl here. It's validating in a terrible way. He wants to sling spell-words fashioned solely for me, the kinds of slurs you'll find for a dime a dozen on any street.

But I don't let him finish. I barely let him start.

"That's why it doesn't work," he says. "Because you're not really a—"

I stand quick and thrust my face into his. "I'm not done," I snap.

His tongue limpens, and his jaw goes slack. No slurs, no spells. No jokes. The words slide down his esophagus and into his stomach, where they froth and rumble.

He tries again. "You—"

I lean closer. "Don't interrupt me."

Again, he swallows his words. His friends aren't snickering now; they realize in fits and starts what's happening to their tall leader. Behind me, the girls cluster. They're still silent, but they're watching.

Someone who isn't silent appears from the gloom beyond the crowd—Wolf-Boy. His scruffy face doesn't smile now. He scowls at Tall-Boy, who's gripping his guts, and then at me. Wolf-Boy thinks he understands, but he's thought that before and been wrong.

Still, he tries. "No need to fight, right?" he asks.

Each word rings earnest. I know he only means the best, can't see the damage he does, how he props up boys like Tall-Boy and shatters girls like the nameless freshman he told to calm down. It would be easy to fall into his oblivious arms and let his furnace warm me.

But I can't.

His mouth opens again to ask, "Why don't we just calm—"

"No," I snap.

Like a scolded dog, he bows his head, and I imagine his ears drooping. I won't let him tell me to calm, or settle, or chill. Not anyone else, either. Good intentions don't matter; a spell-word is a spell-word. Wolf-Boy has his innocent mistakes, Tall-Boy has his humor and viciousness.

And we girls have our vengeance.

I sling spell-words at Tall-Boy. Ones he knows, like *irrational* and *attitude problem*. Ones he doesn't, like *no*. I speak ones specially for him, like *sad* and *worthless* and *empty*. The harder he tries to smirk through it, the deeper my tongue carves them into his body.

Other freshman girls chime in. They only speak the words I use, but an echo is better than silence. We know what this will do to him now, and we mean it. We aren't joking. We are far from calm.

Because girls can be cruel, too.

And I make sure everyone sees. Tall-Boy will turn example at the center of campus. This is the way of college. Sutton University might trigger spell-words to explosions, but we've all been silenced before. Tall-Boy hasn't. He's never been put in his place, has no tolerance to the pressure. It builds quickly inside him.

I strip off my jacket, roll up my sleeves and leggings, expose my midriff and ribs and every spell-word etched into my skin. A new carving tattoos my sternum, and I speak it now. It echoes the first exploding girl. One last spell-word to bring white light bursting from the first exploding boy.

Silently, I thank Allison for teaching it to me.

Goodbye

UNKINDLY GIRLS

On the third morning at Cherry Point, Morgan met the unkindly girls. Dawn had hardly touched the beach, giving the sand a grayish tone. Red rocks dotted the stone path from their small white beach house down to the water. Up the shore, a fishing boat cast off.

Morgan wore the ugliest swimsuit. Dad's decision—a one-piece, dull maroon abomination with sleeves and shorts. She'd never been allowed to wear a bikini, but in the past her swimsuits had looked presentable. The designer must've thought the faintest hint of shoulders and butt would draw too many wandering eyes.

Dad probably agreed. "You're still my baby girl," he'd said when Morgan complained. Six years old versus sixteen made little difference to him. He would scoff when he saw women and girls wear more revealing swimsuits. He'd call them unkindly—one of his favorite words, as if to look appealing meant flipping him off.

But Morgan had spent her life at his side and had seen him lick those chastising lips. She was not to become an unkindly girl. Never.

"You wouldn't do that to dear old Dad, Morgie," he'd say.

She'd come out early to dip into the water, but with so few people wandering the beach, she had her pick of seashells. The more colorful, the better. Hunting for them used to be a treat. Dad would only let her keep three per trip. He said to take too many would damage the ecosystem or something, but the hunt was the fun part.

Now, every shell that sparkled on the beach turned dull in her hands. She let them tumble back to the sand, one by one. A lot had changed at home since last summer. Try as she might to leave it behind, the change had followed her to Cherry Point.

"That is the ugliest thing I've ever seen."

Morgan dropped her last lackluster seashell and looked down the beach, where two girls her age walked the damp sand. One's face was all angles and wreathed in dark hair. The other flashed a soft smile; white stripes patterned her red hair where she'd bleached it. They wore dark, baggy pants and loose-fitting blouses that bared their chests.

Unkindly. The word popped unwanted into Morgan's head. She'd never glanced at other girls' chests the previous summers, but now Dad's eyes dominated hers.

"Like wearing blood," said the pointy-faced girl, still fixated on the swimsuit. "Sickening."

"Isn't it?" Morgan asked, tugging one stunted sleeve. "That's what the tag says. Ugliest Swimsuit, one size fits none."

The two girls giggled, and then the pointy-faced one beckoned Morgan. "I'm Blue, and the redhead's Clown. Follow us. We'll fix you up."

Morgan smiled to herself and obeyed. This wasn't unusual for summer vacation. Somehow, she always made at least one friend.

Neighbor houses squatted a couple hundred feet from each other, but closer to the wet sand stood a dull wooden shop. Water damage darkened its lower walls, and the discoloration gave the shop a sea-worn feel.

Blue and Clown led Morgan inside. Plastic shovels and pails dangled from nails, snorkels lined a metal tray, and bathing suits hung on a circular clothing rack. Plus, there were shelves of the usual gift shop garbage. A tacky ceramic crab clutching a flag in its claw read, "Ain't Life a Beach?"

The shopkeeper, a balding man with a scraggly goatee, let his eyes wander up and down the other girls' bodies. Morgan thought of Dad and how he'd never be so obvious. His shame always forced him to avert his gaze.

Fabric swatted her arm, tearing her gaze from the shopkeeper. Clown shook a plastic hanger, dangling an aquamarine two-piece swimsuit with navy-blue striping. Shiny sequins lay trapped between layers in the trim. They looked almost like scales and made Morgan think of mermaids.

"Lovely, yes?" Blue asked. Her smile was all teeth.

Morgan shrugged, but Blue was right. It was gorgeous.

Blue guided the bikini to Morgan's front. "On you. To die for, yes?"

Exactly Morgan's thinking. Dad would kill her.

Morgan stepped back, letting the two-piece dangle again. "It's pretty, but I don't have money."

"We'll spot you," Blue said, taking the hanger from Clown. "In return, you hang with us tonight on the beach. Agreed?"

Morgan shrank inside. If only it weren't so easy to make friends, Dad would have no one to chastise, and these would be peaceful vacations, nothing more.

Blue laid the swimsuit on the counter. The shopkeeper didn't look at her now, his eyes sharply focused on the cash register. Clown reached inside her blouse and pulled out a black purse. Dollar coins thudded on the checkout counter. Morgan couldn't see their faces, but they made her think of pirate doubloons.

Blue pressed the swimsuit into Morgan's arms. "At the beach, just before sunset." She marched past, and Clown trailed her.

Morgan began to follow them out.

The shopkeeper cleared his throat. "Watch out for them two."

Morgan turned to him. "What?"

He ran his fingernails from temple to goatee, scratching an itch he couldn't catch. "Every summer, they come to Cherry Point and sell dope up and down the beach. Don't get caught in their mess." He began to fiddle with a coin, but his eyes focused on Blue and Clown as they sauntered out the door.

Vacationers, not locals.

They were just the kind of girls who'd make Dad avert his eyes.

*

If they would stop going to the beach each summer, maybe he wouldn't have to see any unkindly girls. Sometimes he saw them at the pool in Syracuse, but nothing would come of that. Too close to home.

When Morgan was little, she'd thought their beach trips were a fun way to spend each summer together after Mom died. Cape Cod, Miami Beach, La Jolla. Different coasts, different kinds of beaches, but always full of sand castles, ice cream, and splashing in the shallows, though never past the sea shelf where the undertow might suck her into the deep. Safety first was one of Dad's rules.

At each beach, Morgan made a friend. She never meant to. They would stumble into each other, or Morgan would see the other girl wearing something pretty. A day would pass, Dad would disappear for a night, and then they would head home.

Morgan tiptoed through the beach house and into her room, where she stashed the aquamarine bikini beneath her sagging mattress. Cool salty air swept through an open window and across her arms. She stripped out of her maroon one-piece and dressed in a tank and shorts. She'd meant to swim, but now a grimmer outlook haunted her thoughts.

She would have to tell Dad about the girls. Since Mom was gone, she'd told him everything, even after she realized he hadn't been telling her everything in return.

Utensils clinked in the kitchen. He was awake.

She stared at her window, thinking about sneaking out, but Cherry Point lay hundreds of miles from Syracuse. If she ran away, she'd just have to come back. He would think her unkindly for worrying him, and he might then worry that she knew his secret.

She traipsed into the kitchen. Dad loomed over the stovetop, his thick yet dexterous fingers sliding an egg from bowl to rim to pan. He wore a blue and white Hawaiian shirt, khaki shorts, and white sandals. Harmless middle-class vacation father—his best costume.

"Morning, Morgie," he said. "Out early?"

"I wanted to swim while it was cool," she said, plopping down on a stool by the kitchen island. The pedestal creaked around a loose screw.

"Your hair's dry." Dad didn't look at her. Somehow he just knew these things. Another egg cracked and sizzled.

"I didn't get a chance. I made a friend."

Dad focused hard on his hands as he slid his graceful spatula beneath the omelet. It flipped and hissed against the pan. "That's nice."

"A couple friends, actually." The cold marble countertop felt soothing under Morgan's palms. If she kept them there, could she keep from getting blood on her hands?

Dad picked up a knife. Its blade slid around the omelet, sawing off brown arms of crust. "Staying safe, right?" he asked, working magic with pepper and cheese. "Staying kindly?"

Dad laid a plate on the countertop. The omelet was perfect, Dad having cut off all signs of burning and crust without losing any of the cheesy yellow center.

Morgan swallowed before biting. "Yes, Daddy. Always."

He would watch her leave tonight. He would see Blue and Clown, and then lick his chastising lips.

*

Morgan didn't say goodbye in the evening. They wouldn't really be apart, after all, though only she would approach the beach, where the unkindly girls sat around a small fire just outside the tide's reach. Coastal winds batted at the flames. A storm was coming.

"Now what are you wearing?" Blue asked. She and Clown had not changed out of loose-fitting blouses.

Morgan wore baggy jeans and a hoodie. She'd told Dad that it was going to be chilly this close to the water tonight.

"Where's your swimsuit?"

"Under my clothes, same as yours," Morgan said. The girls tittered, and she realized their cleavage was still on display, no hint of bikini tops underneath.

Clown tugged a large brown bottle from the sand beside her feet, took a swig, and passed it around the fire, first to Blue and then to Morgan. There was no label. Brine clung to the bottom, as if the glass had been trapped in a shipwreck for a hundred years.

She thought of Dad and passed the bottle back to Clown. "Anything fresher?"

"We'll have something fresher after sunset," Blue said. She and Clown tittered again, the only sound Clown seemed to make. Her hair caught the firelight; its shadows twitched this way and that, as if alive.

As red and purple dusk gave way to black, cloud-covered night, the small fire became an island of light on the beach. Windows glowed down the beach, except at Morgan's house, but the rest of the world was dark. She wondered exactly where Dad was holed up. He could be anywhere the light didn't touch while the campfire illuminated the girls for him.

She'd figured things out after last summer. It wasn't like in the movies where he might've accidentally left out some crucial clue that grabbed her attention or a serendipitous news article happened to link their past vacation locales. She was older now and getting attention from boys at school. The way they looked at her wasn't so different from her father. They were just too juvenile to feel shame. Then there were his comments, his averted eyes, and the nights he'd go out before they left their vacation spots for home. Her brain had linked the chains.

Now she wrapped those chains around her legs. She wondered what heavy thing she'd tether them to and throw into the ocean to drag her down.

"The night's ready, girls," Blue said, standing up and turning to Morgan. "Fancy a swim?" She didn't wait for an answer, just tromped toward the water and expected the others to follow.

They did. Where the tide lapped at their feet, Clown spun around and held out a fist to Morgan. She took the offering, a coarse square that reminded her of dehydrated fruit.

"Ever been swimming high?" Blue asked. "Unforgettable."

And unkindly. Morgan made to pass the square back, but Clown was already running into the tide.

The light was gone. Dad would never know, same as he'd never know about the sequined bikini. Morgan lifted her palm to her mouth, and her lips closed around the square.

"Melts on your tongue," Blue said. She was already knee-deep, the tide drenching her clothes.

Morgan stripped and followed. Salt spray stung her nose. Her mouth filled with the static that blew from Dad's radio when he let her switch between stations. The other girls bobbed, dark driftwood on black waves.

Vague warnings slid beneath Morgan's thoughts. "The shelf. The undertow."

Thunder and waves drowned her out. The girls drifted farther. Morgan meant to follow. Only the thought of Dad anchored her to land. She wasn't an unkindly girl. Never.

Waves rolled toward her. She took a deep breath, stinking of seawater, and plunged beneath the surface. She couldn't see underneath, but somehow she knew that Blue and Clown were diving, too. The ocean became less an undulating wave, more a hand that grabbed Morgan and yanked her deep.

She floated beneath the creaking hull of an aging ship, its underside as glassy and coated in barnacles as the bottle passed between Blue and Clown. Inside, pirates dragged helpless hook hands against smooth walls. Their glass prison was filled with seawater and beer, and their pockets were so loaded with doubloons that they couldn't swim away.

Blue and Clown beckoned Morgan to the surface, their scaly turquoise and orange tails flapping. Neither mermaid seemed unkindly. They just wanted to see selfish men die.

An enormous golden tail rocked the drowning ship. The black sky flickered alive with lightning, painting the silhouette of an enormous woman against the clouds. If Blue and Clown were guppies, she was a shark. Plains of kelp matted her scaly head, and coral coated her arms. One gargantuan hand grabbed the bottle by the neck and slung it at the sky. It shattered in thunder, and its shards sliced every pirate to pieces. Their lungs flopped atop the water's surface, helpless as fish on land.

"Unforgettable," Blue said.

Morgan dug her hands into wet sand and hauled herself onto the beach. The tide splashed across her back, spraying saltwater into her mouth, but her muscles felt too worn to move another inch. Rain pattered the sand. The storm that swirled out on the water had almost reached Cherry Point. Whatever drug Clown had given to Morgan, it seemed to be losing its effect.

Lightning forked overhead, illuminating a smoking mound where the campfire once burned. Morgan thought she saw other shapes closer to the water. She stared hard at black-on-black outlines until the sky lit in another blue flicker.

Two naked bodies lay in the surf, red and white hair swirled around one's head. A bulky figure kneeled beside them. The flicker faded as he turned to Morgan, and he stared until lightning again tore across the sky. Its flash lit his familiar eyes and made his chastising lips glisten.

"I'm sorry, Morgie, but they were unkindly," Dad said. Thunder rumbled, and he paused for it to pass. "You know, don't you? I thought you knew when you told me about them." He started toward her.

Morgan's chest ached against the sand. She wanted to slither back into the water. She felt the lightning coming, the sky's tattling forked tongue, and the beach glowed as blue as her swimsuit. He could see her clear as day.

She lifted her head. "Dad—"

"What are you wearing, Morgie?" he asked, but he didn't say it like a question. He sounded the same as when she was six, the day he told her Mom wasn't coming home. Thoughts of him had shriveled out on the water, but now he was here and real, and he dwarfed every fantastical ocean.

"I—I—I—" Morgan tried to stand, but her legs felt waterlogged. She wondered if that was the drug's doing. She managed to sit up and wrap her gooseflesh-covered arms around her chest.

"It was only a matter of time, wasn't it?" He sounded calm, almost peaceful. He squatted down, drew her into his firm arms, and scooped her up against his chest. Fire beat inside in time to the spitting rain. "You had to grow up someday."

Morgan closed her eyes and tried to forget everything she'd realized since last summer. Dad used to be a good man, or at least that's what she'd believed. She could believe it again, couldn't she? If he just held her like this and warmed her bones against every chilly seaborne wind, she would believe anything he wanted.

"Daddy, carry me home," she said. Lightning flickered past her eyelids. "It can be like it was." She felt him walking, but he hadn't turned around.

"It can't," he said.

Water slopped at her dangling feet. She opened her eyes. The world lay dark between lightning flickers, but she made out frothing waves that encircled them, churned ugly by harsh wind. Dad was walking into the sea.

"Why?" she asked.

"Because I can't feel the way I feel about unkindly girls for you!" he shouted, loud as thunder. "Not my baby girl. Never."

She squirmed, but she'd exhausted herself, and he held her tight. Rain and sea crashed across her, plastering her swimsuit against her skin. He didn't look at her, averting his eyes for when lightning next lit the coast.

He didn't have to avert them for long. Chest-deep in the water, he plunged her under. One hand grasped her shoulder; the other shoved hard against her head. She clawed at his unyielding wrists and kicked at his legs and groin, but her feet were heavy, the water weighing them down. Lightning reflected in Dad's eyes. The storm would watch her die.

Was this how he'd killed the other girls, every summer vacation past? Had he held them first so that they might know a loving embrace before drowning them? Always far from home, those unkindly girls. They were vacationers who might've met anyone on the beach, but instead they'd met Morgan and her father. Dead summer friends were coming to collect. She had been his accomplice, knowing or not, and she would join them beneath the sea. He hadn't been caught for murdering them; would someone wonder why he returned to Syracuse alone this time? Would neighbors ask if Morgan died kindly?

He would tell them so. Someone would come to collect him, and he'd say his daughter died still his baby girl. Always.

Morgan stopped fighting. Her lungs screamed to keep thrashing, but she had to catch his gaze. She stared up at him, bubbles slipping from her lips. The sea calmed for a moment, as if anticipating a mighty wave. Dad glanced down at her.

Lightning flashed. She slipped her fingers beneath the lower rim of her bikini top and yanked it up.

Had he waited, the lightning would have faded and he wouldn't have seen, but even a glimpse seemed too much. His body shuddered backward. He turned his head, eyelids squeezed shut, the sight threatening to drive nails through his eyeballs.

The tide crashed across them, shoving him back and taking her under. It bought her time to break from the shallows. She dove under the next wave. Thunder crashed, but it came warped and uncertain underwater. She thought she might be swimming over the sea shelf by now. Her skin stung with cold as she surfaced.

"Morgie!"

Dad swam against the waves. His drenched clothing tugged at him, but she'd been fighting the ocean for an unknown time, whereas he had a fresh start. He could manage. His fingers snatched her ankle.

If he tried to drown her this far from shore, he'd probably kill them both. Would keeping her kindly be worth the sacrifice?

She looked out to sea for the miracle she'd seen earlier, but there was no static in her mouth, only her tongue. The drug had worn off. No mermaid was coming to save her, same as no one had saved her summer friends in every year past.

She let Dad draw her close and wrapped both arms around his

trunk. He embraced her, too. He might've thought she was trying to hug him, one last desperate grasp for sympathy.

She sucked in a deep breath and thrust downward hard as she could. Flexing her legs, she kicked herself and Dad into the next wave, where the undertow pulled them under. He was stronger and larger, but freed of land, she could move him.

He shoved at her face. Lightning revealed his flailing limbs—he must've missed the chance to take a breath before submerging.

She didn't let go. Her lungs burned again, still faint from the first attempted drowning. She promised them this would be the last. Fighting him wasn't just about Blue and Clown. It was about all the unkindly girls he had already killed and all the ones who might die yet. No more.

Burning faded from her chest, her lungs at last giving out. The surface seemed far away, and she was tired. Ghostly cold ate through her muscles. One more unkindly girl drowned in the deep.

Lightning burned in ferocious flashes, the sky playing catch between two clouds, and the world flickered black and blue. An ocean of fish and seaweed appeared. Vanished. Returned full of faces. Morgan might've believed they belonged to mermaids or dead pirates, but when the next lightning flash brought them closer, she recognized them.

They were easy to remember; none had aged since she'd last seen them. Little girls, adolescents, teens, Blue and Clown among them. All her summer friends.

And there were strangers who crowded beyond, more than Dad should've murdered in the ten years he'd been taking Morgan on summer vacation, more unkindly girls than years in her life. Some were women who might've been Mom's age. Others he must've met when he was younger.

He had been finding unkindly girls for a long time. Noticing them and averting his gaze, he poured his strength into unlatching

Morgan's legs. He didn't seem to realize she was good as dead.

The ocean formed hands in the uncertain darkness between lightning flashes. They hugged him, hugged her. The undertow, the dead—she couldn't tell what helped her hold him anymore. The difference mattered little to an almost-ghost. No more breathing, eating, or sleeping. No more distracting life functions. She could focus now, all secrets bare, and bend her will and body to one last purpose.

The dead wanted him, and she would not let go.

THE LONG FLESH OF THE LAW

The siren's cry came distant and warped, a baying wolf across the lit cityscape. Miracle Robinson would've ignored it, one more howling among nocturnal hunters, if not for the answering chirp close by, drawing her gaze to the curb at her left.

Sandwiched between an SUV and a small sedan, a city cop cruiser parked streetside at a crooked angle. Rainy residue from an earlier storm twinkled over the other vehicles, but on the cruiser it more resembled a sweaty sheen coating naked flesh, the car having foregone any steel frame to instead become a blue-and-white-skinned beast.

Mira swerved right at the next sidewalk corner, dipping under a pink neon sign. She didn't want to see the cruiser and couldn't let whoever drove it see her in return.

Her smartphone's GPS flickered and recalculated her route. She rarely used it, but the city seemed strange tonight. The streetlights cast an odd shine, yellower than usual. Every silent passerby dragged a long shadow, and the street's regular cacophony sounded as strained as a creaky old crate stuffed to bursting.

Another siren cried from far away. There were hunters tonight, yes, but they couldn't be hunting Mira. She'd carefully chosen a dark vest, long-sleeved sweater, and jeans tucked into bland brown boots, the borrowed ensemble screaming *college student*. Above her round cheeks, flushed with the chill, sat a thick pair of old prescription glasses, giving her the look of a wizened librarian beneath her curly red hair. No one would suspect she was only fifteen.

The deception would be crucial when she met up with the others. Petra had heard of a club called Three of Diamonds that didn't check IDs, and they were all set to gather there, unbeknownst to parents. Dad was pulling a late night at the firm. He would come home at three in the morning, eyes red, tie loose, arms loaded with paperwork, too exhausted to guess his daughter had returned only shortly before him.

Mira didn't expect to find a club at the night's end. Three of Diamonds was likely some below-street gimmick restaurant five teenagers couldn't afford. They would order water and cheap food, and they'd cackle over gossip and decide they weren't losers. Mira could be a not-loser with them.

Supposing she ever found the place. The GPS's recalculation had steered her into a dead-end alley, and now it was recalculating again, aiming her southwest. And now again, aiming east.

Her fingers tensed around her phone. She hated doubling back; it was a good way for someone to catch wind that you were lost.

Like that odd cruiser.

She shouldn't have been able to see it after turning the last corner, but there it sat at the curb down the street, looking somehow counterfeit, like a clumsy drawing scribbled against the curb. Had it followed her? Or did every cruiser tonight look warped and strange?

Best to pretend she wasn't alone, wasn't lost. She angled her phone past her chin and muttered to it in a pretend phone call, as if the shitshow GPS were her friend.

So far, it had offered about as much help as her actual friends.

She'd messaged the group chat before tonight's sirens began, first to re-ask the club's name, then for directions. Each time, she'd met laughing faces and notes of *Hmm, can't you find it?* and *It's so easy*, and *Yeah, bitch, hurry up*.

That last one had turned into much-needed advice. Mira hurried around another corner and down the sidewalk, escaping the cruiser's sight again. Hopefully for good this time.

At the next corner, she lowered her phone and reviewed its map. Text and icons had morphed into unfamiliar symbols, and the lines and shapes had ceased to make sense. Buildings transformed into bridges; streets became subways. The map kept spinning, changing which direction led to the waterfront, as if the city were spiraling into the sea.

She glanced ahead, doubtful there was a subway station entrance nearby, and spotted a mouth opening downward, braced by grimy railings. Two cops in blue uniforms leaned against its outer wall, eyes on their phones, their service caps obscuring the subway route.

Mira swerved again. She didn't need them noticing her.

Another unplanned turn, another glitch across her phone screen. She stuffed the brick into her purse. Maybe if she trusted the street, it would bring her to Three of Diamonds by instinct.

But the street was alien, the pedestrians thinning, the cars occasional. Steel shutters blocked shop entrances with a firm grip, less like they'd been rolled down at closing time, more like these businesses had never been open.

The city had turned labyrinthine. It didn't want her to reach her destination. *Head home, little girl.*

Or maybe it didn't recognize her in this outfit, lent by Petra with the approval of London, Stephanie, and Mercedes. The city thought her a stranger, more so than all its tourists, and had no interest in helping her.

Around another corner. And another. Doubling back. Taking a left where she'd gone right. The asphalt became a great gray tongue, its crags sparkling with rainwater. Or saliva.

If she didn't find the club soon, she'd have to give up. And if Dad ever found out, he'd lay into her the same as he had when he'd spotted her friends picking at her clothes outside school, where a smog-belching city bus had covered her laughter.

You don't need to impress those girls, Miracle. They're not true friends.

There was little point in arguing with a lawyer, and besides, she couldn't blame him for ignorance over how girls made friends. How could he understand? What father in the entire history of fathers had ever understood?

It wasn't like she'd ever had a mother around. Not one Mira could remember. For the longest time, Dad had done his best to make up for that absence, ensuring he took her to friends' birthday parties or attending seasonal school concerts. Both of them had wished Mira's mother was around in their own way, but there had never been an obvious rift between them.

She hadn't noticed, with him only occasionally dating, that his only frame of reference to girldom was her. He couldn't see how some of them showed affection by teasing each other over hair and clothes, calling each other *bitch* and *skank*.

And sometimes you decided girls were your friends whether you believed it or not. You just hoped it would become true.

If only she could find them. How long had she been wandering these now-barren streets? She wouldn't check her phone for the time. One more GPS glitch would send her smashing the damn thing over the concrete. She glanced down the next alley, expecting a dead end.

Beyond the scattered food wrappers and soggy newspaper pages, the street looked familiar. Nearly identical to a place she'd passed minutes ago.

No, worse—it was the exact place.

"Piece of shit." She smacked her purse and started into the alley. "You win, city. I give up."

A siren's whoop startled her into spinning around on one heel, striking her shoulder against the brick wall.

Quivering white muscle tensed across the alley's mouth in the shape of that freakish cop cruiser. Its driver side door hung open, and someone had already stepped onto the desolate pavement, a potato chip bag crinkling underfoot.

"Are you supposed to be here, young lady?"

His black boots gleamed with raindrops. A blue uniform crept up his legs and torso, short-sleeved and outdated in a way Mira couldn't specify. His golden badge wore no numbers and appeared as something of a shield and a star at once, with every movement leaning the light toward one shape and then the other. A bristly handlebar mustache drooped around narrow lips and crossed his paper-pale face. Aviator shades mounted a thin nose, and a blue service cap with a black bill fit over dark, slicked-back hair.

Mira unclenched her teeth and forced out an excuse. "I'm just going home."

"No, you aren't," the cop said. "You're staying right here to yak with me."

He had the clipped voice of someone talking in a black-and-white movie. A dampness glistened from his hair to his boots, reminiscent of sweat or fish oil. It even shined off the service pistol at his hip, giving it a strangely animalistic presence, the grip poking from its holster like a dark frog rising from the mud.

"See? You have to stay because I said so." His boots made a sharp *clack* against the pavement as he neared. "Isn't that a firecracker? The others weren't joshing me about switching careers—my last job was peanuts to this one! I've tried out a few over a long time, looking for the shape that's a good fit. This might be the one. Did you know they let you kill people? It's the bee's knees."

Thunder boomed in Mira's chest, her breath quickening. She didn't dare look back, but she felt the alley stretching behind her, offering an escape route if such a thing existed. Hadn't her father advised her about cops, the way he advised his clients? Was she supposed to ask if she was being detained, or did she get that from TV?

Her memories felt distant. Had she ever seen a TV show? Did she actually know her father? Or had he died alongside her mother on the day of Mira's birth? Had she even been born, or was that a dream? Her existence might have always been this alley and the man standing here with his badge and gun. If he had detained her, it was within some city-like tumor clinging to the real universe.

He loomed, his mustache twitching. "I want you to answer some questions. Hearing you answer questions—that's better than music. Better than birthdays and ice cream."

Mira's borrowed boots scraped the pavement, desperate to retreat. She braced herself to smell the cop's breath as he took a knee, his face meeting hers, but his exhalation never struck. There was only the gasoline-and-garbage smell of the city riding a light breeze through the alley. One hand gripped a pencil; the other held a spiral notepad. Its wire echoed his arm hair, and the paper was the same shade of pale as his skin, as if the notebook had grown out of his hand.

"So then," he started. "Mira. Where were you the night of June 50th, 1983?"

Mira. "How do you know my name?"

The mustache arched with the cop's grimace. "Nah, you're getting it all wrong. I ask questions, you answer them. Try again. Where were you the night of June 50th, 1983?"

"I—" Mira started. "I wasn't born yet. That isn't a real date."

The cop's pencil crawled over the paper, its every touch sounding like a jagged fingernail vigorously scratching dry skin.

"Next question," he said, slower. "Did you know a miracle can disappoint? Especially one that's fifteen years old?"

Mira. Miracle. But how could he know? Mira's stomach sucked at her throat. "No. I didn't know that."

"Mm. That's a good answer." The cop scribbled again. White debris flaked from his notepad like dandruff.

Mira didn't think her answer was any good. Maybe he didn't care what she said, only that she keep speaking to him, the way a boy at school used to keep colliding with her in the hallway so he'd have an excuse to talk to her, or the way an elderly woman on the bus last spring had purposely missed her stop to keep telling Mira about how downtown used to be. The cop grew rigid with intent, a pensive dog watching a busy dinner table.

Fresh discomfort rattled Mira's nerves. "Are you going to kill me?"

"I ask the questions," the cop said. "Next up—where'd you get a zany idea like that?"

"You said it. Your job. They let you kill people."

"Sure, I can kill *people*. That's part of the job. But you're just a person. One of you." The cop hitched his belt. "Now, if you brought me to your group of delinquents, that'd be another slice of pie. Then I could do a killing."

"My group?" Mira asked. "You know my friends?"

"Of course, there are all kinds of other swell things I can do to you," the cop said, ignoring her. "For example, I could lock you up somewhere out of the way for interrogation and then forget about you. I could bloat you full of drugs and drop you at Daddy's job. Or we can keep it pleasant, and I can keep asking questions, and you can give the old college try in answering them. Now, let's see—those girls. Petra. London. Stephanie. Mercedes. Are they really your friends?"

He said them in the order she thought of them. She couldn't see anything through those reflective shades, but she felt his gaze crawling with a cold brightness across her skin, her purse, Petra's clothes, as if the shades were his actual eyes.

"I don't know," Mira said.

The mustache curved over the cop's lips. "Are you familiar with a thing called friends?"

His attention poured into her, drowning her. She had to look past him to take in her next breath, catching sight of his flesh-like cruiser. It quaked with its driver's anticipation, ready to pounce. Almost as if his car was not a car but another facet of him, and if Mira could only look at it from the right angle, she would see how the cop and the cruiser were a single creature.

"Have you ever had friends?" the cop went on, eager for another answer. "Would you know?"

The cop wondered the same as her father. *You don't need to impress those girls, Miracle. They're not true friends.* Maybe Dad had known more than she'd given him credit for?

Yes, that was right—she had a past. With a father in it. And a mother, too, though they'd scarcely met, in a time before memory. A world spread past this alley, surviving outside this cop's attention. And hadn't Dad given other advice too?

Don't talk to pigs without me. Even when you're grown.

Mira tried to steady her voice. "You forgot my Miranda rights."

"Miranda? Rights?" The cop stood up, arched his back away from Mira, and glanced left and right. "Is Miss Rights with us now? Or with Petra and the others? Oh, or is Miranda the name you wish yours was short for?"

"It means I don't have to answer questions if I don't want to. And I get attorney privilege."

The cop sighed as if he'd just emptied a refreshing cup of coffee. "That isn't your only privilege. Next question. What is a *turney*, and can you have more than one?"

"A lawyer," Mira snapped. "Like my dad. When you don't want to answer questions alone, you have the right to a lawyer."

"Wait a tic—you *don't* want to answer questions?"

A gleam slashed across the cop's shades, but Mira couldn't tell where the glare might've come from, as if light and darkness belonged to him. The sky rumbled with a new storm's thunder, echoing her heart.

"Mira, use your noggin." The cop flapped his notepad. "A lawyer? Really? Who would ever want to help you? You're a kid. Nobody gives a flying fig about you unless you got a bun in the oven, and even then they hate you for it. Don't they educate you in school these days? They educated me. I've studied lots of neato things. I'm everywhere, and I'm listening and learning."

A chill spread hydra-like up Mira's arms and spine, tainting every blood vessel with isolating cold. She had never felt so alone.

Thunder groaned, another reminder that there was a world beyond this alley. Places, events, people. There was a past—*she* had a past, didn't she? She grasped at anything she'd done, anyone she'd known, even the bad parts. The boy who would always bump into her. Scoldings from her father over the kinds of friends she'd made. A lost mother, out of whose departure Mira had been named Miracle.

She was more than the girl standing here. She had a father, and she'd snuck out of her apartment, and she was on her way to Three of Diamonds to see her friends, or whatever the hell they were to her. No matter what, she had to remember she'd existed before she met this man.

Her hand crawled over her chest and touched fingertips to her purse. She eyed the cop, and then his gun, pulsating, a little black heart at his hip. He shifted, the light falling differently, and the pistol went still.

"Is that gun real?" Mira asked, cautious.

The cop grinned. "Real as anything else."

She didn't like that answer, its implications, but it was all she had to work with right now. "I'm not reaching for a gun," she said. "I don't have one."

"I know." His confidence was a knife in the dark. "But I'm authorized to interpret anything you pull out as one. And then I get to say, *She's got a gun!* and then I get to draw *my* gun and yell, *Freeze!* and then it goes, *Blam! Blam!*" He pantomimed firing a pistol. "And then you die, Miracle. You die, and you don't come back."

Mira swallowed as thunder boomed. "But it's not a gun. It's just my phone. Look." She unzipped her purse faster than she meant to and drew out the flat brick. "See? It's for texting, and watching videos, and sometimes you make calls."

"Who would you call? The cops?"

Mira opened her mouth. Shut it. Watched his dark mustache stretch into a hairy serpent.

"I'm already here," the cop said. "Protecting and serving."

"You're not a real cop," Mira said. "You're—I don't know. Something else."

"Haven't you put two and two together yet? Don't you get it?" He scoffed. "Nah, *getting it* isn't part of your specialty. You don't know dogs from cats about this world, never bothered with an education, you little know-nothing punk. And how can you count on anything when you know nothing? Sure, I could just be me. Or I could be the next cop you see on the street. Could be the job attracts a certain kind. We could all be like me. I could be Ev-Ree-Bah-Dee."

A raindrop struck Mira's phone screen. She could call 9-1-1, but what would they see? A cop, a cruiser, a girl who wasn't supposed to be out tonight. She might as well be trying to nail the cops she'd spotted on their phones outside the subway for loitering, the same way they sometimes scattered her and her friends.

She studied the pistol again. "Where's your phone?"

Lightning reflected in the cop's shades as if he were blinking. "My. Phone."

"You're supposed to have one." Malice slid into Mira's voice as thunder shook the street. "Didn't you study?"

She unlocked her phone and cycled through apps and videos as another raindrop struck, and another, until they were speckling the screen.

But she found what she needed and aimed her phone at the cop to show him.

"See?" she asked. "Look at the cops in the video. Just like you, except they're playing on their phones. You were supposed to do that for a few minutes before asking me questions."

Her mouth went dry, and she wished she could lap up the rain, but she had to keep going, even if trying to trick this thing felt impossible. Possibly suicidal.

"That's why none of this is going right." She lowered the phone. "We started all wrong."

The cop became a statue. A light drizzle patted his hat with the sound of a leaky faucet spitting onto skin.

He reached across his chest and clawed down his forearm. Flesh hooked beneath his fingernails, as pliable as clay. A sickly smell wafted into the alley, and doughy ribbons of sinew pulled free in a wet stretching screech. He went on rending as if scratching loose an enormous craggy scab until the chunk tore from his forearm in a thin meaty layer, leaving a glistening slab in his clawing hand.

It looked like a rectangular glob of vanilla ice cream desperate to melt into the scoops beneath it, but it soon hardened, becoming a phone-like brick in his grasp. Muscles pulsed within, same as his pistol, and threads of tissue wormed into his palm.

"My. Phone." He held it up, and the screen shined the same as his shades. "Like this?"

Mira's teeth rattled around labored breath. "Yeah. And find a wall. To lean against." She aimed a trembling finger past her phone, at the brown bricks of the alley. "There's good."

The cop sidestepped to the wall. Looked it up and down. Mira almost thought he sniffed it before turning his back to the bricks and angling his shoulders against them. His chin tilted down, shades reflecting in the phone screen, phone screen reflecting in the shades, forming an infinity of the cop gazing at himself.

"Do that for a few minutes, and then I'll come strolling in again," Mira said, retreating down the alley. "And then you can ask me questions."

The cop said nothing. His concentration weighed into the phone, determined to get this part right. Maybe the others Mira had seen had put this kind of effort into it, too.

Ev-Ree-Bah-Dee.

She turned from him, determined to shut out the feeling of his stare. Her footsteps sloshed down the alley, its choppy pavement adding the new storm's rainfall to the puddles formed earlier this evening. Sometimes, this city couldn't get enough. It wanted all the rain, all the noise. All the teenagers it could eat.

Not me, Mira promised herself. *Not me.*

She nearly made it to the far end of the alley before the siren's chirp lanced through her heart. Soggy newspaper pages tore underfoot where she skidded to a stop.

The cruiser rumbled across the alley's end, its lights flashing. It had driven along the wrong lane, but she doubted the driver cared. He only wanted to be sure his door faced Mira when it sprang open and the car birthed him into the alley, a white dagger cutting from the cruiser's inner shadows.

"You're getting clever on me," the cop said, sounding tired. "Clever. And devious."

Mira glanced back, half-expecting the same cop to still be leaning where she'd left him, his fleshy cruiser waiting. There was no one. He must have hurried behind the wheel and driven around to cut her off.

"There should be two of you," she blurted out, dredging up any rule he might've missed. "Cops have partners. For their safety."

Thunder crashed, and the drizzle thickened into steady rain. Its drops struck the cruiser, but there was no metallic rhythm, only the pattering of water against a creature's hide. A wet animal stink poured around the cop, into the alley, and a ripple ran through him as if his skin had been a still pond now disturbed by the rainfall.

"I don't like playing with you." His mustache crawled to the right. "It isn't fair, you know. Everybody else gets to sidewinder around the letter of the law, but you want it by the book, and you keep finding more and more rules. It's not fair, you—you're making it not fun!"

The cry shot a tremor through his lips, angling his teeth forward like boulders coming loose from pink mud.

"Never mind," Mira whispered. "I can give you answers again. Like before."

"No more questions," the cop snapped. "I've had my fill of devious girls. Now I'm going to give you the business."

His limbs unfolded from his sides and aimed his pistol into the alley. He no longer shifted in the light or rippled beneath the rain, his bones straining against his skin at the joints before it refolded into place around his skeleton, as if this pose were the right one, his body having waited all night to assume its most natural shape. His arms pointed like a wolf's snout, sniffing out prey before dashing in for the kill. Instead of teeth, plastic and steel now filled his mouth, coated in small hairs and pale porous tissue. His pistol stretched damp and veinous, throbbing with bullets.

Mira clenched her teeth. "Leave me alone."

"I could've done that in a jiffy," the cop said. "You could've been a good little squealer and told me where to find Petra, London, Stephanie, and Mercedes. I could've had something better than a person—people. But you don't know where they've got to. If they'd wanted you to know, you would've found them before I found you. But you're slow on the draw, so you call them friends because you don't know definitions, because you're alone, because you don't have a mommy to give you an education."

"My mom?" Mira shrank into herself. He knew about *her*, too?

The cop cocked the pistol. "Did you think they wanted you? I didn't even want to find you tonight. Who would ever want you when they didn't have to keep you? Don't you know, in your heart of hearts, that if your father had a choice that day, he would've chosen your mother instead of you?"

Brick walls crowded Mira's thoughts. He would allow her past and the world to join her in this detainment, but only when they brought her pain.

Except he was wrong. He had to be. Petra wouldn't have lent Mira her clothes if she and the others hadn't wanted Mira to join them. And her father—she couldn't know his thoughts the day she was born, but years on, he wouldn't wish her gone. She knew her father better than any cop could. And what would he really say?

Don't talk to pigs without me. That was fine; she didn't want to talk to this one.

His gun pulsated with a sickly thump, his mustache twitching into a sneer behind it. Mira's jaw snapped open in a broken-glass shriek, and she hurled her phone toward the alley's end. It struck above the cop's cheek, shattering one lens of his shades before crashing between his boots.

His hand snapped from the gun and grasped his face. "You aren't supposed to assault an officer!"

A bleach-like smell overtook the animal odor as he pulled his palm free. Pale taffy-like strands wriggled from an eye socket of jagged black shards.

Mira retreated a few steps back up the alley, covering her mouth and nose against the chemical stink. Trying not to vomit.

The cop's voice turned raspy. "Don't want to be a cop anymore. Not fun. Should be something else. Something that'll actually want you."

He smeared a hand down his face. Clay mounds bubbled and turned runny like egg yolks, and then he stopped presenting a mustached visage.

Instead, he took on Mira's. Her round cheeks. Her chapped lips. Everything became a mirror except the broken shades, where blue eyes should have stared through her glasses in horror.

"No? Even you don't want you?" The cop-thing covered his Mira-like features. "How about this?"

Another face appeared. Mira knew it from old photographs, half-remembered now. It was a stranger's face, and yet not, with features she barely recognized but her brain did, and somehow the cop-thing had fetched it from her mental photo album.

"She could've lived if she wanted to. It was her choice." The cop-thing wagged a finger. "But she didn't want to hang around you either."

"Don't you dare look like her!" Mira shouted. "You don't need our faces. Just be what you were in the first place—a fucking pig!"

The cop-thing shuddered toward his cruiser. "*Piiig*," he moaned. "Pig, pig, care for a jig? That's dandy. That's just swell. It's your game now, you disappointing Miracle. A pig kind of game."

His face shifted into the mustached cop again, but only briefly. Streetlights flickered around his twitching form, casting half a dozen shadows over the asphalt, each twisting into a different impossible pose of bent-back joints and broken bones.

Mira retreated another step. She wished there were an intersection at the alley's center, but both walls stretched between their neighbor streets. Her boots kept scuffing backward.

"Pig, pig, pig," the cop chanted. "Pig, pig, pig. Miranda can't save you now."

He slapped both hands against the cruiser, and his fingers melted into its damp surface. His legs pressed against it, too, and they sprouted the same tubes as his flesh-made phone.

A vicious grin slid under his mustache, and then his teeth parted, lips tearing, jaw breaking loose and jutting outward. It went on stretching away from his tongue, and then it crawled upward, pressing the thin skin of its underside against his face until the whole mouth folded impossibly around and over his skull, swallowing his head down the now-quivering sphincter of his throat.

Mira at last tore her gaze from him and dashed screaming up the alley. Her borrowed boots skidded over drenched garbage, nearly toppling her, and she had to scrape one hand against the bricks to keep upright, keep running.

A squealing roar gusted against her back as she reached the alley's end, where the cop had first accosted her. She didn't mean to look back, only meant to turn, but couldn't help catching sight of him from the corner of one eye.

Something massive jittered from the twisted amalgamation of cop and cruiser. Both had shaken the air with tension since Mira first spotted them, but they'd quit pretending to be two separate figures, and instead formed this new shape only partly obscured by darkness and rainfall. She made out a mountain of pale flesh and shaggy white hair piled atop four limbs. Lengthy teeth jutted from a sagging lower jaw, large enough to tear her in half. Steam billowed from the creature's open heaving snout, ending in a flat piggish nose, and thick silvery bristles jutted from his hide like the blades of a thousand swords.

One eye shined with headlight radiance. The other was dark, bloody, racing above his thunderous cloven hooves.

At me, Mira realized. *At ME.*

She darted left of the alley mouth moments before the white boar came slashing into the night. Gleaming ivory tusks scraped the brick corners in a vicious screech, and blood splashed from the ruptured eye, spattering Mira's shoulder and arm in red.

Her steps slid under her again, righted, and she hurried down the street, purse clapping her side. Monstrous steps clattered from behind her. The boar was turning to give chase.

She veered right at the next street, left into another alley, right again at its intersection between buildings, on and on. As far away as she could get.

A broken car horn bleated ahead of her. Others answered, chased by a chorus of rumbling engines and brakes against tires. Below, a subway rumbled, and elsewhere she could hear the distant banging of a dumpster lid. And shouting. Footsteps. Laughter.

People.

Mira couldn't know if she'd only been lost on a too-quiet street or if she'd misplaced the universe and now found it again. Didn't want to know. Sirens roared nearby, louder than ever, and she needed to get away before the boar caught up, before others like him arrived in their cruisers, with their guns.

Her boots—Petra's boots—slammed the pavement, dashing toward the next street. The boar's breath steamed into the night, a fire in his belly.

Something that wants you, his voice echoed. *Pig, pig, pig.*

Another squealing roar erupted as he charged. She couldn't catch enough breath to scream again, could only clench her muscles and barrel around the next brick corner.

Onto a sidewalk thick with pedestrians, where she crashed through them. Some glanced her way, yelling *watch it!* but most ignored her, pressing on with their night. If only she could've done the same, if she could've found—

There. Across the four-lane street, a trio of red diamonds formed a downward triangle, aiming toward a golden glow peeking from windows below street level.

Three of Diamonds. She'd made it.

Hooves beat pavement as she reached the curb. No time to wait for a walk sign—she leaped into the busy street and swerved from lane to lane. Some cars halted, blasting their horns. Others took no notice, zooming on as if she weren't darting past them in her pell-mell escape to the opposite sidewalk.

A passing vehicle clipped her elbow as she hit the far curb. The impact sent her spinning to all fours, a pained scream welling up inside her bones.

Sirens wailed and car horns blasted, but the boar's rage shook the night as he rushed into traffic. She felt him three lanes back and threw all her weight onto the hand of her good arm, hated that she had such a thing as a good arm and bad arm now, but she couldn't deal with that in this moment.

The boar was two lanes behind her, halfway across the street.

The siren screamed louder, turning a corner as she scrabbled to standing. She looked either way for a direction, an escape route, anything.

Only as she caught the color and shape from the corner of one eye did she realize the siren was not the sound of more cops heading for this lane. It was something else.

The world slowed as the boar went on charging. Slanted rain darkened the city as she spun to face him, but his remaining eye burned brighter than the sun, an alien fury meant just for her.

And she let him focus only on her.

Let him get one lane away, an oncoming headlight about to slam into her, through her, his hot breath fuming cloudlike over the curb.

Let him have a moment, in the split-second before a red geyser filled the world, to realize as Mira had that the siren was a fire engine ripping through the city streets, finally catching enough of a break in the gridlock to rush toward its destination.

Only for its flat, merciless front to ram into the white boar.

One tusk shattered on impact. The bad eye caved inward with the side of his skull. His middle burst like an enormous overripe cherry, caking the street and sidewalk with blood and drenching Mira from head to toe.

She flinched back, bumping into onlookers as she wiped red rain from her glasses. Cars braked at the fire engine's rear and sides. Crimson gore coated its windshield.

The boar peeled himself off the burning metal in a wet squeal. Cracked hooves thumped against the pavement as rainfall stewed his battered tissue and dripping insides. Mira couldn't make out true muscle and bone within. There was only a meaty bag filled with blood, as if formed by something that didn't understand how the insides of bodies were supposed to work.

He shuffled to one side, becoming less boar-like with each step. Pieces sloughed from his body before morphing into bits of garbage and dented car parts, leaving a trail to the mouth of another alley. His limbs were sloppy noodles, his head falling apart in amorphous shapes.

For a moment, city lights glimmered around him as if he were drinking them in, drawing strength from them, and a tremendous shadow slid over the street, some truer shape beyond any he'd shown in flesh tonight.

Darkness then blinked over the corner, and he vanished from Mira's sight.

Echoes of *Did you see that?* and *Get off the road!* swirled as she stumbled backward. One boot scraped its heel over nothingness. She turned around and plodded down concrete steps, leaving a red handprint on the glass door to Three of Diamonds.

It was not a club. Not a gimmick place, either. Mira instead found a nondescript diner of hardwood floors and landscape prints with seemingly no personality and hardly any patrons.

Except in the back booth. The girls had gathered on soft seats— Petra fidgeting with her hearing aid, London adjusting her rainbow scarf, Stephanie tapping pointy pink nails at a phone screen, and Mercedes fixing her curly hair in a compact mirror.

She glanced up first, gasping, eyes widening, and the others followed.

Mira stood shaking at their table's edge, dripping pig's blood. "Sorry," she croaked. "That I'm late." She turned to Petra. "And sorry. I got blood on your clothes."

The girls stared in silence, and she stared right back, wondering what she'd expected. What she was even doing here.

Sirens howled before she could reach any conclusion, and the diner's windows flared with red and blue light. There would be more than a fire engine now. There would be cops. Either like the last one, or so similar that they left no way to tell.

I could be Ev-Ree-Bah-Dee.

Mira aimed a trembling finger to one side. "I have to—"

She coughed hard, didn't try to speak again, instead staggering from the booth and into the ladies' room. Another handprint marked the door, from her good arm, the one she could lift without throbbing pain.

The sinks were empty. She headed for the nearest one, where the sensor read her blood-coated hand and gushed hot water over her fingers. The gore was clingy and strange, but at least it was dead tissue. Not becoming a cop, or a boar, or anything. She pumped soap from a half-empty dispenser and scrubbed hard, but there was so much. Too much.

Her cleaning slowed as she caught sight of herself in the mirror. White eyes peered through her glasses and a damp sheet of red. Hardly herself. Not a college girl either. Some random teenager, fifteen and exhausted and scared.

The mirror held her gaze even as the ladies' room door swung open. The reflection of Mercedes appeared behind her, and then London, and Petra, and last Stephanie.

They reached the sink as one and clustered in a horseshoe around Mira, not speaking, not hesitating, all of them hugging her and letting the blood seep from her body and into their clothes, skin, and hair. Changing them to become as imperfect as she was.

Their arms coiled tight around each other, and her, as if meaning to squeeze something out of her. It emerged, after a moment, as racking sobs and thick tears.

The harder she cried, the heavier the rain beat down on the city.

THAGOMIZER

Zero miles per hour

Jodie is driving home from the hardest evening of her life when movement at her windshield's corner drags her foot onto the brake. The green sedan screeches a toddler-like tantrum against asphalt, and the headlights peer golden ahead, where she catches the tip of a gray tail sliding offroad, into the black curtain of forest. The longer she watches, the better the trees crystalize out of the dark.

But there's nothing else in the woods. Nothing in the road.

She eases against the driver's seat and glances at crisscrossing tree limbs above, each stripped by November's cold. One of them must have cast a mirage or shadow between the shining headlights and the glare on the windshield. She can't imagine an animal that large would cross the back roads here, let alone vanish between undisturbed trees.

And what kind of animal to account for the size of that tail? An elephant's tail doesn't jut long from behind it like a Komodo dragon's, or wield a set of spikes the length of Jodie's arm. And no elephant wanders loose in the dense wilds of Pennsylvania tonight. She would have seen it. She would have felt the little earthquakes of its footsteps.

Like thunder, she thinks. And then, *Thunder lizard. Dinosaur.*

Which is obviously ridiculous. The "tail" must have been a low-hanging tree limb. The "spikes" were branches. Nothing more.

Jodie slides her foot from brake to gas, and her sedan rolls deeper into the wild.

```
35 miles per hour
```

She sighs to herself as the car regains speed. Night should give an escape from the evening, and heading home should mean an escape from disturbed earth, but here she is, imagining a stegosaur on the road. A favorite of all the dinosaurs.

Against her will, she thinks of Clayton.

It was always stegosaurus with him, to the point Jodie hardly noticed their presence in the house anymore. The way she and her friends chose kitchen themes, Clayton loved spines and spikes and dorsal plates. He had plushies of them, plastic toys, clothes with realistic ones grazing, even cartoon ones lounging on pool chairs with shades over their eyes. The sight of one in a toy aisle, even in recent years, would remind Jodie of Clayton, especially of when he was four and five, bubbling over with questions she didn't have the answers to, some about the future, even more about the past. All before he started learning things on his own and telling her all about them. Jodie had to raise him alone with Trevor away so often, but she didn't mind at the time.

She sinks into a favorite memory: the first time he snuck up behind her in the kitchen, where themed hedgehogs smirked and curled from every corner, and wrapped his thin little arms around her waist.

"I love you, Mommy."

Often a small child is a baby bird, crying for more, but in that moment there was nothing asked for, only a sudden outpouring of affection, and she knew that was the meaning of motherhood.

If only she could have frozen that moment. If she could only feel those arms again, exactly as they were when her son was tiny.

Not the way they became as he grew.

A gray figment strokes the golden cones of her headlights, and she flinches one foot toward the brake.

```
15 miles per hour
```

The sedan slows, and Jodie glances past the now-empty passenger's seat where Clayton used to call shotgun. She scans the woods for hints of an enormous buck, or maybe a Canadian moose that's gotten lost and come this far south to cross the road ahead of her.

Only a black veil fills the passenger's seat now, and the night looks much the same. Jodie can't blame it; she's wearing a black coat over a black dress, and were a large animal to wander into these polyester folds, the night wouldn't see anything either. They can both be the enemies of sight and the keepers of monsters.

The car rolls onward before her eyes can adjust to the naked trees. A shiver climbs her spine as if a back-seat ghost now breathes down her neck, wondering what she saw, annoyed she has no answer.

"Low-hanging tree limb," she whispers to herself, and no one else. "Branches. Not spikes."

There's a special word for the spiky area on a stegosaur tail, the kind of last name you'd give a Gothic heroine's evil fiancé whom she has to leave for her true love before the book's end. Thaddeus? No—thagomizer.

Clayton was the one to tell Jodie about that. He also told her that, despite what's depicted in drawings and movies, stegosaurus never battled tyrannosaurus because millions of years separated each species. A big herbivore like a brachiosaur or stegosaur was probably more dangerous than any carnivore, too. Prehistoric territorial herbivores liked to throw their weight around, same as rhinos and hippos and moose today.

Except Clayton called them "mooses." She couldn't help laughing whenever he fumbled in repeating big words he'd heard on documentaries full of computer-generated animals.

"You don't believe me?" he asked, incredulous.

"I believe you," she told him, thinking how this little boy knew nothing of danger, and she laughed again at hearing him think he knew the threats of the world.

Her laughter came less often as he grew and changed. He remained thin, but what had once been a child a little short for his age sprouted into a gawky teen. The thinness reached beneath his skin, drying the inner well that watered his personality.

Jodie felt the difference most keenly when she would wash dishes and he would sneak up from behind, same as their old game, to wrap his arms around her.

But they were not a four-year-old's arms, and the hug was not a spontaneous show of affection. This new embrace clapped over her biceps, pinning them tight to her torso, and then Clayton would squeeze and squeeze until her spine and abdomen cried.

"Sweetie," she would say, desperate to keep calm. "You're hurting me."

"You don't like my hugs," he'd say, probably swelling a bottom lip she couldn't see. She could only feel his vicelike arms. "What's wrong? Don't you love me, Mommy?"

She tears loose from memory, easier than she used to tear from his grip, when another gray shape slides by in the night. A leathery low-hanging tree limb, with shining black branches.

Her foot leans harder on the gas.

40 miles per hour

This is ridiculous. Even if that first sighting had been an animal and not a tree limb, Jodie's been going anywhere between fifteen and thirty miles per hour, forty now, and increasing speed. The same animal would have to keep at pace—or better—to cross the road ahead of her again and again at the exact right points. Unbelievable for an animal of the size she imagines, and far too deliberate. Animals don't plan that way; she doesn't care how much a large herbivore might throw its weight around.

Night's black curtains blink open ahead where the trees give hints of a small town. If she takes a right at the next fork, she'll probably find a better-traveled road, and then brighter lights, and then places to fill up on gas, grab a snack, take a breather.

But she has many miles to put between her son and herself before she can pull the sedan into the driveway at home.

At least the cold wriggling sensation in her gut offers an explanation for why she's imagining her son's favorite prehistoric creature on a present-day back road. A little desperation to reach home.

And a little guilt, too, that she's set this kind of distance in the first place.

50 miles per hour

Trevor should sit in the car beside her, but why would he? The man is never here. Most anyone in the U.S. military can be sent home on leave when their child dies, but he's chosen whatever hell he's causing overseas instead of vulnerability and support here with Jodie.

"A world of troubles, but people are supposed to be able to raise some kind of child in it anyway," he said once, and he's never elaborated. Jodie guesses he expected his life to be kept in Tupperware back home, unchanging and unperturbed.

And when that expectation fell apart, it must've been less frightening to run from it. Uncle Sam calls, and Trevor serves, an unbroken rule, and he wanders the world with only brief stints home, where he sits in brooding quiet. Hardly speaking, but never listening either. He refused to hear Jodie tell of how Clayton sometimes hurt birds and squirrels in the back yard. Or the chill of him standing over the bed at night when she slept alone.

Or the grip of his strong thin arms.

Last Friday night's car accident when Clayton chased some small animal into the street seemed a blessing. Jodie didn't smile when she got the call or when she met the doctor and then the mortician. She was a good mother full of tears.

But she couldn't deny the relief.

That sense of calm was of the short-lived species. Over the past few nights, a part of her son has been visiting her dreams. She can't remember what he does in them, but she knows the terror of waking from each nightmare, drenched in sweat, and swearing she can hear him asking why she won't stay asleep and stay with him.

"Don't you love me, Mommy?"

Everyone else had the decency to keep their questions to themselves, but she imagined they might wonder, *What kind of mother buries her son on the far side of the state?*

The kind who wants to burden friends, family, and well-wishers with a tiresome journey so they'll pass on the afterparty and she can go home alone. The kind who isn't planning to visit.

She was not expected to speak at the service or burial. Only to cry. Let others tell made-up stories about Clayton's bright future, snuffed out too soon. She forced her eyes to stay open past dry, unblinking pain, past tears, until his casket settled in the earth. She then counted rhythmic shovelfuls of soil until a machine filled the grave and flattened its mound against a dead boy who'd upset the shape of the land.

And as if Clayton's death has also upset the shape of time, that illusory tail slips again off to the roadside.

Jodie beats an open palm against the steering wheel. She doesn't cry out—no one's ever listened, so why bother? Trevor's overseas, and Clayton's in the ground, and God is cracking a strange joke with a cruel punchline.

Why did the stegosaur cross the road?

To scare the shit out of a terrible mother.

Has the same joke and punchline found a terrible father overseas? Jodie can't know, and Trevor, Clayton, and God might be scarce, but she isn't alone in the car. Her crushing guilt fills the air, scentless, unseen, yet as deadly and suffocating as carbon monoxide.

The longer she stretches this already-long journey home, the worse the drive will get. She won't stop anymore, won't slow. When there are no more roads ahead, there will be no more specters of Clayton to haunt her. Dreams, dinosaurs—every figment will sink away.

```
60 miles per hour
```

The sedan slides around a curve in the road. Headlights flare ahead, streak past, and wither in the rearview mirror. It's the first car Jodie's seen in over an hour, but the world already feels a little more normal.

```
65 miles per hour
```

Until something crosses the corner of her eye. She refuses to glance its way, instead cracking a window, and letting the chilly November night slide through the car, stirring the airy guilt into a benign wind. No letting it crush her. No letting it remind her how she taught Clayton to stir powder into milk to make liquid chocolate.

That boy who liked to learn from her vanished many years before Clayton died. On some level, the same length of time has passed since she stopped liking him. A terrible thing for a mother to feel.

But true.

```
75 miles per hour
```

The world ahead becomes a stranger as the road sprints beneath twin headlights. Jodie is no longer driving through the dark woods. Crisscrossing branches above melt into a slushing gray blur, and when a shape whips past her windshield frame, she can't tell tree limb from tail from asphalt.

```
85 miles per hour
```

The offroad grayness becomes liminal. If Jodie can't tell the difference in what she passes, then she could pass anything, anywhere, anytime. Her sedan might have turned into a time machine, only needing the speedometer needle to climb another few notches before she finds herself warped into a prehistoric epoch. She'll wonder where all the autumn-stripped trees have gone, and what the dinosaurs think of her, and how her fossilized body might someday be excavated to puzzle paleontologists. The mother who died before her son was born.

She tries sparing an eye to watch the roadside and keep the solid world in check. If she can capture it, then it can't reshape time, can't slide her back millions of years, can't show her Clayton's favorite dinosaur.

"Low-hanging tree limb," she chants to herself, and the guilt, and the night. "Tree limb, tree limb, tree limb." She can even count them as they pass, like shovelfuls of earth on a dead boy's casket.

```
95 miles per hour
```

The night is a golden cone upon the asphalt ahead. Nothing else exists as offroad grayness fades to blurring black. Jodie can't see the trees for the forest, or the forest for the trees, and when something appears in the road again, rushing through sacred headlightgold, her foot has grown eagle talons and locked itself against the gas.

She expects the calamity of another sudden car in the Pennsylvania wilderness.

But she sees a lengthy stretch of leathery hide, corded by thick muscle and firm spikes the length of her arms. The scales are gray, and the thagomizer's teeth gleam as black as night.

Jodie has only a blink before the tail slams across her windshield, thrashing the sedan into a pinwheel scream.

*

```
Zero miles per hour
```

Black. Gold. Black. Gold.

Jodie tries opening an eye. Squeezes it shut. Opens it—red mud drips from the steering wheel, the remaining headlight flutters gold, fissures cross her broken windshield in patterns of lightning bolts and spider webs—and shuts the eye again.

She prefers the darkness now. She finds a fuzzy peacefulness here, some unknown black lake where child-sized hands might rise from the muddy bank and drag her down to the water. It's cold and wrong, but it's a deep place where her shrieking nerves and shattered bones can't hurt her any worse.

An earthquake rocks through her. It drives bone shards into muscle and shakes Jodie's mind from tranquil inner shores.

Thunder, she thinks for a second time tonight. *Thunder lizard*.

One eye squirms to open, but blood weighs it shut. The other fights off a heavy eyelid and stares past the cone of a flickering headlight. Windshield cracks obscure the woods and the asphalt, but Jodie fights through dizziness and darkness to make out movement past the dark green hood of her sedan, lying half on the road, half off.

This is not a slender tail-like tree limb skirting past her headlights' range. Four thick legs carry a gargantuan bulk longer, wider, and taller than a pickup truck. Dorsal plates clack against genuine low-hanging tree limbs, and its tail thrashes behind. The whole of it is beyond imagination. How could Jodie have ever tricked herself into thinking those thin protrusions of tree were part of this scaly colossus?

She fidgets between her seat and the steering wheel. The hand of her unbroken arm grasps the wheel, and her fingers sink into congealed sludge. She is bleeding, has been bleeding, and will bleed worse if she can't get up, get away, crawl from the sedan before something worse than guilt comes crushing her already-broken body.

But the car is broken, too. The crash dented its frame inward, twisting the doors shut. The hood's been crunched, pinning the dashboard against Jodie's legs. Her foot's still leaning on the damn gas pedal, but it no longer cares how fast she wants to go home.

The world quakes with another footstep. Another. A slender head slides past the windshield as the prehistoric giant reaches Jodie's new prison.

She manages to hit the seatbelt release, but the car keeps her.

No escape here. There's only the night, and a flickering light, and herself, squeezed in place, as if two thin limbs have wrapped around her body from behind, pinning her arms to her torso. Echoes of a boy who won't let go, no matter how far she drives.

And somewhere beneath the scream of chrome and steel collapsing under a prehistoric foot, she can almost hear his lilting voice ask an expectant question.

"Don't you love me, Mommy?"

WITHOUT A FACE

Mercy Harper had kept her distance from the Cassandra Holiday School for Girls for three decades and had missed two class reunions. Her excuses were ready in case anyone asked why she ignored her invitations, surreal observations that while the school had an ugly kind of majesty, its atmosphere was solemn, the stone and timber built around a skeleton of loneliness.

No one ever asked. She told her excuses to herself and buried the memory of what happened to Cassandra. Some days, she couldn't remember the school at all.

She remembered when she found the new invitation. It was delivered not by faceless stamp and envelope, but by a handwritten note nailed to her front door. Someone had come personally. She could forget all she liked, but she hadn't been forgotten.

And deep down, she could never really forget.

She arrived by car the night of the thirty-year class reunion. The school's outside had been repainted a clean white and the window frames replaced to look less disapproving of all they surveyed.

But beneath the surface cosmetics remained the despondent two-floor manor, its interior preserved to Cassandra Holiday's tastes, too lavish for a school. The silvery picture frames that bordered former headmistresses' portraits and the hallway floors' narrow red carpets only emphasized the feeling that Mercy didn't belong, that none of them ever had. This was a place not meant for children, but someone forced children to come here anyway. Even as an adult, she felt unwelcome.

A single enormous room made for the gymnasium, auditorium, and dance hall. What happened in one capacity bled into the others. A lovely winter dance might inspire the girls' athletics by spring.

A night's tragic fencing championship could haunt a reunion.

Five tables under white tablecloths had been set between steel foldout chairs with cushioning, and to the side awaited a self-service bar. There were four women, as few as Mercy expected. No one sane would want to come back here. Still, one of these women had made it her personal business to see that Mercy attended.

There was Grace Scott, her blonde hair tumbling past her waist, always the show-off. Odette Cleary still had that spark in her eyes. She held Gisela Weber's hand the way she used to when they were girls, but Mercy couldn't guess how often they still saw each other. Rosa Fitz stood against the bar, apart from the crowd as ever, but insistent on being present.

That was all. Mercy quietly wondered if it was only ever them here. Out of a class of twenty-eight, how many were living lives too free of this place to bother coming back?

"She graces us," Rosa said.

Grace nodded to her. Odette bowed, and Gisela snickered.

Mercy's memory caught up with her. There was an ominous portent to these particular girls, including herself, being the only ones to gather here. The old fencing team. She would break the omen if she walked away, but she had to know which of them had invited her with a nail in her front door, a tiny impaling sword of steel. It was impossible to come right out with the question.

She sat at the table and lied to them. "It's lovely seeing you all. You've aged nicely."

Gisela covered a laugh with her hand.

"Apologies," Odette said. "She started drinking early."

Gisela always had the makings of a drunkard. The night before their first fencing tournament, Ms. Holiday had given the team a little gin, and Gisela spent an hour singing before she fell asleep. Had she drank enough this past week to visit Mercy's home with a hammer, nail, and invitation?

"These reunions aren't easy," Rosa said. "It's more a responsibility than a party. Sometimes we need encouragement."

Likely it was her. The nail was Rosa's sort of direct approach. Mercy examined her long enough to start seeing double—no, there was someone against the gym wall, far behind Rosa, near the eastside exit. Wonderful. The presence of anyone outside this group of five would break the link with the past.

Mercy turned to Grace. "Who else is coming?"

"No one, dear. We didn't even think you would show."

"Then who's that?"

But when Mercy and Grace looked past Rosa, the wall was empty.

Mercy sank against her seat. "They must've left."

"Must've wandered in by mistake," Gisela said. Red veins stenciled her eyes. "But who would see this building and come here by mistake?"

"Has it been closed?"

A group shrug worked its way through the meager reunion.

"It's a large building," Mercy went on. "They must do something with it through the year."

"Says who?" Gisela asked. "Is there a law that says they have to do something with it? Maybe it's here for us." Odette pulled her close and filled her glass with dark liquid.

Grace brushed back her hair. "The school has carried something of a stigma these last few decades since Old Lady Holiday was sent to the asylum."

Mercy's blood turned icy. Grace came out and said it, just like that, as if it was nothing. As if it was ordinary. With that approach, she likely sent the invitation.

Odette smiled. "I don't see why. Cassandra deserved it. The school should've given honors for surviving. Especially poor Mercy here."

Poor Mercy. Odd choice of words. Had she let the years cloud her memory? Sometimes words were so strong they beat the past into the shape they liked. Or was this a trap? Odette might have set a snare with an invitation as bait.

They all remembered her. Mercy had been afraid of that. It meant any of them could have sent the invitation, and the likely reasons why were just as frightening.

She excused herself. The nearest washroom was attached to the changing room near the gym. So long as she didn't glance inside and see its long wooden benches which broke the path between the twin sets of lockers, where she once lay bloody and beaten on the tile floor, she would be fine. Then again, nothing here could stop her from walking out the front door, heading home, and getting on with her life. Nothing physical and real.

She stepped inside the washroom and doused her face with cold water. The porcelain basin was as spotless as the day she left. Many nights she and Grace had worked across its surfaces with toothbrushes.

Behind her, a toilet flushed. She looked to the mirror to see which stall had feet planted under its door and met eyes with the past. Her reflection wasn't a middle-aged woman with crow's feet around her eyes and a raven's blackness in her solemn smile. Instead the mirror showed her at fifteen, slim, smooth-faced, laugh lines hardly formed.

And behind her stood the fencer. A fencing foil slid down her side, its knobby, harmless end pressed to the sleek washroom floor.

She wore a white uniform and a fencing mask so dark that there were no features, only a faceless empty place. Still, her height gave her away.

"Ms. Holiday?" Mercy spun around, jaw clenched so hard it hurt. No one stood behind her. No feet lingered beneath the stalls. She didn't even hear water running, only her heart's drumming in her ears. Back at the mirror, her reflection showed her as she was.

The front door hadn't gone anywhere. She could still leave.

Gisela was singing upon return to the gym. Another drink and she would be passed out.

"Do you remember how Cassandra would give us a cap of gin the night before tourneys?" Grace asked Odette. "We were so anxious, she had to settle our nerves."

Mercy retook her seat. "I thought that was just that first tournament."

Grace noticed her and winced. "Every time. Everyone but you. That can't surprise you. She must've known what was going to happen when we started spreading rumors."

We? So Grace knew. Likely they all knew.

Rosa piped up. "I don't think Mercy knew the rest of us were lying."

"Does it matter?" Grace smiled at Mercy. "Old Lady Holiday was a witch to all of us, but she was only a monster for you. Gave us the gin, gave us the best equipment, gave us help. Are you surprised? You had the shortest arms, dear. The least reach."

Mercy hadn't thought about the others when it happened. Her only focus had been the fencing championship, that no matter how Cassandra treated her, she only had to prove herself against the opposing school's team. She hadn't considered the game of chess Cassandra played over who challenged who and which girls had the best chance to win in the end. What she knew was that day in the changing room, when an anonymous fencer towered over her.

Silent, she beat at Mercy with a fist and the hilt of a foil. Broke her nose. Broke her fingers. Meant to break her spirit, but the body would do.

And then for Cassandra Holiday to intervene in the nurse's office, begging Mercy to keep quiet so the game wouldn't be delayed for an investigation. Telling her Grace or Rosa could win, if only Mercy forfeited her match. As if she wasn't the same height as Mercy's mysterious assailant.

But no one else on the fencing team knew that was the start. They only heard Mercy's stories.

"I'm sorry," she said. "I wasn't listening."

Gisela laid her head on the table and giggled.

"I asked if you knew the rest of us were lying," Odette said.

Rosa added, "What's done has been done for over three decades."

"Do you hear footsteps?" Mercy turned around in her seat. They were the steps of her assailant on the tiled floor of the changing room, the only sound she made besides striking Mercy. "Do you think Ms. Holiday was invited?"

"Don't you know?" Gisela snickered and this time the others echoed.

The past echoed, too. After the championship, when Mercy told the girls in secret about what Cassandra had done in the changing room, they laughed at her. She had been assaulted, they had no doubt, but not by Cassandra. Cassandra had no faith in Mercy's ability, but they didn't believe she would sabotage one piece of her team to bolster the others. Too high a gamble. Grace, Odette, Gisela, Rosa—they were only willing to get onboard when Mercy rerouted her story away from the assault and into rumors that brought Cassandra's sanity into question.

Here in the gym, more than a quarter century since, nothing had changed. Mercy would always be one apart. And behind them, back at that wall, wasn't there a masked fencer with a hand to her mask where the mouth would be, covering up a laugh?

"I don't have to think things when I know them." Mercy slapped her hand hard on the table surface. The strike echoed through the gym and silenced the laughter. "I know someone nailed an invitation to my door. Someone wanted me here. One of you."

Everyone but Gisela shook her head. She was passing out on the table.

"Then who else? The fencer I keep seeing?"

"The what?" Grace asked.

"There's someone else here. I see her. Do I have to be the one to say it? Rosa, I'd think you'd be willing to say it. Ms. Holiday is here. She nailed the note to my door."

The laughter was gone from their eyes. Now they shared the same worried look as when they first heard Mercy's stories years ago.

Grace traveled to the bar and found herself another drink. "Cassandra Holiday is dead."

"What did you think happened?" Rosa asked. "They took her to the funny farm and she lived happily ever after? Three days in, she stole a half dozen other patients' pills."

Mercy pounded the table again. "If that's true, how is she here tonight?"

"She isn't."

"She's right there." Mercy shot up from the table. "I see you! I'm not afraid of you anymore!" She knocked past unconscious Gisela and darted for the eastside exit, the door having only now softly closed behind the masked fencer.

The east hall lay lit but empty. The sound of footsteps drew away. Mercy chased after. Cassandra had to be in her eighties by now if she was still alive, and it had to be her. There was no one else. Not unless the girls were right, that she couldn't have been the changing room fencer.

The hall's décor changed after passing a few rooms. The red carpet gave way to tile flooring not unlike the changing room while the silver-framed portraits melted into white drywall. Somebody waited ahead.

Mercy was catching up. Her legs hadn't felt this spry in years.

More than one somebody walked ahead of her. To either side of the hall hulked mountainous men in white coats and slacks, their white shoes' footsteps drowned by maniac screams and a distant, endless sobbing. Between them, their meaty hands ushered away a tall, lithe figure, her upper body wrapped in a fencing coat.

No, not a fencing coat, Mercy realized. A straitjacket.

The figure glanced over her shoulder. Mercy expected to see the featureless fencing mask, but found only the sunken, sallow face of Cassandra Holiday. She was younger than Mercy now.

Mercy halted, expecting that if she averted her gaze even for a second that the apparition would vanish. It would leave her on red carpet once again. She stared as long as she could while Cassandra and her escorts grew more distant, but she couldn't keep from blinking.

When she opened her eyes, the asylum hall was gone, but the red carpeting had not returned. A dim, gray corridor loomed before her, built from the bones of Cassandra Holiday's School for Girls, but bereft of its skin. Years had eaten at this hall. It looked the way the school always made Mercy feel. This should have been validating, but it only made her run back to the gym.

The door gave an awful screech now. There were no tables in the gym, no self-service bar. Someone had pulled out the bleachers where parents and visitors once sat to watch sporting events like the fencing championship. Thick layers of dust caked the seats still standing; the rest had collapsed. Spray paint dressed the walls, high as the ceiling, with various curses and symbols. The floor was a ruin of holes.

Mercy forced her eyes shut and then open again. This vision stayed. She hurried across the battle scars and out of the gym, where she found the door to the restroom and the adjoining changing room.

"Nothing can stop me from leaving," she told herself, and then wondered if that was true. "Grace? Rosa? This isn't funny."

"Funny farm," she heard Rosa say. From the changing room.

Mercy lingered in the opening, uncertain she wanted to see the changing room's state. It might be an empty, harmless relic, a graveyard of old sins, or it might be a vision of that night. She wasn't sure which she feared the most. She stepped inside.

The roof had collapsed, clearing away the lockers and benches. By some miracle, a hanging curtain remained over an alcove for girls who wanted privacy. Mercy wondered, had she changed behind it on the night of the championship, would she have been spared the mysterious fencer's wrath? She doubted it. Cassandra had come with a purpose.

And she would come again. Mercy expected her to appear any minute now from behind that curtain, her soft footsteps now crackling with debris. The rest of the fencing team was gone. They had left her to this.

"No," a cold voice said. "You left them."

A white glove gripped the curtain and slid it gently aside, revealing the fencer. Tall as the lockers, she strode without hurry across the ruined changing room, foil in hand, face obscured in blackness. She paused a few feet from Mercy.

"You expected this was an invitation to revenge," the fencer said. Her voice was a loud whisper, throaty and condescending. "But you couldn't keep away."

Gooseflesh dotted Mercy's skin. The room had turned frigid. "I knew you were here. They were lying before."

"You were all lying." The fencer stepped closer. "Even to

yourself. What was it you thought earlier? Words may beat the past into the shape they choose."

"One of them nailed the note to my door. It couldn't be you. You couldn't have known which of us started the rumors. Could've been Grace. Rosa."

The fencer neared and now Mercy saw the mask did not entirely obscure her face. Within the blackness there was gray bone, eyeless sockets, and an eternal grin. "It was only ever us here. The only two people in our little world." The foil clattered on the debris-strewn tiles. "Rosa was tall then, you know. Grace, too. In fact, the entire fencing team was made up of unusually tall girls except you. You had no reach."

Mercy knelt beside the sword. She was close enough to grasp its hilt. They had gone to a great deal of trouble to chime in with her stories back then. But it would've been best not to lure her here, force her to confront the past.

The skull in a fencer's mask breathed over her. "You wonder who nailed the invitation. Well, who wanted you here the most?"

Mercy's fingers locked around the hilt, much as they might the handle of a hammer. The changing room transformed.

In the gymnasium, Rosa had joined Grace's side at the table, while Odette, diving as deep in her cups as Gisela, danced her fingers through Gisela's hair. The three conscious women were chatting noisily when Grace noticed someone had entered the gym.

"Is that you, Mercy?" she asked.

A fencer watched from where Mercy first entered the gym that night. She held both arms behind her back. Her featureless mask appraised the room.

"We thought you must've left after that outburst." Grace tapped the table. "Come join us and drink. We'll make amends by morning."

"Where did you find that old thing?" Rosa's stoic demeanor broke into a giggling fit. "And how did you fit into it?"

Mercy crossed the gym's threshold on soft footsteps, arms hidden until she had nearly reached the table. Then she showed them.

"It's the championship," Odette said. "Don't you see? She never had her shot."

It was Rosa, the least inebriated, whose eyes widened first. She understood. "Where did you get that, Mercy?"

Mercy raised her arm past her shoulder, fingers gripped around a hilt, but not of a harmless fencing foil that bent like a blade of grass. Rising above her head, she wielded a steel rapier. The guard, engraved with the pattern of a rhododendron, sprouted into a stiff, sharp blade. It was meant for thrusting but was sharp enough to slash.

Mercy brought it down in a swift curve and slashed Odette's throat open.

Grace shot out of her seat to run, and the still-moving rapier plunged through her upper back. Mercy supposed it must have found her heart. She fell across her foldout chair and onto the floor.

Rosa folded and braced her chair to her front, a makeshift shield, but her gait was uncertain. Like the others, she had been drinking too much tonight. Perhaps if she had been as sober as Mercy then she, too, would have seen the past, understood that she didn't belong here. Cassandra Holiday's School for Girls was Mercy's place. No other alive.

She strode up on Rosa, took the front of the chair to one arm, and drove the rapier into Rosa's middle. The chair slammed the floor between them. Rosa gurgled something obscene and fell at Mercy's feet.

At the table, Odette was dying, trying to hold her throat together and wake Gisela. Neither was possible. When she saw Mercy coming, she tried to run and only fell on the floor beside the self-service bar.

Mercy paused at Gisela, sleeping, and squeezed her hand as if Odette could still reach her. She was defenseless, but Mercy couldn't leave this incomplete. There would only come another nail, another invitation. She thrust the blade through the back of Gisela's neck.

The gym became silent except for the warm breathing within the fencing mask. Mercy slumped into the same seat she'd taken before and let the mask thump onto the reddened tablecloth. The sword hit the floor beside her, a tinny strike on wood. Sweat coated her face, but it was done now.

The featureless mask gazed up at her. It really was hard to tell whose face was behind these things. Looking over the table and floor, at the figure who stood near the edge of the gym without her fencing uniform, Mercy didn't need to know. Right or wrong, she had made sure. And there was no one left to remember.

She reached across the table and pulled the old fencing team's drinks to her. A little something to settle her nerves.

LAST LEAF OF AN URSINE TREE

Elle knows Mother's time of the month is near when she looks out the bedroom window and sees the bear appear in the driveway. About the car's size, she is a beast of brown shaggy fur, tremendous snout, and scraping claws.

"Of course it'd happen today," Mother says, shoving bags into the back seat. She glances from car to window and snaps impatient fingers at Elle. "The bear will have to follow behind. We can't be here when the landlady's back. If she's on her time—you don't want to see. She's got a big tyrant bear, the prehistoric kind. Don't just stare at me, move!"

Elle hurries clothing into her worn pink backpack and clutches Leaf, her green stegosaur stuffy, named for the shape of his spinal plates and missing a plastic eye. Residue of her life dots the room in crayons, papers, and garbage. The landlady will know they came back while she was in Florida, squatting in an empty house without paying the rent. She might change the locks this time.

When Elle steps outside, Mother's bear takes the back of her overalls by the teeth and carries her toward the car.

"Didn't I say move?" Mother snaps. Her hair frays in dizzying swirls. "Want me to give you what your brothers got?"

Elle shakes her head, hugs Leaf, and lets Mother's bear shove her into the car's passenger seat. She watches the tiny house sink into trees' shadows as Mother reverses out the driveway. Her bear follows as if birthed from that place, a forest of monsters.

Except even leaving gives no escape. The monster's slobber soaks down Elle's spine.

*

Monthly cycles didn't always bring bears. Elle's schooling is dodgy, but she can tell from what she's gleaned in scattered history lessons that bears used to be wilderness creatures, circus servants, sometimes meat. She doesn't know when things changed, or how, or why.

But she's known Mother's bear all her life. And other bears, too.

Once Mother parks the car amid downtown's brick and concrete, her bear follows, and passersby take notice.

"Wonder if it's the little girl's," an elderly woman in a blazer says to her phone. "I remember when mine came the first time. Still miss him some days."

Mother snaps her fingers—Elle is staring again. Her bad habit. Easier to forget a growling stomach when lost in someone else's life.

"We'll eat tonight, I promise," Mother says. "Need to stretch the cash a little until I get paid."

She orders Elle to follow into a downtown corner store, sit behind the counter with her coloring book, and remain silent through Mother's shift. Elle obeys, laying Leaf against her chest as she scrawls orange and blue crayons over Disney princesses, but she watches and listens to the store's comings and goings.

Kids her age run circles around an older woman, but she has no bear to terrify them into silence. A goateed guy leads a bear inside, grabs deodorant, and leaves. Mother says men don't have bears or cycles, but Elle knows some do. She learns a lot by staring.

Teenagers giggle over Mother's bear as the above-door bells jangle their entrance. Older than Elle, but they act like the human body is a mystery or taboo.

"Babe, you're coming to my place tonight, right?" one of them asks another. "Should get some party tricks."

"Bridget," a light voice says with a groan. "It's my time."

"Really?" the first voice asks, louder than necessary. "I don't see your bear."

"I know, but it's coming. I feel it."

Elle wonders if she'll feel it soon, too. And if not soon, when? Twelve years old, her first blood, her own bear—signs she waits for sometimes when staring. Someday she'll see a person-free bear and know it's hers.

A longing sharpened whenever Mother threatens Elle with what her brothers got.

*

Mother shoves their bags into the front seat and bundles them each under blankets in the back as night brings a chill to downtown. The bear sleeps beside the car, sharing ursine warmth, but she's also a giveaway that people are living out of this car. Marauding cops will send one of their own on cycle, and then a badge-approved bear will balance out any confrontation.

Or they'll wait for Mother's cycle to end, when her bear again vanishes into shadows.

Elle wakes to Mother's cursing. A blue-uniformed figure withdraws from the windshield, having pinched a cream-colored ticket beneath one wiper before the nearby bear could rouse.

"Damn busybodies," Mother says.

She rearranges the bags and starts the car, muttering to herself about how she misses New Orleans. An oft-repeated sentiment, how once upon a time she was comfortable and ate well. Her nostalgia stretches to cover secret wounds, but Elle can't blame Mother for it. A better time and place than where they've come from.

Better than what Mother's become.

She moves the car each night, but sometimes parking feels almost as expensive as rent, and food isn't cheap. They are never starving, but their bellies are never full, either, and Mother tries to balance hunger and patience, but eventually hunger wins. Elle can tell money is scarce by counting Mother's curse words.

She can likewise count her age climbing by the week, by the year. Someday, she'll feel what Mother calls *that first hot knife in your gut*. Elle isn't sure if she'll see the bear beforehand, a friendly omen, or if pain will sneak up on her.

But she knows her body is bones and dirt. Mother can hardly feed either of them. If one-eyed Leaf the stegosaur were edible, Mother would cook up a spiny-tailed dinosaur stew. When Elle's bear appears at her first blood, it will be a creature of bones and dirt like her. Too weak for commands.

Too weak to fight Mother's bear if she decides to give Elle what her brothers got.

"It was necessary," Mother said once. "There's strength in bloodshed. Something has to die so someone else can be born. You're only here because they're gone. Be grateful."

Elle was then expected to thank her mother. So she did.

*

Mother's bear is gone when she drives them out of the city, back to the house in the woods.

"Landlady's got to be in Florida again by now," Mother says. "We'll get a couple months' peace before she next checks in."

Elle hardly understands how she mistook this place to be a forest of monsters when they last left. Only in returning from weeks downtown can she appreciate the unspoken perfection of the tiny house, near invisible from the road, tucked between rows of fluffy-leafed trees down a narrow stone path. It is cozy and green and good.

But night will come. It always does.

Mother is off her cycle, the bear gone, so why does Elle hear prowling outside her bedroom window? Why does a shadow cross the line of light beneath her bedroom door?

The hunger has grown. Mother has failed to feed the bear, or the bear has failed to feed Mother. Elle has no idea which carries responsibility there, but they share a need for food. When the bear returns, will Mother stop those jaws and claws?

Or will she let someone die?

*

The bedroom door moans as something large and powerful presses in from the hallway. Elle scarcely has time to wake up and understand what's happening, let the chilling immediacy of it infect her bones, before a dull grunt ripples through the wood.

Mother's bear is in the house.

Mother's bear is breaking down the bedroom door.

Mother's bear is hungry.

Elle leaps out of bed and forces up the window, about to squirm through. A flash of grim premonition sees her caught halfway in and out, the sill snagged against her bony hips. She instead scurries under the bed, where her breath sends dust bunnies quivering.

Leaf lies abandoned at the bedroom's center. No time to go back for him.

The door crashes open on squealy hinges, and a cloud of hot breath surges across the room. Floorboards cry beneath massive paws. The bear's moonlit bulk knocks the bed firm against the wall, and its screech forces Elle to cover her mouth against a sympathetic scream.

Forepaws stop at the window, where a slobbery muzzle presses through the gap above the sill. The bear can't fit, but she's distracted now, thinking her prey has slipped outside.

Elle has to do better than let the bear think this, better than staring. Time to run. She crawls from under the bed, through darkness, toward the outline of her bedroom doorway. Her crawling is gentle on the floorboards. Nearly gone.

Moonlight glints off Leaf's remaining plastic eye. He is so close, Elle can stretch into the depths of the room beneath the bear's hindlegs and grab the soft stegosaur by the tail. The rescue will take seconds.

Elle holds her breath and reaches out. Fingertips brush wood, a dust clump—there, stuffed cloth. She wraps her hand around and yanks Leaf close.

His eye clacks against the floor.

The bear shudders in surprise and then tears her head from the window. The moon glints white in her slobber, and a savage moan seeps from her body as she twists to face the bedroom doorway. Never would Elle have thought this monster could be so graceful.

She crushes Leaf to her chest and flings herself out of the room. Behind her, the world quakes in muscle against doorframe, claw against floor. The bear is coming, and she's faster and stronger than any little girl in the world.

Elle dashes screaming into Mother's bedroom. It smells of ancient perfumes and bad dreams.

The atmosphere cracks with a finger snap as Mother startles awake and orders everyone to knock it off. The bear freezes in the hall. She will never disobey Mother; that is not the way of blood-called bears.

Elle can't be so silent and still. She shrinks to the floor, and her tears soak Leaf's flank where she squeezes him against her face.

Mother snaps her fingers again, and again, but no impatience can fight this panic.

"Give me a break, Elle," Mother says, pleading. "She'd never hurt you. I love you. Enough."

Elle swallows a sob. After all Mother's threats, how can she say that? Baffling that she might even mean it, only hurting Elle's brothers out of necessity.

But they're dead all the same. Elle might be dead someday, too. Should she be grateful?

Mother can't hide her needs. A mother bear must feed to make more bears. Something has to die so someone can be born, and Mother is hungry like Elle.

Between hunger and love, eventually hunger wins.

*

Daylight comes, a chance to catch up on rest, but Elle is afraid to sleep. The bear prowls outside the shut glass, the wooden walls, somewhere in the shadows of the trees, maybe peaceful, maybe waiting for Elle to quit watching. Quit thinking.

There's no winning a fight against that monster, but could Elle win against Mother? She doubts it. Child against parent might as well be child against beast, and Mother is a bear in her own right.

Elle glances out the window, where Mother's car sits lonely in the driveway. If only she'd catch word somehow that the landlady will soon return from Florida, on her cycle and with her big tyrant bear in tow, that would bring salvation. Elle and Mother would have to flee this house and sleep together in the car downtown. No chance for nocturnal bear attacks.

Unless Mother chooses one.

The fantasy dissolves under Elle's stare. No one is coming. Couldn't someone leave then? Elle should pack her things into her ratty pink backpack and sneak herself and Leaf out the window.

Without a bear rattling her nerves, she might fit. Might even escape.

But where would she go? In the house, she misses downtown. Downtown, she misses the house. Mother has her memories of New Orleans to crawl into at night, a time when she was comfortable and ate well. Even her bear remembers.

Elle has no better days to hide inside. Her life has always been one house or another, squatting or renting, living out of the car in between, her constants being Mother and her bear. Elle scarcely has a past.

She may not even have a future.

*

Nighttime stabs a hot knife into Elle's gut. Sleep-stickied lips tear open to scream as Elle envisions a bear claw driven into her gut, eyes flashing open to slobbery jaws and soulless hunger.

But her bedroom lies empty. Only Leaf joins her on the bed while shadows cling to the walls.

Blood seeps between her legs and dots her pajamas.

Shouldn't there have been some warning? Where is her bear? Is she so malnourished she can't even call the most meager of bears to her? She gets up to wake Mother, who might help in the bathroom for cleanup and a pad, but heavy breath says she isn't alone in the bedroom.

He rises from the dark, tall and gaunt. His jaws feel immense, his claws terrible. He is Elle's bear. Finally.

And yet for all his bear nature, he is bones and dirt compared to the prowling beast outside. Stronger than Elle, and maybe Mother, but not mightier than her bear.

Elle runs fingers through his soft coat and inhales the newness of him. She could command him to fight Mother's bear, even though he'd lose. They could creep out of the house, and she could ride him elsewhere, maybe all the way to New Orleans, however far that is.

She could have him eat Mother when her period ends. That would stop everything. No more Mother, no more cycle, no more brother-eating bear turning an ursine appetite toward a daughter. But would Elle's cycle match Mother's, binding them?

Too many rogue possibilities swirl in Elle's head. Were she to threaten Mother and fail, Mother might have her bear devour Elle before she finds another chance.

Elle has control of herself and her bear, nothing else.

She places Leaf on the floor, pats his one-eyed head, and then kneels beneath her bear. She gives him a long stare, scrutinizing and memorizing his sharp teeth, wet dog-like nose, and glittering black eyes.

"You have to do what I say?" Elle asks. "Anything?"

The bear watches her and gives a halted groan.

"Okay then." Elle tells him what she wants.

His ears twitch. He's hesitant, showing it in the hair and muscles bristling up his spine. He might think waiting will change Elle's mind.

But she's had practice at staring, and the longer she drives her command into him, the more he's compelled to obey. Her first blood has come. She is a bringer and commander, and he is her bear.

"Do it," Elle says, and then she repeats her command.

The bear closes his teeth around her skull. They descend by inches, as if he thinks his throat's engulfing darkness might change her mind if he takes it slow. She says nothing, lets the bear's jaws fold around her head, the teeth puncture scalp and cheek, and at last the bear hurries to bite down, crush her skull, snap her neck, anything to end this. He is so large, and she so small, that he can crunch, tear, and gulp down thin flesh and weak bones and pajamas until he has devoured everything the world has known of Elle.

She is gone.

And yet, she lingers. The bear's insides spread to fit a little girl of bones and dirt. His menstrual-enchanted digestion tugs at her body and feeds him, her bear, and his strength feeds her. Round and round the strength of bloodshed goes, like light circling the rim of a stuffed stegosaur's only eye. The bear grows into nocturnal blackness until he fills every shadow of Elle's room, a tyrant bear of the prehistoric kind.

He—she?—they are no longer bringer and brought, bleeder and bear. Unity has drawn them tight in the darkness.

Across the house, another bedroom breathes the faint scents of sleeping Mother.

They could go to her now, but instead they'll wait. To come upon Mother by surprise in the dark would be too much like the thoughtless hulk prowling outside the house. They're a different kind of bear, one who wants Mother to see what's become of her daughter. She ended Elle's brothers, after all. A mother should know the fates of her children. She should be grateful.

After that, Mother can see what it really means to die so someone can be born. A little girl is coming, and she's faster and stronger than any parent in the world.

They aren't sure if they'll still exist at the moment Elle's time of the month should end. Mother might vanish down this same throat, and then her bear, and when the cycle would stop had Elle lived, they might fade into shadows, or themselves, leaving only Leaf to show the landlady they were ever here. Or they might live on as girl and bear in one body.

The future is no certainty, but when has it ever been? They won't worry about it yet. There is only this moment and what they plan to do. Daylight is coming to wake Mother in the tiny house tucked in the trees.

And this morning, it is a forest of monsters.

HOPSCOTCH FOR KEEPS

I was watching TV when Mom called me to the living room window. "Kim, who's that?" she asked.

Our old apartment in Johnson City faced Market Street, and across Market Street sat the blacktop park. It had no name, but it did have a basketball court, skateboard dip, metal spinner always too hot to touch, and an open stretch between the monkey bars and slide.

The hopscotch kid was on her knees in denim overalls, drawing hopscotch squares in pink chalk. Other kids were playing outside, but not with her. She was alone.

I didn't know who she was and shrugged at Mom to show her. Kids came from all down our street and a couple others.

"Still a couple hours until dinnertime," Mom said. "You should play with her."

I wanted to play my Sega instead, but she told me to, even though it was a hot summer afternoon and I could melt. I took a can of grape soda from the fridge to rub on my forehead.

Hot, watery air made the cars lazy when I crossed Market Street. The angry sun heated the blacktop and cooked us in sour sweat so that every kid left a snail trail. I saw Jordan hanging upside-down from the monkey bars and waved. He stuck up his middle finger like his dad did when driving, so I stuck mine back at him. He dropped off the monkey bars, and I followed him smiling toward the slide. We stopped at the pink chalk lines.

Some other kids hung around the hopscotch kid's squares then, but no one hopped. We never played hopscotch anymore; that was for babies. I'd finally be eight in two months, catching up with the rest of my friends.

Except Phoebe. She was eleven, but hung around us anyway, and sometimes let me play with her Skip-It or listen to her Walkman. Earlier that summer, she got real sick and had to leave for a couple weeks. The grown-ups wouldn't tell me why, but Jordan's dad told him it was because Phoebe took too many pills. Mom only gave me one pill for a headache sometimes, but I guess some moms are bad at math.

The hopscotch kid stood when she had drawn twelve squares in ones and twos. Her grin was big as the sun, like a grown-up's mouth glued onto a kid's face.

"Who's first?" she asked.

Jordan smeared one chalk line with his sneaker. "This is baby stuff."

I nodded. A car crawled by, and I flapped my T-shirt to take in the worthless breeze.

"Fine, I'll go first since everyone else is chicken," the hopscotch kid said. She stomped to the first square and then hopped one leg, two legs up the pink chalk squares. She fell at the last one leg square. Other kids laughed, but she kept grinning. "Who'll do better? None of you."

Phoebe went. She made it look cool with her bouncing jean shorts and red light-up sneakers. She finished without stumbling. I wanted to go next, but then everyone was arguing that they could go. Jordan and three other kids went before I got a turn. I couldn't finish it, but I got as far as the hopscotch kid.

She went again and made it to the end. "Let's make it interesting," she said. She got on her knees again and started drawing more squares. The air got sticky while we watched. She drew way past twenty, almost reaching the street.

Jordan wanted to be first.

"Not so fast," the hopscotch kid said. "What's your bet?"

He pulled two dollars from his pocket. Ice cream money. My soda can had gone warm, and I daydreamed about strawberry ice cream on my sticky tongue. I hoped the truck would come by soon.

The hopscotch kid pulled two dollars from her overalls. "Winner takes all."

Jordan started hopping, but he tripped even earlier than the hopscotch kid had on her first try. She hopped past his last square, almost to the end, before she dropped. He wanted to go two out of three.

"Maybe later," she said, pocketing four dollars. "Who else wants in?"

Most other kids backed away, but Phoebe wasn't chicken and neither was I. Jordan stayed with us, too. He wanted to win back his ice cream money.

The hopscotch kid leaned over me. "What do you got, shrimp?"

I held up my soda.

She nodded. "I'll do a dollar for that."

I tripped where I had to split my legs at the fifth and sixth square. The whole time, I hadn't meant to open the can, but when the hopscotch kid grabbed it, all I wanted was grape soda. I didn't have skin anymore, just sweat.

Phoebe was next, and the hopscotch kid asked what she had. "My credit's good for you," Phoebe said.

I didn't know what that meant, but the hopscotch kid stamped her foot. "You got to bet something," she said. Her grin got bigger. "Or everything. You could bet everything. I'd totally play for that."

Phoebe backed away and scratched her arm. Looking at her, bigger than the rest of us but nervous now, I thought maybe Mom was wrong, that we shouldn't be playing with this hopscotch kid.

"I'm not chicken," Jordan said. He elbowed Phoebe aside.

"What are you betting?" the hopscotch kid asked. "I don't play for what I already got. Put up something for me to win."

Jordan shrugged. "Fine. I bet everything. But you give me all four dollars when I win."

The sun had to be angrier then. It got so bright that the hopscotch kid's teeth shined. "Four dollars against everything, sure. But I go first."

This time she didn't drop. She made it all the way to the end, almost hopping into the street. Cars crawled behind her. The air was so wavy and the sun so shiny that I couldn't see her too well, just a rippling blur across the blacktop.

"Your turn, champ!" she shouted. "Reach me. Come get your four dollars."

Jordan walked to the first hopscotch square and started leaning and stretching like a track runner.

The hopscotch kid turned blurrier, shinier. Looking at her hurt my eyes, so I looked at Phoebe. She was sweaty as me but didn't fan herself or grab the soda can, even though it sat at her feet. It would've been nice if she'd held my hand. I could've been brave then; I knew it. Brave enough to try after Jordan. To bet everything.

Jordan hopped one leg, two legs, one leg. He made it halfway and started to wobble, but his arms balanced him. He kept hopping.

I couldn't see him too clear after that. The hopscotch kid's shiny blur covered him. They were two smears hiding in the sun's white glare. What did we do to make it so angry? The blurriness got so bad I couldn't tell what was out there. Kids, cars, chalk, street—it was one big mess until a shape followed the pink chalk squares out of the blur, walking toward me and Phoebe.

It was the hopscotch kid. She was alone.

I asked where Jordan was, and she grinned at me. "Must've gone home," she said.

The air still rippled where the hopscotch squares hit the street, but I could see again. Jordan wasn't on the sidewalk. He wasn't anywhere. He'd hopped into that shiny blur and vanished like he was eaten by the angry sun.

And the hopscotch kid grinned.

I didn't know what I was doing, shaking all over. My hand grabbed the grape soda can. I wanted to run home with it, but instead I threw it at the hopscotch kid. It hit her in the forehead and exploded on the sidewalk, all purple and fizzy. Everything smelled like grape. Blood bubbled up the slit in her skin.

I meant to say sorry, but instead I shouted, "Bring him back!"

The hopscotch kid stomped through the purple puddle and loomed over me. She should've blocked the sinking sun and cast a shadow, but the glare brightened around her. "He's mine now," she said. "You want to play for him? Make your bet."

I didn't know what she did to him, but it wasn't fair. "I'll tell on you."

"Tell?"

"To your mom."

"Tell my mom?" The hopscotch kid giggled, sharp and mean. "What mom? What do you think we're doing out here, shrimp?"

She shoved me over. I landed in the spilled soda and scraped my palms on the blacktop. Even the puddle was warm as it soaked into my shorts.

Phoebe started in, fists clenched, but the hopscotch kid backed off. A red line cut down beside her temple and around her cheek. She was still grinning. "We're not playing horseshoes, girls," she said. "This is hopscotch. And I play for keeps."

I didn't want to play anymore, but her horrible white teeth

made me feel like I had to. "For Jordan?" I asked.

"For him? You'd have to play for everything." The hopscotch kid snatched the leaky soda can off the blacktop. "Everything and a replacement can of soda."

Phoebe took my arm and helped me up. "She'll get you a new one," she said. "Then we play for Jordan."

"Don't go getting in trouble," the hopscotch kid said, but I was already in trouble and she knew it. "No breaking something so Mommy grounds you, no offering to do chores. I won't be here once the sun drops, and the only way you're trying for Jordan is through me. Bring my soda. Then you hop the chalk."

I went to cross Market Street alone, but Phoebe came with me. She didn't say anything else, just followed me toward my apartment. A car paused in the street and crawled past after we crossed. I thought how it might be easier to get hit and have an excuse to drop hopscotch than try getting my mom to stop me. She'd wanted me outside. We heard her snoring in the bedroom.

"Where's your bathroom?" Phoebe asked. I told her, and she went.

I looked out the window at the blacktop, where the hopscotch kid batted the last grape soda drops onto her tongue. Shadows stretched long from the slide and monkey bars, but not from her. Nobody else was on the blacktop. The ice cream truck rolled up, but it didn't play its music and didn't stop, like the ice cream man knew he shouldn't talk to the hopscotch kid.

I never wanted to go outside again, but Jordan was stuck somewhere. He wasn't coming back if I stayed home. I had to try, no matter how the hopscotch kid made my hands shake. She looked up at the window, cheeks all shiny, and I felt the blacktop turning into a deep dark hole, sucking me down. I got cold even though I was still sweating and couldn't stop staring until a soda can hissed behind me.

Phoebe was pouring grape soda into the sink and covering the can's opening with her hand. She frowned when she caught me looking. "You ready?" she asked.

I didn't talk, just walked back to the door.

Phoebe carried the open soda can. "I was never here." She went into the hallway and looked back. "Coming?"

"We can make her give Jordan back," I said. "If we find her mom—"

"Didn't you listen?" Phoebe shook the can at me. Soda sloshed inside. "She doesn't have a mom, or a dad, or anybody. It's just her. You think that thing's really a kid out there?"

I didn't know what she meant, but it made me think I had to go. My sneakers squeaked on the hallway linoleum. Phoebe offered her free hand. I took it, squeezed hard, and let her lead us outside.

To the hopscotch kid.

The air was hotter, the heat rising off Market Street and the blacktop to make up for the afternoon getting late. Phoebe didn't let go of my hand as we crossed in front of honking cars. I touched the spot where Jordan vanished, the edge of pink chalk squares, but didn't feel him there. The hopscotch kid had put him far away.

She saw the soda can was open. "You drank some of mine?"

Phoebe shrugged and let go of my hand. "Don't be a baby about it."

The hopscotch kid snapped the can from her and grinned at me. "You'll go after me," she said, and then gulped down grape soda. "But I'm here to win. Don't think because you're a runt that I'll go easy. Jordan's worth a lot. Maybe even more than everything you got."

The new can crumpled in her fingers and clattered beside the one I'd thrown. Its puddle was gone—the sun drank it—but the hopscotch kid stared at where it used to be, like she was seeing something on the blacktop. Or not seeing something. I couldn't tell.

"You go before her?" Phoebe asked. The hopscotch kid nodded too far, like she had a heavy head. "Fine. But I'm going first!"

"That's not how we play," the hopscotch kid said. "That doesn't count!"

But Phoebe had already started, one leg, two legs, up the chalk squares. She hit the middle and wobbled, spread her arms to keep steady, and then kept going.

The hopscotch kid leaned close to me. She had grape soda breath. "This doesn't count," she said. "And when I catch her, she's gone. You'll be alone then, Kim. You want them both back, you'll have to win twice before sundown. Once the sun's gone, so am I."

I didn't ask how she knew my name.

Phoebe was all I could see. I thought her hop should count. She wobbled one more time near the end, and it looked like the sunshine might get really bright again and catch her. She straightened, kept going, one leg, two legs, and finished at the street's edge. Not shiny or blurry, just far away.

She waved at me and the hopscotch kid. "For everything!" she shouted.

The hopscotch kid stepped up to the first square. She looked pale and sick. One leg bent, but not like Jordan's had, more like she couldn't help it. She hopped one leg, two legs, stumbled, kept going. Her two leg squares took the longest.

Around halfway up the chalk, she turned shiny and blurry again. It hurt my eyes so bad that I saw three pink squares together once, but she still put a leg on each. I couldn't tell her shape anymore.

The blurriness cleared, the shine dulled, and she was the hopscotch kid again, just wearing overalls with two ordinary legs. She fell out of the chalk squares and hit the blacktop.

Phoebe and I ran to the center of the chalk.

The hopscotch kid had creamy purple fizz in her teeth. "Short game," she said, but I didn't think she meant her last hopscotch bet. She grinned at Phoebe one more time. "Think you're so smart? This doesn't hurt; I'm just going home. You'll still have to deal with the ruin to come."

She stopped moving and talking. I could've put my head on her chest to hear if she was breathing, but I didn't want to touch her.

Instead I shoved Phoebe. She was too big to move, but I tried anyway. "How do we get Jordan back?" I asked. "She was the only way! What do we do now?"

"Now you go home," Phoebe said.

"But Jordan—"

"We have to be far away from this thing." She took my hand again, walked me across Market Street, and left me at the apartment doorway.

I didn't wake up Mom. I watched out the living room window at the blacktop. The hopscotch kid hadn't moved from where we left her beside the chalk. She was alone. She stayed alone until evening, like the sun was hiding her from people.

The way her face looked, still a shine in her teeth even just lying there, I knew Phoebe was right. That wasn't a kid out there. When people finally noticed her under the streetlights and an ambulance came, they thought they were trying to help a girl like me, but all they touched was what the hopscotch thing had left behind. No soda, just the soda can.

If she ever came back, she wouldn't look the same. Maybe her flavor would be orange soda, or cherry.

Or whatever flavor Jordan would be. I couldn't really sleep that night. I kept dreaming about him in a shiny white place, blinded and screaming, the sun always chasing. Every time I tried to grab him, a dream of Phoebe would pull me away. Then I'd wake up.

I didn't tell anyone that Phoebe had been in my apartment, but someone must have known because she went away after that. Johnson City police officers asked me about her, but I didn't tattle.

I didn't even know what she did. They asked me about Jordan, and I told them the hopscotch thing took him.

They said I was brave, but they were lying. They didn't believe me.

Mom wouldn't say where Phoebe went, just that we couldn't be friends anymore. "When you make a kid mistake, you get a kid consequence," Mom said. "Phoebe made a grown-up mistake, so she has a grown-up consequence."

It wasn't fair. Mom's the one who made me play with the hopscotch thing when I just wanted to stay inside. I yelled that it was her fault, and I hated her. Later I said I was sorry, but that was a lie. She cost me my friends.

We moved out of Johnson City before summer ended. Our new windows face other people's yards and a smaller street.

Since then, the nameless blacktop park has been gutted and its playground equipment torn down. I guess it got a bad rep with one kid dead, another sent away, and another vanished. It's a Walmart parking lot now. No one draws hopscotch squares there anymore.

If Phoebe comes back from wherever she went, she won't find the old place, or me. Just like she won't find Jordan.

But I might. We don't have a blacktop park, but we have a driveway and that's pretty much the same. Every morning, I take chalk outside and draw squares in ones and twos. Before the school bus comes, I practice hopping. I think the hopscotch thing might come back some bright summer day, and I need to get good at hopping before then. We can play for soda if she likes, but she'll tell me to bet bigger things when she hears what I want.

My old home. My friends. The blacktop park. My life back the way it was. For all that, I'll hop the chalk, and I'll play for everything.

For keeps.

MAGICAL GIRLS CHILD CRUSADER SQUAD

Erin Bird is sixteen years old, and it's time to save the world again.

She isn't the first to spot trouble this afternoon. Can't be when she's sitting in her narrow bedroom in her parents' cramped house, which she clutters with plastic toys and stuffed animals, some she hasn't played with in years, others new to her, untouched since she scavenged them from lost-and-found boxes around the city. They're a statement art piece, something for school when she has time for it, but she hasn't figured out the meaning yet.

An altar to the thoughtless kid she used to be, with hardly any say or responsibility? A goodbye to someone whose grades aren't crumbling against universal disaster, and to a time when continued life on this planet didn't rest with a handful of teenage girls?

But childhood-Erin hardly knew who she was. You learn a lot about yourself when your body changes, when you dive frightened into battle, and when you risk death every week.

When you watch someone you care about take that risk and never come out the other side.

The trembling melody hits her ears at a frequency only she and her Bandmates can hear. That peppy whistle that signals a transformation. Every Bandmate can feel when another makes the change, and no one makes that change unless there's a threat.

Even if sometimes Erin wants to change anyway. Badly.

She presses pale hands against the edge of her creaky bed and hurries to the bedroom door for a cursory listen—no sounds of her parents lurking. They must not be home from work yet. Long hours, bad pay. That's what lets Erin get away with saving the world.

She crosses her room, pops open her window, and slides over the sill, whistling as she goes. Any ordinary teenager would plummet from the second floor, but her tune resonates with the enigmatic dimension of the Ur-Song. Time skews and bubbles across her skin. The pain is brief, the stabbing prick of an ear piercing, and when the bubble bursts open in a bright magical flower, Erin burns with rippling light.

And Erin soars.

Her clothes have changed with her. A breastplate of humming magi-music battle armor coats her torso, music notes gleaming across its black design with pink trim. Matching gauntlets and greaves guard her limbs, along with a dark skirt and leggings. Her auburn locks flare into lengthy snakes before the transformation covers her scalp in a fusion of medieval knight helmet and the billed flat-topped hat of a majorette.

But she doesn't lead her Bandmates. That's left to Rochelle.

Erin sees her now, a golden missile zipping over flat rooftops, the skyline climbing higher and higher toward the city's center. They're not an uncommon sight in the city anymore. Like the regular attacks by otherworldly monsters and strange phenomena, the locals expect someone to show up and save the day. People can get used to anything, and they've had months to get used to the Magus Nocturne Band.

There's no restrictive energy dome binding Erin or the others to this place. The Bandmates could fly anywhere in the world, but they keep close to the city. This is where vicious forces threaten to plunge the universe into musical chaos, and it's the Ur-Song's chosen battleground of mysterious destiny.

It is also home.

Soon both girls are zigzagging between skyscrapers downtown, where another radiant pair streaks toward them—a bright green rocket for Cici and a burgundy one for Vivian.

There are five members to the Magus Nocturne Band. They started as five, too, and then they were down to four, but now they are a squad of five again—sort of. Verity is still a rogue guitar solo more than a Bandmate proper, but at least she isn't trying to kill the rest of them like she used to.

For now. It's a start. Except she is chronically late.

"What's the situation?" Rochelle asks.

She keeps her dark hair cropped short beneath her Bandmate helm. Her armor is black with gold trim around her lean frame, and its vibrations radiate through the air, casting a golden sheen across her tan eyes and amber-brown skin.

She glances to Erin, her lips pursed firm, but Erin only shakes her head.

"Just felt the hum," Vivian says, tapping the side of her head. Coils of black hair jut here and there, uncontained by her helm, and they circle her russet cheeks.

"It was me," Cici says, face reddened around the gasping black circle of her mouth. "A little south of here. There's something banging and clattering down the street, calling static from everybody's radios, phones, car speakers. You name it, this thing's got it buzzing."

Erin blanches. "Is it one of Shatterine's monsters?" she asks.

Cici nods, but there must be more to it than that. She isn't usually this shaken by the devastation Shatterine brings to the city, not since the first couple weeks after the Ur-Song changed their lives. Now she's nervous, and tears glitter in her eyes.

Vivian floats toward her and rests a gauntleted hand on her shoulder. "Tell us, Cici."

"It's from that day with Marcy," Cici says, solemn. "When she—you know."

The girls grow quiet, but Erin can hear the thing distantly over the city's car horns and everyday rumble, something that bangs and clangs and wrings the songs out of the air, turning them to hushing static. Corrupting the Ur-Song.

Sent by Shatterine, malicious conductor of the Concerto Apocalyptico.

"It's the monster we were chasing that day," Cici goes on. "It got away when we turned back."

"But it won't get away today," Rochelle says.

She sounds confident, but there's a twisted nerve in her voice. The Bandmates are keepers of secret knowledge and terrible truths, but even they don't know everything. To them, a Bandmate fell that day. To most other people, Marcy's death was a freak accident, almost unexplainable. The locals, Marcy's family, her other classmates and teachers—they never knew she was a member of this rocketing-around-the-city, saving-the-world Magus Nocturne Band. Some of them even think she took her own life.

Erin knows better, every Bandmate does, but since that day they've worried that one of Shatterine's monsters wields a special power to cancel out the Ur-Song, cut its influence from their bodies and leave them powerless.

Marcy was flagging at the back of the Band that day while they soared through the city, but she was the one to alert the others. Maybe she flew too close to the monster before they arrived.

Erin can't be sure—none of them can—but they must be thinking and worrying the same. Nothing else would put that nervous fright in Rochelle's voice.

"We should fly low on approach," Erin says. "Just in case."

Rochelle nods agreement, and her word conducts the Band. They skirt through the city only a few feet above the street, not as quick as usual, dodging pedestrians with their strollers and phones and dogs on leashes. Cici runs a hand over a big dog's head in passing, and Vivian chuckles with thunder, green lightning coursing over her limbs.

Erin wishes she could pretend this moment was the precursor to any other battle. They're always in danger, but people can get used to anything, and there's no one more malleable to threats than a group of teenage girls.

Still, the nervousness sticks to them as they swerve past cars and rush down a residential avenue. Deep down, Erin worries every battle has been as life-threatening as this one, only none of them realized it until Marcy dropped from the sky. Invincible teenagers. Silly children playing war with powers from another dimension.

They've almost reached the clanging, music-twisting abomination. The thing they were chasing the day they lost Marcy. Maybe they should turn back, but Rochelle powers on, and the rest follow.

"Hear the radios?" Cici asks.

Yes, Erin hears them. Static gasps and undulates from each speaker with anti-music. Whatever this creature is, it's tied to the Ur-Song magic, which means it must be Shatterine's doing.

Rochelle draws her flute-blade, and her golden aura flares sun-bright. The others draw their weapons too, each burning with her own radiance, together forming an ambient concert with their magi-music battle armor.

They're an incomplete performance. Beside them gaps the empty space where Marcy used to fly like a dazzling silver star.

But Erin has heard before that you go to war with the army you have. Even if their numbers are few. Even if they're too young to be diving into war in the first place.

Together the Bandmates stare down a street of brick apartments, cracked sidewalks, and aging cars with old-fashioned stereo systems, each singing static to the tune of a crystalline behemoth. Geode-like growths tower from its back in a messy amalgamation of color. They scrape together at each girthsome step, summoning the static to answer the two-story elephantine beast's lumbering march through the city on legs as thick as eighteen-wheelers. Crystal tusks jut from its face, and a cruel white glare says it knows exactly what it's doing to the music.

It might even know what it did to Marcy.

Residents have already fled indoors. Some are likely losing their minds, especially if they're the type of people used to hearing music in their heads all the time, those cranial tunes now bent toward malicious static. Anyone new in town might try to call the cops, but residents who've seen this kind of weird conflict play out a few times? They already know that the cops never show up for problems like this.

Only the Magus Nocturne Band dares face Shatterine's underlings or her mutations of the Ur-Song.

Erin waits for Rochelle's command. So do the others, everyone hovering at a standstill. They've made it this far, but getting close might mean ending up like Marcy.

"Enough," Rochelle says, flourishing her flute-blade. She speaks like she can read every Bandmate's mind. "We can't let her memory distract us."

"She's barely been gone, Ro," Vivian says.

"We could be gone too," Cici says. "Erin was right about flying low, but how close is too close?"

Rochelle opens her mouth to speak and then purses her lips. Always calculating, always deciding the best course, but the Band never lost anyone before Marcy. Her death has beaten fracture lines through the group. If they fly toward this particular monster with too brash an attitude, then everyone might go dripping from the sky like a storm of teenaged raindrops.

Cici shakes her head. "Can you hear it? The city's crying for us and singing for a doomsday choir."

"Here I thought you were the give-up girls back when we'd spar," a stern voice says. "But this is just pathetic."

Another light pops across the rooftops and descends into the Band's airspace, and now they are five again, the way they started. Not Marcy—she's never coming back—but Verity flares beside the Bandmates, her once-terrifying white visage now sharpened to blue-hot fire. She never mingles with the others at school, and she eats alone in the cafeteria by choice, but out on the battlefield? She's here when it counts.

"Spar?" Erin asks. "That's what you call trying to kill us?"

"Don't blame me for your weakness," Verity says, and she aims her guitar-sword at the monster. "And that thing's weak, too. I'll show you."

Cici pleads for her to wait, and Rochelle commands it, but Verity rockets forward on her own. It isn't like Erin and the others can stop her. They could hardly survive her when she was their enemy.

"Well?" Vivian asks. "We letting her go alone? I never signed up for that."

She blasts off like a crimson shot, burning on Verity's heels, and Rochelle, Cici, and Erin chase after her.

Verity strafe-floats beside the creature's crystalline back. It swipes a lazy paw at her, but it seems more concerned with pumping musical static into the world. Almost like it isn't much of a threat to five of the Ur-Song's warriors.

Except it has to be a threat. A terrible one. Because if it isn't any danger to them, then what happened on the day Marcy fell?

"Careful!" Rochelle snaps.

Verity waves a hand over the creature's hide. "Nothing's happening. You're all quaking in your boots like there's something worthy for me to fight." She braces her guitar-sword to her chest, and her elegant brown fingers shred a flurry of notes.

Rochelle eyes Erin, then Vivian and Cici, before raising her flute-blade to her lips. A pleasant tune sweeps out, and the other Bandmates follow her cue to play their own magi-music weapons. Vivian and Cici synchronize with Verity. Erin fumbles briefly with her great cello-mace, but she manages to hold it in mid-air and play.

Their little concert buckles the air around the crystalline behemoth, summoning the Ur-Song from the black depths of un-matter and all-melody. It has no thoughts, no body, only the absolute emotion of music.

Darkness coats the monster from its hindlegs to its glimmering tusks. It calls on the static again, but if it means to use musical powers to assault the Band, it should have tried when they first showed up.

Missed its chance. The Ur-Song takes it like a parent tucking a child to their breast, and the darkness swallows the abomination into pure music once more.

A tinny jingle lingers as the Band quits playing and the Ur-Song fades. The city is once more at peace. The radios fall back in line, and the cellphones, and podcasts, and every other sound people try to play forgets its static and remembers its own tune of instruments and voices and life.

"That was—" Rochelle starts.

"Child's play," Verity says. "Almost makes me miss knocking the rest of you around. How did you ever fight me, quaking in your boots over that great big slow-ass?"

Vivian cracks a smile, and Erin opens her mouth to make an excuse.

But Cici speaks first, aiming a thumb over her shoulder. "I'd better jet; I got to help prep my little sister's quinceañera for Saturday."

Erin raises a hand. She wants them to wait first, maybe discuss how they were frightened to face this thing. To talk about Marcy. If the crystalline behemoth didn't kill her, why is she dead?

But Cici zips off, leaving a nature-green lightning bolt leading out of the neighborhood. Rochelle and Vivian take off next, the work done.

Verity hesitates, hovering above the street. Is she soaking in the victory? Wondering the same thoughts as Erin? Or is she forever late to arrive, late to leave?

Erin's raised hand shifts into a wave, as if that's what she almost meant to do. Verity doesn't return the gesture. She grunts something unintelligible and then rockets off across the city. Not quite part of the team yet. She's fought against everyone more times than she's fought beside them, but enough visits from Shatterine or her malformed monsters will tip that scale.

Should the remaining Bandmates live that long.

*

Erin returns home as her parents arrive from work, one and then the other. They question why she's getting home so late, and her answers are noncommittal, the kind of vagueness that can't be interrogated for inconsistencies later, not that her parents have the time or energy.

"Friends," she says, with the adolescent shrug every adult expects.

A good enough answer for her parents. Her mother opens the front door, mumbling about studying for a math test Erin forgot about.

Her father pats Erin's back. "Glad you've finally found a peer group," he says, with the clinical perspective of a guidance counselor. "These are the best years of your life. Every boy should have high school friends to reminiscence about later."

Erin doesn't argue that she might not have a later to fill with reminiscence, or that she's spending these *best years* fighting an extradimensional war for humanity's future.

Or that, despite what she lets her parents believe, she's as much a girl as her friends.

*

Of the five girls in the Magus Nocturne Band, Erin has the easiest time hiding her secret from family, teachers, and classmates. Rochelle and Vivian have known each other forever, and they need to be careful how they appear together when they share silhouettes with the gold and burgundy Bandmates. Cici knew Marcy the longest, but that isn't an issue anymore. No one knew Verity, and it took the Bandmates time to figure out which of their classmates was Shatterine's right hand before Verity's change of heart.

But once upon a time, Erin was the odd one out, the loner, only coming into the fold when she first underwent the change. In some ways, she still feels like the odd one out, despite Verity's presence, despite her Bandmates never treating her like less than any other.

She never really knew herself as Erin until it happened. The night was crisp when the Ur-Song first swept its musical hand around her with the time-melting tune of magical girl transformation.

The change brought a panic of differing bodily shapes and feelings. More alarming was how much she liked it. How this new shape and form felt right.

And still feels right every time it happens. It feels so right that everything else that has always felt wrong has morphed into a shadowy barb stabbing inside her. It's the fuzzy vision and vertigo that hits after coming inside from a bright sunny day. Clothes, school, outdated ways of addressing her—nothing fits anymore.

But really, it never did. The change not only smashed her present, but it remixed her past to a new melody. Every memory glitters with broken-glass hints of yesteryear, the understanding that she has always flowed down this river, with the Ur-Song bringing a welcome awakening in more ways than one.

She's been hiding for over a year now, letting most of school, her entire family, anyone who sees her outside the Magus transformation think she's a boy, same mistake since always, since ever. No sense blaming them—not like she knew either.

A guilty part of her wonders if she craves Shatterine's attacks on the city. They're a convenient excuse to whistle those magical notes and usher in the transformation. Time skews and bubbles, and when it bursts, Erin doesn't look the same. It isn't solely the uniform. It's everything she dreams.

Her Bandmates are respectful. They try not to refer to her in school, even though she sits with most of them for lunch.

But everyone has such sexist expectations. As the presumed boy of their friend group, teachers and parents alike look to her to be the rock in the aftermath of Marcy's death. They feign worry over mental wellness, but really they want to offload the responsibility onto younger shoulders, and their assumptions about Erin make her an easy mule.

No one knows about the nightmares. Not even the other Bandmates.

Erin never heard Marcy hit the ground, none of them did, and yet she imagines the noise while she's dreaming. The desperate sputtering out of a silver star. The whistled-air plummet of a friend, so stunned by her unexpected surrender to gravity that she can't even scream. And through the wind rushing in Erin's ears, the hum of her armor, the clanging of the crystalline behemoth, and the car horns and city commotion below, she hears a wet, bodily crunch.

It's only her imagination, isn't it? She couldn't really have heard the sound of muscle and bone shattering across asphalt and blocked it from her conscious memory—right? Psychological denial has to be an intention of TV shows.

She tussles with her sheets for the umpteenth time since that day. The city's urban rumble fills the night, and Erin thinks of the roar of a falling star. Of a presumed suicide by parents and teachers. The worry that those presumptions might be true in some way, as if Marcy chose to cut the cord on her flight-giving armor, and the chord with the Ur-Song, transforming back to her mundane fragile self at the worst possible moment.

Because if her death wasn't the crystalline behemoth's doing, what was it? Why is Marcy gone?

None of the Band can say. They only know she isn't coming back.

At least they're aware of the when and how, that Marcy was brave and heroic. Her parents haven't a clue, and they can't be shown or told. Her death will never make sense to them.

Being part of the Magus Nocturne Band means keeping the Ur-Song's secrets. The Bandmates are blood sisters, battling together against horrors from beyond sound, bleeding in each other's arms, patching wounds, making excuses, crawling into quiet places for a chance to sob or scream, leaving homework unfinished, tests failed, extracurricular activities as a bottom-of-the-barrel priority because some days they can barely remember to eat.

When was the last time any of them got a decent night's sleep?

They know each other better than their parents ever will. Rochelle's mother has no idea that the streak of light that saved her from the crushing blow of a toppling streetlamp was her own daughter. Vivian's grandparents have never heard her relieved laughter after Marcy saved her from a cross-universal harmonicane. Cici's fathers will likely never find out what their daughter's intestines look like, while the rest of the Band will never forget those crimson tubes sliding over Rochelle's hands.

That was a Verity-inflicted wound. They almost failed to put Cici back together, but they managed in the end, pushing her intestines back in, forcing her skin shut, ending the transformation and then reigniting it. She could barely get the tune through her lips gone blue.

None of them second-guessed that maybe they were in over their heads. They each made their peace with the Ur-Song's expectations. Who else would save reality from Shatterine?

This is the cost of war. Everything Erin used to think of as normal adolescence has been beaten to tatters. That's how it is when only the Magus Nocturne Band can fight Shatterine and save the world.

And yet there's so much else.

Today has been kind to them. No dead bystanders, no cars malformed into great pipe organs. No Bandmate depowered and plummeting while her friends flew on, unaware for several minutes that their team of five had dropped to four. The crystalline behemoth was no challenge at all. Its presence didn't nullify the Ur-Song's power.

But with every Bandmate intact at today's end, that leaves only more questions surrounding Marcy's death. Erin can't figure out any answers.

Do the others wonder the same? Erin can't be sure. She hides too many feelings about these transformations, these battles, and likely there's plenty the others keep to themselves, too.

Who can she talk to, then? Her parents would love for her to open up about her friend's death, but Erin doesn't know how to share some of the truth without sharing everything, and it would be easier to explain she's really a girl than to tell them about the Magus Nocturne Band.

What would Marcy do? Erin desperately wishes to know, but Marcy will never have a chance to come clean with her parents, or fail tomorrow's math test. She wanted to be an archeologist, even though she never figured out which college major she would need to make that happen.

She was only sixteen years old when she fell from the sky. A life barely lived.

Erin tears free of her sheets, wants to tear out of her skin, but if she whistles and transforms, the others will feel it in the Ur-Song, same as she does when they transform. They'll think Shatterine's attacking tonight, as if today's monster was a bluff. Erin can't tear them out of their lives for nothing.

But she can't sit alone on her bed on the cusp of nightmares either.

*

Sneaking out is harder without transforming and flying, but Erin's exhausted parents don't rouse when she gets dressed, shuffles downstairs, and heads out the front door.

The city glitters in the night. Grass crunches underfoot, beaten by daytime heat growing more intense each year, now relieved in the cooling starlight. Erin travels potholed streets, passing clustered houses, apartments, and the chain-link fence guarding a nearby row of warehouses. Her path rounds a bodega's corner and leads onto a block she seldom visits and a house she's only approached from the air.

Back when she called the girl who lives here an enemy.

Verity's house is broad and plain, with a pale fence, wide garage, and manicured lawn, all screaming American dream. From what she tells, her parents are absent as often as Erin's.

While the first five members of the Magus Nocturne Band gained their powers at the same time and directly from the Ur-Song,

Verity gained hers from Shatterine. The Concerto Apocalyptico conductor wanted a Bandmate of her own to battle the Ur-Song's forces. Even after turning over a new leaf, Verity is hell in magi-music battle armor. She must have fought the Band two dozen or more times before they finally convinced her she could never be more than Shatterine's pawn.

She's one of the Band now, but that doesn't mean everyone trusts her. Likely she doesn't trust them. It's enough to fight on the same side, and for her to feel independent in making that choice.

Erin clambers up the tree outside Verity's room, where she tosses pinecones at the glowing glass until the curtains part and the window opens.

"Bird?" Verity asks. "What the hell's your problem?"

"Can I come in?" Erin asks.

Verity stares a moment, and then she retreats from the window with a dismissive hand, clearing the way for Erin to scramble inside.

Musician posters coat the cream-colored walls. Music sheets litter the desk, and a guitar and amplifier fill one corner. This place has known instruments since before the Ur-Song came into Verity's life.

She crosses her purple pajama-sleeved arms over her chest. "Well?"

Erin putters back and forth in front of the window. Where to start? Talk about life, and Marcy, and all the futures that haven't happened? About the crystalline behemoth, and how not one Bandmate lost her powers today, and what that means? At how there's a math test tomorrow that Erin hasn't studied for and can't begin to understand because her head's too full of devastating musical storms, invading harmonic monsters, and Shatterine's plan to swallow the city in a hellish elegy and complete her corruption of the Ur-Song?

All that comes out when Erin finally looks to Verity is: "Will you kiss me?"

Verity blinks earthen eyes. "Why?"

"Because I haven't kissed anyone before," Erin says. "Or been kissed. Because we might die next time Shatterine possesses the city with another mind-slayer ballad, or unleashes a giant dino-song at the school to hunt down all the kids while she figures out which ones are secretly us, and I don't want to die without being kissed like—like—"

She can't get Marcy's name out before tears rush down her cheeks in a croaking sob. Face covered, she turns to the window, trying to get herself under control. Even though she despises the teachers and parents who expect her to be a rock, there's some part of her unused to showing genuine feeling. She's become too good at keeping secrets for her own health.

"I'm sorry," she whispers, composing herself.

Her body jolts when an unexpected hand slides onto her shoulder. Verity draws Erin close, a hand in her hair, another at her back, as if she's a cat being petted.

"Do you think I don't feel bad about anything I've done?" Verity asks. "Everybody has regrets. They don't have to say it. We're all like that, one way or another."

"But if that monster today was harmless—what if Marcy died for nothing?" Erin asks. "What if you fought us for nothing, and we're fighting Shatterine for nothing? What if none of it means anything because it's one power of the Ur-Song against its own corruption, and everything would've been fine if it just never bothered with our world in the first place?"

Verity leans back and brushes Erin's hair out of her face. "Except you don't really feel that way. You like the way the transformation makes you feel, right?"

Erin swallows and gives a surrendering nod.

"And you know this world would be fucked anyway, don't you?" Verity asks. "It doesn't matter that the Ur-Song is here, or Shatterine. There've always been grand powers hurting people, and grand powers fighting each other, and eventually one or another wants its kids to go to war. That's who we are right now. If it wasn't us and here, it would be someone else, somewhere else. This is the disgusting way things are, everywhere." She pushes a fist under Erin's chin. "But at least *we* get to fly."

Erin fights against a smile and loses.

"I'm not going to kiss you, Erin. Maybe in other circumstances, but—" Verity stares off into the distance and then bores her gaze into Erin's eyes. "You got classic survivor's guilt, traumatic fear of death, and probably half a dozen other psychological problems neither you nor the rest of our magical musical parade have had diagnosed or looked after because everything we do is a goddamned secret, and we never have the time. Right now, you need a good night's sleep. And you need to grieve."

Erin wipes her reddened face, still smiling. "You said *our* parade."

Verity raises her eyebrows in surprise. "Slip of the tongue. Tell the others, and I'll tie yours around your neck and choke you with it." She chins at the window. "Good night, Bird."

*

Erin scuttles down the tree outside Verity's house and back to potholed streets. She feels ridiculous, having come out here seeking formative experience, but a comforting weight blankets her heart in Verity's kindness.

And uncertainty scratches underneath. If this is the way things are, what does that say about how things will be? Is there a future if everything stays the same? Or is time a gray, unchanging sludge with one point in history indistinguishable from any other? TV shows and video games suggest an end goal to any war, a journey climaxing against a big bad, some kind of improvement beyond the final battle, but is that true for the Bandmates?

For the world?

Erin is torn from her dour thoughts by the sounds of jangling chimes. They're coming from somewhere beyond the chain-linked fence, where the warehouses loom dark and untouched. The musicality makes her wonder if Shatterine is up to no good here.

The conflict between Verity's comfort and the world's uncertainty melts down Erin's exhausted bones. Why now? She has that math test tomorrow. A friend lies cold in the ground, her memory hot and aching. Verity is right, Erin needs to process her grief, but how is she supposed to do that when she and the Band are always saving the world? How does Shatterine have the energy to wreak havoc nearly ever damn day?

For a moment, Erin wants to look the other way and keep strolling up this sidewalk. Go home. Give herself a break for once, because she never gets a break, none of them do.

But she can't. What's she supposed to do, let Shatterine hurt someone? Call the cops and hope they'll actually show up? At the last school incident, they'd cowered in the parking lot and street until the Band dispersed Shatterine's polyphonic demon.

It's up to the girls. Always has been.

Erin puts her fingers to her lips and whistles a magic tune. The Ur-Song tears through her, pain first, then relief at her transformation. Guilt follows, and then the exhaustion beneath everything else. Too many conflicting emotions battle inside her heart.

"As I suspected," says a dry yet pretty voice, like crystals scraping together. "I've known your little harmony squad looks different between mundanity and musicality, but you're the most different of all."

Erin turns from the fence to the street, now aglow in sickly violet. The air ripples as if heat swarms off the asphalt on a hot summer day, forming a geode ring around starry darkness where a chalk-white woman floats at its center. Gemstones dot her lengthy purple hair and jagged glittering armor, like a fairy princess gown fused with an ankylosaur's spiky hide.

Shatterine.

Erin raises her great cello-mace. "You're the one who's about to look different when we smear your face over the sidewalk for what you did to Marcy."

Shatterine rolls her glowing yellow eyes. "Please," she scoffs. "We're alone for the moment. You can drop the pretense—I had nothing to do with your dull gray tragedy."

Erin springs off the sidewalk and swings her cello-mace overhead. The geode ring swallows Shatterine and spits her out a little to the left, dodging Erin's blow.

"You blame me because you need it to be my fault," she says, raising a pointed index finger. "If it isn't my fault, the universe is backwards, inside-out, made-up nonsense. So, it must be my fault, yes? Except you know better. The silver one died because she lost faith in the Ur-Song."

The fingers of Erin's gauntlets clink against her cello-mace. She pauses, pensive, thinking over the past few weeks. Marcy was dejected, sure, but faithless? Never. She always put on the brave face, always backed up Rochelle's commands like a Magus Nocturne Cheerleader.

But then, Erin is always pretending in her own way. Couldn't Marcy have pretended in another?

"She fell," Erin says through gritted teeth.

"But why?" Shatterine asks. "Her armor shouldn't have allowed that."

"She changed back. In mid-air."

Erin doesn't like this explanation either. It sounds too much like adult presumptions that Marcy no longer wanted to live.

Shatterine clicks her tongue. "The gray one lost the Ur-Song. She let its music wither inside her, a plant bereft of rain or sun, overshadowed by her dreams of boys, and college, and archeology, and everything else she wanted out of a future that had nothing to do with your little squad. Maybe if she'd made a choice, it would've mattered. If she'd given up the Band, the Ur-Song might have let her go, but she kept going through the motions. To fly like a bird with a broken wing is to fall, eventually. And so she did, when the Ur-Song likewise lost faith in her. It made an example of her, and that's the real reason she's dead."

Erin rockets forward again, this time with a guttural battle cry, and she thrashes her cello-mace at Shatterine's armored head. She expects another teleporting dodge.

Shatterine instead crosses her armored forearms overhead and guards against the blow.

Her grin glows beneath melodious metal sparks. "I see the same shadows in you. Faith in the Ur-Song, indeed. But you want more, don't you? How couldn't you? You're so young."

Erin flinches back, withdrawing her weapon. Can't she even make a dent in this fiend?

"Don't be ashamed of it," Shatterine says. "No one else sees your struggle. They think the disparity between one life and another means nothing, and you let them believe it, for your sake and theirs. Your alleged friends think you have it the easiest. Maybe they accept you, even love you, much as teenagers can understand love. But they'll never see you as one of them."

Erin lashes out again. She doesn't know what to say, has never had much chance for conversation with Shatterine. She's certainly never wanted it.

"If I die, and the Ur-Song returns to complacence, what will become of you?" Shatterine keeps grinning. Why won't she stop grinning? "To defeat me is to defeat yourself. This battle would end, and then the war, and that means no more transformations. Don't you see? You need the Ur-Song's power to channel through me. How else could I have given it to Verity?"

"It's the Ur-Song's gift," Erin says. She swipes at Shatterine again, and again, but her cello-mace can't manage a strike unless Shatterine lets it happen. "You abuse the power."

"Shouldn't you?" Shatterine asks. "What else is it good for? I thrive with this power permanently, and you could do the same. Give up your everyday mundanity. You'll never get the chance to fully enjoy an ordinary life anyway. The war will drain you dry. But take Verity's place as my right hand." Her eyes gleam like twin suns at dusk. "Lead the Concerto Apocalyptico, and you'll never have to pretend you're that boy again."

Erin realizes for the first time that this is not simply the Ur-Song's war—this is personal.

She hates Shatterine. And more than that, she hates how Shatterine's words dig into her heart with sadistic longing. There are buttons in that organ, and Shatterine knows how to push them. She might even have tempted the other Bandmates, offerings tailored to each of them.

But that would mean they each refused. And it might mean Shatterine knows something about them. Maybe not their names or where they live, but enough to beckon and seduce.

Erin hovers in the air, her armor thrumming with a pink aura. Was Shatterine another high school kid at some point? She might have been chosen before the rest of them, a lone soldier in the Ur-Song's power, helping fight what was then a meager corruption before she decided to enhance that corruption for her own sake.

If what she says about the Ur-Song's faith in its soldiers is true, she might have turned against it preemptively, a need to remix the universe before it lost patience and faith in her.

Better to reign as the devil than plummet like him.

"I could never join the likes of you," Erin says, almost spitting the words.

Shatterine's grin is eternal. Like she knew this would be the answer, same as Erin. But then, why ask it?

"See you around, little squadling," Shatterine says, sinking into the violet-tinted darkness of her geode ring. "Hopefully not smeared on the sidewalk."

Erin rushes into the air again, but Shatterine vanishes into a chasm of disharmonic crystals. Only scraping music and the hum of Erin's armor linger.

She has no time to compose herself—a trio of bright lights rush onto the street, where their tailwind shakes the nearby chain-linked fence.

Vivian glances up and down the block. "We felt you change. What's up?"

"Status situation," Rochelle says. "Come on, Erin, speak to me."

Cici grips her shield-cymbal. "Yeah, where's that Shatter-slime?"

Verity soars in like a blue comet a moment later than the others, even though her house is closest to where Erin transformed.

"I'm so sorry," Erin says, forcing a hollow giggle. "Thought I saw Shatterine in the warehouses. False alarm."

Rochelle looks perturbed, had likely been hard asleep. Vivian and Cici give a good-natured chastising, but Erin can tell they're relieved she's okay. Each one speeds home, back to their individual lives.

Verity watches Erin for a silent minute, and then she, too, zips away. Maybe she's relieved like the others. Erin has to remember that everyone but Verity is grieving, and she shouldn't give them more to grieve about. None of her troubles, especially when nothing really happened. Physically, Shatterine tonight was as harmless as that monster in the afternoon. Doubtful she's figured out who Erin is by one transformation on the street.

Erin soars toward her neighborhood, and then past it, to the city's edge and the highway beyond. Small towns glitter in the night around the forests and hills and rivers, keeping secrets from the darkened world.

She could vanish into that darkness. Never turn back from the magical girl, never fight Shatterine, or her friends, or anyone. She could forget the Ur-Song's war.

But what of those friends' futures? And what would happen if the Ur-Song felt her lost faith? If it loses faith in her?

*

Back home in bed, nightmares bring vicious songs, their lyrics playing cruel questions. If Marcy were alive, would Erin have considered Shatterine's offer? And if another friend dies, will Erin change her mind? If she finds herself plummeting, powerless, will she regret turning that hand away and sticking with the Band?

I thrive with this power permanently, and you could do the same.

Give up your everyday mundanity.

You'll never have to pretend you're that boy again.

She hates the temptation. And she hates the uncertainty over whether Shatterine is right about Marcy. Verity said there have always been grand powers, always a decision to create child crusaders, and they're the recruits in the Ur-Song's enigmatic destiny.

What happens to a warrior who's given up the war? And what can a grand power demand when one of those soldiers has so much to gain and everything to lose?

The answer might be a dead teenage girl, broken across sunbaked asphalt.

Morning comes, and Erin's exhaustion and stress must be visible; her parents warn that she doesn't have to go to school today if she isn't feeling up to it.

She's grateful. She almost wants to tell them a truth as a reward, but which one? That she wants them to call her Erin now? That she wishes to start hormone therapy? Or that she's kind of a superhero, kind of a soldier, and there's nothing they can do about it because only she and her friends can fight Shatterine's corruption of the Ur-Song? How would she even explain to them what the Ur-Song is? Could they ever understand last night's temptation?

Only Verity knows how she would act under Shatterine's grasp. She alone knows she could come out the other side.

Erin hopes she never has to find out for herself. She thanks her parents but says she should get to school. Can't miss that math test.

She doesn't know the functioning behind half the formulas, and manages even fewer of the answers. These tiny numbers are more complicated than Shatterine's plans, Marcy's fate, all of it, but at least when it comes to class, Erin can ask for a make-up exam and hope for her teacher's mercy. There's no such thing as a do-over on the battleground.

The others call her over at lunch. Chatting, laughing, eating, grieving, maybe asking themselves, *Was Marcy not okay? Were we all too exhausted to notice?*

And then killing the thought when no one else says anything, a random discordant note to be ignored while the Band plays on.

There might never be answers. Sometimes people die and leave behind an infinite ellipsis going *dot-dot-dot* into the sunset.

Erin's on the verge of tears at one point, but she holds them in like usual. Maybe everyone feels this clutching uncertainty. Or their minds might be focused on school. Erin will never know the difference.

But some things can change. She looks over her shoulder to the lunch table where Verity sits alone, the way she likes it, and lifts one hand in a cautious wave.

Verity smirks and offers a sarcastic wave in return.

It's a start.

*

Evening brings open books and sharpened pencils—time to study. Erin will absorb these equations if it takes all night. Maybe some life lesson hidden in the numbers will help crack the code on herself and her existence someday. She can win the fight and still do all the things Marcy never had the chance to do. All the things Erin wants to do.

Should she and the others live that long.

She's about to review one of the formulas from today's test again when her ears tremble with a familiar magical tune.

That Ur-Song whistle. One of the Bandmates has manifested her majorette helm and battle armor somewhere downtown, Erin can feel it, and a distant explosive *boom* tells her this is no false alarm.

Her gaze falls to her notes with a sigh. She's probably going to fail the make-up math test too, and the homework that follows. Her grades will keep deteriorating toward the end of junior year until they're too poor for any decent scholarships.

If the girls ever defeat Shatterine once and for all, Erin isn't sure what kind of future she'll have left to sort out in the world beyond. And if they don't, she supposes she'll still be here, fighting the Magus Nocturne Band's extradimensional fight. She might die before it matters, a life not yet lived, like Marcy. A name yet unclaimed.

One by one, the Ur-Song might lose its patience, starting with her.

But anxiety-driven stalling won't change what Erin has to do right now. Her friends need her.

She stands by the window, takes a deep breath, and slips outside with a whistling tune between her lips. The Ur-Song's magic bubbles around her, cladding her changing body in humming magi-music battle armor. She then soars off like a pink firecracker toward the city's silhouette against a bruise-colored sky, where a new monstrosity threatens life as she knows it. She'll try to make it home before her parents notice she's gone.

Because Erin Bird is sixteen years old.

And yet, it's time to save the world again.

AUTOTOMY

Until the April after I turned ten, I woke up each day to my mother's humming. Off-key, voice sometimes cracking, there was always a good morning song in our house. I used it to find her through my always-dark world, and then I'd give her a hug that could burst the stars.

On the morning without a song, I found a stranger washing the dishes. She didn't lean against the kitchen sink's creaking counter the way Mom did. And there was something else missing besides her hum. I waited until the sink water ran so loud that I could sneak past, into the den, without her noticing.

Dad's morning toast led me to his chair. I smelled the strawberry jam.

"Where's Mom?"

Dad's newspaper ruffled. "Washing dishes."

My words bubbled out, no forethought. "There's a stranger in the kitchen."

The newspaper folded as Dad lurched out of his chair, the recliner's gears screeching, and crossed the house. No one argued on the far side of the stairs. He came back after a minute. "You scared me. Mom's still at it."

"It's someone else."

"I saw her myself."

What someone sees has always been more important than what I know. I couldn't explain my senses; it never came out right. "She doesn't smell like Mom."

Dad gave a big, bellyful laugh. "Lily, your nose could count spots on a cow. Maybe Mom smells different today, but that's still Mom."

He didn't understand. It wasn't that Mom had put on a new deodorant or perfume. The stranger didn't have the human scent particular to Mom.

She didn't have any scent at all.

I went outside, hoping Mom would come dancing back from the pond or the grocer's, the delicate way she always walked, to run off the imposter. Instead it was a long, lonely day at the chicken coop. I listened to them scrabble after the corn I threw into their pen. Chickens have an overwhelming stink, enough to drown out many scents, especially a scent's absence.

That's how the stranger snuck up on me. The whining hinges of the chicken coop scraped my nerves. I waited to hear Dad's laugh or Mom's hum, but there was only the clack of the closing gate. Two dry, coarse surfaces rubbed together and then cracked.

The stranger was breaking chicken eggs between her fingers. Runny yolk pattered in the dry soil.

"No chickens," she said. Even in the midday warmth, I shivered. Those were Mom's vocal cords at work, but they were instruments in the hands of a novice.

"Mom, can I see you?" I held out my open hands.

"Do you see with your fingers?"

"Like we used to do." My fingertips found the stranger's face.

She snapped back. "Dirty." Her footsteps, not dancing at all, sped toward the house.

My hands grasped and released the air. Even in that brief

touch, I recognized Mom's bent nose, sharp cheeks, puffy bags beneath her eyes. Identical, as if a plastic mold had been taken of Mom, grown from her.

Almost the real thing.

I spent that weekend avoiding her heavy, purposeful footsteps. My house became like the stranger, an intrusive imitation. The furniture arrangement hadn't changed, but I kept banging my hips against hard edges, and every touch felt alien.

How could Dad not notice a difference? Didn't he ever pay attention to Mom? She didn't watch nature programs or do her chores in eerie silence. She never asked weird questions like the stranger, who snuck up on me by waiting against walls, still and quiet.

"How do I make more of you?"

I had nearly banged into her. "More of me?"

"More children."

"You have to get married."

"But I'm already married."

Mom was married to Dad. The stranger wasn't married to anyone I knew. "First there's marriage. Then babies. You have to wait awhile and then it happens."

"There must be a way to speed up the process."

I knew more than that. Sara Pei told me things. I wasn't about to share with this stranger who visited Mom's pond, but not to swim, or watched movies with Dad instead of talking to me so I wouldn't feel left out.

Monday at school seemed almost normal and made me wonder if I was losing my mind. But then I'd think about the stranger's deliberate steps, her silence, her lack of scent, and no one on Earth could convince me that thing was my mother. She waited for me on the school steps where Mom used to wait. I almost didn't notice, my cane making gentle arcs across open stone until it prodded her foot.

"You have a doctor's appointment."

I couldn't argue. This was school, I was a kid, and I only knew the world I could touch and smell and hear. Everyone else saw my mother's face. I followed the stranger's footsteps along the dusty road.

"Right as rain," Dr. Kowal said when she finished checking me over.

Usually I joked about whether I could do Dad's crossword puzzles now, but nothing came out.

Not with the stranger standing next to me, saying strange things. "How about her skin?"

"Well, I'm no dermatologist, but her skin looks healthy. If you're worried about breakouts, I'd say she still has another year before that burgeoning adolescence comes roaring in. But you never know with hormones. They change everything, even mood, and they're never predictable."

"That is troubling." The stranger said it like Dr. Kowal had given me a year to live, which made Dr. Kowal laugh.

I didn't laugh. If I tried to explain my mother's absence, they would blame it on the changes inside me. Dr. Kowal probably couldn't explain how my adolescence would do away with Mom's scent. I forced a smile and took a lollipop like a good little girl before Dr. Kowal could diagnose my mood.

Dad was snoring in his recliner when we finished the walk home, but the stranger shook him awake. "I need the basement cleared out." He left his chair and brushed past me.

"She just wants it, and you do it?" I asked.

Dad laughed, his first response to everything, like language was a joke. "What she wants, she gets. Don't marry a man who'd do any less for you. Or a woman, either."

An expectant silence stalked his suggestion. Whenever Dad joked over who I might like, Mom scolded him, said it wasn't a joking matter and I had to be allowed to sort my feelings myself.

But the stranger only said, "Your father is right," and then waited for him to do her work.

Dad paused. That was the moment he might've noticed something was wrong. But he walked to the basement, probably laughing inside until the concern gave up and left his head.

From then, the stranger spent most of her free time in the basement. She was never late to walk me between home and school, only now she carried the basement's damp odor. At night, clanking metal pipes, clinking glass tubes, and a thumping engine sang me to sleep. Sometimes animals cried, I thought, but by the time I hurried out of bed to the basement doorway, there was nothing.

Her footsteps quieted so she wouldn't wake Dad. Nothing masked the basement's stink when it crept through my bedroom door one night.

"Downstairs, Lily."

Sleepy, I wanted to argue it was a school night, raise hell with her. My mood was going to change. I was entitled to fights with my mother.

Except no matter how sleepy I was, I knew this was not Mom. This was a stranger, the kind of person I was supposed to tell grown-ups about, never speak to, never take her candy. Yet everyone was okay with her. I had no say. Out of bed, through the house, down to the basement. Fluid pumped through pipes and crackled on heated glass. A pounding piston hurt my ears. The basement's scent was strong, but I smelled something new underneath, hard to distinguish, like baby powder mixed with mustard.

A hand in a rubber glove grabbed my wrist. Before I could yank it away, mealy warmth dotted my hand. The stranger let go. I rubbed at the space, smearing the gristly cream on my fingertips.

"Good, no burns," she said. "Bed."

I climbed the railing back up the stairs. A knife could scrape away my hand's skin, let it slither off to its new life with the stranger's weird cream. I settled for turning up the kitchen faucet's hot water until it scalded my fingers. The cream washed away. The stranger worked through the night, loud machines stewing her strange gruel that wasn't supposed to burn.

Dad called me to the den the next morning. The stranger was with him.

So was the cream.

"Your mother cooked up this moisturizer for the dry days," he said, chortling. "She's getting into witchcraft."

I was starting to hate his laughter, the way his cheeks slapped wetly against his gums and teeth. More disgusting, I heard a sick, gooey smack, the cream being squeezed between fingers and spread over skin.

He was letting the stranger coat it across his back. And he was going to make me, too.

"Don't hurt your mother's feelings, even if it smells like a hot dog stand."

If a smile can make a sound, then I heard the stranger's smile. "Yes, Lillian. Don't hurt my feelings."

I wanted to scream, *You're not my mom*! Dad would have laughed before he scolded me. I wanted to run. They never let me go anywhere on my own, but I didn't care. Outside, across the dusty soil, past Mom's pond, to places unknown.

Instead I rolled up my shirt. The stranger's rough hands plowed "moisturizer" down my spine like she was scrubbing the kitchen sink.

I let her. I should've fought, but I didn't. Each evening, we did it again, her stewing slime below, me and Dad letting her rub it into our backs.

The itching started after three days. Not a surface itch like dead skin cells, but beneath. My skin felt restless, like it had better things to do than hang onto me. Something moved underneath, something that wasn't my muscles and bones.

Dad didn't notice. He said the cream made his skin look smoother than it had in years. I didn't ask to touch him and check. If his skin felt wriggly under my fingers, I would've dug my nails into his flesh to tear it off.

The itchiness settled, or I got used to it. Maybe that was the burgeoning adolescence, Dr. Kowal's prophecy come to pass. I didn't like to think my body accepted the cream, that restless feeling, any of it. I missed Mom's scent, her humming. Maybe she couldn't undo what the stranger had done, but she could sit with me while it happened.

But I couldn't even search for her. Our property was the gravel driveway, the fake lawn, the chicken coop, and the fence that bordered the back yard before the path to Mom's pond. Every time I tried stepping outside that world, a hand pulled me back.

It was never Mom's. "Don't wander." The stranger's grip was cold.

I don't know how many times I tried. Even at night, she found me before I'd set ten steps on the path to the pond. Her grip cold, she dragged me home, cane clattering on dry earth.

The last time, she asked, "What would I do if something happened to you?"

She would have to find someone else for her cream. "You'd have Dad."

"He's older. Dirty."

"Dad isn't dirty. Mom loves him. You'd know that if—"

If she was Mom. We both knew what I meant to say. I thought she might hurt me. Instead, her cold fingers stroked my scalp, my neck, my back. I shuddered away from her. Was she trying to show affection?

That was only the first time. She started asking how school

was going, if I needed new books, if other kids were good to me. At night, she took the cream to my back, less a sponge to a basin, more a mother's comforting hand to her daughter.

She wasn't going to hurt me. Much worse, she was going to love me.

Soon she took to humming while helping at the chicken coop, to walking in a dainty dance. Her speech's rhythm became familiar. I think that made me forget the absence of scent, the past several weeks of strangeness. My brain let its guard down on my mouth.

I closed the chicken coop. "Thanks, Mom."

Once it was out, I couldn't put it back. Maybe it meant nothing to the stranger, but I wanted to rip my tongue out and let the chickens peck it apart.

With enough practice, there would be no distinction besides the smell. She would fill Mom's space in the family, her replacement so complete that maybe, someday, she would generate her own scent like Mom's. I'd think I imagined the whole thing as a kid, a side effect of my inevitable adolescence. There would never have been a stranger. Just some silly, fearsome fantasy. That might be why I did what I did. Not hope that Mom could come back.

It was shame. And hate.

The next morning, Dad headed for work while the stranger walked me to school. After an hour, I left class with a bathroom pass, left school, walked home. The dusty road was a stable path I could trust. The piston was at work downstairs, the stranger with it. I crept through the house anyway. Dad kept his cell phone with him and the stranger kept Mom's, unused, but we still had a landline. I called the police.

If I'd said my mother had been replaced by a lookalike, they would have laughed me off the phone. So I lied to them. Told them everything I could think of, that I'd been hurt, that there were drugs in the basement, that I'd been pulled out of school and was being kidnapped.

I had to blame Mom. It wasn't her, it was the stranger, but there was no choice. If I'd stopped to think, I wouldn't have called, but this wasn't about thinking. This was about Mom, remembering her, risking forgetting her. This was about my hate for the stranger, and I was going to ride that hatred to its end, whatever shape it took.

Dad used to worry I would fall down the stairs when I was little, but I understood their danger. Mom knew I did. The stranger knew nothing. She was surprised to hear me tumble into the basement, my cane clattering behind me. The basement air hung thick with odd odors. The cream was worst in its raw form, whatever that might be.

"Be careful with that." Cold hands touched my arms. "You could've hurt it."

Soft spots were forming over my limbs, and one shoulder ached something awful. "They're coming," I said, voice strained.

"Who?"

"I don't know. They're coming to take me away. I ran from school, but they're coming."

The stranger stepped back. I wasn't sure she believed me until her frantic muttering began. There were words in her ramble, but not English. Dizzy from the fall, I wondered what the stranger would make of braille, if her other language had a form for my fingertips.

"We're leaving." Her cold hand yanked me to my feet by my injured shoulder and made me cry out. "We don't have time for shouting. Outside." Her nails scraped a glass container beneath her other arm.

The cream. Wherever we were going, she wasn't done rubbing it on me.

The sun had grown relentless since I came home. Sweat

pooled down my back, made my shoulder ache even worse. The stranger kept on muttering to herself, interrupting and snapping as if a committee was in session, each member at odds with the others. Her Mom-like composure ran slick down her arm and onto mine.

"Did you tell them about the moisturizer? Do they understand that if they take you, it could interrupt?" She expected everyone to understand her ways without explaining them.

"I tried. They didn't care."

I must've heard the car before the stranger knew it was coming. When it slowed nearby, her grip tightened. The engine stopped; a door opened. No police siren, but someone else.

"He wants to take you away?" the stranger asked.

Here was my chance to calm my world, but I didn't. I nodded and let things happen.

"Excuse me, are you—" The man's question ended in a gurgling scream, the way a throat might sound while drowning. He thumped on the roadside.

When the stranger snatched my arm again, her hand was warmer and damper than before. "Was that the only one?"

I shook my head. My every word and gesture made the world a worse place, but I couldn't stop. The stranger led us off the road, toward the barren fields. She must have liked it out there, where the sun baked away the scents, made the world more like her. I felt lost without my cane, my shoes teasing around pebbles and uneven earth. Behind us, another car pulled over. A bystander was calling the police.

The stranger went back to her muttering.

Ten minutes on, a heavy vehicle tore across the sand, the pebbles ricocheting off its bumper. Growling to a stop, its doors creaked open. The stranger pulled me tight to her side.

This time it was the police. "Stay where you are. Hands above your heads."

I couldn't. She wouldn't.

She freed my arm, and I should have run, but I was numb by then, my mind, skin, legs, everything useless. Glass shattered. Warm cream slopped across my shoulders, down my back.

A sickening crackle spat chilly drops across my limbs. That was the moment the stranger stopped trying to be Mom. She was bursting open, air twisting as if making way for her, the wriggling, wet creature she really was, what I couldn't see. Close enough to touch, put a shape to, but I wouldn't. The wet sounds were already too much. She was too fluid for me to understand.

I'm not sure the officers understood either, the way they started screaming. They could take all my senses right then. None of her shrieking, none of her musky taste, none of the damp runoff her limbs threw across mine.

At last, she had a scent of her own. I've never smelled anything like that before. There's no food, place, person, dead or alive, that can compare, only a frosty alien mist. It hurt to breathe beside her.

Guns fired, but that didn't stop the stranger quick enough to save the officers. Gurgling throats, falling men. Something happened between her wetness and their bodies, but I slammed my hands to my ears and rolled my thumbs over the canals to drown out the noise. Blind, deaf, damp, aching, I started screaming and didn't stop for a long time. Even when other people surrounded me, stroked my hair, wrapped a blanket around me, put me in the back of an ambulance, I wouldn't unclench my ears, not until Dad's arms picked me up. I don't know how long that took. The screaming stopped and the crying started. I think I cried until I fell asleep.

They kept me out of the investigation. I picked up bits and pieces. No one could figure out what the stranger was making in the basement, but I doubt it was baby powder and mustard.

Dr. Kowal found no trace of it on my skin. That used to comfort me. Not anymore.

Investigators only found soft, shriveled tissue beside the dead police officers, like a water balloon left to leak in the sand. The news said the officers died putting down an unidentified animal. Mom was declared missing, maybe killed by the same. They chalked up my phone call to a wild imagination. I said nothing, let authorities invent their own story. Maybe that satisfied them.

I have my own problems these days. People are dead because of me. The stranger's gone, but still—maybe I deserve what's going to happen.

Dad developed a rash down his back. He figured it was sunburn. Eventually the skin sloughed off in thick layers, and he needed grafts, but after surgery he seemed normal. His laughter has died.

I don't think his knowing Mom was gone for those weeks we spent with the stranger would help any. It's best he thought he had a little more time with her than he really did.

Lucky him, not so lucky me. They sent me to therapy for the trauma and my adolescence. I cooperated at first, but after a couple years, I didn't think it was helping. No matter how the counselors helped adjust my mood, they couldn't find Mom, only make me feel better about her absence.

I never want to feel better about that. Plain and simple, I miss her. I want her scent back.

Maybe if she was here I wouldn't be so scared. She'd listen to me and not repeat a word I say to anyone. I could tell her how I smell like the stranger's mustard/baby powder cream now, even when I rake deodorant under my arms and drown my skin in lotion. I could tell her how I dream about the stranger, not disguised as Mom, but the fluid thing she was at the end.

I could tell her about the sight. Not from my eyes, but across my body, as if a million little nerves are poking from my pores. That restless feeling is back. My skin has had enough of me, ready to wriggle off my muscles and bones and walk to greener pastures where it can be its own girl. Part of me once thought it might be the adolescence again, or the guilt, but not now.

Soon I'm going to find out firsthand what happened to Mom. We won't be together, but I'll have answers before what happens to me happens. At least the itching should stop.

I wonder if Dad will notice a difference this time.

THE TURNING

Week 1

They say the turning takes nine weeks, give a day or two. That's what Krissy's heard, and that's if she believes the news that the curse is real, and then she has to believe that the people in suits have a clue what they're talking about. A lot of faith to ask of a fourteen-year-old, but she's trying. Faith might be all she has left, a kind of magic that's forever dripping from this sieve of a world.

The turning begins in the feet. Her toenails have split already, talons budding at her toes' roots, and her soles stretch thin against the bone.

This doesn't get better from here, but she'll pretend it doesn't get worse. She meets her friends at school, texts them after, takes selfies for social media. If nothing else, she'll keep a record of these final weeks—scratch that. She'll leave a record.

Week 2

Krissy coats greasy moisturizer over the scaly patches at her elbows and knees. Easy places to hide from friends and parents alike, and aside from her feet, nowhere else has shown signs of turning. If she can hide the symptoms long enough, maybe her body will fight the change same as a bad cold, and no one will have to know.

Maybe she won't end up like those kids who get pulled out of school or mentioned on the news.

Her friends flit around her, oblivious hummingbirds. Beautiful creatures, and she envies them now, their ordinary skin that hasn't gone leathery and alien at the joints. Or are they, too, hiding the turning?

The change soon spreads to her chest, thighs, and spine, the last discovered when she turns her back to the mirror one morning and glances over her shoulder. She can't reach that far around herself to moisturize. The skin morphs unhindered.

She's still staring at her reflection when Mom opens the bedroom door. Mom never knocks.

Week 3

Krissy's parents pull her out of school and forbid her from seeing friends. A lump has formed on the crown of her head, and her school has a no-hats rule. There will be no hiding the budding crest. She hopes it will crumble, a brittle shell that flakes into strange, leathery dandruff.

The doctors seem less optimistic. They've seen this before, she knows, and they'll see it again when her turning has finished. Supposedly the kids who finish then vanish without a trace.

By mid-week, her nose and lips begin sticking forward, her jaw having jutted up toward her cheekbones. No pain, only discomfort in body and soul. Heavier filters coat the few selfies she still snaps from her phone camera. A craving for fish invades her stomach, but feeding the changes will only encourage them, right? She forces down tonight's bland chicken cutlets and underbaked macaroni and cheese. Everything would taste better had it come from the water.

Mom says they'll try another specialist next week. Krissy tries to tell her, "Okay," but a strange squawk rolls out instead. Dad half-chuckles into a fist, half-chokes on cheesy noodles, and Krissy abandons the dining table on awkward, narrow feet.

Alone, she texts her friends about the specialist. Every word lies to them about her prospects or claws after commiseration in her parents' uncomfortable behavior.

A couple of friends respond with compulsory one and two-sentence answers. The rest ignore her. They're probably afraid they'll catch the turning. No one really understands why it happens, after all—genetics, disease, witchcraft? The news calls it a curse, but deep down, it's a mystery.

Whatever the cause, her friends have decided they had best leave her alone. Krissy wonders if she would do the same in their shoes.

Her feet hardly fit into shoes anymore. The talons have grown too long, curling hooks that might snag every fish in the sea.

Week 4

The specialist turns out as unhelpful as the other doctors, and why wouldn't he? If some miracle cure were found to stop or reverse the turning, that news would spread faster than the curse itself. Instead, online articles only fearmonger about whose kids might turn next. Talking heads fret about social impact. Religious types of various denominations tell everyone to pray.

Krissy can't say who's right or wrong.

Non-answers aren't good enough for Mom. "Couldn't she stop it if she tried?" she asks, finger twirling her curly hair so tight that strands snap apart. Dad imitates a friendly-faced statue and stands just as useless.

"The infection isn't psychosomatic," the specialist says in a patient tone, but he doesn't understand the core of the question. Mom isn't looking for solutions.

She's looking for someone to blame.

Krissy's thumbs have grown thick since last week, but she's learning to type on her phone despite that. Once settled into the back seat of her parents' car, she logs into her phone's Discuss app, where she's found a chatroom for other kids afflicted with the turning. She doesn't know their real names, but Catburger, LimeSpine, BrutalCornflake5, and others help stave off her loneliness.

Unlike her school friends, they don't turn to ghosts. These friends turn like she does.

"I wish you wouldn't talk to those people," Mom says, as if the curse worsens by association. "You're not like them. They're stuck this way, but you aren't. We'll figure this out."

Krissy tries to answer, but her whine belts out in a high-pitched pterodactyl screech.

Mom glares over her shoulder. "Want to try that again, young lady?"

A tangled explanation drifts up Krissy's tongue, knotted with thoughts on community and shared experiences, but she only utters a lower, softer screech, choked at the end with a single, quiet word: "Please."

Mom turns to the windshield again, shaking her head. Krissy turns to her screen, but she listens hard.

Mom: "I can't."

Dad: "It's okay."

Mom: "How is it okay? She's turning into a fucking dinosaur."

Dad: "Actually, pterosaurs were flying reptiles, not true dinosaurs."

There is a cold, angry pause, and then a game of verbal tennis begins, one-on-one, with Krissy its only audience. She might as well be a ghost; her parents shout about her like she doesn't haunt the seat behind them.

More like she's inside them, nesting in their minds at all times. She's still chatting on her phone when Dad makes his peace offering via pizza and movie night. Krissy wants anchovies for the first time in her life, and Dad obliges. They make it partway through *Beetlejuice* until the scene when Geena Davis and Alec Baldwin malform their faces to scare away the intrusive family, and Mom abruptly shuts the movie off.

She doesn't have to say why. Alec Baldwin's stretched prosthetic face looks too similar to how kids like Krissy turn out in the end. How she'll turn out by the end.

This doesn't get better from here.

Week 5

Her parents' arguments become daily occurrences, drifting between hushed angry whispers and high-volume shouting matches. Krissy's learning to tune them out, but words crash through her walls both physical and mental. Group. Changes. Normal. Abnormal. Solution.

They don't feel her problems of a crest jutting from the crown of her head, snout stretching knifelike from her face, ears melting to earholes, or dark hair falling out in clumps on her pillow each night. Her rigid fingers struggle to turn shower nozzles, and her toothbrush snags on sharp teeth that grow unbecoming for yearbook photos and selfies alike. She's given up eating with utensils.

These are all symptoms to her parents. At their core, Krissy is the problem.

Her online friends echo the same, their parents unfeeling. That's why they have each other. They're calling themselves the were-dactyls now, with dactyl-men being vetoed for lack of inclusivity. She imagines were-dactyls would sound cool aloud if she could still speak any language but screeches.

She asks where LimeSpine has been. No one knows. BrutalCornflake5 suggests maybe her parents took her phone away. Another were-dactyl suggests LimeSpine physically can't use the phone anymore. Krissy glances at her ever-thickening fingers and wonders how long she'll keep the power to tap a touchscreen.

Catburger has theories, and they develop into group discussion. There is the always-question: how did the turning begin? Same as puzzled doctors, politicians, and clergy, the afflicted teenagers can only speculate. But those grown people with their complete yet underdeveloped brains keep clawing for solutions, not answers. They'll only consider an origin if it might provide a cure.

Catburger suggests there can be no cure. What they're dealing with has lingered too long for any modern remedy. Archeologists used to fret about curses from dead people in ancient cultures they didn't understand. Nothing but ethnocentric superstition, especially when those archeologists should have been keeping an eye on the paleontologists, who never guessed what graves they might be digging up.

Finding the fossils of dinosaurs and the species that shared the world with them could mean looking for trouble.

There might have been magic in those Mesozoic days. The animals might have only been as conscious as crows, but every little girl who's traded food for trinkets with a corvid or three knows that, like their cousins, crows have a magic to them. They have judgment and revenge, too. Why should ancient animals be any different?

Anger might dwell in the bones of the dead, so potent that even fossilization couldn't break it. A revenge that lingers, buried in the earth until some crawling thing that dared stand on two legs and dominate the world comes digging. Finding. Unearthing magic that they can't feel, let alone understand, but they've freed it just the same. They had vengeance spells in prehistory, sure as they have them now.

Ask any crow.

Week 6

Webbing has grown down Krissy's arms. She struggles to wear shirts, the sleeves crumpling at her wrists.

Worse, her fingers have fused. Each day, their joints migrate farther down her arm. By the end, each upper limb will become one great webbed hand—a wing. She eats by sliding her snout along her dish. Grabbing at things becomes her feet's job; maybe that's why the turning begins there.

Still, she has lost the power to type on her phone. She can only scroll down the chat as her online friends wonder what's become of her, and then their discussions and questions carry on:

How might pterosaur magic compare to crow magic?

Did you know a flock of crows is called a murder?

If pterosaurs knew murder, could they curse each other?

And if so, why should we pay the price?

They talk and talk until Krissy can't keep up. She's lost to them. Goodbye, were-dactyls. This must be what happened to LimeSpine. It will happen to each of them, and then they'll have nobody, not even each other.

Every single one will finish their turning alone.

Week 7

Krissy's clothes no longer fit around her changing body. She drapes her shoulders in blankets and hugs them around her torso, but they come loose often and her parents shout over decency. Dad's hair thins at the crown, same as Krissy's weeks ago. Maybe he'll turn, father like daughter, the first adult in the world to succumb to prehistoric vengeance spells.

But no, he's only stressed. Mom, too. They speak softly now, but Krissy still hears them through the walls.

Dad: "What can we do?"

Mom: "I don't know. I just want our little girl back."

Can't they see that she's right here? Different, but still her. Their words hurt worse than shifting bones and jutting snout and the fish-driven hunger that burns her guts. Hasn't she been punished enough? And for what sin? She doesn't deserve wrath from the ancient world. What has she ever done but exist?

Her parents buy more blankets and hang them over the windows. If Krissy can't be decent, can't look human, then they don't want her seen.

Her world grows dark, cold, and lonely. She should sink into depression and never climb up from bed, but the turning shoves rage through her leathery skin. A pterodactyl screech shakes the air, and she flaps her still-forming wings. Her room swirls with small, dusty tornadoes.

And she gets an idea.

Week 8

Krissy keeps to her room by day. Her parents only whisper now, their murmurs scarcely creeping through the walls. They have a solution in mind; she can tell. They don't know what it is any more than she does, yet, but she has her own projects.

By night, she clambers out the back door. It takes twenty minutes to unlock and turn the knob the first time, but she's getting faster at slipping out into the dark. Walking on four limbs has become easier than two. Her wing-knuckles help her lumber onto the porch, and her foot presses the screen door shut without a sound. Letting it crash would wake her parents, and they wouldn't understand.

She spends the night hopping off the porch railing and toward the back lawn, desperate to catch the wind. Her wings spread, flap, collapse, and she slams into the dewy grass.

And she tries again.

Week 9

Both Mom and Dad call out from work this week. They spend daylight hours with Krissy, haunting her bedroom the way shadows crawl from the sun, but they won't touch her. Her hide is leather and scales now. Alec Baldwin's stretchy prosthetic face in that *Beetlejuice* scene has nothing on hers, a hard, beak-like snout lined with flesh-rending teeth.

She lets her parents pretend they're better than they have been. Whether they know about her nighttime excursions is irrelevant. She can't stop.

She won't be stopped.

At mid-week, she realizes why she can't catch the wind. The porch doesn't stand high enough for strong gusts; she can't catch what isn't there. She must climb higher.

Night falls, and the rooftop beckons. Clambering from porch railing to shingles isn't easy, but her feet have grown proper talons over these nine weeks, and they help her find purchase on the way up. The turning begins in the feet, but it might end in the wings, one way or another.

The sky offers plentiful starlight and a gracious full moon. She eyeballs the chimney's silhouette and scrabbles up its shaft, onto the top, high as she can climb. To drop from its peak might break her.

But then, to never try might break her, too.

There's no point in a running leap. Her legs don't work that way anymore, and strength rises in her upper limbs. It's now or never.

She leaps.

Her wings slash to either side. Their webbing trembles. Every inch downward stretches into a small yet immeasurable unit of infinity. She has time to consider a crushed skull and snapped neck. Her parents will think she meant to kill herself. Will they be relieved?

She thrusts downward, rushing air fights her webbing, and at last her wings catch the wind. Nose-turned-snout turns upward, and she shoots from the yard, past the trees.

Toward the stars.

Once she gets going, flight becomes easy. Wind rushes around her crest, and she tilts her head in time with her wings to shift direction. She doesn't know if that's necessary, but the steering feels right. Lush trees bristle beneath her.

With air rushing around her earholes, every sound from the world below dims in the night. There's a peace here she hasn't felt in—ever? She can't be sure, but it feels good and right to fly. Like she was meant for it.

A familiar screech pierces the darkness. She turns and twists toward the clouds, and now she sees that the wind carries many riders. Winged shadows slash across the corn-yellow moon. She isn't as alone as her parents have made her feel. She screeches back, not even sure what she's saying, and the calls bounce across the sky in the greatest song she's ever heard.

Maybe this does get better from here.

An hour passes before she thinks of her parents again. She's exhausted and could really use a snack and rest. Home slides beneath her talons, the rooftop trying to catch her, and she lands harder than she meant to. Practice will make perfect. A chittering noise bubbles up from chest to throat. Is that laughter? She doesn't know, but it feels right as flying.

She glides from rooftop to porch and is about to jimmy around the screen door when the back door behind it swings open, a rectangle of light breaking the darkness.

Dad's silhouette carves the light, and a grave smile paints his face. "We were worried," he says.

The screen door crashes behind Krissy, and she knuckle-walks onto the kitchen tiles, where a chemical stink coats the air.

Mom's awake, too, much to Krissy's surprise. She holds a glass measuring cup over a metal pan. "Hey there, sweetie," she says, jostling the pan. "We have fish. You like fish nowadays, right? We haven't been fair about what you're going through, but we want to fix that. Don't we?" She says this last question to Dad.

He nods, but his smile shows no cheer, no supportiveness. He's a grim-faced statue tonight. Something's wrong.

Hard to tell if Mom knows it. She smiles like it hurts to let her lips touch, her teeth filled with happy promises. She holds the pan out toward Krissy, arms stretched to their limit as if she's afraid to let her daughter get too close. A whole catfish lies inside, drenched in what must be cooking oil. Must be.

"Dig in," Mom almost sings.

Krissy looks to Dad, who nods again. Her fish-craving stomach dances with joy, but her thoughts hesitate. She wonders exactly what happens to the other kids who've finished turning. Are they taken by the government? Do they run away?

Or have their parents done something unthinkable?

Krissy begins to retreat, but Dad slides behind her. One flat, weathered palm presses between her shoulder blades; the other encircles her narrow neck in thick fingers. "We're sorry," he says.

"So sorry," Mom echoes. She seems to mean it, there are tears in her eyes, but she carries the pan close now. "Eat the fish, sweetie." Her voice fills with a mournful lilt, her betrayal of the deepest and final kind, a solution to their daughter-turned-problem.

Krissy flaps her wings and sends the air billowing through the kitchen. Mom grabs the fish up in her bare hands and lets the pan clatter. The oil doesn't smell like water and fish-stink—it wears that chemical smell.

"Open up, sweetie," Mom says. The fish dangles closer.

"Krissy, it's mercy," Dad says, fingers clambering toward her snout.

Mercy for who? Not for her, not when she's caught the wind and found the night. Mercy for them, then. Her family has turned into a dark egg, and now a rancid evil hatches behind Mom's eyes. She presses the fish against Krissy's teeth. The chemical taste trickles onto her tongue, as does the fish's meat. Her stomach orders her to take it, hungry like never before.

Behind her, the screen door crashes onto the porch, torn from its hinges, and wood splinters from the back door. Dad releases his grip, and Krissy feels him spin around. The catfish flops from Mom's hands and smacks wet against the kitchen tiles.

Dad: "Who are you?"

Mom, her voice cracking: "Another one?"

Glass shatters in the living room, the picture window bursting inward. A blanket writhes on the carpet, as if deciding on its own that Krissy's parents' sins must be seen, but then it shakes free of a crested head, toothy snout, and great leathery wings.

Another one. Another like Krissy.

A window cracks apart in one of the bedrooms, and two more kids-turned-pterosaur swoop into the living room through the picture window. Others follow from the bedroom hallway. Despite their wingspan, their upper limbs fold neatly against their torsos, letting them squeeze into the kitchen, snouts aimed at Krissy's parents. A pterodactyl screech bursts up one throat.

Krissy can't discern its entire meaning, but no matter what else, it's a song for her, and she answers. She returned home alone, trouble come to roost, where her parents tried to nourish her in the worst way. They thought she would always be alone. Would die alone.

But these other changed adolescents are birds of a leathery feather. Whatever angry magic swirls inside her likewise swirls inside them. Her parents have blotted up the windows for too long and forgotten that birds have flocks.

And for some birds, their flock is called a murder.

They rush at Mom and Dad, their prehistoric screeches drowning out human screams. Krissy isn't much help, but the others make quick and bloody work. Not because they're weredactyls or true pterosaurs. Not because they can. They're quick because they're a flock of shared experiences, and they've had practice in their own houses, each forced to break free of some terrible eggshell the way Krissy has to break free tonight.

But she doesn't have to do it alone. She's never really been alone.

When the kitchen clamor settles, the flock shuffles on wing-knuckles and feet into the living room, where the night's mouth gapes wide with glassy teeth. The largest of them hops onto the picture windowsill, talons gripping tight. Wings catch the wind with ease of practice made perfect, and their downdraft gives the others a boost for thrusting themselves skyward. One by one, they glide up and away.

Krissy is the last to climb onto the windowsill. She looks to the stars and moon, where sibling shadows cut the night. Her talons crush brittle glass and brace to follow her flock toward seas and sunsets and mysterious futures. The turning begins in the feet and ends in the wings.

But the turning is just the start.

WE WHO HOLD THE MEDIAN

The median was free most Tuesdays for Lulu's and Sofia's gathering, but today blue uniforms and yellow tape blocked off the rounded end where cars stopped at the intersection of Scarlet Avenue and Fishkill Road. Tattered denim decorated the sun-yellowed grass, and blood-brown residue stained the concrete. Some impatient driver, one eye on their phone and the other on a fussy baby in a car seat or a frustrated spouse, had wanted to beat the stoplight.

One of the first lessons Lulu had learned after her parents kicked her out—on the street, there were no wolves, cougars, or bears. Downtown was a concrete wilderness, its beasts were light-runners and curb-hoppers, and they had a hunger for panhandlers.

"Rest in peace, Hairy Dave," Sofia said. The wind teased scraggly black hair into her grinning face. "Median's ours."

Lulu slinked up beside her. The sun beat down on her, but she hugged her clothes tight to herself against a chill. Everything she owned clung to her body. If she left her extra clothing in an alley somewhere, it wouldn't be waiting when she returned. People only paid attention to her when they came to take, never to give.

Squat, disinterested buildings bordered each intersection corner, watching small crowds leave their parking lots to gather where the police ambled back and forth.

Little to be done now; Hairy Dave was dead, and few cared for the fates of panhandlers in this town.

Lulu and Sofia stood invisible among fellow onlookers in that no one wanted to see them. Still, hands clutched at purses or double-checked pockets for wallets. As if the girls would beg at the roadside had they hands for thieving.

Especially not now. The median was a lucrative strip of grass surrounded by concrete that split this stretch of Scarlet Avenue in two. Its tip ended at a four-way intersection, where it watched cars slide back and forth along Fishkill Road, tugging clouds of crumpled fast-food wrappers in their slipstreams. Some Scarlet Avenue drivers likely believed the stoplight had it out for them.

If so, it had a soft spot for panhandlers. To work the driver windows here was to pluck riches from idle cars. The warehouse district, the derelict strip mall—dangerous places, and never generous.

"This'll change everything," Sofia said. None of the crowd noticed.

Only Lulu. "Someone else might think so, too," she said. "How'll we protect the territory?"

Sofia side-eyed her as if the question was silly, but the median wouldn't protect itself. "Dave's curse. Always worked for him."

Lulu kept her mouth shut then. More to keep Sofia placated, not because the plan was a good idea.

Hairy Dave had long ago called a curse on anyone who'd take the median from him. Curses were the kind of thing people who owned cars and houses didn't worry about, but depending on the neighborhood, such words might as well be laws. The girls snuck in and out on Tuesdays while Dave stalked off to far parts of town, allegedly to tend pigeons as if he lived on some Manhattan rooftop, but they had never tried to claim his spot. Magic or no magic, he was a big man, and the kind of quiet settled in him which Lulu didn't want to test. She had known men like him.

She supposed he kept a different kind of quiet now.

Rumors of a curse might even keep someone from taking this patch from her and Sofia. Doubtful that Sofia believed in curses, and probably most others didn't either.

But now blood anointed the concrete, and blood was thicker than words. They were only two scrawny street kids, nothing to their names but the clothes on their backs. They hadn't owned any curses yesterday.

Hairy Dave's demise left an inheritance of superstition and malice that might protect them yet.

Sofia kept them to their usual haunts until the median was clear. By weekend, police were tearing down their yellow tape and finding other locales to haunt. Urban maintenance then washed the blood away. Gawkers stopped by, the kind of middle-class snobs who wouldn't spit on thirsty panhandlers to give them a drink, let alone toss them a buck, and left colorful twenty-dollar wreaths as if they had known Dave. The flowers shriveled in the heat.

When all other parties lost interest, the girls moved in.

"Wish they'd left the blood," Sofia said, grinding the sole of her thin shoe against concrete. "Would help make the curse look legit."

Lulu nodded, her attention on the intersection and the cars rushing alongside the median. Blood was a healthy reminder that every panhandler was only ever seconds from becoming a smear. To drivers, they were already no better than roadkill until they were worth a memorial. Better to stare dead ahead and pretend there was no one in the median begging for a dollar to live.

That was harder for drivers to do at the median. The stoplight was temperamental. Sometimes it went red and Sofia would approach a car, only for it to turn green right away and let the driver zoom off while she stomped and cursed. Other times, it would linger, letting Lulu pace down the line and sow guilt car by car while Sofia made her desperate sales pitch.

"Look, I know times are tough, but it's not just for me," she would say. "My young friend's family didn't want her anymore. Can't you spare a buck?"

Windows cracked and reluctant drivers offered dimes, dollars, even a crumpled twenty from one trucker, anything to make them go away while the red light glared through windshields and into brains.

"Bless!" the girls shouted each time, but only Lulu meant it.

The sky's colors grew heavy as evening set in. Soon they would have to start back toward the strip mall. Lulu said as much.

"No, no, we're done with all that shit," Sofia said, tightening her scarf. "We'll camp here. Keep the territory. Everyone needs to recognize this median belongs to us."

Lulu glanced at the red stoplight, brighter than Dave's blood. That insectile eye had watched Dave's death.

"What about curb-hoppers?" she asked.

Sofia rolled her eyes. "Stick to the grass and don't sleepwalk. Dave got careless; we won't."

Summer day ebbed to dusk, inviting heat from the sun-soaked pavement. Lulu paced the grass, looking skyward, hoping to see constellations, but there were no stars tonight. Black clouds hid the cosmos and filled the air above with the cries of unseen birds.

"Back up!"

A hand tugged Lulu from the concrete's edge just as a pickup truck screamed past. She looked down too late, would've been struck had she not been pulled back. Her downward gaze caught the intersection, where she spotted a man crossing Scarlet Avenue, bathed golden in the pick-up truck's headlights.

Her eyes shut tight. She didn't want to see this.

Sofia steadied her, yellow grass crunching underfoot. "No wonder you almost died, wandering with your eyes closed. If you're too tired to keep an eye out, take a nap. I'll be lookout."

Lulu listened for screeching tires, a heavy thud of metal against flesh, another thud of limp, doll-like flesh flopping to asphalt.

Nothing. She opened her eyes and glanced at the intersection. The truck's red taillights shrank away, having crossed Fishkill Road without hitting anyone.

"But I thought—"

"Doubt you thought much of anything." Sofia knocked the side of Lulu's head. "Stumble out here at night, and you're street pudding."

They locked eyes until Lulu turned, nodding, and let oily hair fall into her face. *Street pudding like Dave*, she thought, but didn't say. She sat on the grass, eyes open, heart thudding. The sky remained black, and she was afraid to glance too long at it. To stare might summon another screaming vehicle.

"What's Dave's curse? Like, what did he say it'd do?"

Sofia edged toward the median's tip. Her dark silhouette gave an exaggerated shrug. "Just that trespassers would be sorry. Probably meant he'd get you, but that was when he was alive." The stoplight glared red and reflected in her eyes. "Why?"

Lulu glanced at the intersection. In this darkness, she must've imagined the man. "We're sure he's dead? That someone else wasn't killed here the other night?"

"Do you see a big bearded bear of a man?" Sofia asked, stretching her arms to either side.

Lulu gave a slight headshake.

"If he wasn't dead, he'd be here. He wouldn't get chased off, not like Old Madeline. You're the one who told me that."

Lulu remembered. It was how she knew that people didn't always keep the territory they claimed. "It was Kings who chased her off. They weren't going to panhandle, but they wanted money or fun, and then they ran her into her intersection. A truck was turning right, but signaled left—"

Sofia snorted. "Bullshit."

"You don't believe someone used a turn signal?"

"I'm an atheist."

That made Lulu laugh. "Well, it was wrong for Old Madeline."

And she'd had ended up like Dave, a red memory beneath yellow tape and blue uniforms. Lulu had shut her eyes that night, but she told it like she'd seen it. The screech, metal-on-flesh thud, flesh-on-street thud—they painted a distinct gory picture.

"Street pudding," Lulu murmured.

"Kings won't come here, if that's why you're fussing." Sofia smiled at an oncoming car. "Nobody messes with the median."

Headlights turned Sofia's pale face golden as they rushed by, illuminating a man towering behind her at the median's very end. Lulu tensed, but when the car was gone, so was he. Only Sofia stood at the median's end.

Lulu sprang off the grass and glanced down Scarlet Avenue. No one walked to the left or right, but she had seen someone, a familiar broad shape. Where had he gone?

Sofia looked each way, too. "Who'd you see?"

"Don't know." Lulu shivered despite the heat. The night held a gelatinous shape overhead, and the weight filled the air around her. "You think a car really killed Dave?"

"What else?" Sofia asked.

"Kings? Or some other gang? Dave had a way of drawing lines and daring people to cross. Maybe somebody finally did."

"Yeah, they're called drivers." Sofia kicked at the grass, now dark as the sky. "They don't see us unless they have to stop. Whoever killed Dave doesn't even know they're a murderer. Probably thought they hit some overgrown possum. Ease up, will you?"

Easier said than done. Obedience would be a relief, but Lulu's muscles tensed each time a car approached the intersection.

No sign of Hairy Dave in the crosswalk. Pedestrians wandered the sidewalks; that was normal. Street life meant keeping on the lookout for someone who wanted what you had. Often the ones richer than God.

A slender sedan passed, headlights aglow, but no ghostly visage appeared. The night sky grew so thick that Lulu felt she could drink from it. Sofia talked a good game, had to be tough to live out here, keep Lulu safe, but how often had she been pushed? Who had challenged her? If one night came to blows, would she win? Lulu didn't want to find out.

Sofia scoffed. "Fine, you want to keep looking, you be lookout."

Before Lulu could answer, the streetlights blinked, drowning the intersection in near-total blackness. Only the green glare of the stoplight broke the night.

When it turned red, the streetlights flashed alive again, illuminating a bulky form stepping at Lulu's left. She turned at the brush of an arm, the scent of hair and musk.

No one else stood in the median except Sofia.

"What's your problem now? Just a summer brownout, you know how it is in this town." Sofia scoffed again, harder this time. Her patience was dying. "Scared of your own shadow, that's you."

Shadows didn't bother Lulu. Shadows meant there was light. What scared her was a world too dark for shadows. A world of the invisible. Anything could live in that darkness.

Anything could reach out and touch her.

Sofia shoved at her, not so hard she might fall out of the median, but enough to make a point. "What am I supposed to do with you? Too jittery to rest, too freaked to be a good lookout. You'll be jumping at the next mosquito buzzing by."

"It's not shadows," Lulu said.

"What's the problem then?" Sofia snapped.

Another car passed, this time glaring its high-beams, and Lulu caught him full-on—a hulking bearded beast of a man draped in three brown coats and denim jeans, standing at the median's tip with one arm stretched out. A finger pointed outward, almost to the horizon. He vanished with the headlights.

"Dave," Lulu muttered.

"Dave? *Dave?*" A nasty giggle slipped through Sofia's teeth. "That curse isn't real. He made it up to scare people, and we're using it the same. Don't let it use you back. There's no such thing as curses."

"He was pointing away." Lulu staggered along the grass, desperate to glimpse another sign of Dave. Or Dave's ghost.

"Away. Away." Sofia repeated it like an echo and turned to the spot where blood had stained the pavement on Tuesday. If that stain had returned, it was too dark now to see. "Dave is done. It's our time now. I see nobody; I hear nobody. You're losing it, Lu."

Lulu listened as wind teased her hair, and she realized that hearing nobody seemed strange. Pedestrians walked the sidewalks, but they might as well have been phantoms for all their silence. Nowhere in town sat this quiet.

A place this quiet should have been dead. The median felt unnatural, an alien territory not only for having always been Dave's, but for being an intrusion. Didn't this town know how roads worked? A double-white line should've been enough to keep cars from crossing lanes, but no, these reckless drivers needed concrete to dissuade them from plowing their steel on wheels into each other face-first.

And as with all stretches around the road, onlookers appeared. Telephone lines for birds, medians for panhandlers. Every person needed a place.

But the median was not a person and it seemed more than a place. There was a presence here. No matter how often Lulu had followed Sofia to work the windows here on Tuesdays in Dave's absence; the median was his. It would buck them off like an angry horse.

Another car crawled toward the intersection from far up Scarlet Avenue. The stoplight glowed green, but Lulu felt a merciless aura breathe off its garish glow. It would turn red in time. The car would hold still, its headlights would glare over the median and crosswalk, and Sofia would have time to spot Hairy Dave in his favorite haunt.

"He wants us to leave," Lulu said.

Sofia paced from the median's concrete tip to the crunching grass. "There's no one else here. Quit freaking on me."

"But I saw Dave."

"So what?" Sofia's voice climbed to a shout. "Let's say you did see his ghost—what then? He's dead! He can't talk, he can't eat, he can't fuck, he can't kill, so what's the big deal? What can a dead man do?"

Lulu didn't want to find out. She remembered blood on the median and saw it melt from brown crust to running red. She wondered if Dave had ever spilled it here fighting off pretenders to his hairy throne, consecrating it in the splash of battle to build his curse in sterner stuff than mere words.

He must have formed an understanding with the median. It wouldn't have let some errant driver murder its friend, the king to whom it paid fealty.

What then? And what had he done to his killer since?

The crawling car approached the intersection as the stoplight ticked yellow, and the driver slammed the gas. An engine roared, high-beams flashed.

Hairy Dave blinked into brief existence. Lulu made to cover her eyes, but too late—she caught a better look at Dave's stern, bearded expression, hairy-knuckled hand, and pointing finger.

He wasn't pointing away to the horizon. He was pointing behind Lulu, toward the slender end of the median.

At Sofia.

The stoplight flashed red, and the car squealed to an unhealthy stop, washing the median in too-bright light. Dave bled away.

Lulu narrowed her eyes. "It wasn't a curb-hopper."

Sofia approached the car while it was their prisoner. "For the last time, knock it off. Don't scare away what's ours."

But the volatile stoplight did that for them, abruptly turning green to let the driver speed free. Sofia stumbled back, a sudden wind kicking up her clothes and hair, and she glared at Lulu like it was her fault.

"If you don't want to be here, then go!" Sofia snapped. "No one's taking this spot from us. We made more cash today than we did all last week, and no way I'm letting the best thing that's happened to us go to waste. It's ours, understand? And Dave can't have it anymore."

Lulu swallowed bile. "Because you took it from him."

No cars approached from afar and none slid through the intersection from right or left. Not even the wind breathed across the median.

Sofia strode toward Lulu, lips parted in a snarl. "And?" She shoved Lulu's chest. "What of it?"

Lulu wanted to back away, but her heels teetered on a concrete edge. There was no median left to take her.

"When?" she asked.

"When do you fucking think? The night he was killed." Sofia shoved Lulu again, harder this time. "I swear, you're the most addle-minded girl on the street. He had something that could better our lives, so I took it. We took it. And it's already paying out. We need food and shelter. You think someone's likely to stroll by and hand that to us? Has anyone ever handed you anything, you whiny brat?"

A car tore down Scarlet Avenue, headlights breathing a radiant death. Lulu teetered at the median's edge, heels sliding toward asphalt. She would've slipped onto the street already, but her jacket bunched in Sofia's fists.

"I can get another Lulu the pitiful puppy," Sofia went on. Her arms straightened, lowering her fists. Lulu's head dipped toward asphalt. She grasped at Sofia's arms, but if she fought, she'd fall for certain. "Or you can heel and be quiet. A curb-hopper killed Hairy Dave, and that's how it is now, no matter what really happened. Aren't you smart enough to get that?"

The oncoming car cruised closer. The driver couldn't see them on the dark median, but Hairy Dave loomed in the encroaching headlights, coming at Lulu from all sides, eternal blame making black holes of his eyes.

She began thrashing. "But Dave's curse!" she shouted. He thought this was her fault, but it wasn't. "He's cursed us!"

"I'm so sick of you," Sofia said. Her arms drooped, and her fists sprang open, letting go of the bunched-up jacket.

Lulu flailed off the median. Her back slammed against hard asphalt, knocking the wind out of her and shaking her joints. There wasn't time to move. Headlights flared across her face, would've blinded her before their car crunched across her body.

Two legs broke the light and a bulky shadow fell across her. His finger pointed at the median.

Tires screeched. The car swerved sharply, ran at the median, and hopped the curb.

Lulu knew the noise without looking—metal against flesh as the car's hood collided with Sofia—but the rest was new. She had never been this close before to hear limbs crumple, a spine and skull slam into a windshield, bone and glass cracking together as if they had always been one frail substance. The car screeched to a stop, burning tire treads through the grass, but Sofia's body didn't jostle free from the hood. She lay slumped, unmoving. The driver screamed, but Sofia didn't make a sound.

Joints and back still aching, Lulu scrambled to her feet and hobbled across two lanes of Scarlet Avenue to the far sidewalk. She made out the pedestrians now, chattering and holding up phones. She could hear the driver in the median, a young woman screeching and shouting for help.

But there was nothing Lulu could do. Sofia had played with curses and concrete. What had she expected?

Lulu looked back as she limped beneath a yellow streetlight. She couldn't make out much of the median under the starless sky, but she knew that blood once more coated the pavement, and maybe bits of clothing and hair dotted the grass, scraggly and dark like it used to hang from Sofia's head.

An indistinct shape slid from the car, likely the driver, and hurried along the hood, still shouting for someone to help her. Not to help Sofia, who did not move. They looked alone here, she and the driver, but Lulu knew better. Hairy Dave kept his usual quiet, and he was nowhere to be seen.

That did not mean he was gone.

THE MANY SINS OF CLARA GREENSTONE

A hundred rumors swirled about Clara in the time we lived together at St. Mary's Home for Girls, that spring and summer of 1946.

The sisters called her a devil, and that might have been true, but they called everything devilry. Hard to trust their know-how when they'd paint with such broad brushes.

Me and the other girls were more inventive, saying Clara was a goblin, or a wolf in girl's clothes. Ellie called Clara a spirit, but I'm certain that wasn't right. I touched Clara many a time, and whatever else she might've been, her body was solid flesh and bone.

But I could never blame Ellie for having wondered about spirits and ghosts in a place like St. Mary's. The house had an edge to it. I'd never been in a graveyard then, but I've walked them in the years since, and St. Mary's felt much the same. At night you could believe a hand might reach from dark corners, and maybe it would belong to one of the sisters in her habit, or maybe it would be something grimmer. I sometimes hoped to see little Jenny spring from the shadows, smiling like I'd only imagined anything bad had ever happened to her, or she'd been hiding for a game and took it too far.

But she was too young and sweet for that awful place to spit her out once it had swallowed her. St. Mary's was an old house even then, built atop the kind of stones to remember dragons and from the kind of timber to miss its nature as a forest. When you walked its halls, you knew it reminisced on age-old cruelties as easily as it forgot the children it had wiped from the earth. To talk of such things was a sin. That never stopped us. We understood enough about the place that caged us to be wary of it, and we had inklings of what it wanted to do with us.

It wasn't like nobody ever died on the grounds. A wealthy man had left the property to charity, and there were whispers that he'd passed away somewhere in those halls. He might not have been the first, and he certainly wasn't the last.

There were the dead girls, too. I couldn't know them all—a Myrtle by flu, a Sylvia by her own hand, not to mention the ones who went missing. Dorothy vanished two weeks after I arrived, supposedly adopted, Evangeline the silent girl disappeared one Christmas Eve, maybe a runaway, maybe not, and of course, there was Jenny. The sisters said she fell out a window, and her body had been taken away in the night.

They wouldn't hear any word besides about it, as if we could forget Jenny and her pretty hair as easily as the house and the sisters wanted, but a few of us twenty-odd girls knew otherwise.

We said Sister Agnes fed little Jenny to the thing in the attic.

*

Clara came to St. Mary's Home for Girls on the first day of spring that year. There was nothing much special to her at first glance, wearing an ill-fitting yellow dress, her secrets hidden under the hem. That was the afternoon Sister Agnes bled Wendy's fingertips during our needlework lesson, a punishment for stealing. Not that Wendy wanted to steal; she just felt the need now and then.

But none of us dared explain that to Sister Agnes. We'd only have faced the same, or worse.

There was always worse when it came to Sister Agnes. Mother Caroline was supposed to be in charge, but I never knew her to be anything but the soft-voiced matron who read us Bible passages and said what fine young ladies we'd grow to be someday. Every sister should have been equal beneath her, but Sister Agnes ruled that home with a cold-fingered grip. Her punishments came cold, too, different from the other sisters. When you pissed off Sister Grace, she would snarl and holler at you from wherever you'd misbehaved all the way to the narrow closet. You at least had some warning you were about to suffer.

But Sister Agnes never raised her voice. That afternoon at needlework, she closed her hand gently but firmly around Wendy's and pricked each finger one after another, as calm as she might shut a nursery door at night.

I'll never forget the chill in me then, or the way Wendy's shrieking rattled my teeth.

After that moment, while Sister Joan wiped freezing water over Wendy's fingertips amid her crying, Clara's appearance in our lives seemed too small a thing to give our attention.

"Clara Greenstone, they call me." A proud declaration Clara gave upon entering the long bedroom where we all slept.

"How do you have a family name if you don't have a family?" Ellie the Gossip asked.

"Oh, I've a family," Clara said. "Don't know where they got to, but they're mine."

She was annoying from the start, a choppy-haired little creature with too big a voice. Sweet earthen eyes glimmered from her head when she wanted, but they could fill with green mischief just as fast. She never once called me Colleen, always shouting *wee girl* at me and some of the others, the ones she liked. That tree root of a girl stood a head shorter than me.

Over the years since, I've thought I should've noticed

something more to her that first day. Some sign she wasn't right, or that St. Mary's was in for a change.

Not like I was looking for it. Clara took her lessons like any other girl, swept and mopped the kitchen and halls, listened to Mother Caroline read from the Bible, which the sisters always told us was a special treat. The days brought the same gauntlet as always, each of us hoping we wouldn't be the one to catch hell from any of the sisters.

Clara was a model resident then, only speaking when spoken to, her peepers wide as the ocean and drinking up everything about the home, the sisters, and the rest of us. She was watching, learning, and knew how to hide her true nature. We would only know her strangeness when she wanted us to see it.

Later, it seemed to me she wasn't sure why she'd ended up at St. Mary's and might have been looking for the reason.

We were all like that once.

*

Things began to change a few nights later, when Sister Grace caught Ellie whispering after lights out.

To be fair, we were all whisperers that night. Mother Caroline had dozed off while reading to us, and we were still giggling about it past bedtime.

"Even she's bored by it."

"No, she's sleepy 'cause she's old. Ancient. She remembers those stories from when they happened."

"She met Jesus and Moses and all of them."

"God calls her *grandmother*."

That set all of us laughing. I can't remember who started shushing for quiet at the rest of us, but she wasn't alone. Even I had to speak up.

"You'd better hush," I said. "Or Agnes will let the attic eat you all like she did Jenny."

"You're such a worrier, Colleen," Ellie said, scoffing. "She wouldn't give us to the attic." But on the word *attic*, I heard the confidence rot off her tongue. "Not for something as small as whispering."

The difference between Ellie and everyone else was that she forgot how to be sneaky. She didn't know how to speak and listen for the sisters at the same time, and in the long bedroom where all of us slept in our twin rows of cots? Whispers found their way.

Ellie was mid-chatter again when Sister Grace burst through the door, breath fuming in the dark. She launched herself at Ellie's bed, snatching away the sheets and then squeezing rough fingers around her chin and cheeks.

"The last words out of your mouth in the night should be your prayer to the Lord," Sister Grace said. "See the other girls? They're all bedded down like we left them, in case the Lord should need to take any of you in the night. But here you are, little Elaine, chattering with your devil talk."

"It wasn't," Ellie said, her voice distorted between pinched cheeks. "It was only—"

Sister Grace was a black shape against windowlight when one silhouetted arm dropped from Ellie's jaw and the other swung palm-first across her face. The blow cracked thunder down the room, jolting our spines straight against our cots.

I remember blood. There's no way I could have seen any in the dark, but somehow the red drops stuck in my memory. Ellie crumpled beneath Sister Grace, and her sobs ran muffled against her sheets.

"Each of you lie with hands clasped," Sister Grace said. "Let Elaine the Gossip's pain remind you of your sin."

She didn't need to explain further. As Sister Grace stormed out and snapped the door shut behind her, we understood Ellie had taken the blame for all of us..

I thought that would be the end of the night's whispers. We'd all been properly silenced, and the only sound in the room should have been Ellie's sobs as she cried herself to sleep.

But Clara's cot lay beside mine. "Wee girl?" she called. "So that's how it is here?"

I didn't dare speak in case Sister Grace still prowled outside the door, but I nodded. Clara shouldn't have seen, should have taken silence as a hint.

"So it is?" she asked. "Well then, we shall see." She sighed, rolled over, and fell fast asleep a good hour before I did.

And then her sins began.

*

I had never seen boy's clothes inside St. Mary's before Clara tugged up her yellow dress the next morning and showed off an old cotton shirt and a tattered pair of brown shorts.

"Where'd you get those?" I asked. "Did you come in with them?"

"I came in with many a thing," Clara said, and she tapped her lips like there was nothing more to say.

From then on, you never knew how you'd spot Clara in St. Mary's halls. One moment, she'd be wearing her dress, and the next she'd have thrown it off and gone strolling between lessons in that shirt and shorts, sometimes with a newsboy cap atop her choppy hair.

None of us told on her. I wasn't that type of girl, and as for the rest, you never knew what was secretly a virtue on Monday and a sin on Tuesday. Would pointing out a mischievous girl be an act of loyalty to the sisters or a gesture of pride? Anything could be a sin in those days.

Clara made a game of it, seeing how long she could get away flaunting the wrong clothes before one of the sisters popped around a corner. She'd stroll two steps behind the sisters in her shorts, but when they'd turn around, she'd be in her dress as if she'd never been wearing anything else. I even spotted her wearing them in the back of Mother Caroline's Bible reading, confident the matron's eyes had gone too frail to notice.

The dancing nearly did Clara in, but only because of the rest of us. She'd sometimes hike up the shorts to the tops of her thighs and hop around crook-legged.

"Dance, my merry girls," she'd say. "What's wrong, your legs turned to fish?"

We only stared. Dancing was a sin, wasn't it? So was laughter. I sometimes felt a giggle in my throat, but whenever I did, I'd swallow it. To laugh would have damned me to punishment and given Clara away.

Never. Not if I could help it. She wore the shirt and shorts to bed now and then. She sometimes even slept naked.

The sisters only caught her in the end because she wanted to get caught.

And she only wanted that because of me.

*

One night, I felt a small finger poke between my shoulders, and I rolled over to find the vague shape of Clara kneeling between our cots.

"They'd better not catch you up," I whispered, ready to roll back to sleep.

Clara held a fist to my eyes. "Worth the risk for sweets." Her fingers bloomed into petals around a thumb-sized parcel—a paper-wrapped morsel of chewy candy.

I might have questioned where she got her boy's clothes, but I was too much of a child to wonder where she'd found candy, to think if she'd stolen it. Didn't care. A sweet was a sweet, and we rarely got them. There was no reason to deny myself. I thanked Clara, plucked it up, and popped it into my mouth.

Candy was special in those days. Maybe because children didn't know many other pleasures in this world, but to me, the sweetness was a kind of magic. Best to savor it. If Sister Grace's rants spoke any truth, candy was the closest to any heaven I'd ever get.

I never asked Clara if she only gave a piece to me, or if she'd found one for every girl down the long bedroom.

But certainly I was the only one to get caught.

It was my mistake, not Clara's. Being half-asleep already, I didn't think of anywhere to hide the candy's paper wrapping. It drifted to the floorboards in the night, right beneath my cot, where Sister Grace later snatched it up.

Again, I wasn't the type to toss another girl to the sisters' teeth. "I found it somewhere," I said, almost a shrug in my voice. That wasn't like me.

"It went missing from Mother Caroline's room," Sister Grace said. She was a shadow even in daylight, the paper twisting between her gnarled pointer finger and thumb. "She's too soft to correct you girls, but I'm not. It's a sin to steal."

It was a sin to lie about stealing, too, and she gave me five lashes with her narrow switch for each sin. And then it was a sin to cry, and I got five more. They came in licks of fire across my bare back, and no matter how I clenched my teeth, they stung all the same.

And I thanked her. Not for correcting me, which she must have thought, but for punishing me herself.

For not fetching Sister Agnes.

"The wounds will heal," Clara said that night, her hands reaching down the collar of my nightgown to inspect my back. "But the scars might linger, and lingering things can be all the worse. My fault, wee girl."

"They're not my first," I said, shaking her off and turning to her. "And would you not call me that? I'm taller than you, not your wee girl."

Clara chuckled, a springtime brook in her throat. "Wee not in size, but in years."

I was eight years old then, and I could have sworn she was younger, but like I said, I was a child. What did I know? Had I been half as smart as I thought I was, I'd have understood the gleam in Clara's eyes, shining even in the gloomy room.

"Sister Grace," Clara said, licking her lips to taste the sound. "Funny name for her, don't you think?"

Her revenge on my behalf began the next day.

She tried her trick on Sister Joan first, yanking up the hem of her yellow dress to show off her shorts and then letting it fall back down. Sister Joan ordered her to come close and made her yank up the dress again, but there were only underclothes beneath.

"What we hunting for, sister?" Clara asked, and Sister Joan walked away red-faced.

The game then began in earnest. Clara would pop around a corner wearing only her shirt and shorts, no dress to hide them beneath, right in Sister Grace's sight. Sister Grace would chase her around the corner, stumbling at the end and nearly falling, but when she caught up, Clara would only be wearing her dress again.

There was more to her scheme than sleight of hand. I swear that sometimes she darted past me, Sister Grace on her tail, and something more like a boyish face grinned beneath her choppy hair and newsboy cap. She'd then spin around and look like the same girl I knew.

That was when I noticed her hair never seemed to grow.

"How do you do that?" I asked one night that week.

"Do what?" Clara asked, as if she were the picture of innocence.

I shrugged against my pillow. "Any of it!"

"Ah, because I must." Clara shrugged back at me. "I've no choice in it. They deserve to be vexed, so I have to vex them."

"You can do it because you have to?" I scowled at her, as if a grim look could ever goad that girl into plain-speaking. "Makes no sense, Greenstone."

"Plenty of folk do things only because they have to," Clara said, nestling her head into her pillow. "And this here burden's mine. Them habit-wearing beasts, they see some half-feral girly boy-y flustery little bit of nonsense, they want to make that make sense. And they'll cut that little creature into the shape of sense."

"Cut?" I asked.

"Sometimes. If they have to." Clara grew quiet. "And sometimes, because they can."

The game took a turn three days later, after Mother Caroline's Bible reading, when Sister Grace caught Clara by the arm while we were leaving the home's library. Clara still wore her shirt, shorts, and cap.

That is, until Sister Grace stripped them off her body there in the hall. Down to the skin.

I've come to doubt my eyes at times. I can only tell what I saw: Clara didn't look like I did without her clothes at that moment. She had other parts, things I'd never seen before then, and myself and the others, we covered our mouths against squealing and laughter.

Sister Grace dropped the clothes and went sheet-pale.

Clara smirked in that crooked way I came to know as hers. "Why Sister Grace, I hadn't a clue we could runs naked around this place. What a paradise St. Mary's be!"

She hopped over the pile of clothes and bolted down the hall.

Sister Grace chased, and I think she only managed to grab Clara's arm again because Clara wanted to be caught. Wanted to make a fool of the woman who'd lashed me.

"How did you do it?" Sister Grace asked. "How did you hide this?"

But when Clara whirled naked in Sister Grace's grasp, she

had lost the parts strange to me and now resembled me beneath my clothes.

"What's the matter, sister?" Clara asked, her eyes wide as the world, her lips pouty and innocent. "Thought you'd seen something you been missing all your long life?"

Clara's was a sin of nonsense and silliness, and that might have been good for five lashes, but Sister Grace had a different idea. She left her switch where it belonged and instead dragged Clara down the hall.

They headed for the narrow closet.

The sisters only punished me there once, and I forget why. *Closet* is a generous word. It was an uncomfortable slit in one of St. Mary's wooden walls. The ceiling caved down and away from the door, tightening the channel the deeper you went, though there wasn't much floorspace to wander. Barely room to stand, sides too tight for lying down. You could only sit curled up, spine crying, limbs stiff.

Most girls came out aching, hungry, exhausted. Some would wet themselves, though I never did.

I had the feeling then that Clara would come bouncing out as if no time had passed. Despite what she called me, she was the true wee girl. The narrow closet would only make her skip a meal or two, but she would somehow find comfort there.

I also had the feeling that, while it was the first time Clara would be thrown in the narrow closet, it would not be the last.

I'll never forget the last.

*

The sisters set Clara free a day later, and it was as if Sister Grace had made a mortal enemy out of the world itself.

No obvious vengeance visited her life. Not even practical jokes. I only noticed from the day Clara first emerged from the narrow closet that nothing seemed to go Sister Grace's way anymore. She would prick her fingers during needlework, or trip while heading up a stairway she had climbed a thousand times. A slice of bread she'd placed fresh on her plate would turn either soggy or stale in her mouth—I could tell when she spat it back out. She and Sister Joan nearly came to blows over how the bread was stored until Sister Agnes settled them.

Did anyone suspect Clara? I certainly did, but then, I knew her better than the other girls. And Sister Grace didn't suspect; she *knew*. Once she'd been told Sister Joan wasn't to blame, Sister Grace decided her every misfortunate, proven or not, was Clara's fault.

And she was going to make Clara suffer.

After that, Clara never went more than a few days between visits to the narrow closet. She'd sit inside it a few hours, sometimes a whole day, but she never seemed to have too hard a time. I never wished worse punishments for my friend, but I sometimes wondered how she escaped worse fates, like lashings.

Or like Jenny, gone up those attic stairs and never seen again.

*

Jenny had been a scrawny creature with the palest skin and the longest hair. Her locks were dark and shiny. Not in the greasy way a couple of the girls had it, but in the way the night sky shines in its darkness. It went down her back, past her hips. If I had ever believed the sisters that she'd fallen out a window, I might have thought she'd somehow tripped on that hair.

But I didn't believe the sisters. I believed the other girls when they said Sister Agnes had fed Jenny to the thing in the attic, and I had better reason to believe than anyone.

Unlike the rest, I remembered the last time I'd seen Jenny. She was wearing her nightgown at mid-morning because she had dropped back on her cot after wake-up and missed her morning lessons. It was the third time. The rest of us had tried to wake her, and we would have tried harder had we known what Sister Agnes would do.

I watched them from far down the hall—Sister Agnes in her black habit, flying like the reaper on the wind, her hand clenched tight around Jenny's arm. Some punishment waited above, I knew that even then, but I couldn't have known what. Sister Agnes dragged Jenny up and then returned a few minutes later, the attic door slamming shut behind her. If Jenny cried, I didn't hear her. No sound ever escaped that place.

No children, either.

Days passed before Sister Agnes, calm as if explaining the weather, told us Jenny was dead and said a window had done it.

"An accident," Sister Agnes had said. "No one to blame."

But I blamed her anyway. The words hugged my teeth and hopped on my tongue, never jumping out of my mouth, but they were there. Sister Agnes and the others knew something was wrong at the top of St. Mary's, and they gave one of us girls to it for their own reasons.

Had she been living at St. Mary's with us then, I like to think Clara would have saved Jenny. How would she have done it? I don't know. Maybe it was just the hollow wish of a desperate little girl who thought her friend invincible.

It was one thing to prod Sister Grace or Sister Joan, but there was murder in the eyes of Sister Agnes. Around her, we kept ourselves low.

If you'd asked me a few years later, I'd have said those sisters needed a good night out, the touch of a lover like most of us would someday feel, in ways the sisters would never know.

But if you asked me later, and now, I'd say this: Every single person in this world is deeply hurting somewhere inside, and the sisters of St. Mary's Home for Girls might have never thought it to themselves, but in their hearts, they believed we were to blame.

*

As the weeks went on, it became mine and Clara's custom to inch our cots together at night. Were one of the sisters to come stalking the long bedroom past bedtime, I had to trust that Clara's tricks would make them doubt their eyes.

Pressed-together cots might seem like nothing in the grand scheme of the world, but the closeness made all the difference when Clara and I could hold each other's hands in the night and whisper so softly that only we could hear each other. In that darkness, we confided our secrets across pillows and sheets and clasped hands.

"You don't belong in this place, you know that?" Clara asked once. "It don't suit you."

"I've been here since I was six," I said.

That felt something like an answer. Having lived in St. Mary's for two years, I had to belong, didn't I?

"If anyone doesn't suit this place, it's you."

Clara edged closer, her elbow sinking into the crevice between our cots. "How'd you come to get here?"

"Mama brought me," I told her. "*Just a little while*, she said. She and Papa would lift me in their arms and kiss me and bring me home once he came back from the war." I let this settle between us, as if a pause between words could be anything like the long years without my parents. "But I guess he never came back, since neither did she."

"Fool of them," Clara said. "Never had parents myself, mind, so I've no idea what's decent in them."

I screwed up my face, catching her in a lie. "You said you had family."

"I said it, and I had them." Clara explained it like this was the same simple concept of telling me feet went on the ground instead of the ceiling. "But there's more to family than parents, and more to an origin than a home. I grew up in the dark places, some lively toadstool, a mishap sprung from wet and green. They kept thinking to put me into other wet places, like a marsh or a church. You know, a priest once tried to baptize me. But I swallowed all the baptismal water in one gulp, not spilling a drop."

I giggled, and it fought away any cry inside me. "How did you come here?" I asked.

Clara rolled her shoulders, tugging my hand. "I lost my way, same as you. A many precious things get lost in this world. A many wild things, too. And the mean. Many a mean lost thing wound up here, walking in them habits. And crawling about in the up-there."

I didn't ask what she was talking about. She meant the attic.

"A mean lost thing lingers in that place," Clara said. "Stay away from there. Never let that cold one, Agnes, take you away."

By then it was only one among many secrets we swapped about the sisters of St. Mary's. How Sister Grace's middle had swelled over the course of a few months before she went away for a while, and then one day came back as almost her usual self. How Sister Joan hid dirty magazines behind a loose floor plank. How Sister Agnes might have blood on her hands.

And how none of the sisters, and not even Mother Caroline, would visit the attic alone. I came to believe something terrible happened up there long before Jenny disappeared, worse than all the beatings and lashings and starving, maybe even before St. Mary's had become a home for girls. And I came to believe it happened again since to anyone who lingered there. To Jenny.

Now and then, I would glance at the long bedroom's ceiling and shudder as if I could see clear through to the attic.

And I kept hoping never to see the real thing with my own eyes.

*

Three days later, Clara pushed Sister Grace too far.

We were at breakfast. Someone had placed the milk jug on a high shelf, likely Sister Joan, but she wouldn't come out of the washroom that morning to fetch it for Sister Grace. Many times I'd seen Sister Joan at a sink basin, scrubbing her hands until her fingers bled, as if a sin lived beneath her skin that she couldn't wash away. The other sisters couldn't talk her out of these trances, but this instance of furious washing had put Sister Grace in a bad mood.

She came into the dining room with the milk jug, a fury in her steps. Clara stood beside me, as she'd taken to doing, but I felt her trembling, like she was holding in laughter that could shake the world apart.

"Don't," I whispered. "Not today."

"Too late, wee girl," Clara said, and the answer almost sent her snickering. "What's changed is changed."

I saw what she'd done when Sister Grace stumbled on an uneven floorboard. The milk jug slipped from her fingers, twisted in the air, and shattered against the table's edge.

Glass sprayed, but the pale explosion that should have been milk instead spilled a hundred white marbles in every direction. They bounced and clacked free across the floor, rolling around our feet, into the hall and under furniture. Three of them ricocheted off my foot. One of them spun in place, and I saw the same creamy cloudiness beneath its glass as I would've expected had they been milk.

Or *still* been milk. Once that impossible thought came to me, I couldn't shake it away. Likewise, I couldn't escape knowing who'd done it. To look at my friend would have been to incriminate her, but after everything I'd already seen, even understanding that it made no sense, I knew Clara—that unexplainable girl—had changed the milk into marbles.

No one ran to collect them. Whichever of us moved so much as an inch would be admitting their sin to Sister Grace and would take the blame and punishment for everyone.

Clara moved more than an inch. She hopped onto the table as if the marbles were skittering white mice, and then she yanked up her dress to reveal her cotton shirt and grimy shorts for the first time since Sister Grace had stripped them off her body.

"Oh, thank me lards above, Sister Grace, you found me marbles!" Clara shouted. "I feared I'd lost them, I did!"

With her knees crooked, she stamped her toes and heels against the tabletop, dancing a merry jig to Sister Grace's pale horror.

There was no fighting it this time. My throat trembled, and a coughing giggle shot out my mouth. The sound was so queer that I giggled again, harder this time. Ellie must've found it funny, too—she laughed next, and then the rest of the girls bawled with aching bellies and tearful eyes. I bit my cheeks to try and stop it, only for a snort to escape louder than the giggling.

Laughter was a sin. Dancing was a sin. Marbles were probably a sin, too.

I don't know what dancing over marbles and making little girls laugh could be, but Sister Grace took that for many sins put together.

She grabbed Clara by the scruff of her scalp and hauled her off the table, only to slip on marbles and nearly crash to the floor. That sent another hushed cloud of giggling over us girls.

Sister Grace didn't look at us, let alone chastise. All her hatred was bent toward Clara— one girl to suffer the world's punishments—and she dragged her enemy down the hall, into the narrow closet, where she slammed the door shut and locked it.

And it stayed locked.

I expected to find Clara free by lights-out, at worst by morning, but she didn't appear at breakfast the next day.

One marble rolled under my shoe, and I kept it. There was no other sign of my friend that day. Clara remained in the narrow closet for a second lights-out in a row.

After a third night with no whispers beside my cot, no hand to hold in the dark, I started to worry.

Between lessons, I watched the narrow closet for any sign of it being opened, but as far as I knew, the sisters didn't bring Clara food or water. Did Sister Grace alone know there was a child locked in that slit in the wall? No, the others had to notice Clara's absence from lessons, meals, and the bedroom.

They had decided she was not their problem.

But I decided she was mine. I tried to bring her water in a small cup, which I meant to spill at the closet door so it might run along the floor to her.

Sister Agnes caught me before I could reach, her cold fingers grasping my arm. Her grim mouth set in a line, so much like the other creases haunting her face.

"For Clara," I said, though Sister Agnes hadn't asked a question. "So she'll drink."

"She is Sister Grace's charge," Sister Agnes said. "Let us ask her."

Her voice was an icy rain, and I followed, chilled and shivering, to where she found Sister Grace at the pantry.

"Dear Colleen has thoughts on Clara's punishment," Sister Agnes said.

Sister Grace looked to Sister Agnes and then to me. "She's where she belongs."

"But she'll die!" I shouted through tears.

Sister Grace snarled. "What would you know, little devil?"

I knew three days without water meant death. And death for a sinning child such as Clara meant Hell.

"If you cause a fuss now, we'll have to correct you," Sister

Agnes said. "You've been lashed already, and the narrow closet is full. We'd have to find somewhere else to put you. Am I speaking plain enough?"

I nodded; she was. Without meaning to, I looked to the ceiling, where the attic dwelled at the height of the house.

I remembered what she'd done with Jenny.

*

The sisters forgot about Clara, or pretended to. A peace settled onto them like a comforting summer breeze without our runtish troublemaker prancing around in boy's clothes, turning milk into marbles, or making Sister Grace stub her toe on misshapen floorboards, as if Clara could somehow be faulted for that last one.

While the sisters bustled in contentment, I mourned my friend. And hoped for a miracle.

And then I got one.

Seven days after Clara's internment, Sister Grace caught Wendy playing with a couple of marbles she'd snagged from the dining room. Sister Grace hauled Wendy up by the arm and dragged her to the narrow closet that instant for stealing.

Which sin caused one of us to be bled, another lashed, another locked away, and another sentenced to the attic all seemed interchangeable, never pairing with any specific punishment. In those days, I thought there must've been a complex system to how the sisters ran St. Mary's. Since then, I've realized that no one really knows what they're doing, and the world is chaos.

Sister Grace must have known the same that day when she wrenched open the narrow closet, ready to stuff Wendy inside.

Only for Clara to come bounding out alive.

"Top of the morning, Sister Grace!" she cried, loud as a foghorn. She seemed no thirstier, no hungrier, not even any dirtier than when she'd been thrown in the narrow closet a week before.

"Might I break me fast now? Sure's been quite a wait."

Sister Grace shrank back from Wendy, Clara, and the narrow closet. She darted gasping around the corner, a shriek in her throat. Wendy slunk away, probably to hide in case Sister Grace came back.

I wasn't going anywhere. I charged against Clara, nearly knocking her back into the narrow closet. Her spine struck the door, and she held me while I hugged her waist and sobbed into her chest.

"How?" I asked from somewhere amid my mess.

Clara only smirked. "Fret not, I wasn't in there long, wee girl. Only stepped from the day they shut the door to the day they opened it. Easy trick, you see. Always about the tricks and japes to save a life. Good humors, you know?"

I cried harder, hating her. Loving her. Wishing I understood her in the slightest.

"Now then, easy, easy," Clara said, cooing to me. "If you can't laugh, I'll laugh for you. The humor's like your soul's sticking out an extra arm they don't expect. That one piece of you saying, *No, sir, no, ma'am, no any of you. None of you's going to make any sense of me.* And you mustn't let them."

That evening, I overheard Sister Grace's shouting through the door to Mother Caroline's room. "If it does something wrong, get Sister Agnes, Sister Joan, I don't care," Grace said. "I'm not touching that *thing* again!"

Some days, I think that should've been the end of St. Mary's as a whole. The sisters were outwitted. Why should they be allowed to taunt and beat us? Why should they determine sin?

When night fell, Clara and I shoved our cots together for the first time in a week. I expected she'd be too exhausted for whispering, but I should have realized Clara would never do as I'd expect.

A melancholy seemed to have settled into her. "I touched these walls and asked them who they used to be," she said. "I wonder if they're what led me here to St. Mary's, you know? Can they recall being some forest I once knew? Maybe they're what's left of me family."

"This place is all that's left for any of us," I said, and I wiggled over the cots until we both lay across Clara's and I could clutch her tight. "We're all we got."

"No, little mercy," Clara said, and she kissed my forehead. "You'll be out of here before I am. Wait and see."

That was the only instance she ever called me anything besides *wee girl*—until the end, that is. As if she knew something about me that I didn't.

Sometimes I awoke in the dark hours and thought there was a bulky shape beneath the blankets of Clara's cot, far larger than any of the sisters. It breathed slow and cumbersome, as loud as a bear. But by morning, the blankets would have settled to their usual state atop her.

She was a creature of her own kind, and her boldness was infectious.

I don't blame her for what happened to me after; it was entirely my own choice. If anything, she should take credit. I'm glad I became that sort of girl, one whose heart filled with courage and bravado.

But those traits couldn't save me.

*

Curiosity must be a sin, and I was no angel. I wanted to see Sister Joan's secret.

It was a not a well-kept secret. Plenty of us knew which loose board in the closet by the library hid Sister Joan's dirty magazines, even if she snuck this fact under the noses of Sister Grace, Sister Agnes, and Mother Caroline.

I waited until Sister Joan had taken to one of her self-inflicted tortures at the washroom sink, and then I pried the board off and dug out her secret. Most of the magazines were rolled up, and one had been scrunched as if thrust into its hiding place in a hurry. Each hid black and white photographs of naked people inside. The sisters might have called nakedness a sin, but everyone was naked sometimes, so I couldn't see what made these magazines dirty over any others.

The question distracted me until someone gripped my shoulder and wheeled me around.

Sister Joan hunched close to me, face red as an apple. Had she been alone, maybe we could have let the secret lie together. But she wasn't.

Sister Agnes stood behind her. "Where did you get these, Colleen?" she asked, cold and smooth as a frozen lake. "How did you smuggle this filth into our holy home?"

Confusion tied my tongue in knots while they led me away from the loose board and magazines, chatting about sin and the severity of punishment. No way would Sister Agnes believe me over another sister.

We were nearly to the stairs before I realized where they planned to take me, and then all I could do was scream. I'd have confessed anything, done anything, let them do anything they wanted so long as they wouldn't put me up in the place where Jenny disappeared.

But Sister Agnes did not know mercy. Not even for children.

The attic door was a black mouth. My limp legs crossed its threshold, never stepping but dragged by two grown women into that monstrous cavern, a place that darkened the deeper we went. It spanned the whole of the house, you could tell by the slant of the rooftop above us, but it seemed far vaster, as if it burrowed through to other houses, their attics, and everything that haunted them. There was no light except what little drifted up the stairs, and it would follow the sisters away when they shut the attic door.

Only a steel chair broke up the dust and cobwebs. Leather

straps trimmed its armrests, and rusted bolts gripped its legs to the floor. Sister Joan strapped me down while Sister Agnes glanced back and forth, as if standing watch. A tremble worked down her fingers.

Even that horrid slab of ice given human form was afraid. I started to scream again, but it did no good. Sister Joan finished strapping me to the chair, nodded to Sister Agnes, and then they left me. The door slammed shut, harsh as a coffin lid.

I tried to hold stiff for a while as though, if I stayed a decent and quiet creature, they might return and free me.

But bravado never cures fear. It can only comfort a frightened heart.

When courage died, I screamed in mourning until my throat went hoarse. Rocking back and forth did no good; the chair was too stiff. And did I really want to lie on the floor? Something worse than darkness might have lurked down in the dust.

Tears trickled from my eyes, and I put real fire into sobbing. I hoped if the sisters heard me, they might come back and take me downstairs for a lashing. Crying was a sin, after all.

Night sealed the attic's blackness, and then I knew for certain I wasn't alone.

The noises were ordinary at first. Scratching, scuttling—mice, I hoped. Rats, at worst. Nothing I didn't already know lived in the house.

But stare into absolute darkness long enough, and you'll see shapes.

Something else huddled at the far end of the attic, larger than a rat, its head bowed beneath its shoulders. Subtle breath stirred the dust, but somehow I knew it didn't need to breathe. This was for me to hear, so I'd know my eyes weren't playing tricks on me. What lingered in the attic was like Clara in a way, its secret only noticeable because it wanted to be noticed.

I didn't want to notice it, be noticed by it. I wanted nothing to do with it. I just wanted to eat supper and use the washroom, to sleep in my cot beside Clara and whisper about what I'd found that day.

Spend enough time in St. Mary's Home for Girls, and you'd learn the sin behind desire. To want was wrong. To wonder and be curious were wrong, too. We were born with too much sin for God's good world, and that was why we'd ended up in St. Mary's. A place to cleanse us of the sin of desire, along with every other kind. We would become pure creatures before we left these walls.

Or we would die trying.

"Now then, what kind of thoughts be those for my wee girl?" a voice whispered beside my ear.

I screamed my way out of a trance. My eyes narrowed, adjusted, still making out the huddled shape in the dark ahead. It couldn't be what had whispered in my ear. I knew that voice.

"Clara?" I asked. "How did you get up here?"

"I've a better question," Clara said. "What do you get when you cross a country with a bomb?"

One of her nonsense thoughts, passed to me as if we still lay beside each other in our cots instead of holed up in that hellish attic. I shrugged the same as I would have in the long bedroom.

"An explanation," Clara said, and I could almost see that crooked grin on her choppy-haired head.

I tugged at my leather restraints. "Will you let me out?"

"I can't touch you, not in the way I'm here." Clara whistled gently in my ear. "But tell me a joke, and we might be free from the dark a brief moment."

Another sound brushed against my world—that breath in the attic, closer now. I peered again into the darkness, where the black shape had left the far wall. It sat nearer on the attic floorboards. Too big to be Clara. It had to be the same gangly thing that had eaten Jenny many months before.

Clara snapped her fingers. "Come then, tell me one."

"I can't," I said. It came out breathy, half-gasping. "Clara, it's too dark."

"I know darkness like this," Clara said. "I *am* darkness like this. And I know the joys and armor of playing the fool. There was once a clown called before a king, and the king could have ordered the clown's throat cut, or stretched, or broken from his head at any moment, but the clown kept his humor."

The blackness coated my eyes. I felt Clara's presence, her hand hovering near mine, as if we were about to clasp them in the long bedroom. My fingers stretched to reach her.

Across the floor, the shape slid closer.

"Listen, I want you to hear this," Clara said. "It's important. You ready for it?"

I nodded as if she could see me.

"What kind of cake do you make with twenty clams?" Clara's smirk crackled across the attic. "A stomach ache."

I wanted to laugh with her, but the shape in the dark scuttled closer. Its footsteps were dry dust against wood, and its arms might have reached the roof had they uncoiled from its body.

"Giggle for me," Clara said. "Can't you remember the marbles, or did you lose them, same as I did?"

I forced a smile onto my face, a fake thing I could wear against the scuttling shape. That day in the dining room with Sister Grace and the milk made into marbles had freed something inside me, but I didn't know how to get it back. Not in that attic.

"I can't," I said, half-ready to sob. The shape's breath crossed my feet.

But Clara's breath touched my ear. "You have to. Whatever's up here, it's got a mouth carved for eating sense. Only got to stick an arm free of that mouth and it'll snag the thing's lip, no going down that miserable throat for you. Come on, where's that silver tongue?"

The shape craned its neck. A round head reached toward my lap. I looked to the ceiling as if I could see through the attic, the rooftop, all the way to the stars.

"How am I supposed to laugh when it's this scary?" I asked, choking at tears.

"Wee girl, there's always too much to be scared of," Clara said.

Arms encircled the seat, and there was no knowing whether they belonged to Clara or the shape in the attic.

Clara lowered her voice to a whisper. "You must keep your humor, else you'll end up like them sisters below. Hollow things of sense, that's all. Come now, your time here is nearly at an end. If you can't think up your own, repeat after me. Ready?"

I swallowed, closed my eyes, and nodded again.

"What do you get when you cross a potato with an elephant?" Clara asked.

"I don't know," I said.

"Mashed potatoes." Clara giggled in my ear.

And I might have giggled. More than that, I repeated her word for word and Clara giggled back at me, a proud moment while fearful sweat coated my skin.

And the darkness giggled too, just like any of us.

But that made no sense. Who else could be up there? Could the other girls hear me through their ceiling?

I looked down to face the source of the giggling, only to find a head in my lap taking firmer shape the more it laughed. A monstrous mouth formed from the outline of its pale shape against the blackness, and then even finer details came to me as if this thing couldn't hold them back anymore.

I knew that face. "Jenny?"

Her eyes shone clear in the dark, and her familiar long hair spilled around it. Not someone eaten by a thing in the attic, but maybe a *thing* herself. I couldn't know for certain. All I knew was that I'd found her again for the first time since Sister Agnes dragged her up the stairs and likely put her in this monstrous chair.

"Jenny," I said again. "What happened to you?"

She tilted her head and laid it heavy again in my lap. Her lanky arms tucked around the chair, and she began to moan.

"You know her?" Clara asked.

"She was—" I started to say *my friend*, but could I? Wouldn't a friend have known better? "She was one of us. Last time I saw her, Sister Agnes brought her here. She told us she'd fallen out a window and died."

"Don't know about any windows, but she don't seem to be whatever she was back when you knew her."

Had my hands been free, I'd have stroked and petted Jenny's long locks. I could only look on her, lower my head, and nuzzle my face against her still-shiny hair. She was more solid than Clara then. Anything might have become of her since the day Sister Agnes led her up these stairs. I could think whatever I liked—that Jenny had died of fright up here, or that Sister Agnes had strangled her in an icy grip. Or maybe Jenny was forgotten, left to thirst and starve like Clara in the narrow closet, only with none of Clara's tricks to get her out.

But my speculating wasn't a shadow in that darkness. I would never know what had truly become of her, or quite what she had become. Only that I wanted to help her.

"She'll lay a suffering on anyone if she's like this." Clara sounded grim like I'd never heard her. "You cannot be leaving her this way. Not here."

My wrists and ankles tensed against the leather straps. "What do I do?" I asked.

"Exactly as you'd want anyone to do for you in this vicious place," Clara said. "You must catch Jenny up in your arms and kiss her and bring her home, the way it should be for all sweet children wronged in these places. The way it should be for you and me."

Tears brimmed again in my eyes, and I pressed my face harder into Jenny. She smelled of dust and regret. Without any help, she would be left to haunt this place.

Clara breathed closer in the dark, lips against my cheek. "She can't be left here, another loss from a war with no end."

"Which war?" I asked.

"The war them grown beasts wage on the wee ones of the world," Clara said. "They mightn't have tanks and growly guns like the war your papa faded into, but it's full of weapons all the same, of lashings and narrow closets and all the ways they wish to cut you until you make sense for them. Never do it, little mercy. Never make sense for them."

Had I the means, I'd have cut my palm and seen Clara cut hers, and we'd have forged a promise in blood for it.

But she had other thoughts, her voice straying deeper into the attic. "You take her," she said. "And I'll be here instead."

I raised my head from Jenny's. "You can't! You don't deserve that, and you're still alive."

"It is a hungry place," Clara said. "And I've nowhere to be. A rest in the dark might do me fine. It'll help me grow, same as I did in my first darkness, all a toadstool of a creature. Might be I become worse. A thing more frightening than Jenny, breathing through their ceilings and down their necks. And they won't know how to make me laugh." Twin lights glittered in the dark, a green glint in her sweet earthen eyes. "Not like you. But please, another joke. Thinking you got a knack for them now, and it might give good Jenny a moment's joy."

I couldn't deny her then. First I told a terrible joke, and Clara told one too. We both giggled, and Jenny laughed with us. The darkness never brightened, but it softened. No matter how the attic meant to eat our laughter and quiet us, Clara was always bigger, louder, closer, and her voice bound Jenny and I together.

Somewhere in my jokes, I stuck out that extra arm of spirit like Clara had said, the one no one expects. And then I asked more silly questions and stuck out another. No leather straps bound these soulful arms to the chair, and they were enough to catch Jenny up and kiss her.

And I would bring her home, wherever that might be. I would come for Clara, too. We'd laugh again over each other's jokes, even the really nonsense ones. Especially the really nonsense ones.

I think, before Clara came to St. Mary's Home for Girls, had I seen Sister Grace, Sister Joan, Sister Agnes, and even Mother Caroline all brandish cleavers and slaughter one of us girls, and then cook her up and serve her for supper, I wouldn't have said a word. I would have torn flesh from that girl's bones with my teeth, grateful I'd been spared. It would have been a silent meal, feasting on one of our own, everyone terrified that the first to speak might be devoured next.

Wasn't that what had become of Jenny, deep down?

But Clara changed the home. Changed me. She saw me through to morning, when the attic's darkness at last crept away from its door. The shape of Jenny lingered with me. I couldn't see her suggestion in the blackness anymore, but the nonsense arms of my soul clung to her and wouldn't let her go until she was free of the place that had stolen her life.

When Sister Joan and Sister Agnes returned to release me, they found me dry-eyed and smiling.

"Back so soon?" I asked. "I'd like to stay longer."

Sister Joan's face began to redden. Nothing unusual there, but I swear I saw a nervous crack in the ice of Sister Agnes.

"Before you wish me good morning, I need to tell you something I learned up here. Why did the groom choose bread for his best man?" I smiled wider for them. "Don't you know? It makes the best toast."

*

Papers were put in order to transfer me from St. Mary's to a secular home for girls, with a note on disturbed behavior. Really, the sisters decided if the attic couldn't unmake me then I had to be out of their control.

Which I was. Too many arms springing from my soul, too much nonsense in one wee girl.

I saw Clara in that final week at St. Mary's, but she wasn't herself. More like the well-behaved boring girl she'd pretended to be when she first arrived. I tried to press our cots together at night, to whisper and hold hands, but she seemed confused, like she didn't know me anymore.

Part of her had to be resting in that attic in Jenny's place, I decided. Waiting for something, but I couldn't know what until long after I left the home.

A kind family adopted me soon after my transfer. You don't need to know the details, but I was happy and far from St. Mary's. There were hills and yards and streets and other children. They laughed and played, and they were sometimes cruel, but never so much as the menace I'd seen before. Nothing like the narrow closet, the attic, or the cold glare of Sister Agnes.

Three years passed before I found out what had become of her, though it happened only two months after I left St. Mary's. The newspaper was never clear on the specifics, but she'd had some sort of accident on the stairs. I could guess which ones, where they led, and who she might have found there.

Not so much my runtish choppy-headed friend. More the great bear-sounding shape that had formed along her cot some nights.

A creature of her own kind, with a mouth ready for Sister Agnes.

That was when I let Jenny go. She was ready, had been ready, and only needed to know there wouldn't be a Sister Agnes anywhere she went to stuff her inside the attic again. I found an open place at the edge of a great woods and—

It's hard to explain how you unravel your soul from another. I said, "Goodbye," and then Jenny drifted away.

Sometimes the end is only a released breath.

Sometimes it's the shutting down of St. Mary's Home for Girls. I read about that in the newspaper, too, something about how the sisters no longer felt capable of caring for the girls. They could pretend it was their idea all they liked, but Clara was to blame. To thank. The sisters couldn't unmake me, but she had unmade them. A little bit for me. A lot because it tickled her to do so.

I could only hope some of the other girls had found solace, some humor to make their souls hard to swallow, before they split apart into the rest of the world.

And what of my friend? What of Clara?

*

I'm old, now. I've been old for a long while, I think.

The years have given me two husbands and a wife at different times in my life, and I've outlived them all. They've also given me two children, three stepchildren, and six grandchildren so far, but there's another on the way and perhaps more to come.

I think of children every day. When I watch them play, St. Mary's climbs up the spine of my memories, a threat to take my little ones. They'll never end up in a place like that, but tell it to the attic in my mind, full of paranoia and fear. The nightmares never go away.

These feelings surprise me. Shouldn't my soul be too crooked to hate St. Mary's anymore? After so many years, am I really still angry?

Yes, I am. Even anger that's as weathered and ancient as mine may still linger like a forgotten ghost in a dark attic. Cruelties thrived in that place, some I won't say, others lost to time. Though nothing I could do would ever change that inside me, I didn't want that house to outlast me.

So tonight, I drive across four states to reach St. Mary's Home for Girls. For the last time.

The house has been put to use one way or another over the decades, but it's never held a consistent function since the sisters shut it down. Maybe its true self has always sought the torment of children. It waited for its former owner to die so it could hurt them before, and now it waits to reclaim that purpose again.

It has waited too long, and time's run out. I park at the curb and spring the trunk of my car, where two jerry cans of gasoline await a purpose of their own. If I'm to be old, if I'm to die, then I'll see St. Mary's die first, and may all its cruelties burn with it.

But not Clara.

I find her standing on the warped steps beneath the front door, as clear as when I first saw her wearing a yellow dress long ago. She doesn't wear the dress now; she's got on her shirt and shorts and newsboy cap, attire any girl could wear today without much hassle.

Times have changed, but Clara stays the same.

I shake my head and laugh as I lug the jerry cans to the steps. "How?" I ask, as if she's ever given a straight answer to that kind of question.

Clara giggles. "Got here same as always, wee girl. I stepped from the day you left and into the day you came back. Easy trick." She smirks in the way she always has.

"If you're skipping years, how come I'm still *wee girl*? Aren't I older than you now?"

"Never!" Clara laughed. "Never, never."

"Still a choppy-haired little thing," I say. "You've been waiting all this time?"

"Not in the slightest, never the patient sort." Clara stretches, yawns. "Slept a bit, though, and I've grown quite large in the dark, not so much that sweet small thing you used to hold hands with at night." She pauses, her smirk working against some greater burden inside her. "Never really was."

And I've known that. Always, always, there has been more to Clara Greenstone than sins and laughter and anything we simple creatures can imagine, whether our souls are shaped like sense or as crookedly nonsensical as mine.

Clara holds out one hand and takes a jerry can. She then holds out the other hand and takes mine. Our fingers close around each other's for the first time in decades, hers as smooth as the little girl she appears to be, mine gnarled and shaking with age. We pour gasoline together over the steps and into St. Mary's doorway. Twin puddles conjoin and slither down a once-familiar hall, into dusty darkness primed for new flickering light. As if St. Mary's has been desperate for a drink.

When it's time to cleanse the house, I nearly drop the unlit match, but Clara grasps my wrist in both hands and holds me steady until I can spark the flame and throw it where it's meant to go.

The house moans as fire engulfs its doorway. Like it knows.

Once the entrance begins to burn, Clara snatches up a cloud of fire in her hands and runs giggling deep into St. Mary's Home for Girls. The walls remain thick timber that might remember when it used to be a forest, but somehow I see through them, clear as windows.

I watch Clara bound into the library where Mother Caroline used to read the Bible to us, its shelves emptied, and across the loose board where Sister Joan used to hide her magazines, and then into the dining room where Clara once turned milk into marbles and danced a jig for Sister Grace. Clara carries the fire around the corner where she once ran naked, and into the long bedroom where all the girls once slept. The flames dance into the narrow closet, and through the washroom, and when Clara reaches the top of the house, she throws the fire into the attic where it can burn the darkness and its terrible hunger, so no more girls like Jenny will ever be caught there.

Clara does it all laughing and running and dancing, and I might dance and laugh with her down in the lot as she steps through another darkness, to some other place in the world. Our freedom and our crooked souls and our giddiness are each a sin, growing fast as fire. The sisters used to teach us so.

But this last night at St. Mary's Home for Girls, the joy of sin runs free.

BENNY ROSE
THE CANNIBAL KING

On Halloween night, 1953, Blackwood Mercy Hospital burned to the ground. The building collapsed long before the fire was put out, and by end of the rescue team's tireless search, forty-one bodies were recovered from the smoking ruin.

Six were not. Five children, one adult.

Town council said the hospital fire was a freak accident, an open-and-shut case, but the kids of Blackwood know better.

They say Benny Rose did it.

ONE: HALLOWEEN 1986

Sticky pine limbs dragged at Chase's arms as he picked through the woods. He was glad for the cover of his old-school Dracula costume, but the black sleeves had to look like someone had been sick on them by now.

That might happen before night's end, the way Donnie sounded behind him. They hadn't watched each other's intake at Rachel's Halloween party like they planned, and they couldn't exactly complain about it. Neither was older than seventeen.

Every few steps, Donnie stumbled against Chase's back. "I think your shortcut's kind of a long cut."

"I think you're drunk," Chase said.

"Could be both of us are drunk."

Chase didn't feel drunk, but if they were late to meet their ride, he'd probably be called that and worse. Cutting through the woods seemed like a good idea to make sure they weren't late, especially when no one would drive them from Monterrey Court. They were out-of-towners, and that seemed to matter in Blackwood.

But the town's back end was practically Vermont wilderness. Crickets owned these woods.

The trees weren't so thick that Chase couldn't see the stars, but those lights were tiny twinkling dots, and the moon was hardly a hairline suggestion lost in the sky. It was easy to lose direction.

"This isn't right. Supposed to be at Gleason."

"No, Loveland." Donnie stumbled into Chase yet again and leaned a hand between his shoulders. "Why's this town shaped like two ugly pretzels had an uglier pretzel baby?"

Because it was grown piecemeal, not planned like some places, but Chase didn't say that. Donnie wouldn't remember by morning anyway.

He let off Chase's back and began patting at his costume. "Did I leave my movies at Rachel's?"

"She'll get them to you at Christmas. Focus on your feet." Chase reached back to steady Donnie, whose bare arms stuck from a short-sleeved white ninja costume. Pine needles clung to his skin and hair. Chase held on anyway. What else were friends for? "One foot in front of the other. Yeah, like that. On you go."

On Donnie went, and then down he went on hands and knees. His costume was probably a mess, but Chase could only see it by the faint glow that breached the trees ahead. Still holding on, he pulled Donnie to his feet and led him somewhere to rest.

"I think I see light." And evidence of civilization, too. The trees here had been tamed, their lower limbs sawed off to look tidier. Chase drew Donnie to sitting and set his back against one of the trimmed trunks. "I'll check it out. You sit tight."

Donnie swung his head up and down, his face gone pale. "I like that. You go, I stay."

Chase gave him an encouraging shoulder clap and pushed past a row of pines. They had to be near something if there was light. Too weak to be a streetlight. He hoped it was something other than a vacant roadside. That wouldn't be much better than wilderness unless it was the exact right spot on Gleason Street, or Loveland Way, to meet their ride.

Past another row of pines, he made out the source of the light.

Two back yards stretched from the trees, their lawns neat and trim. White fences bordered the two-story colonial houses, keeping the property lines firm and creating an avenue of grass to the sidewalk, where a sad little lamppost tried to light the street. Only blackness stretched past that.

Behind Chase, the cricket orchestra quieted so that Donnie could retch in peace. Good, he might be more helpful now.

Chase took a step back, his heel crunching pine needles. "This can't be Gleason, unless we're pretty far south." He turned toward Donnie. "Not Loveland, either, but maybe somebody knows where the—"

Back through the pines, Donnie's tree trunk stood empty.

"Donnie?" Chase looked to the light again and then back to the tree. Donnie's white costume should've stuck out even in the dim. "Not funny, buddy. I don't feel like being scared right now."

Nearby crickets remained quiet. Chase's gut turned, as if facing the houses again and urging the rest of his body to turn, too. Turn and get out of here.

He swallowed and felt cold in his throat. "Where you at, man?"

He compromised with his gut, didn't step forward or back, but sidestepped so he could get a better look around the tree. Donnie might have crawled to the other side, to puke in privacy.

One white pant leg stretched back from behind the tree, flat on the ground.

Chase's heart said everything was fine, he'd been nervous for nothing, but his gut still said to go. "Donnie?"

The leg quivered, kicking at needles, and then twisted to one side. Dark fluid ran across the ground. Donnie might have pissed himself, but Chase didn't think so. The fluid was too slow, too thick. It seemed like blood.

He turned around and started toward the houses. Pine needles crackled beneath his shoes. Not too fast, not enough to show his lungs were losing it, not enough to show he was scared in case Donnie was now sober enough to pull a prank. He crossed into the soft grass between yards.

A footstep crunched needles behind him, easy to hear now that he wasn't crunching them himself. And then a second footstep, a third, one after another. They weren't Donnie's staggering feet, too sure of themselves, and no one called out to Chase. Whoever walked behind him was quiet.

He couldn't help walking faster. Trying to run, he realized just how unsteady he was, how the drinks had loosened his muscles. His balance wasn't as bad as Donnie's, but he wasn't fast.

The footsteps behind him didn't run either, but they were certain, evenly paced steps, and getting closer.

Chase gulped cold air, drying his mouth and throat for the sake of greedy lungs. He slipped between the houses. Toothy fences rippled to either side, both homes saying they wanted no part in his trouble. They didn't have their outside lights on. The neighborhood was asleep. His tongue a dry sponge, he couldn't get his voice to leap past his lips and wake everyone up.

He almost hit the far corners of the houses, where one fence curled around a front yard and the other paused at a driveway, but he skidded to a stop twenty feet from the sidewalk. There was no road here, only an open circle of pavement. Lampposts dotted the sidewalk of the circle's rim, but they were all weak.

Across the circle, a billowing white shape floated through the consuming darkness. It kept its distance from lampposts and weaved as if carried on the wind. Was that what got Donnie?

No, it was a white shirt on someone wearing all black otherwise. The floating was only the trick of a bicycle in the dark, its orange reflectors stealing bits of lamppost light. Chase kept on toward the sidewalk and licked his lips, about to call to this kid. Maybe they knew a way out.

His voice started up his throat when a swift white shape slid up on his left and dug into and across his neck. Hot fluid ran down his chest.

It didn't make sense, this opening at his throat. Blood was supposed to stay inside, not run across his fingers when he tried to collect it. Was it always this warm? Something soft but hot scraped his face, burning his eyelids. He was falling, didn't know where until the ground slammed his front. Sharp hot points tore up his spine. The pain, heat, and coppery stink reminded him of a schoolbook about the food industry, of animals hanging on slaughterhouse hooks.

He tried to speak, but nothing came out, and there was nothing to see.

But he could hear. The crickets were loud again in every direction, no longer disturbed by what they'd witnessed. Under their song, a footstep crashed down on his left, and then another ahead, the same slow pace as whoever had followed him, approaching the sidewalk. That wasn't fair; that's where he'd meant to go.

From the paved circle came a metal grinding, the sound of a bicycle's pedals and gears as it turned around. The kid was leaving.

Take me, Chase tried to say. No words came up, only blood.

And then the footsteps returned. One, two, past his side. A hand caught his ankle, lifted his leg, and dragged him back toward the pines. Blades of grass cut at his open throat, and then pine needles stabbed his wounded flesh. When the hand finally set him down, sharp pain hit his back again, and he realized that was no slaughterhouse hook.

Those were teeth.

TWO: OCTOBER 27, 1987

Desiree St. Fleur slapped her tray onto a lunchroom table opposite the new girl. They were both juniors, and new kid status shouldn't have been anything special at their age, but Blackwood was a pothole of a town. New things were rare.

The new girl's eyes widened. Desiree had heard the phrase *deer in headlights* before, but had never seen it on a human being. From her lengthy pale face to the tan of her long hair to her thin cream sweater, everything about the new girl screamed trembling doe. She must have been nervous over the lunchroom's dull roar, or its curious sour milk odor. Not over Desiree in her leather jacket, white T-shirt, and acid-washed jeans. No way.

"Got a minute?" Desiree stuck a hand across the table and introduced herself.

The new girl licked her lips and offered her hand in return. "Gabrielle Walker."

"You look anxious." Desiree prodded the plastic grilled cheese on her tray. Tuesdays were always grilled cheese, and for some reason the sandwiches never came out right anymore.

Gabrielle's eyes stayed wide, like she expected Desiree to lunge over the table any minute and claw them out. What town did Gabrielle come from that made such timid people? Surely towns couldn't get tinier than Blackwood.

"Did Mrs. Hatcher tell you to stay away from me?" Desiree asked.

"No one's sat with me." That made sense. Gabrielle had been eating alone since her first day and probably expected to spend the school year that way.

Desiree went on poking her sandwich. If she dropped it on the floor, she imagined it would bounce like a rubber ball. "Where you from?"

"New York. Not the city. Feels like I have to say that to everyone."

"Rumor has it you live on Glade Street."

"Yeah, with my grandma. It's kind of a weird place." Gabrielle's eyes settled. She was all smiles now.

Desiree flashed white teeth between rich black cheeks. "Any plans for Halloween?"

"I don't know anyone."

"You can't hang out with Grandma on the biggest night in Blackwood."

"Grandma's friends had free tickets, so they're taking her to Atlantic City."

Likely Gabrielle came from somewhere big, even if not so big as New York City. She'd only been in town for a couple weeks and hadn't grasped the hopelessness of her situation or how Halloween was its only escape. Blackwood had no mall, no movie theater. Kids milled around town square on nice days and anywhere else they could on others. If they drove, they drove someplace else, because in Blackwood there was little to see and only the woods to hear.

Halloween was different.

Blackwood had one thing that no other town had in the world.

Benny Rose, the Cannibal King, and all the stories that came with him.

Gabrielle was oblivious. An idea slid into Desiree's thoughts. She saw it clear as if she had painted it in her bedroom. Jack-o'-lanterns, and horrors, and Gabrielle's frightened doe face.

"I was going to invite you someplace," Desiree said. "But maybe you could invite us to yours instead."

"Us?" Gabrielle asked.

"No one's parents live in the old folks neighborhood. We could have a little get-together, stay up late, eat pizza. It'll be nice. Nobody would bother us there."

"Like, a party?"

"Nothing that big. Just me and a couple friends who might be into it. Halloween's a big deal in Blackwood."

"Not on Glade Street. No one's even decorated."

Desiree knew that, had seen it herself last year, but didn't want to think about that night right now. This was different. "Then you're not getting the full experience. When it comes to Halloween in Blackwood, go big or go home."

"I have nowhere else to go." Gabrielle seemed forlorn, the way Desiree liked to think she herself looked while staring into space.

An air of majestic sadness, she thought, an idea too pretentious to repeat aloud.

"All I'm saying is, everyone loves Halloween here. Getting into the spirit is a—" Desiree almost said hazing, but didn't want to sound too scary.

Gabrielle rescued her. "A rite of passage?"

"Exactly. Show my friends you're cool, make them your friends. It's a win-win."

"I don't know."

"You said you don't know anyone. Wouldn't you like to?"

Gabrielle prodded her grilled cheese, mimicking Desiree, except half of hers had been eaten. Timid or not, they made strong stomachs in New York. "It'd be nice to hang out."

"Then it's a date. Let me know which house and we'll come over Saturday." Desiree pried her tray off the table. "And, you probably know, but don't tell Grandma."

Gabrielle offered a shy, tight-lipped smile.

Desiree chucked her lunch in the trash and headed back to her friends. Sierra Jacques and Jesse Sanderson sat side by side at the end of one lengthy table, isolated from the lunchroom's busy crowd. Sierra's boyfriend would've come bothering them, but he was a senior and had a different lunch period this year.

Jesse traded disgusted looks between her rubbery lunch and an open paperback of *The Catcher in the Rye* propped between russet fingers. Her face seemed sucked into the book, ringlets of hair dangling against the pages. Some of the pages were almost as yellow as the blouse she wore beneath her weather jean jacket. The book must've been a school copy, an old one.

Sierra's dark curls circled her darling brown sourpuss. Every part of her tense body held statue stiff within her pastel-pink dress except her burning eyes, darting up and down at distant, oblivious Gabrielle.

"A picture would last longer," Desiree said, dropping into Sierra's way.

Sierra's hot glare fell on her. "You two got pretty chummy."

"Getting jealous on my account, too?"

"No. Paul's enough. She'll find out."

"It's not her fault he said she's pretty." Had it been only once, Sierra might have let it go. But Paul said it every time he caught Gabrielle out of the corner of his eye, at least when around the girls. Like he was determined to make Sierra jealous.

It worked. "He won't be saying that when the school hears how many of his football buddies she's slept with already."

Desiree pictured that sweet doe face covered in tears, eyes wide with betrayal once Gabrielle realized it was Desiree's best friend who started the rumors. A few weeks in Blackwood and already a school pariah. The rumors would never die, even when other girls pointed the finger at Sierra and her friends as the source. There would be trouble. And then there would be Mom to deal with.

Desiree leaned over the table and pouted. "But princess, I thought you liked my plan."

Sierra's glare softened. She hadn't told her lies yet. "Yeah, yeah. Is she coming?"

"I got a better idea. A Halloween slumber party at her place while Granny's out of town."

Jesse closed her book in an exhausted slap and shoved it away with her lunch. "Weird, her living in that neighborhood. I thought you had to be old to move there."

As if summoned by the word *old*, Mrs. Hatcher slowed in passing their table. Her gaze fixed on Desiree from a face carved in Paleolithic limestone. "Miss St. Fleur, girls are supposed to love James Dean, not dress like him. We've talked about this."

Desiree didn't recall that. She recalled standing in silence while Mrs. Hatcher criticized her leather jacket and cloudy black curls, wondering if Mrs. Hatcher taught history because she'd lived it. Desiree didn't see a resemblance to a dead movie star in her clothes.

She nodded anyway as if yes, this time it would sink in, and Mrs. Hatcher passed by to chastise someone else.

"She wishes she had your style," Sierra said, making Desiree and Jesse laugh. "I don't see why she gives shit to you when you don't give it to anyone." Her eyes narrowed. "So, what's the new plan for Snow White?"

Desiree told them. Jesse flashed a nervous smirk.

Sierra grinned ear to ear. "Maybe Mrs. Hatcher should watch out. There's a cunning mean streak inside you."

Desiree didn't really agree. If all went as planned, Sierra's jealous itch would be scratched, Paul would drop his fixation, and Desiree would've spared Gabrielle a nasty junior year.

And all it would take was tricking her into thinking they were friends, and then stabbing her in the back.

THREE: HALLOWEEN 1987

Desiree almost made it out in peace. She had her shoes on, night bag packed with pajamas, toothbrush, and cassettes of *Thriller*, *Whitney*, and *Self Control*. Later she realized she had not asked if Gabrielle had a tape player.

She was halfway down the stairs when her mother reared up behind her. "And what are you up to?"

Desiree froze. She had been too quiet, which made Mom suspicious. Her foot slid to the next step and from there it was easier to descend. If she could get out of the house without responding, then she was good as gone.

Mom stamped the floor. "Why are you dressed like you're going out?"

Had a zombie eaten her brain? Desiree turned back, wearing a black leather jacket and matching tank top and jeans. No pirate costume mistakes on Glade Street this year. If anything happened, she could drift into the dark, where clothes, skin, and hair alike would blend with the night.

"I'm dressed like I'm going out because I'm going out. It's Halloween." Dammit, she'd spoken, been slowed down.

Mom was reeling her in. She wiped a hand down her tired face, lighter than Desiree's and deep with worry lines. She was five years

Dad's senior, and since he'd left, she seemed to have aged another ten. "After what happened last year, you expect me to let you go rampaging out of here?"

When Desiree didn't answer, Mom stormed into Desiree's room, muttering under her breath. Glass smashed against the floor—paintbrush jar?—and then came a snap, the sound of canvas being cracked across one knee. Mom had probably grabbed the nearest painting. And Desiree had been working so hard on that dancing elephant watercolor.

That wouldn't stop her. She hit the bottom of the stairs and walked briskly to the front door. She could get away if there was no back and forth, all the shouting one-sided. Mom wouldn't chase. To chase would make her look silly, and she'd be damned before she looked silly.

"I'm your mother. You are a teenager. I have a say in these things so long as you're under my roof."

Not one more word, Desiree told herself. She grabbed the cold doorknob.

"Why are you doing this to me?"

It was a dirty trap. Desiree almost didn't twist the knob. Tricking her into an apologetic reply would be like throwing a lasso around her waist. Every extra word meant another tug. Mom would keep her home that way, shouting until Desiree was too exhausted to go anywhere. If she was going, it had to be now.

No matter how hurt Mom pretended to be.

Desiree twisted the knob and whipped the door open. Her bike awaited by the mailbox at the end of the gravel driveway where she'd left it. Mom shouted something about how she was never supposed to do this alone, but the wind snatched the exact words away. Desiree walked her bike onto Magnolia Court and made a right at the maple trees that bordered the yard.

Good as gone.

Her mother never hit her. She criticized Desiree for dressing how she did, but never raised a hand over it. She seemed to think that qualified her for sainthood.

But over the past year, on days like this, she broke Desiree's things. At first they were small things. A cassette tape unspooled, a favorite cup smashed on the floor. More often now, she was likely to break a treasured painting to pieces or throw a sketchbook in the mud.

And on days like this, Desiree would've rather been hit.

She didn't realize she was silent crying until she heard the jingle of another bike's bell. Sierra knew if Desiree's bike wasn't at the mailbox, she wouldn't be at home. She didn't ask about Desiree's tear-stained cheeks. They dropped to walking their bikes, as slow as Desiree needed. She loved Sierra for that. For many reasons, but some were feelings Sierra could never return, and so Desiree never offered them. Simpler that way.

Once they hit the end of Magnolia Court, they turned onto School Bus Road and hopped back on their bikes. Autumn wind rushed across their faces and slipped cool fingers through Desiree's hair. Her tearstains faded from windswept cheeks.

Sierra's curls were bound up in a red bandana, the knot twitching behind her head. She wore the same baggy white shirt and black pants pirate costume as last Halloween. Her night bag and purse bounced at her back, bound to her by cord, as she turned from School Bus Road onto Main Street.

"Either you need to get a car or I do," she said.

Jesse had a car and had agreed to meet them at Loveland Way. She wouldn't go farther north unless that was their destination. Her father had filled her with terror at adding unnecessary miles to what was already an old car.

Main Street was the quickest route across Blackwood, and the busiest. Dormant streetlights hung with plastic bones, dimpled by fake bite marks. Jack-o'-lanterns clustered every storefront. Local businesses put up mannequins or cardboard figure effigies of Benny Rose, sometimes in a brown coat, other times covered in bandages and burns, always a pale face with coal-black eyes. Down a ways in Blackwood Square, the middle-schoolers were putting together their costume contest with the help of town council members, setting up folding chairs and sweeping leaves off the pavilion. Cardboard bats, ghosts, and Benny Rose faces plastered the wooden walls.

"Remember doing this stuff?" Desiree asked. "Feels like it's been forever."

"We've been on these bikes since forever." Sierra had taken to bumming rides since Paul and Jesse got their licenses and access to cars. "I'm not used to this shit anymore."

"They say you never forget how to ride."

"Tell it to the cramp in my thigh." Sierra leaned her chin over the handlebars. The remains of rainbow streamers poked out of their ends. She had cut them off with scissors at the end of ninth grade, like they were such grown-ups already.

"We can always call Paul," Desiree said.

"If we call Paul, that'll ruin the surprise." Sierra started huffing and puffing. "Pedal through the pain, baby." She passed Desiree by a few feet.

Desiree didn't see the need to rush. They left Main Street and rolled onto Loveland Way. Jesse would find them soon.

Eastwater Park stretched to the left, its lawn covered in red and brown leaves. To the right, a row of small houses lined Loveland Way, where a herd of trick-or-treaters marched down the sidewalk. The leader was a Bride of Frankenstein, maybe eight years old, the only one trying to be scary. The others were smaller. They dressed as baseball players, dancers, and *Star Wars* characters. Urging them on from behind was the lone adult. A Freddy Krueger claw poked from his right sleeve, but no costume, makeup, or mask. Maybe his wife told him that would be too scary for little kids.

Or maybe this was his version of Benny Rose. The Cannibal King ate not only people, but stories that didn't belong to him.

Desiree remembered being that young right after moving to Blackwood, when she would take off with Sierra and girls long forgotten, and later with Jesse once she befriended them. Back then even Desiree's mother would've scoffed at chaperoning them on Halloween. Her father never made a fuss about it either while he still lived in Blackwood.

Nowadays, when he called from Danby, he always asked if she was being careful. The words *stranger danger* had seeped into Blackwood. She'd heard that phrase on the news before, but it was a city thing, nothing to do with their little town. In the past couple years, it had become the law of the land here, too. Benny Rose's infamy had been co-opted by neighborhood watch groups. *A monster doesn't have to look like a monster to be one,* the paper flyers often said. *He could be anybody.*

A car horn tooted behind the bikes and then rode alongside them. Jesse beckoned from her rusted red sedan—the only thing she could afford. "Going my way?"

"Thank Christ." Sierra glared at her, sweat sliding between her eyes. "Can't you come get us for once?"

"Can you pass a driver's test?"

"Stop the damn car and let us in."

Jesse braked in the middle of Loveland and helped the girls stuff their bikes into the meager trunk, their front wheels jutting out its open mouth and the lid bound by a bungee cord. It would squeak around the bikes once the car got moving. They piled into Jesse's car, Sierra calling shotgun.

"Are you Benny Rose?" she asked.

Jesse wore a brown raincoat that opened over a blue sweater and jeans. "I couldn't think of anything else."

Desiree leaned from the back seat. "Sierra, don't judge. You're wearing last year's pirate costume."

"It was last minute." Sierra patted the fluffy white shirt. "And you're not even wearing a costume."

"Sure I am. I'm—that guy from the beginning of *Friday the 13th: Part V*."

The girls were quiet, and then Sierra asked, "The guy who died in the outhouse?"

Desiree had forgotten that. They had only seen the movie once when someone at last year's Halloween party put on the LaserDisc. She could've and should've named Michael Jackson, or really any rebellious figure in a leather jacket, but her brain had settled for that one.

She started laughing and the others joined her. Mom was forgotten.

Loveland curled around Eastwater Park and straightened out where a slender wooden bridge crossed Lemon Fair River. The surface churned just beneath the wood, the river having swelled since autumn began thanks to a stormy early October.

Jesse's car thumped over the bridge's wooden planks. Last Halloween, they had ridden their bikes downriver to the party on Monterrey Court. They were three pirates then, Sierra and Desiree dressed the same as Sierra now, and Jesse wearing a blue captain's coat with a fake parrot glued to the shoulder. They hadn't been invited and kicked themselves out before anyone noticed, but it was a fun night until what had happened later when Desiree was alone.

Gray skies hung overhead now, still a ways until evening, but in the dark, it was hard to tell where the water's noise was coming from. Even a longtime Blackwood girl could get lost.

Sierra began to sing "Jessie's Girl" as they reached the far side of the bridge, which made Jesse giggle. Desiree caught her smile in the rearview mirror. It was past time to put on her good mood. She would need it here.

Pontiac Drive slipped between Lemon Fair River and rows of pine trees that pretended at being a forest. A little north of the bridge, gray-green hedges half-hid a wide oaken plaque embossed with enormous golden lettering. It read, *Glade Street Retirement Community*, and then in smaller letters, *est. 1963*.

The car turned left at the sign and started up a paved slope that breached the rows of pine trees. Glade Street curved. At first Desiree could only see a couple small houses to either side surrounded by green, but after coming around the bend, the rest of the neighborhood opened.

It was too round to call a dead end, but it was wider than any cul-de-sac she had seen before. If there was another proper word for the street's shape, she didn't know it. Most of the two-tier colonial houses surrounded this paved circle, facing each other and the featureless, dormant fountain between them. Pine needles floated in its stagnant water.

Desiree hadn't come as far as Gabrielle's house a year ago. She didn't think her friends had ever come here at all. In the light and at the center of it, she felt old age breathing from all sides, draining her. People died faster in places like this. With no kids around, and the trees cutting them off from the world, Desiree pictured an outdoor crypt.

"This place bums me out," Sierra said.

Jesse hugged the car to the right-side curb and worked counter-clockwise toward Gabrielle's house, 13 Glade Street. "It just needs some love."

"Its personality needs a colonoscopy. We'll be doing new girl a favor, scaring her. No wonder she didn't know Halloween is Blackwood's thing."

Not one porch was decorated for Halloween. Not even

a jack-o'-lantern. The glut of pine trees that surrounded the neighborhood in green felt out of season. Glade Street had no autumn leaves to rake.

The houses were stark, near featureless, and cut from common cloth. Each was painted canary yellow or sky blue, the shingles reddish-brown or blue-black. Green, trimmed lawns hid behind white fences that pointed up like mean underbites. The fences hugged the fronts and sides of their houses to keep them from the sidewalk and each other. All driveways were empty except a few houses up from Gabrielle's, where a gray-haired, stiff-shouldered man squatted with a plastic cherry-red jerry can, gassing up his push lawnmower. Olive spots dotted his pink scalp.

Gabrielle's house had the only driveway with a bicycle outside the shuttered garage. Desiree wouldn't put it past the neighbors to complain over the eyesore. No fun allowed. Jesse parked in the driveway just past the white fence, and they carried their bags up the stone walkway. Sierra knocked on the front door.

The lawnmower's rumble dragged across Desiree's nerves. She glanced over her shoulder at the man down the cul-de-sac as he steered the mower toward the lawn for one last trim before winter. Was he looking at them out of the corner of his eye? She must have imagined it. He couldn't be the same man from last Halloween.

But she felt cold anyway.

The front door creaked open and Desiree turned to Gabrielle's beaming face.

She coughed out a laugh. "I can't believe we're doing this. I mean, welcome! Happy Halloween."

Sierra put on a grin, hugged Gabrielle, and asked to come in. Jesse smiled sheepishly and followed.

Gabrielle leaned toward Desiree. "What's wrong? Do you need water?"

Without looking back, Desiree cocked her head over one shoulder. "Who is that?"

Gabrielle craned to one side. "That's the HOA guy, Arthur Donovan. His wife is out of town with Grandma." She leaned past Desiree, swung her arm overhead, and shouted at the top of her lungs. "Hi, Mr. Donovan!"

Why did she do that? Desiree looked over and offered a pursed smile. Arthur Donovan probably hadn't heard Gabrielle, but he saw her arm, lifted a hand in a half-hearted return wave, and went back to mowing.

Not Wallace Shaw then. Desiree's nerves tried to settle as she followed Gabrielle inside.

The door opened on a foyer, where ahead climbed a stairway. A shut door on the left probably led to the garage, and a narrow hall stretched past the stairs to a dark kitchen. To the right, the living room opened where Sierra and Jesse looked for a place to drop their bags. Gray sunlight peeked through a gap in the picture window curtains and slanted across their bodies. The furniture had been pushed to the walls. A small Panasonic television haunted one far corner, and the door to a half-bath hung open at the other.

The house smelled musty, like old people. Desiree wasn't surprised.

"I figured we'd set up in the living room," Gabrielle said, stepping toward Sierra. "There's space for sleeping bags, or someone can use the couch if they want. Grandma's chair reclines, but it's kind of worn. I got popcorn. We can order pizza. You can put your coats anywhere."

Jesse slipped off her brown raincoat and draped it over the sofa.

Desiree tightened her jacket. "Thanks, but it's chilly."

Gabrielle looked alarmed. "Oh, I can turn on the fireplace if we move the couch."

Sierra giggled. "You're way too high-strung, Gabs. There's no parents, no trick-or-treaters. Just be cool. Deep breaths."

Gabrielle sucked in air and then blew it out. Jesse patted her arm.

Desiree approached the picture window and pressed the curtains open. Each house could see the others across the cul-de-sac, but other picture windows were already smothered in closed curtains. Sparse lampposts dotted the sidewalk, one every two or three houses. Stronger light would've disturbed the elderly residents, Desiree supposed. Arthur Donovan's yard was empty.

At the circle's opening, Glade Street curled around the pines from where the girls had come. That was where Paul would probably wait long past dark.

Sierra's hand clapped Desiree's back and made her jump. "You're high-strung, too. What's up with you?"

Desiree looked over her shoulder, where Gabrielle was leading Jesse to the kitchen. "You still want this?"

Sierra screwed up her face. "Of course I do. Where's your bite?"

Desiree gnashed her teeth and grinned.

"There's my girl," Sierra said. "When this is over, we might be friends. But she'll have to earn it first."

FOUR: AND NOW, THE WEATHER

Black clouds loomed over Paul Boyle as he drove his yellow '83 Toyota Corolla along Loveland Way. He wouldn't have noticed had Adrian Olsen not pointed them out. Now, he couldn't unsee them. The boys had been having a good time. They had a costume and a plan, WBWR was taking a break from Whitney Houston to pound out some Bruce Springsteen, and Paul was going to see Sierra.

But now there might be a storm.

A little rain wouldn't hurt anyone. A lot would crash the festivities at Blackwood Square, send the kids home early. Paul's parents, too. They were volunteering at the festivities this year. No clear skies meant no festivities, which meant no reason to stay out. Tired from volunteering, they wouldn't have noticed his breaking curfew tonight, but if they came home early, he'd be in trouble later.

And then there was the beer he'd stolen. He and Adrian each had one in their hands. An empty can rolled on the floor between Adrian's shoes.

"Should we head back?" he asked.

Paul took a sip. "Don't pussy out on me."

"Me? I'm not the one who's pussy-whipped by a junior. Only reason we're out here is 'cause Sierra keeps your nuts in a box of Cracker Jacks."

"You don't think we'll have fun spooking a few girls at a slumber party?"

"It's fun for you. If we're stuck out there when Sierra's done being scared, she'll want to spend the night snuggling up with you. What do I get?"

"It's four girls. Two for me, two for you." Paul elbowed Adrian's arm.

"Pretty sure the Fonzie impersonator ain't up for that."

"Then Sierra gets me and Fonzie while you snuggle up with Jesse and the new girl, and everybody gets a Happy Halloween."

Adrian turned to the road, grinning. "This new girl's never heard of Benny Rose?"

Paul shrugged. "They don't have him in other towns." The car turned right at the bridge and rumbled across.

Adrian glanced out the passenger window. "River's looking mean."

Paul tried not to look but couldn't help it. Lemon Fair River churned away from him, its surface white and frothy.

"Might already be raining up north. Maybe this isn't such a smart idea."

Paul stopped the car at the edge of the bridge. "I'm trying to have fun with you, man, maybe even get you laid tonight, but you want out? Then go."

Adrian stared at him. He was a big guy, bigger than Paul, liked his football just the same, but he had limits. If there was one kind of bullshit Paul could not stand, it was small-town bullshit. Never living anywhere besides Blackwood seemed to weaken the nerves. He had moved from Jersey when he was ten, and right away he could tell the people here were cowards. Even the ones he liked.

"Cautious Man" faded from the radio and a nasally voice filled the car. "And now, Tyler Cavanaugh with the weather."

"This is going to be one atmospheric Halloween, kiddies. We're talking thunderstorms up and down the east coast. The good news? For us, it's all noise. We should stay dry on our side of Vermont and have a beautiful if tempestuous Halloween in Blackwood. So if you hear howling in the trees, that's not Benny Rose coming to get you. It's only the wind."

The mention of Blackwood's boogeyman felt like a blessing. "I Wanna Dance with Somebody" popped on the radio next, and for once, Paul didn't mind.

He smirked at Adrian. "See? Nothing to worry about."

Adrian stared a moment longer and then clapped the dashboard. "Let's roll out, then. How long do we have to wait?"

"A couple hours. Depends on Sierra." The car continued over the bridge, up Pontiac Drive, and onto Glade Street.

Adrian finished his second beer.

"Slow down. We'll need a place to piss."

Adrian waved at the pine trees crawling past the windows. "Nature's bounty surrounds us." They snickered.

The car came to rest where Glade Street opened. Paul thought he saw someone peek from behind the curtains at the nearest house, but far as anyone here knew, he and Adrian weren't doing anything wrong. He forgot about it when he cracked open another beer.

*

Tyler Cavanaugh has been WBWR's weatherman and nighttime disc jockey for thirteen years. His weather predictions are close to true more often than not, and he has meteorological reasons to believe everything he says.

But this Halloween night, he is dead wrong. The cold front will shift inland, the storm will slam across the Appalachians, and no one will know how bad it is until Blackwood is already drowned in thunder and rain.

FIVE: GHOST STORIES

The sleepover had been uneventful so far. Gabrielle ordered pizza and made popcorn on the stovetop while Channel 11 played monster movies. Thunder rumbled while she and Sierra were watching something with zombies in it. Eventually a black and white movie about giant ants replaced the zombies. Each time Gabrielle seemed ready to drift from the TV, Sierra egged her back, priming her for the big scare later.

Desiree hovered at the kitchen's edge, polishing off one last slice of pepperoni pizza. Jesse paced between counters behind her, stirring a coffee mug full of Pepsi like it was a glass of rum. Ice clinked, and thunder growled, closer.

"It's not a big deal," Desiree said. She wasn't sure whom she was talking to.

Jesse gulped her Pepsi and placed the cup on the table.

"We're grown now," Desiree went on. "This is what we do, right? Give each other a hard time, pull pranks. Gabrielle said it herself. It's a Blackwood rite of passage. This is how she becomes one of us." She considered her pizza slice. "I'm never having kids."

"Why not?" Jesse asked.

"Where do I start?"

Jesse smirked. "It's okay. My aunt and her *friend* don't have kids, either."

Desiree offered a bright-eyed smirk in return and then took it away. "Having kids changes you. Giving birth, adoption, it doesn't matter. If they're with you, you're a parent, and you don't stay the same. And if I'm the reason my mom is the way she is? I don't want to turn out like her."

"I don't think you have to. Maybe you don't hate your mother. Maybe you just hate the way she makes you feel."

"Oh, thank you, Mr. Donahue. Are you going into television, or do you want to be a mom after high school?"

Jesse shrugged. "I mean, I want to get married. Kids, I guess? But I'll never make them miserable with school sports and things like that. Afternoons are for cartoons, books, and potato chips. They'll be the laziest little brats in the world."

That didn't sound so bad. Desiree put one arm around Jesse's hip and hugged her side.

Sierra tapped a flashlight on the kitchen doorframe, snapping them to attention. "You two ready?"

Desiree wasn't, but she finished her pizza slice and followed Sierra to the living room. Jesse trailed after them.

Sierra started flicking off lights. "Time to pay the piper. It's Halloween, babies."

Giant ants made *whoop-whoop-whoop* noises from the TV. "It's only Halloween until midnight," Gabrielle said, shutting it off.

"Not in Blackwood. Witches ride all the way to dawn."

Jesse giggled. "Second star to the right, and then straight on 'til morning." Sierra gave her the stink eye.

Desiree looked out the picture window—soft, near-silent rain fell across Glade Street—haunted by her reflection. She shut the curtains against even the frail light of the sidewalk lampposts and darkness covered the living room.

Sierra switched on the flashlight, sat with it against her black pirate pants, and gathered the girls into a circle on the floor. "It's not a real Halloween sleepover without Benny Rose stories. Not a real Halloween at all."

"Who's Benny Rose?" Gabrielle asked. Desiree envied her ignorance.

"What a weird question in Blackwood," Jesse mused.

"Who's Benny Rose, huh?" Sierra tapped the flashlight's head against the carpet. "Just who is Benny Rose? They say this used to be an ordinary town. Some still think it is. They're not scared of the Blackwood Devil." Her voice flattened. "Not like they should be. Not like they were when he was their neighbor."

Sudden thunder made all the girls jump. Sierra had to be grinning in her head, but she kept a straight face in front of Gabrielle. Rain drummed the roof and rattled the gutters.

Sierra drew the flashlight under her chin, round cheeks casting deep shadows around her eyes. "Back in the fifties, Blackwood wasn't such a nice place to live. Kids went missing. Their bodies would turn up weeks, sometimes months later with chunks of flesh chomped off, their exposed bones gnawed. The police and newspaper started getting notes, all the letters cut out of magazines and pasted onto paper. It was the killer telling how he ate his victims. Grilled, baked, chopped in a stew, but most of the time, he said he ate the kids raw. And every note was signed, the Cannibal King.

"This went on for months. Nobody knows how many victims, not even today. They only know how many were found, and his letters hinted there were many, many more. Well, having sent a bunch of notes, it was only a matter of time before he got sloppy and left fingerprints for the police to check. They found the Cannibal King. His name was Benny Rose, and he worked in the morgue of Blackwood Mercy Hospital. You'd think he'd have enough to eat down there, but dead people couldn't entice the appetite of

Benny Rose. He liked to eat them alive. Have you seen the hospital, Gabs?"

Desiree felt Gabrielle's hair swoosh back and forth from her shaking head.

Sierra must have seen. "That's because it's gone. When Benny heard the cops were in the hospital, coming to arrest him, he lit up an oxygen tank, and the explosion set the hospital on fire. There was no getting out, but he decided if he had to die, he wasn't dying alone. Over forty people were lost when the blaze brought the hospital crashing down on their heads. Afterward, combing the rubble, firemen found a severed hand that didn't belong to any of the other bodies. The fingerprints matched the ones from the notes—Benny Rose's left hand. They figured the rest of him was burned or crushed in the rubble. Blackwood PD said the case was closed and everyone tried to move on.

"But some people still see him. Now he's got a mean meat hook sticking out of his left wrist. He guts people in the front and then hangs them up by the spine. Kids still go missing to this day. They say we never find the pieces anymore because Benny got smarter. He doesn't let anything go to waste. He eats everything—meat, bones, and soul."

Thunder rang again as if it had been waiting for Sierra to finish. She let the living room fill with the percussion of light rain.

Jesse swallowed. "That wasn't scary."

Sierra's eyes burned over the flashlight.

"I mean, it's scary the first time, but we've all heard that one a hundred times."

Desiree bit her cheeks not to laugh. It had been one of the most typical stories. Sometimes Benny was a janitor or a doctor, sometimes he was a cop or an orderly. Other stories were wilder, where he stalked the streets like a vampire. A few said he never ate anybody, that he made up the cannibal gig to hide his selling kids' organs on the black market. If the teller made it gory enough, the story would stick.

Doubtful he ever did those things. Desiree's mother said the whole incident was blown out of proportion, that as far as she knew, someone named Benny had been suspected of killing five kids a long time ago and died before anyone found out. That maybe Blackwood would be better off if everyone minded their own business. Five kids, hardly notable enough to earn the monikers of Blackwood Devil and Cannibal King.

Mom didn't understand. Blackwood was never going to be better than a small town. It would cling to what little history it had until the end.

Faint light prodded the edge of the room. Sierra was at the curtain, looking out at the thickening rain.

"What's wrong?" Desiree asked.

"Thought I heard something."

"Oh, hardy-har," Gabrielle said, and then laughed.

Sierra didn't laugh, but she didn't antagonize either. She only glanced at Desiree and tossed up impatient hands. Paul wasn't here, or wasn't ready, maybe hadn't seen Sierra's signal.

She drifted back to the circle and passed the flashlight to Jesse. "Your turn."

"Oh, I'm not good at telling them," Jesse said.

"You sure love listening to them, freeloader."

"I always forget something important and have to go back. Mine are never scary."

Sierra snatched the flashlight and held it across the circle. "Desi, please, save this slumber party. You know some good ones."

Desiree's hand closed around Sierra's fingers and the flashlight. She could take it and tell any of the old stories she had stashed away. They were all new to Gabrielle anyway.

But another story wanted out. It was a spider in her mouth,

its legs creeping past her lips. She could crunch it in her teeth, swallow it, but it was going to come back again someday. Best to let it out, even if it scared her worse than it would scare her friends.

She drew the flashlight to her chest. "I have one in mind. And it's special because it really happened to me."

Jesse snickered. "Bologna."

Sierra scoffed. "We're by ourselves, nerd. You can say bullshit."

"It's not bologna or bullshit." Desiree leaned over the flashlight. She hoped it glowed in her teeth. "Why do you think my mom's been so bad this year?"

"Because she's a cranky bitch."

"Why do you think she flipped out last Halloween? This Halloween?" The girls were quiet. "I went somewhere she told me never to go. I saw Benny Rose one year ago, on this very night, in this very neighborhood."

Gabrielle stiffened. Jesse pressed her shoes together and curled her legs against her chest.

"We were with you that whole night," Sierra said.

"Not the whole night," Desiree said. "Remember, we split off since you were sleeping over at Jesse's. I had to bike home by myself."

"And you came here?"

"Not because I wanted to. It was so dark that night, I didn't know I'd turned onto Pontiac. The river was running, but I couldn't even tell which side I was on, so of course I couldn't see the Glade Street sign. You know how it is. The dark plays tricks, especially on Halloween."

Sierra nodded, the flashlight reflecting in her eyes. Her pirate costume was scarcely visible in the living room, a ghostly reminder of their outfits that night.

"So I was riding my bike uphill," Desiree went on. "And it didn't take me long to realize I'd gone the wrong way. I didn't turn right around, though. Maybe I was still confused, and no one's house lights were on. It was late. You know these old people, going to bed early. The only lights were those weak lamps. That's when I saw a man in the dark with me."

Jesse curled up tighter.

"What did he look like?" Gabrielle asked.

"That's what threw me at first," Desiree said. "He was naked and even whiter than you. I thought he was some old guy with a mental problem who wandered out of his house with no clothes on. And that got me a little on edge anyway. You never know what they're going to do, do you?"

Sierra's mouth lost its smirk.

"But then he turned to me." The menace drifted out of Desiree's voice. She was there again, not far from the mouth of the cul-de-sac, exactly a year ago and moments before she spotted the naked man.

The neighborhood had no definition in the dark. The few lampposts offered pale, frail light, and the houses were little more than bulky suggestions beyond their manicured lawns and stern fences. Desiree couldn't name the feeling in the air. She only knew there was a welcoming presence and a gut feeling that she did not want to be welcomed here.

Her bike stopped. One foot leaned past the pedal and onto the pavement, and it might as well have stepped into a bear trap. She froze in the middle of Glade Street, as if her stillness might keep the neighborhood from knowing she was there. She was afraid to turn around. There might be something behind her. If she was lucky, she would only find one of the residents, who might tell her indignantly that she wasn't welcome here after all.

But the welcoming atmosphere wouldn't leave. It insisted.

She couldn't be sure whether she actually saw something ahead of her in the dark or whether her brain fed her imagination enough to get her moving. She often imagined things. Later, the encounter did not seem real.

The man stepped from between two houses, so pale she at first mistook him for a tall stretch of white fencing, and crept to the edge of the grass. Each step was graceful and deliberate, and his black eyes reflected the nearest lamppost. She thought that maybe he didn't see her, that her hair, skin, and jacket blended enough with the night that she was a barely visible wraith in the street. Then she remembered her pirate costume's white shirt and the orange-yellow reflectors that lit her bike under car headlights.

Those eyes could see her. They were watching.

"Desi?"

Thunder crashed, shaking Desiree out of memory. She was in Gabrielle's house on a different Halloween with three anxious girls who sat around her.

Sierra waved a hand, interrupting the flashlight beam. "You okay?"

"Yeah. Of course." Desiree forced a laugh. "Scared me so much, I kind of sank into it. I got quiet back then, too. I didn't scream, but only because I couldn't, like my lungs were screaming but it wouldn't come up my throat. The whole time he walked toward me, I was frozen stiff, like he was turning me to stone.

"Then he smiled at me. That's when my body came alive again and I swung around and pedaled the hell out of there. Didn't look back. If I looked back and saw him chasing me, I don't know what I'd have done. If I fell or froze again, he might've had me. Funny thing is, I wasn't lost when I got back to Pontiac. I have no idea how I ended up there after we split. But I knew the way home and went as fast as I could. That was the last I saw of him."

Desiree lowered the flashlight. The room took on an eerie chill.

Jesse shivered. "I'm glad you told one. That was way better than what I would've told."

"And you think that was Benny Rose?" Gabrielle asked.

"Mom said it was one of the old people," Desiree said. "Wallace Shaw, who had dementia. But I don't believe her. Yeah, that was Benny Rose. And if I hadn't pedaled like crazy to get out, I wouldn't be sitting here telling you three about it."

Desiree kept to herself that her mother was worried, that she had shouted Desiree to tears before she could explain. She promised she wouldn't break curfew again, but not because of her tears. It was the man who watched her on Glade Street. Mom could say his name was Wallace Shaw, but that wasn't the name Desiree thought when she remembered the pale figure in the dark.

The name she thought was Benny Rose. It had been only natural to tell the story tonight.

Sierra was at the window again. She returned to the circle in a huff.

"You can stop pretending there's something out there," Gabrielle said. "I'm plenty spooked, I promise. Especially since there's no Wallace Shaw here."

Desiree didn't like that. "Are you messing with me?"

"Grandma introduced me to everyone when I moved in. There's no one with that name."

"Maybe he died," Jesse said, sounding hopeful. "Or, you know, moved away."

Both were possible. Desiree didn't want the flashlight anymore and passed it across the circle.

Sierra slipped it to Gabrielle. "Okay, you want to creep everyone out? You tell one."

Gabrielle accepted the flashlight, less like she wanted it, more like she was predisposed to take things that were handed to her. "Is every ghost story in Blackwood about Benny Rose? This has to be the least haunted town in the world if there's only one ghost."

"When I was little, I didn't even know there could be other ghosts," Jesse said. "It's a local quirk. We make them up all the time."

Or stole them. Benny had been applied to every urban legend Blackwood kids could get their hands on. The couple on lovers' lane who hear of an escaped mental patient on the radio, the babysitter who gets a call from inside the house, the murderous hitchhiker, the hook-handed man. Only in Blackwood, the killer was always Benny Rose.

Gabrielle looked thoughtfully at the flashlight. "We didn't have Benny Rose in New York."

"Then any scary story." Sierra nudged her knee. "Come on, you got to know at least one ghost story."

"I guess I know one. Kind of like Desiree's, though, it happened to me."

Sierra propped her chin on her palm, enthralled. Desiree and Jesse waited.

Gabrielle didn't set the flashlight under her jaw. Its beam aimed off to one side, brightening one half of her face and leaving the other in shadow. "It was on a stormy night like this. A couple and their kid were on the Jersey Turnpike, and everyone was driving way, way too fast. They couldn't slow down, that was too dangerous with all the traffic, so they kept speeding. And the rain got worse. But the thing about rain is—"

Thunder rumbled. The storm unleashed a shower of tiny hammers, drowning the room in its harsh drumming song.

"Rain sounds one way when you're outside, but another from the inside. Even in a car. Everything got still and heavy, like it was realer than it had ever been. And somehow, the kid knew what was going to happen. She had a bad feeling seconds before the tires skidded and the car flipped off-road. When a rescue unit came, they found the couple dead, but their kid was still alive. Her relatives told her it would be okay, that her mom and dad were in a better place. She thought she'd never see them again.

"But she was wrong. Their ghosts came to her at night and asked why she didn't say anything before the accident. She knew what was going to happen, so why didn't she tell them? And every night she saw them, it felt like she was the one who was supposed to die. The dad used to say that if a mother bear is starving she'll eat her cub, because if she dies, the cub will die anyway, but if she lives, she can always have another cub. That's how it was for the girl. If her parents had lived, they could've had another kid, but she lived and can't have more parents. Now there's just her and the ghosts."

Gabrielle lowered the flashlight and handed it back to Sierra, who cradled it in her lap. Desiree couldn't see anything, but thought she heard Jesse swallow. The rain was too loud to be sure.

"Sorry," Gabrielle said. "That wasn't the right kind of ghost story."

The flashlight slid toward Jesse. "Your turn," Sierra said, her voice shaky.

"I need to use the restroom, but don't start without me." Gabrielle left the circle and opened the door in the living room's corner. The light went on after it shut, leaving a narrow yellow line beneath.

Desiree reclined across the floor. *This was a bad idea,* she realized, but she didn't want to be the one to say it.

Who then? Jesse followed Sierra's lead, and sad story or not, Sierra had an axe to grind. A petty, jealous axe. This was Desiree's idea; she had to rein it in. If Sierra wouldn't call it off, somehow, Desiree would have to spoil it. At the least she would give Sierra the chance after Jesse's turn.

But then, any Benny Rose ghost story would seem trite after Gabrielle's honest reflection. Sierra didn't understand. In too many ways, she was still a kid. If Jesse passed the buck again, and

Paul still didn't show up, Sierra would try one-upping Desiree. Her next story wouldn't just take place on this street, but in this house. The walls would be painted black, a common meeting spot for the servants of the Blackwood Devil. Hadn't they heard about Satanists in the news? Not in Blackwood. Here, Benny Rose took the crown from even the King of Hell. Where Gabrielle's stairs now climbed, there once towered a great gray mountain of fleshless scalps and hollow sockets. Decayed, each piece was the small skull of a child. A pale, naked fiend had piled them on top of each other, piled them until they climbed past the blackened ceiling, the house itself dwarfed by this morbid geography.

More than five skulls. Too many skulls to count.

And atop the mountain, there sat the Cannibal King himself. He was too high up to make out his features, but his black eyes broke up his white shape and shined down on Desiree. He was not a ghost, but alive. He had to be. If he was dead, then there was no afterlife defined by justice. What did it say about the universe if a man like him ever found happiness?

"Desiree?"

The flashlight lit her face. She knocked it away and struggled off the floor.

"Did you really zonk out twice?" Sierra asked. Jesse snickered beside her.

Desiree hadn't meant to. "I was bored imagining the next lame story you'll tell."

"Whatever, Bride of Benny Rose."

Desiree glanced at the bathroom, still occupied. Paul wasn't here yet. She lowered her voice and leaned toward Sierra. "Call it off."

Sierra sneered. "Will you ever stop being so fucking contrary? You want to be like this with everyone else, I get it, but do you have to do it with us?"

"I set this up for you, princess. Please."

Sierra waved at the curtains. "I can't even call it on. Paul hasn't flashed his headlights. That was his side of the signal."

"So there was nothing out there."

"His car. I was trying to keep Gabrielle creeped out, but like you said, it'll get lame. I can't keep this up forever."

Desiree listened to thunder pretend it could take the neighborhood apart. Lightning flickered behind the curtains. They would think up something else to scratch Sierra's itch, but not tonight. This was for the best.

But why would Paul park his car out there and not show up?

Gabrielle emerged from the bathroom, casting brief light across the living room before she snuffed it out. "Is it still Jesse's turn?"

"Maybe that's enough for tonight," Jesse said.

Something scraped the window. A tree branch? No, the pines were nowhere close to the picture window. Sierra was up first, pushing the curtain aside. Rain muddied their view of Glade Street.

It had better not be Paul. Desiree was too tired for this shit.

Gabrielle sat on the couch close to where Desiree stood. "What is it?"

Sierra shook her head. "It's coming down so thick, I can't even see the sidewalk."

But it could be Paul. "Gabrielle, listen," Desiree said. "When we invited ourselves over, it wasn't just for telling stories. It was—"

The front door creaked open. A blue flash lit the foyer, broken by a black shadow, and when it died, footsteps stamped up to the living room doorway. Sierra aimed the flashlight.

A broad figure blocked the doorway, his brown coat billowing. A vicious meat hook curled from his left sleeve and gleamed in the flashlight beam. His pale right hand dragged something dripping and bulky beside him. The light crossed its head.

It was Paul, hanging limp from the figure's thick fingers. Blood smeared his face and bubbled out of his mouth. "Sierra?" He lifted his head. "Help me."

They forgot how to scream. Gabrielle's gasp stuttered into her lungs, and Desiree imagined her widening eyes in the dark. The blood on Paul's face slithered with rainwater. It was pinker than Desiree thought it should be.

Sierra punched the wall beside the window. "Jesus, Paul."

He grinned through the watery makeup. "Hey, babe."

"Is that Adrian?" Sierra hit the wall switch, lighting up the living room.

Adrian pulled the hood off his brown raincoat, his expression smug. In the light, his meat hook was clearly plastic. He let go of Paul, who clambered to his feet and wiped fake blood off his chin. Adrian hadn't been part of Desiree's plan. It was supposed to be Paul dressed as Benny Rose, alone and on-time.

"Meatheads," Jesse hissed, stepping behind Sierra.

Sierra pointed at the boys' shoes. "You're getting water all over Gabrielle's carpet."

"It wasn't supposed to storm," Paul said.

Sierra looked to Gabrielle. "Tell them to get the hell out."

Gabrielle glanced at the carpet and then the boys, wringing her hands in front of her jeans. "If you could go in the kitchen, Grandma would appreciate it."

The boys slipped back into the foyer. It hadn't been fun enough for them to scare the new girl. Paul had wanted to scare Sierra, too. If he'd stuck to the plan, the scare would've happened right after Sierra's story, before Gabrielle brought down the mood. Now Desiree didn't know if they owed her an apology.

She leaned toward Gabrielle's face. "Are you okay?"

Gabrielle nodded *yes*, but was it a lie? Desiree didn't know her well enough to tell.

Sierra pointed into the dark beyond the foyer. "The kitchen. Now."

Adrian started toward it. Paul lingered. "It was a joke. Sometimes you got to take one to make one."

"No, you don't pull that shit on me unless they clear it first." Sierra gestured at Desiree and Jesse.

"You don't pull that shit without warning on a bunch of girls alone in a house at night," Desiree said. "It matters."

Adrian hesitated at the edge of the living room's light and turned around. "You're not alone now. You got big strong dudes to protect you."

Desiree rolled her eyes.

Adrian shrugged at her. "Oh, right, Daddy left, so boys suck, huh? Not our fault."

Desiree supposed she should flinch but didn't. It was nothing she hadn't heard before. She wasn't even sure how to feel about it after Gabrielle's story.

Sierra stamped her heel. "Get in the kitchen, caveman."

Adrian stifled a belch. "Hey, ask the new girl if there's any beer. We ran out."

"Old ladies don't drink beer."

"Tell that to my Great Aunt Harriet." Adrian backed up toward the kitchen's darkness. "She used to let me—"

White hands reached out of that darkness and grabbed his shoulders in thin, bony fingers. He pulled against them, but he was clumsy. Half in the light, half in the dark, he teetered on one leg.

A pale face followed the hands like a skull rising from tar. Its mouth opened wide, drinking the night, and clamped its teeth onto Adrian's neck. Hot, thick blood bubbled up from his blistering skin, and he let out a high-pitched gurgling shriek. His arms flailed, punching the darkness and dragging the meat hook across something behind him, but it was only plastic, and whatever grabbed him was real.

The white face tore the flesh from Adrian's neck. He dropped the hook with a clack on the tile floor, stopped punching, and groped lazily at the wound. Blood seeped down his hands. The white face hung over the red river as if breathing it in while chewing Adrian's flesh.

Chewing, and at the same time smiling.

SIX: THE CUL-DE-SAC

Paul scrambled for the front door, shoes slipping on damp tiles. Sierra and Jesse chased him, screaming their heads off. Desiree tried to scream too, but nothing came out. It was like last Halloween, the sound trapped inside her.

Adrian might have screamed again, but he didn't have a throat anymore. The face that had eaten it now raked its lower teeth up his cheek, ripping away a chunky strip and carving new recesses into his skull. It made no sound but the squishing flesh between its teeth and the splash of blood across the floor. A burning stink filled the air.

Gabrielle shoved Desiree from behind. She hadn't realized she wasn't moving, transfixed by the horror show at the kitchen's edge. Trying to escape brought them closer to those black eyes.

"It's looking at me," Desiree whispered, crossing the foyer. Lightning flashed through the kitchen windows and its open back door. Adrian sank into the blue glow and vanished when the girls turned their backs on him.

Gabrielle kept shoving until Desiree was out the front door and then slammed it behind them. Rain spattered their hair and clothes, and stung Desiree's eyes. Her hairdo fell in a soppy mess across her forehead. She made out Sierra on the street with Paul, jogging down the sidewalk. Jesse was far ahead. They were passing her car, but Desiree didn't know why, and there wasn't time to stop and figure it out.

Sierra punched Paul's arm. Her bandana had slipped off, letting the rain pound her hair flat. "What the hell was that?"

"I don't know." He sounded stunned.

"We didn't plan that!"

"Neither did I."

"What about Adrian?"

"I don't know!"

Sierra punched him again. "What the hell do you know?"

Gabrielle's front door whipped open behind them and banged inside the foyer. Desiree spun around.

A naked, maggot-white man stalked into the rain, where frail lamppost light shined off his wet hide. Desiree saw him clearer than she wanted, even shrouded in the downpour. Hairless skin squeezed his bones, a skeleton with only the barest layer of flesh. A distended gut, like that of a starving man, spilled around pronounced hips. His genitals hung limp underneath.

She hoped he might move like a zombie in the movie Sierra and Gabrielle had been watching, arms extended, his gait shambling and clumsy.

But his steps were deliberate, a pacing predator at the edge of hunting grounds. With his shoulders hunched, he became a cougar ready to pounce. He first sneered at Gabrielle and then he caught Desiree's gaze and smiled again. This was no mindless zombie. This thing knew exactly what he was doing.

He was familiar.

"Benny Rose?"

Desiree couldn't look away until Gabrielle shoved her again. They ran through the deepening puddle that was once the cul-de-sac, its fountain overflowing.

The white thing followed, not running, but not slow.

They caught up with Sierra. "Where are we going?" Gabrielle asked.

Sierra pointed at Paul's car at the mouth of the cul-de-sac. Through the downpour, it was more a vague, car-shaped impression facing them with round glass eyes. Jesse was already at the front passenger's seat, yanking the door open. Paul ran to the driver's side and hopped in. Sierra raced to the back, hauled open a door, and waved Desiree and Gabrielle inside before following. Thunder shouted for them to hurry. The doors clapped shut.

Sierra locked the back. "Drive, dammit."

Paul turned the key.

This was the point in horror movies when the car should stall. Desiree expected it to happen here if stories were coming to life tonight, but the engine growled alive.

Paul switched the headlights on as the bony thing reached the hood. The glare defined every crease of his ghastly pale skin. He looked to either headlight and then started toward the passenger's side.

"Drive!" Sierra screeched.

Paul floored the gas and pushed forward. The hood's corner hit the thing that killed Adrian. The figure crumpled on impact, vanished from sight, and the car lurched over it. They made a harsh, slippery turn, and then slid toward the mouth of the cul-de-sac where pine trees braced the narrow street.

Jesse slapped the dashboard, urging the car faster. Paul was laughing like he hadn't just lost a friend.

Desiree twisted in her seat to look through the back windshield. Streaking rain washed the glass and the car was heading farther every moment from Glade Street's lampposts. The world had been swallowed in the storm. Still, when lightning flashed, there was no mistaking what she saw.

Their hunter stood from the flooding pavement. Like they hadn't run him over.

SEVEN: LEMON FAIR RIVER

The car slipped briskly along Glade Street's curve toward Pontiac Drive. Trees raced past the windows, their needled branches scraping where rainwater weighed them down. Sierra shouted while Paul drove, his backseat driver. Desiree clawed at her knees and thought about clawing out her eyes, but that wouldn't change what she'd seen.

"You said Benny Rose?" Gabrielle's eyes looked no wider than when Desiree had approached her on Tuesday at lunch. Wasn't she scared right now? Or was she always scared?

"I don't know what I'm saying," Desiree said.

"I thought he wore a big coat and had a hook for a hand."

Desiree shook her head, not in denial. She used to imagine a man charred everywhere but his face until last Halloween in Glade Street. If that had been Benny then and this was Benny now, there was no coat, no hook. He was a white worm grown to the shape of a person.

"He's whatever the storyteller wants him to be," she said.

"I want him gone."

Desiree felt she'd brought this on them by suggesting a Benny Rose-themed prank in the first place. *You reap what you sow*, Mom sometimes said, but that couldn't be true; real life didn't work that way.

Still, her poison flowed into Desiree's brain. Their joke had summoned Benny Rose.

The car jolted to a stop midway down Glade Street's slope to Pontiac, where the sign reminded readers that the neighborhood had been established in 1963. Pine trees blocked most of the cul-de-sac's light.

Sierra punched the back of Paul's seat. "What's the problem?"

"The water," he said.

Thunder growled, but it wasn't alone. Angry water surged past the hood of the car, the headlights shining on a frothing current. Lemon Fair River had overflowed. In the dark, with sheets of rain and pine needles coating the windshield, there was no telling how deep the flood went.

"It's the elevation," Jesse said. "The whole neighborhood would be like this otherwise. We're stuck."

"We're not staying here." Sierra grabbed Paul's shoulder, making Desiree think of fingers on Adrian. "Drive."

Paul reversed the car a few feet and then charged into the water. The hood splashed hard against the unwelcoming surface, splattering the windshield. Its wipers swept back and forth, but there was no clearing the surge. Freshwater spray struck the driver's side windows.

Through the back window, Desiree couldn't distinguish the dark pines from the stormy sky. She would have to wait for lightning to tell her if Benny had followed.

Paul reversed the car again, as if gearing for a running jump, and then plowed down Glade Street's dip a second time. The headlights crested a choppy surface. They were making headway.

"It's too deep," Jesse said.

"Couldn't we use your car?" Desiree asked.

"I had the keys when we ran." Jesse looked down, shamefaced. "But I dropped them outside. They might be on the lawn. I'm sorry."

"Your car wouldn't do any better," Sierra snapped. "Be quiet so I can think."

Floodwater chopped at the windshield's edges. Unless the current subsided, they weren't going to make it down Pontiac Drive, let alone across the bridge to escape Lemon Fair River. The floodwater was rising even now.

Lightning lit the sky. Desiree looked back so fast it made her neck twinge, but she only caught the final blue flicker. Was there something white walking between the trees? She couldn't be sure.

The car hood leaned slightly south. Paul turned the wheel against it and the tires squealed. South was the way they wanted to go, but it was too early. They hadn't cleared the pines.

"Now what?" Sierra shook Paul's shoulder. "Hey, what's happening?"

He smacked the steering wheel. "What do you think's happening? It's flooding."

"We're flooding, too," Gabrielle said, dragging her feet onto the back seat. She was the only one without shoes.

Water pooled on the car floor around their soles. It was only a little now, but there would be a lot if the car kept pushing.

Something scratched past Desiree's window. She flinched away. Benny was coming for her. She pressed into Gabrielle, who shoved against Sierra.

"Will you two knock it off?" Sierra shoved them back.

Another scratch at the glass. Lightning flickered silently across a pine branch that had caught on the rear passenger door. It swept past as thunder followed the lightning. Another branch thumped against the trunk, while more brushed past the sides. Desiree knew a tree might have come down, or several branches had been torn off different trunks, but each scratch felt like thin fingers around her.

"We have to get back to land." It sounded strange, something she might have said as a joke in last year's pirate costume. The water inside the car was halfway up her shoes.

"How?" Jesse asked. "If the water can pull the car—"

"If we don't go now, it's going to pull the car with us in it."

"But I can't swim. If we went—"

Jesse cut herself off and looked left and right for solutions. When she found none, her trembling hand cracked the car door open. Floodwater rushed across her lap.

"Shut that thing!" Paul shouted, reaching for her.

Past the passenger seat, Desiree couldn't see whether Jesse hopped into the water or the water tugged her out, but she slipped from the door and let it hang open while water spilled through the car. Sierra shrieked orders. Jesse answered in a choked scream that dug into Desiree's nerves. She didn't think about what she was doing, only grabbed her door's crank and rolled down the window. Rain swept inside.

Gabrielle turned to her. So, her eyes could get wider.

"Are you nuts?" Sierra reached past Gabrielle.

Another lightning bolt cut the sky, but there was no need to look back this time. Movement in the rearview mirror—something white dipping into the floodwater. Then the lightning faded, and there was only Jesse in the current, clinging to the door for dear life.

Desiree slid out the open window. The girls made *What are you doing?* faces at her, and she beckoned them to follow.

Didn't they get it? The car was doomed, and if the flood pulled them away, they would be lost to the river. It wouldn't matter that Jesse was the only one who didn't know how to swim. Everyone would drown.

Desiree mounted the car roof. Wind spat rain in her face and tried to shove her off the car's slippery hide. Behind its trunk hung a haze of blackness, the world swallowed by Benny Rose. Was he back there?

She scooted toward the front windshield. Paul blasted the horn. He was shouting something, but between the windshield wipers, rushing water, and thunder, he might as well have been a mime.

Jesse seemed a hundred miles away, a piece of nighttime that flailed against the current. Desiree slid onto her belly and stretched an arm across the open door. She couldn't reach. The car roof thumped behind her, taking on the weight of first Gabrielle, then Sierra as they scrambled out the window.

"Hold my legs!" Desiree shouted.

They skidded, Gabrielle almost slipping off the side and into the floodwater with Jesse, but they grabbed on to Desiree's legs. Paul clambered out his window, a big man fighting through a small hole.

Desiree leaned far over the side of the car, her waist flying free. Thin fingers had her by the ankles, and she thought of Benny Rose.

"Jesse, grab on!"

A hand shot from the dark current, found Desiree's forearm, and held on tight. She began to pull Jesse against the car. Sierra and Gabrielle felt the extra weight and tugged. Paul might have been helping. Desiree couldn't tell. Her skin was numb with cold.

Together, they hauled Jesse onto the hood and then up the windshield, coughing and sputtering, but alive.

The car lurched, and Desiree skidded toward the passenger side. Soon the flood would float them away. It had places to go and wanted them to come, too.

Desiree waved everyone toward the trunk. Gabrielle understood and slid down the back windshield, where she hopped into waist-high water. Desiree and Sierra pressed Jesse behind her and then Desiree followed. Paul and Sierra were last. The current dragged again, but they held hands and kept the chain strong as they trudged up Glade Street's slope. Lightning flickered across the pine trees, turning their black mass into individual standing sentinels.

The chain yanked back where Sierra froze behind the others. Gabrielle looked over her shoulder from the front. "What's wrong?"

"Watch your step for branches!" Sierra shouted.

Desiree didn't feel any branches underfoot. Each needle-filled piece of tree floated on the water's surface. Jesse glanced back, mouth hanging open. Even weakened from her ordeal, she realized at the same time that the branches wouldn't sink. They pressed harder to reach less-flooded land.

It was too late. Desiree should have realized where the white shape went when it disappeared and didn't reappear.

Benny was under the car.

His tall, wet shape thrust out of the water behind Sierra, bony body dripping. Desiree screamed a warning, but thunder drowned her out.

Benny's arms snapped cobra-like at Sierra's shoulders and yanked her back toward the car. His teeth crunched into her shoulder. Her mouth opened, silenced by thunder and cast red by the car's taillights. She let go of Paul's hand and slapped at the fingers on her shoulders and the face that chewed toward her neck.

Paul let go of Desiree, grabbed Sierra's arms, and tore her away from Benny. There was blood everywhere. Desiree couldn't see it, couldn't distinguish it from the water that soaked every inch of her, but she felt it in her bones somehow. This was Sierra, her best friend. This couldn't be happening.

There was no such thing as Benny Rose.

Paul hauled Sierra out of the water and against his chest, cradled in his muscly arms. "I got you! Don't be scared!"

Gabrielle tugged, but the chain was split. With only one hand held, Desiree felt lost, moments away from freefalling into the current. Jesse turned her head like she didn't know what happened to Sierra, why Paul wasn't with them. Hadn't she seen the skeleton man?

Desiree pressed ahead and helped Gabrielle tug Jesse out

of the water. Slippery hands slid through her fingers, but she squeezed them tighter. They came to the edge of the flood and dragged themselves onto what had become the shore, their sopping clothes weighing them down.

Desiree let go of Jesse and swirled around. There was Gabrielle. Sierra in Paul's arms. The car, its taillights illuminating nothing, not even the dark trees around them.

Where was Benny?

Paul set Sierra onto what passed for land. Her injury became obvious this close to the neighborhood's first lampposts. A tear opened her shirt above the right sleeve, where raw, red tissue peeked through blistered skin from shoulder to chest. Blood spread down the once-white fabric.

Desiree reached out and took her hand, the skin tough like it had been left too long in the sun. She needed a doctor, burn cream—where to start? They had nothing to bind the wound. "Paul, she needs to be carried."

"Just a minute," Paul said, coughing. His hands were on his knees.

"We can't stay here!"

He started to stand. Water splashed behind him as white hands clambered up his back, shoulders, onto his face, dragging him backward.

Sierra spun around. "Paul?"

He skidded down the slope into ankle-deep water. If he was screaming, the storm ate his voice. The way he thrashed, he should've shouted for help. Why wasn't he screaming? Why weren't they helping?

Benny's legs swung around Paul's waist and gripped his torso. It made Paul jerk back, putting his face to lamppost light where Benny had touched him, and it was clear then why he was so quiet while all the girls shrieked.

Blisters blotted his forehead, erasing one eyebrow and leaving the socket below as raw as Sierra's shoulder. Scalded tissue rippled down his cheek, had eaten away part of his nose, and fused his cheeks and lips into one mass of burned flesh.

He couldn't scream. Whatever muffled noises he might have made died under rainfall and the girls' panic. One wild eye pleaded at them.

Sierra thrust herself past Desiree and reached for him. "Paul!"

Benny twisted Paul's head around and bit into his skull like an apple. Skin sizzled under a white, wormy tongue. Paul crumpled to hands and knees, where water lapped at his hips and elbows.

Desiree's arms circled Sierra's waist to stop her. Jesse grabbed her, too, and they hauled her toward the lampposts. "It's too late!" Desiree shouted.

Sierra went back to high-pitched screaming. She couldn't fight the girls, too weak from her injured shoulder. Her feet stumbled, sliding up the narrow stretch of Glade Street. "Someone help Paul!"

EIGHT: WINDOWS

Gabrielle led them back to the cul-de-sac. The falling rain had to sting Sierra's wound, but they didn't have anything to cover her with. She didn't seem to notice, kept moaning for Paul under her breath.

"We need to get somewhere dry," Jesse said, dancing from foot to foot like she thought that could shake the water off. "Somewhere he can't get us. Go through a back yard, the trees?"

"If Pontiac's flooded, so are the woods where they dip behind the neighborhood," Desiree said.

Glade Street's development was now a fortress with a treacherous moat. The cul-de-sac wasn't immune, either. The street seemed alive with raindrops making ripples in pooling water.

"We have to go back," Sierra murmured. "Paul's alive."

Desiree tried to put Paul out of mind, to not picture his limbs and face stripped to bone, being eaten alive.

She looked around. There were houses everywhere. The girls didn't have to be alone in this. She touched Gabrielle's arm. "Which neighbors do you know best? Who's home? We need somewhere to hole up."

Gabrielle shoved wet hair out of her face. "Grandma's friends went with her to Atlantic City. We can try Mr. Donovan's house."

She hugged the sidewalk and started clockwise around the cul-de-sac. Desiree helped Jesse pull Sierra along.

The rain fell harder. If Benny was already here, he was probably watching them from where the winding part of Glade Street met the cul-de-sac. Desiree glanced back every few steps, but saw no one. She was in the light; he was in the dark. He could see everything.

A flicker danced at one side of the cul-de-sac's mouth. Someone's picture window curtain had just opened and shut. It was another option if Arthur Donovan didn't open his door, but it would mean heading back toward the neighborhood's entrance. Benny liked an ambush. It was in his smile, the look of someone who knew exactly what he was doing and enjoyed it. What had Sierra said this past week when they cooked up tonight's dumb plan? *Cunning.* He had a cunning smile.

Gabrielle slipped around Arthur's white fence, up the driveway, and along the paved walkway to his front door. Her knock was gentle, even polite.

"Mr. Donovan, are you up? We need help."

Desiree pressed Sierra into Jesse's arms and joined Gabrielle at the door. "A little more aggressive." She rammed her fists against the wood, stinging her knuckles.

Sierra bucked against Jesse and turned toward the mouth of the cul-de-sac. "Paul, come back!"

"Quiet her down."

Desiree raised both fists and pounded, one-two, one-two. Gabrielle mimicked her. No one answered.

"Paul!"

"Shut up," Jesse snapped. "You're going to get us killed."

"But Paul!"

Desiree heard a sharp crack and turned her head. Sierra clutched her shoulder with one hand, her cheek with the other.

Jesse lowered a trembling open palm. "Sorry. That's what they do in the movies."

Gabrielle gave the door a departing kick and retreated down the walkway. "He has to be asleep."

You know these old people, Desiree's story echoed. *They go to bed early.*

But not all of them. She looked to the house beside the cul-de-sac entrance where an eye of light had opened and closed. The curtain didn't part again, but only a couple minutes had passed. Whoever had glanced through their picture window would still be awake.

"Someone's in that house," Desiree said, pointing.

"I forget whose house that is," Gabrielle said, but she led the girls down Arthur's driveway.

Desiree helped guide Sierra. She trembled under Desiree's touch. Jesse trembled, too.

Benny didn't have to linger at the narrow part of Glade Street. He could appear from any back yard. Desiree would've felt better to see him, at least know where he was.

Halfway down the sidewalk from Arthur's house toward the cul-de-sac entrance, another curtain slid aside and then shut.

Desiree left Sierra to Jesse and rushed ahead of Gabrielle. "Did you see?"

Gabrielle shook her head. Raindrops dribbled off the end of her nose.

"Someone's awake here." Desiree darted up the driveway and slapped her palms on the picture window. "We need help!"

Tapping the window reminded her of how the rain sounded while they were inside Gabrielle's house, telling ghost stories. Could these old people distinguish fists from rainfall?

Gabrielle darted up the slick stone walkway to the front door of 5 Glade Street and slammed her body against the wood.

"Help us!" Again, no answer. Gabrielle retreated. "I didn't see anyone."

"And I didn't imagine them," Desiree said.

"Then I don't get it."

Desiree punched the window and turned to the driveway. Sierra's sobs were loud at the sidewalk, where she and Jesse quivered beneath a lamppost. They looked so lost, Sierra about to collapse, Jesse struggling to hold her. Rainwater seeped into Sierra's wound.

"Next door," Desiree said.

She led them clockwise, back in the direction of Arthur's house. The greater the distance they put between themselves and the cul-de-sac entrance, the safer she felt, even if Benny had moved on.

Glade Street's homes were similar in evening sunlight, but now they lost all definition, their meager differences dissolved by darkness and rain. The girls were trapped in a neighborhood of identical sullen houses.

Across the cul-de-sac, near Gabrielle's house, an upstairs curtain parted and a head's silhouette peeked out at the rain. The curtain stayed open longer than that of the picture windows, but it still shut after a few seconds. Next door to Gabrielle's house, another window lit up and then darkened. And another, closer to the entrance. Islands of light flickered in and out of the rain. Everyone wanted a glimpse.

Desiree stalled at 6 Glade Street's fence. "They're watching us."

Gabrielle stared out at the cul-de-sac, where the fountain drooled over the pavement. Another window glowed orange and then darkened. "Why won't they help?"

Sierra sank against the nearest fence. Her shoulder left a red-brown smear down its white paint. She had been rendered useless, her bravado gone. Jesse tensed her jaw, making it look like her head was about to burst. Gabrielle's breath hissed in and out and made clouds in the air. Everything they were an hour ago had fallen apart.

Desiree reached for Sierra's arms and pulled her up. It probably hurt, but she couldn't squat here. "Gabrielle, take her with us. Jesse, this way."

Desiree headed up the driveway of 6 Glade Street and took a sharp turn onto the lawn. Her shoes squelched in spongy soil around the corners of the house, toward the lightless back yard. A stunted stoop led to a flimsy-looking door, and if the houses were as similar as they seemed, Desiree expected it led to the kitchen. She pulled open the screeching screen door as Jesse came around the corner, followed by Gabrielle and stumbling Sierra.

Desiree planted the sole of one shoe against the door. Jesse followed her lead.

"On three. One. Two." They kicked. "One. Two."

The back door flew open under the second kick. No wonder Benny had crept into Gabrielle's house. He might have waited for thunder to cover the noise, but nothing much stood in his way. Desiree ushered Jesse inside, then Sierra and Gabrielle, and followed them. She shut the door behind.

But she had no idea how to keep it shut if Benny came looking.

NINE: 6 GLADE STREET

Their shoes squeaked across kitchen tiles and left puddles from the door through the foyer. Here, the interior differed a little from Gabrielle's house, the stairs being on the opposite side and a half-bath hanging open by the front door, but the foyer still led to the living room. The place smelled the same. A standing lamp cast furniture shadows through the doorway and across the girls.

Desiree heard an old woman yelp from the living room.

"I'm sorry, Ms. Carmine," Gabrielle said. "We've been banging on doors and no one answered, but we need a place to hide. Our friend's hurt."

Desiree stopped behind the others. They wouldn't enter the living room, as if needing an invitation from Ms. Carmine after breaking into her home.

She was a stocky, gray-haired woman who had been watching TV from a rocking chair. Her eyes darted over cauliflower cheeks. "I don't understand." Her voice crooned more like an old lady in a cartoon than a legitimate human being.

"There's somebody after us," Desiree said. "We're staying here."

Sierra collapsed dripping wet on the living room carpet. Her shirt rubbed a red-brown stain down the living room doorframe. "We have to call nine-one-one. They have to help Paul."

Jesse hauled her off the floor.

Ms. Carmine chewed her lower lip. "I'm sorry. I hadn't set my hearing aid until right now." She eased out of her rocking chair and waddled toward the doorway. "I'll fetch some towels. Come in and warm up."

Jesse thanked her and drew Sierra toward the couch where she could soak the cushions. Desiree stood aside to let Ms. Carmine pass. A wire dangled from her ear, but Desiree had a feeling it had been set since before they came by. It was simply too much trouble to answer the door. Ms. Carmine, and probably most people on Glade Street, wanted to watch TV and pretend there was no trouble outside their homes.

Jesse began to pace between the picture window and the gas fireplace where a small fire crackled. Its flames made her shadow dance. The TV show was black and white. Desiree didn't recognize it.

Gabrielle drifted to the lamp's corner, where a yellow rotary phone sat on an end table. "Do you think she'd mind if I used her phone? I want to call Grandma."

"Your grandmother can't help," Jesse said. "We need an ambulance."

"And tell them what?" Desiree asked. "That Benny Rose is after us? *Oh, thanks, girls. That's only the hundredth time tonight.* It's pointless."

"A naked psycho bit our friend. There's nothing else to tell." Jesse wasn't convincing.

Gabrielle already had the phone to her ear and was asking information for a Marriot in New Jersey.

"They have to help Paul," Sierra muttered.

Jesse stamped her foot, making the fireplace flames twitch. "I'm begging you, stop saying that. I keep seeing his face." She looked at Desiree. Raindrops clung to her jaw. "What did it do to his face?"

"I think Benny's touch burned him." Desiree pointed to Sierra's shoulder. "Benny burned her, too."

And he had chewed chunks of Adrian's flesh, but Desiree kept that to herself. They had already forgotten him, it seemed. None of them had seen how far Benny ate through the boys. It might have gotten worse. *Meat, bones, and soul.*

"Paul."

Desiree sat on the couch beside Sierra, wrapped an arm around her waist, and pulled her head into a hug. Wet hair slithered across Desiree's shirt, but it didn't matter.

"We have to do something about that bite," Jesse said. "Is she going to be like him? A zombie or something like that?"

Silly as Jesse sounded, Desiree studied the area around the bite. Blisters rippled, but Sierra's skin stayed a healthy brown. She wasn't turning into the bone-white, sickly thing that had bitten her.

"Grandma's not answering."

Gabrielle hung up the phone and drifted to the fireplace, where she knelt on the floor. Firelight flickered in her eyes, wet with tears.

Jesse approached the phone and traced one finger across the holes where numbers stared.

She looked at Desiree. "Do you really think it's Benny Rose?"

Desiree stroked Sierra's head. The thing outside looked like the man she'd envisioned atop the mountain of skulls. He looked like the man from last Halloween, too. That was no Wallace Shaw with dementia who chewed Adrian's neck and burned Paul's face. She had believed that man a year ago could be Benny Rose while telling stories. And now?

She gave Jesse a quick nod. Thunder crackled, the rain hitting louder and then softening as if a window or door had been opened and then promptly shut.

Jesse started pacing again. "Some stories, he's alive. Others, he's a ghost."

"He came through Gabrielle's back door," Desiree said. "That thing has a body." A body with organs; a stomach filled with burned flesh. "He's hungry."

"And he ate them." Jesse swallowed. "He fucking ate them."

Desiree couldn't remember ever hearing Jesse say that word. It felt unnatural.

Sierra's breath rattled out. "Tell the ambulance where to find Paul."

Desiree held her tight. "Even if they wanted to help us—hell, even if we told them it's Benny Rose and they believed us? They're on the wrong side of the river. This storm's flooded Blackwood. We're stuck on Glade."

Sierra began to sob in her arms.

Jesse approached the fireplace and spread her hands over Gabrielle. "Where did he even come from? Stories don't just pop to life."

"Maybe we did it." Desiree turned to Gabrielle, who still watched the fire. "We shouldn't have tried to scare each other. The prank with Paul was like a summoning, you know, like they talk about in the news? Satanists summon demons. We were asking for trouble. We should've had a Halloween with no Benny Rose, no ghosts. Gabrielle shouldn't have had to tell about her parents."

Gabrielle blinked, her stony face a gargoyle come to life. Desiree wasn't sure what to make of her anymore. She wasn't sure what to make of any of them. This was beyond them.

Mom was right. They should never have come to Glade Street, should've stayed home with their parents this Halloween.

Except Gabrielle couldn't.

"I'm sorry," Desiree said. "About the prank. And him."

Gabrielle brushed tears across her forearm, but only smeared more rainwater over her face. "I actually thought there was a reason they died. Like, I already survived the worst thing that'll happen to me. If I can handle that, I can handle anything. But then tonight happened."

The rain grew loud again, like they were back outside, and then muffled. Had Ms. Carmine opened a door?

Gabrielle looked to Desiree. "Don't feel bad. You didn't do anything wrong. If you all weren't here, I would've been asleep in my room when he—"

Her voice died in her throat, and her eyes widened at something behind Desiree.

Ms. Carmine padded from the foyer into the living room doorway. She did not carry towels. Raindrops slid around her wrinkled cheeks. Desiree felt the bad thing happening before she saw it, as if this damp, elderly woman were an omen for what crept out of the storm.

Benny Rose slid naked from the darkness behind Ms. Carmine. Shadows danced up his face, cast by the living room fireplace, and stretched his smile up the sides of his hairless head.

Ms. Carmine glared into Desiree and spoke out of the corner of her mouth. "Well, what are you waiting for? Get 'em, Benny! Get 'em!"

TEN: THE BLACKWOOD DEVIL

Sierra tore screaming out of Desiree's arms and scrambled on hands and knees toward the TV corner. Desiree grabbed the couch edge closest to the fireplace and shoved it across the living room as a barrier. She meant to push it all the way to the entrance, but that would've been too close to Benny's gaze. She stumbled back, passing the picture window where Jesse and Gabrielle had retreated.

Benny lurched past Ms. Carmine. He hardly looked at her. His foot planted on the central couch cushion and lifted his head toward the ceiling, where his eyes reflected the TV's black and white light. He was choosing a target.

And he wanted Desiree. She could feel it as she backed into the far wall across from the doorway. There were no other exits. Sierra cowered against the TV stand. Gabrielle stood in front of her, expression frantic, and Jesse had her shoulders to the wall.

Benny slid one leg over the back of the couch. He was coming, one step at a time. He didn't have to hurry when his prey was trapped.

Desiree grabbed Ms. Carmine's rocking chair to heave at him, but it wouldn't do any good. Paul had run Benny down with a car and yet he'd stood again seconds later like nothing had touched him.

Lightning flickered in the foyer behind Benny and under the living room curtains.

Desiree hauled the chair past Gabrielle. "Jesse, the curtains!"

Jesse snapped the curtains open, her gaze glued to Benny. Desiree swung the rocking chair against the window. The glass chipped.

In the reflection, Benny hit the carpet and dragged his other leg over the top of the couch, landing him in front of the fireplace. His sagging gut and genitals hung black against the fire.

Desiree swung again. Glass exploded into the rain. Benny's reflection burst with it, but she felt him approaching, still smiling. If he had breath, it was on her. She had to get away. She scraped the chair across the bottom of the window, clearing away the largest glass teeth, and then swirled around to throw the chair at Benny. It banged against him and hit the floor somewhere; she didn't watch. She clambered over the windowsill and dropped onto the wet lawn.

Jesse and Gabrielle followed together. Gabrielle fell shrieking into the grass beside Desiree. A chunk of glass had sliced her palm open. Rain washed the blood down her forearm.

The window was empty behind them.

Desiree staggered to her feet and cupped her hands around her mouth. "Sierra!" No one had taken the time to usher her along.

Her hand grasped the sill and pulled the rest of her up. She was a frail, unsteady blotch against the living room's light.

"Hurry up!" Desiree reached for Sierra's hand to drag her over.

Benny's face loomed above her. She didn't seem to realize it as she slid her knees onto the sill. He didn't cut her attention until he grabbed her from behind and plowed his face into her lower back, where his teeth ripped at skin, muscle, and spine.

Her scream blasted like a siren. Desiree grabbed Sierra's arm and wouldn't let go, even with Gabrielle's hands on her shoulders trying to pull her back. Paul had been hopeless when they abandoned him, but this was different. That was Paul. This was Sierra.

Desiree tugged her from Benny's grip. Skin and cloth slid from under his fingers, and muscly flesh stretched away from his teeth. Sierra snapped free and fell over the windowsill onto Desiree.

Desiree rolled Sierra over and stood. "Get up. We have to go."

Sierra couldn't talk anymore, only screech and sob. Her back was a ragged red cavern where Benny had bitten away tissue and nerve. Desiree tried not to look.

Benny chewed but didn't wait, his white fingers already grasping the sill to follow. Glass crunched underneath them. Flesh vanished in a bulge down his narrow throat as he leaned out the window.

"Get up!"

One of Sierra's legs started to stand and then gave out. Fine, Desiree would drag her. She tucked her hands under Sierra's arms, hefted her bloody back against drenched chest, and began to drag her across the lawn. Her legs left muddy trails in the grass. She was dead weight, alive but unwieldy.

"Don't pass out on me. You have to kick. Help me, Sierra."

No response. She didn't even cry or scream anymore.

"He's coming!" Jesse shouted.

She and Gabrielle were already at the sidewalk and drifting into the wider circle of the cul-de-sac.

Benny landed in the grass. Sweeping rain washed the blood off his smile. He strode after Sierra's limp legs, making deliberate, calm steps between their muddy strips.

Dragging her put an ache in Desiree's back, but she couldn't stop. "Pedal through the pain," she said. "Remember, Sierra?" The question wasn't fair. Sierra said that back on Main Street when Benny Rose was nothing but a silly face in store windows and plastic bones tied to streetlights.

Now the real thing reached for her leg.

"Get off!" Desiree dragged harder, lifted higher, but she couldn't go any faster than this. She was already lagging.

Benny's head recoiled in a disgusted sneer. His eyes never

leaving Desiree, he swiped at the ground, where his fingers scraped Sierra's shoe.

"No!"

He swiped again and caught Sierra's ankle, gave it a tug.

"Let her go!" Desiree yanked Sierra back.

Her ankle slithered out of Benny's hand and flopped on the grass. His smile was back. He faked grabbing her again, let Desiree shriek. His lips peeled back, and lightning flickered across his teeth where bits of flesh dangled.

Sierra started to slip from Desiree's grasp. Their limbs were wet again in the merciless rain, and every step sank Desiree's shoes deeper into the mud. She had almost reached the sidewalk herself when Jesse and Gabrielle rushed to her sides and helped pull Sierra into the street.

Benny followed, but he was in no rush. Behind him, Ms. Carmine watched from her broken window. Her expression was lost in the storm.

Desiree's limbs sagged. None of the girls were all that strong, but they couldn't leave Sierra. Tonight had been for her pleasure, and pettiness, and pride.

Benny came up on Sierra's leg. His fingertips dragged along her shin, protected from his touch by thin costume fabric.

Desiree's shoes slipped on the flooded pavement and threw her splashing on her back. Sierra fell across her legs. Jesse and Gabrielle grabbed Desiree around the middle, pulled her out from under, and tried to cushion Sierra's head. Her eyes were closed, all limbs limp. She hadn't made a sound since before Benny dropped from Ms. Carmine's window.

He strode around her side and reached for Jesse, who scrambled back into Gabrielle. Both of them darted away from his touch. He lunged at Desiree next and sent her slipping back in an awkward crabwalk. Her splashing palms scraped rough pavement.

He had isolated Sierra. His smile dared them come closer. When no one did, he crouched over her and clasped his hands around her head.

Gabrielle scrabbled up from the cul-de-sac puddle. She took Jesse's hand and reached for Desiree's.

They were letting this happen. How could they let this happen? Sierra wasn't even conscious; she couldn't fight back. Desiree wanted to charge Benny, slam him off Sierra, pick her up strong as Paul, and run like never before. Benny was still smiling as he leaned closer to her head.

Desiree grasped Gabrielle's bleeding hand and let herself be hauled off the ground.

"Don't look," Gabrielle squeaked.

They ran. Desiree didn't know where they were headed. Up the sidewalk, between two houses, out of sight from the lampposts. Somewhere Benny couldn't see them. Somewhere they couldn't see what he was doing to Sierra.

ELEVEN: THE WEAK ONE

They darted through—how many back yards? Desiree couldn't pay attention. They seemed too few to escape the truth of Sierra's fate and yet infinite in their meaningless sameness. Gabrielle let go of the others' hands to open gates and usher Desiree and Jesse through, a mother deer herding fawns away from a wolf. She stopped behind them to close each gate—it seemed pointless. No fence would stop Benny Rose.

Desiree couldn't say that. She had to keep one hand over her mouth to muffle sobs. There wasn't time to stop and cry for Sierra any more than for Paul.

But didn't Sierra deserve the time?

"What do we do?" Jesse whispered. "We should kill it, right? Crack its stupid head open?"

Gabrielle nodded like this was a plan. Her hair was matted to her scalp again and slopped down her shoulders.

Desiree lowered her hand from her lips. "He isn't stupid. He could've tried harder to get Sierra, but he let us exhaust ourselves, trip over our own feet. He was—" She swallowed a sob.

"He was having fun," Gabrielle said flatly. She had only realized this minute exactly what they were dealing with.

"Okay then." Jesse passed through another gate. "How do we

use that? How do we make it not fun for him?"

Gabrielle lowered her head. "Die?"

They slowed behind one house and tucked against its dark rear. Thunder blasted the sky, but lightning was taking a break. Jesse was a pair of white eyes in the dark, wider than Gabrielle's had ever been. If there were tears on her cheeks, they were mixed with the rain.

Desiree had always thought Jesse was the weak one among them, but maybe it had been Sierra all along. She'd fooled everyone with her fiery attitude and spite, but it was camouflage. Benny might have liked her for that.

Now someone else had to be the weak one. Maybe Jesse. Or it could be Gabrielle.

Or maybe it's me, Desiree thought.

Jesse shivered again. "He'll catch us. He's going to eat us one by one. Why's he doing this to us? How do we make him stop?" She so badly wanted someone to tell her what to do, but Sierra wasn't here anymore.

Desiree covered her eyes. "I shouldn't have left her."

"She was out," Gabrielle said. "She would've told us to go."

"I wouldn't have listened."

"Why there?" Jesse asked. "Why'd you have to pick the house where someone loved this thing?"

Desiree bit her tongue. There were no words. It was easier to be angry than to mourn.

"She's probably the witch who summoned him," Jesse went on. "Like you said in her house. Satanists popping up everywhere, summoning demons. Our town has people like that. We have the Blackwood Devil."

"It was the closest house." Desiree's teeth chattered and she clenched them. Benny might hear.

"There were people looking out their windows all around us. We had our pick."

"They wouldn't open their doors."

"They're probably scared of him, too."

"But why would they be?" Gabrielle asked. She started toward the next gate, another back yard. "She told him to get us, but he was doing that anyway. He only wants us. Isn't that like Sierra's story? Benny Rose doesn't eat just anyone. He eats kids."

As they passed between houses, Desiree glanced down the gap toward the cul-de-sac. No curtains parted, but people were watching; she could feel it. Glade Street's residents were still keeping tabs on the girls who ran from Benny Rose.

"It's all of them," Desiree said.

Gabrielle and Jesse stopped at the gate and looked back at her.

"They're all on his side."

There were warnings all the way to Glade Street that they should stay away. The river, flooded. The sign that read *Glade Street Retirement Community* hid behind hedges. No decorations, no life, only that ugly feeling of decay and the sense last Halloween that Desiree was welcome in the way that a predator welcomes prey. This was the only neighborhood in Blackwood that was guaranteed to have no kids.

Until Gabrielle.

Desiree wiped rain out of her eyes and followed the girls into the shadow of the next house. Her chest ached, her breath heaving in and out. "They don't want kids in their neighborhood. They want us dead. They're on his side!"

Jesse grabbed her hand. "Not so loud, Desi."

"We're just kids!" Desiree clamped her free hand back over her mouth. "Sierra's just a kid."

It was her turn to be the weak one. Benny would have her next. He'd had his eyes on her since he bit Adrian and was disappointed— no, since last Halloween. The longer they stayed out in the open, the sooner it would happen.

They stalled at another back door. Gabrielle pulled her socked feet onto the stone stoop. "We can go back to my house, hide and get my shoes, but he might be there. He might be anywhere."

Desiree approached the back door and pulled open the screen. No, she refused to be the weak one. Someone else could have her turn.

She planted a muddy shoe against the door, looked at Jesse, and cocked her head to one side. "When it thunders."

Jesse planted her shoe beside Desiree's. When the sky shouted again, they kicked. This time the door flew open in one blow. Jesse ducked through first. The inside smelled the same as the last two houses, an unsettling elderly odor. Desiree wanted to know what these people bought that made their houses smell like this so she could avoid it for the rest of her life.

"And what about whoever's in there?" Gabrielle asked. She squinted through the rain, but the roof was not familiar. "From the back, I don't even know whose house this is."

Desiree ducked behind Jesse and waved Gabrielle inside. "It's our house now. Benny won't hurt them, but we're not like him."

She closed the screen door gently so Benny wouldn't hear. As in Ms. Carmine's house, their shoes squeaked across the kitchen floor and into the foyer. Gabrielle's socks made squish-squish noises behind them. There wasn't time for stealth. If someone was home, they'd probably already heard the door crash open despite the thunder.

There were doorways to either side of the stairs that led to the living room and garage, but the lights were off. The girls hurried upstairs, where a line of light cut across the second floor hallway from beneath a shut door. It was all Desiree could see, but she heard someone brushing their teeth. Rain pounded worse up here, echoing through the roof.

She slipped past Jesse and led away from the light toward a dark doorway, where she found a light switch on the wall. Grotesque lime wallpaper gave the bedroom a sickly character. A king-size bed took up the room's center and a vanity and mirror stood across from the footboard. Beyond that, two dressers hugged the far wall beside a closet door, where a fire extinguisher sat on the floor. Desiree ran to grab it, leaving muddy footprints on the bedroom carpet.

The toothbrush swishing sound stopped. Footsteps made the hallway floor creak. "Who's out there?" a man asked.

Desiree flicked off the light and darted past Jesse and Gabrielle. The opening bathroom door lit up the hall, but it would be too late for the man to see her. He was in the light; she was in the dark. His silhouette wore an outline of flannel pajamas and spectacles, lenses reflecting light. She was only sorry to break the spectacles when she swung the extinguisher at his head.

"Sorry, Mr. Donovan," Gabrielle said as if she'd been caught gossiping in class.

He collided with the wall and slumped to the floor.

Jesse flipped on the bedroom light. With the bathroom light, they could see that a bruise formed on Arthur Donovan's temple, beneath wispy gray locks.

"Did you kill him?" Jesse asked.

"We need to tie him up," Desiree said. "I didn't hit him that hard."

TWELVE: SILVER BULLET

They dragged a chair upstairs from the dining room. Arthur was heavier, but they got him seated and bound him with sheets from the linen closet across the hall from his bedroom. They dried off with his towels as best they could. Gabrielle used one to wipe the mud off the back door. Benny would have no reason to pick this house over any other.

Not trusting their knots, Desiree went to the garage to find tape. Instead, she found things that would help start a fire. At first that made her think of using the living room fireplace to dry their clothes, but if Benny found them, they wouldn't have time to get dressed. She didn't even want the downstairs lit. Still, she brought those things upstairs and stuffed them in the linen closet in case Benny came up looking. She didn't share that with Jesse and Gabrielle. They were frightened enough.

When all their downstairs business was done, they shattered a few of Arthur's drinking glasses into a plastic pail and scattered the shards up the stairs.

"Will that stop him?" Gabrielle asked, wrapping a bandage roll from under the bathroom sink around her wounded hand. She had left her muddied socks there and swapped on a pair that belonged to Arthur's wife. If only they could find shoes that fit.

Desiree finished emptying the pail at the top of the stairs. "It might slow him down."

Jesse stretched across the floor beside Arthur's bed. Gabrielle sat beside her, back against the footboard. They didn't sleep, but they didn't seem entirely awake either.

Resting sounded nice, if only Desiree could. She paced in front of the bedroom window that faced the cul-de-sac, now and then parting the curtains to catch prying eyes. The neighborhood was quiet except for the rain. If anyone saw brief light in Arthur's window, they would assume it was him.

These goddamned dinosaurs. Did Gabrielle's grandmother know her neighbors had summoned this thing? If not, did they warn her? No, Desiree didn't think so. The Glade Street Retirement Community was founded over twenty years ago. Benny Rose was the status quo. What was a dead granddaughter to the Glade Street Homeowners Association? They had a legacy to uphold. When they first conjured him, had there been an ordinary neighborhood in this place? And after Benny was awake, what did town council do?

Desiree imagined them seated in a makeshift meeting room in town hall. It wouldn't do to be anywhere that official meetings took place. This was off the books. They slung their expensive jackets over the backs of chairs, loosened their ties, and drank coffee or lemonade, or whatever. A creaky oscillating fan did little good to ventilate the stuffy room. They were sweating, she could smell it, but that wasn't from heat alone.

They were nervous. Grown men having to gather and decide what to do about a haunted neighborhood, where an undead hungry thing had been summoned to eat children. The first to speak had to admit that, and no one wanted to be it.

At last, one of them would've folded his hands on the table with a sigh and said, *Well, what are we going to do?*

They went over disappearances, deaths, and so on. No one

wrote notes. There could be no record of town council acknowledging the supernatural. What genius suggested rezoning the neighborhood to a retirement community? Someone who wanted to live there. It might have been HOA guy and captive Arthur Donovan himself. The town must have spent a fortune buying homes from normal families who hadn't already moved away and then selling them at a loss to the elderly.

It was a perfect con. Now they had a neighborhood with no kids and the means to keep it that way.

Muffled crying tore Desiree from her thoughts. Jesse was against the footboard with Gabrielle now, hands covering her face while Gabrielle rubbed her shoulder. Their clothes were slowly drying.

Jesse's fingertips scrubbed her cheeks, leaving them a redder brown. "You know what you were saying earlier?"

"I don't remember," Desiree said. Earlier felt like a hallucination.

"About never having kids. Sierra didn't want to, either. It would've been nice for her to talk about it, like we did. But I guess it wasn't going to matter for any of us."

"It matters." Desiree took another peek around the curtain—nothing out there—and joined Jesse and Gabrielle on the floor. "What are you going to do when you're older? Get married, have lazy kids, and that's it?"

Jesse looked off to the side, almost embarrassed. "A veterinarian. I think that'd be cool."

"And you?"

Gabrielle leaned her head against the footboard. "I don't think I'll live that long."

Desiree snapped her fingers in Gabrielle's face. "No, what are you going to do? Marry a rich guy? Have cats? Be a movie star? Tell me."

"Nursing. I want to be a nurse." Gabrielle lowered her head. "I did, at least. I don't know anymore."

"What about you, Desi?" Jesse asked. "What do you want?"

"I'll teach."

Jesse burst out laughing. "You want to be Mrs. Hatcher?"

"I'll be an art teacher. It's different. I'll be cool and live with cool, weird people, and sometimes we'll paint up the sides of buildings. And I'll listen to all the kids. The other teachers will hate me, but everyone else will love me." Desiree placed her hands on their knees. "So, we all know we're getting out of here. We all have something to do someday."

Gabrielle looked incredulous but nodded. Jesse smiled again. Desiree stepped away from them. Good, they both believed her.

If only she could be that easy to convince.

She went back to the window and pressed the curtain aside, was about to let it drop back in place, but caught it for another look.

There were people in the cul-de-sac. Three of them, their fat umbrellas blooming over their heads. Two stood beneath a lamppost near the narrow part of Glade Street. The third walked the fence of Gabrielle's house, approached Jesse's car, and then turned around and went back the way they came. Curtains parted in another window, revealing a lit living room.

Desiree ducked back and let the curtain hang. "They're looking for us."

She expected the girls to stiffen, maybe cry again, but they only stared at the vanity.

"That reminds me of another Benny Rose story," Jesse said.

"No more," Gabrielle said. "Please."

"This one's different." Jesse looked up at the vanity mirror, reflecting the windows that faced Arthur's neighbor. "People like to think he walked out of the darkness and into Blackwood like that was his whole story. Nobody wants to remember that they had to have accepted him, even liked him, for him to get away with what he did as long as he did. They didn't suspect this nice man from the hospital was eating their children. He acted like any one of them. He'd read the newspaper, get a cup of coffee, and then he'd go sit on a park bench. Feed the birds. Watch the children play.

"And that's why Blackwood can't let it go. He's not just Benny Rose, the Blackwood Devil, the Cannibal King. He's Blackwood's shame. And he's made it so everybody, no matter how much fun they're having together, is a little bit afraid of each other. You never know who anyone really is." Jesse wiped her eyes. "Sierra wouldn't have liked that one. God, I wish I hadn't slapped her."

Desiree glanced at the curtain, but she didn't touch it. All those people out there, Arthur in here, Ms. Carmine who sicced Benny on them, had all probably seemed like nice people before tonight. And tomorrow, they would go back to seeming like nice people. No one in Blackwood would know any different.

"There has to be a way to stop him," Jesse said. "What's his silver bullet?"

"His what?" Gabrielle asked.

"Silver bullet."

Jesse stood and approached the vanity. A rotary phone, jewelry boxes, and containers of makeup covered the space beneath the mirror. Her fingers sifted through them, found a pair of steel scissors, and held them up to the light.

"A silver bullet is the only thing that kills a werewolf. Or for vampires, a stake in the heart, sunlight." The scissors stretched open and snipped closed. "How do we kill Benny Rose?"

Gabrielle looked between Jesse and Desiree. "What do the stories say?"

"They don't stop him in the stories," Desiree said. "He always gets you in the end. Even when it seems like you got away."

Last Halloween had seemed like a close call, but tonight it turned out to be a warning.

"Sometimes the storyteller changes it, makes Benny lose." Jesse set the scissors down and turned from the vanity empty-handed. Arthur's wife must not have owned any silver. "But those aren't the ones that stay. Only the best ones get retold—the more gruesome, the better."

Desiree grew impatient. "Who cares about the stories? We're dealing with the real thing."

"All stories matter. They tell us truths about things that never happened. Maybe we'll learn something from one of them."

"We won't. They're made up by kids who don't know anything, to scare other kids who don't know anything." Desiree glanced out the window again. There were more people outside, but still far away. "Like us."

Jesse made a pleading gesture. "We've hardly tried anything."

"Who says it takes something special to stop him?"

Desiree kept the underside of that question to herself. Who said even something special could stop him? For all they knew, what was already dead couldn't be killed. Getting run over by a car should've broken bones and left Benny a crumpled mess, but he still came for Sierra and Paul.

"In the older stories, the ones about the hospital, he burned to death," Jesse went on. "We could burn him. Chop off his left hand."

"We could eat him," Gabrielle said, snickering.

A dry chuckle joined them, sending chills through Desiree's bones. She and the others turned to the chair in the corner.

"You can't stop him." Arthur's head hung over his chest, but now an open-mouthed smile split his face. The bruise on his temple shined purple. "He's out tonight, and he won't stop. He's Benny Rose, and Halloween is his holy night. You Blackwood youngsters know that. You've known it all your lives."

THIRTEEN: ESTABLISHED 1963

Desiree crept from the window. Her fingers plucked up the scissors as she crossed the vanity and approached the side of the chair in case Arthur felt like kicking. His slippers had come off, revealing scaly feet that scraped the carpet. He didn't look like much for being head of the neighborhood; just an old man tied up in his pajamas, but twenty or thirty years ago, he would've been stronger. And how strong did anyone have to be to summon a demon?

It was time to find out. "What did you do?" Desiree asked.

He looked at her, uncomprehending, but she hadn't hit him that hard.

She held up the steel scissors. Jesse and Gabrielle slunk behind her. "What did you geriatric shits do? How'd you summon Benny Rose?"

"Oh, that. Witchcraft, little girl. Don't you know? Our community's a little congregation for the fallen one. It's not only Halloween. It's the solstices, the equinoxes, all the Sabbaths of the Devil that take place when the veil is thin between our world and Hell."

Desiree gaped at him. Was he being real with her? She couldn't be sure what was genuine in the wake of Benny Rose being more than a story. The look in Arthur's eyes sang smug mischief.

She pointed the scissors at his hand, bound to the armrest. "Why's Benny Rose trying to kill us?"

His eyes fell on Gabrielle. "You already know."

Gabrielle glanced at Desiree as if asking permission to speak. "Does Mrs. Donovan know?"

Arthur cackled, dry and mean. "Come on, Gabby. You're not really interested in what Marian knows. Ask me about Judy."

Gabrielle eyed her bandaged hand. "Does Grandma know?"

"Why do you think she let Marian and Mable take her to Atlantic City when she had you newly arrived? And so soon after she lost her son and daughter-in-law."

"Because they had free tickets."

"Free tickets to what, Gabby? The car they drove there? The casinos? Do hotels take tickets now? In my day, they taught kids real things."

"But she could've stayed. If she was with me—"

"Judy knows what'll happen to you. I expect she doesn't know what'll happen to her, how she'll feel. Nothing in life comes free. She'll find out the cost when she comes home, and then get over it. She'll have a whole neighborhood of shoulders to cry on."

Gabrielle's eyes went wide. She darted past the chair and out of the room, her face beet red.

Desiree almost followed. "Don't talk to her. Talk to me."

"Nothing I say is going to help you," Arthur said.

She blinked and, briefly, he became the negative of her mother, contrasted in appearance but both specimens of the same manipulative species. He wasn't going to be intimidated by being tied here, not even by scissors. They were only teenage girls. What could they do?

Fine, he could be obstinate all he liked, but he had no idea what he was in for. Desiree slid the scissors into her jacket pocket and headed for the hall to fetch the things she'd found in the garage.

Gabrielle leaned beside the linen closet, her fingernails scraping the wallpaper. Tears glistened on her cheeks. "She could've said so." She swallowed hard. "Grandma could've just said she didn't want me. I don't have anywhere else to go, but I could've run. People do that, don't they?"

Desiree didn't have an answer. It wasn't something she'd thought about any more than she ran from her mother on a daily basis. But this was something else. Gabrielle's grandmother wanted to live alone bad enough to feed her own flesh and blood to Benny Rose.

Sniffling, Gabrielle drifted toward the bathroom and ran the tap.

Desiree watched her go and then opened the linen closet and picked up the things she'd brought from the garage.

"There was another girl with us," she said, loud enough for Arthur to hear. "Her name was Sierra. And we loved her like you can't know, did things for her we didn't like. That's how much we loved her. And she didn't take anyone's shit. She dished it out. Sometimes even when the person didn't deserve it. So think of this like she's here with us."

She returned to the bedroom with a small white matchbook and a red jerry can of gasoline, big as Arthur's head. He hadn't needed to keep matches and gasoline locked away. There weren't supposed to be troublemakers on Glade Street to find them.

"But I have a feeling you deserve it. You killed my best friend."

Arthur wasn't smiling now. "You won't."

Desiree sloshed the jerry can in his direction and set it between the bed and chair. "Don't tell me what I won't do. Don't even think I won't."

He gritted his teeth and looked to Jesse, who turned away. Then he looked to the doorway, where Gabrielle reappeared, still red in the face. He would have no friends here. At last, he turned back to Desiree, the fight having drained from his eyes.

"How did you summon Benny Rose?" Desiree asked. "I don't care if you think it'll help us. Tell me."

"Oh, that? That was easy. To get Benny Rose here, we had to do—" Arthur leaned as close to her as his binds allowed. "Nothing. We did nothing. He's been here since before we knew we could use him."

"Since Blackwood was founded?"

"Not that far back, no. Since the hospital burned down."

Arthur's smile returned. It reminded Desiree too much of Benny. She thought of taking the jerry can and smacking the amusement off Arthur's face.

"You know that story, don't you, girls? Blackwood Mercy Hospital." He nodded at the window. "It was here."

That explained the strange shape of the neighborhood. The cul-de-sac used to be a parking lot, the hospital a wide, rounded structure to one side.

Desiree could imagine. She could even see it burning. "And after, you knew there was something here."

"There was no Cannibal King before the hospital burned," Arthur said. "Don't you know anything?"

Desiree gritted her teeth. Arthur wasn't making complete sense, but she couldn't let him know that or he'd have her twisted around his finger. If he was smart enough to trick Blackwood town council decades ago, he could try tricking three high school girls.

"What's out there then?" she asked. "A ghost?"

"How should I know? What's a ghost anyway?" Arthur rested his head against the back of the chair. His neck was a stretch of wobbly skin. "You step in mud and the footprint washes away, but step in cement and it doesn't. An ordinary day is like mud, but when something really bad happens, it sticks around. Forty-seven people died in the hospital fire, but only forty-one were found right after it collapsed. They hushed up whatever else went on with that.

The town built a new residential subdivision and called the case closed, except for the stories."

"But town council knew about him. They had to know or they wouldn't have given you the neighborhood."

Arthur raised his eyebrows. He hadn't expected Desiree to figure that out, had he? "Town council had a problem. We had a simple solution. If there's a neighborhood with a thing in it that eats kids, don't let kids live in that neighborhood. So, they gave it to us. Problem solved." He looked over Desiree with gray, apathetic eyes. "Benny keeps things safe for us. Nice and quiet. Any riffraff come on Halloween night, they won't come back. And everyone knows. It spreads, like roots from a tree. Hasn't anyone in your life told you not to come here? They don't know why, but kids should stay away."

Last Halloween, Benny Rose had stood in the middle of Glade Street, knowing Desiree was there, hungering for her. *Fee-fi-fo-fum, I smell the blood of Blackwood's young.* Not every kid was so lucky to get spooked and pedal away. Some kids came to Glade Street on foot, with friends or alone, and that was the end of them.

Mom was so angry last Halloween. She'd been a firecracker since Desiree's father left, but this past year ticked it up a notch. Had she even known why?

Desiree glanced at Gabrielle. She looked so innocent, the nicest resident of Glade Street, though that bar was much lower than anyone in Blackwood knew. "And what about her? It isn't her choice."

"Gabby's case is unfortunate, but we can't have her upending the neighborhood. It'd be inconvenient. You'd understand if you got older, wanting to keep things the way they're supposed to be. Not the way everyone keeps changing things to be."

Desiree dug her nails against the matchbook. "How many kids?"

Arthur flashed a big-teethed, shit-eating grin and shrugged against the knotted sheets. "Youngsters never respect the rules, but scary stories? Those, you'll take to heart."

Desiree leaned close to his head. Her breath tickled wisps of gray hair around his ear. "I think my friend would want me to hurt you now."

The glee died in his face. "Hang on. Maybe there's a way."

Jesse stepped closer, and Gabrielle leaned from the doorway.

"There's a hole behind Mable's house. You know hers, don't you, Gabby? Two houses down, between yours and mine. Every Halloween, the hole opens and he crawls out. On November first, when he sleeps, we close it. And then a year later, he opens it again. Can't say it'll help you, but who knows? Might be worth a gander. It's the grave of Benny Rose, after all."

Desiree stuffed the matchbook into her back pocket and headed for the hall. "We'll be right back."

Jesse and Gabrielle glanced at each other and followed. Desiree closed the door and led them up the hall toward the bathroom where they couldn't be heard. Rain pounded harder on the roof. Thunder sounded distant, on its way out of Blackwood. That should have been a comfort, but she had a feeling that most of the neighborhood would be searching if the storm couldn't keep them indoors.

"It's way past midnight," she said. "Halloween's over. Benny should be back in his hole." If Arthur was telling the truth.

"Remember what Sierra said?" Gabrielle asked. "In Blackwood, Halloween goes to dawn. Could we hide here until then?"

"We won't make it to morning. They're already looking for us. Soon they'll be opening their doors to let Benny hunt. They'll talk to each other, too. Eventually someone will realize Arthur's AWOL, or Benny's going to come to the house that doesn't open. And then he's going to get in." Desiree rubbed her aching eyes with the heels of her hands. She'd pulled all-nighters before, but never on the run. "Like I said, he's not stupid."

"Then we can't stay," Jesse said. "But the story's true. And this is the site of Blackwood Mercy Hospital. If we get out of here, he shouldn't be able to follow, right? These are his hunting grounds."

"We could try to forge the flood again. Maybe someone has an inflatable raft?" It sounded ridiculous as it left Desiree's mouth. "If we go, we'll drown. If we stay, he'll eat us."

"What was Mr. Donovan saying about the hospital?" Gabrielle asked. "Forty-seven dead, but only forty-one found? I don't get it."

He could have been trying to give them an unsolvable puzzle. He had every reason to stall for time, let the neighbors realize his absence. Benny would come. Grave. Hole. "I've never heard a Benny Rose story about the hospital and a hole."

"A lost Benny Rose story," Jesse said, transfixed as if she'd found a map to buried treasure. "*The* lost Benny Rose story. The one that's real. If we check it out, we could find something to stop him. Like, putting a ghost to rest? Or a vampire going back to his coffin by dawn?"

"Silver bullet." Desiree didn't want to hope, but Jesse did, and that meant it mattered. "And do we think Arthur's on the level?"

Jesse and Gabrielle shook their heads.

"Me neither. He's hoping Benny will spot us and follow us there. If we went down a hole, we'd be trapped. Why don't the neighbors up and shoot us and feed him our bodies?"

"They might not have guns," Jesse said, and then, her voice flattening, "He might not like to eat the dead. Like in the stories."

Desiree shuddered. If the only answers were in that hole, what choice did they have? "We'll check it out."

"What about him?" Gabrielle asked, thumbing at the bedroom down the hall.

"He could get loose. None of us are too good at tying knots.

Someone should stay and guard him while the other two sneak over to the hole." Desiree opened the linen closet and drew out another few sheets. "Help me tie these together. Whoever stays behind might have to escape out the window."

"It should be me," Jesse said. "Gabrielle knows which house we want and you shouldn't be alone with him."

Desiree scowled. "Why not?"

"Because I'm upset about Sierra, but you're heartbroken and mad like I've never seen you."

"Why shouldn't I be?"

"You should be. But I don't want to see this place go up in flames like the hospital after he says one wrong word."

That wasn't fair. Desiree was angry, but she hadn't really done anything. She never got to do anything. Every semblance of misbehavior was blown so wildly out of proportion by her mother, by everyone, that she hardly talked anymore. Jesse would've had better reason to worry about Gabrielle. Or Sierra.

Except Sierra was gone.

Downstairs, a phone jangled. A split-second later, another phone rang from inside the bedroom. The girls looked at each other, uncertain. Both phones rang again.

Arthur called from behind the door. "That would be my neighbors. If I don't answer, they'll know something's wrong."

The girls held still, as if the phones could hear them move. Another twin ring.

"They'll know you're here. Better let me talk to them."

"Who has the deepest voice?" Gabrielle whispered. "To pretend we're him."

The downstairs phone rang. The upstairs phone started to, and then cut off mid-ring. Desiree dropped her sheet rope and opened the bedroom door. The chair hadn't moved an inch. Arthur's fingers drummed the armrests. He looked pleased the way Desiree expected she'd look if she was about to be rescued. She darted toward the front-facing window and pushed the curtain aside.

The neighbors remained distant, dark figures in slightly thinner rain. At Arthur's driveway, a bone-white, naked shape crept out of the lamplight toward the front door.

Desiree charged back into the hall. "He's here!" She grabbed the fire extinguisher off the floor where she'd dropped it and chucked it downstairs. It hit the foyer's tile floor, where it cracked open at the top and swirled toward the living room, spraying white mist. However Benny hunted, she hoped the noisy cloud would throw him off.

Wood cracked downstairs. The girls carried the bound sheets into the bedroom, where Gabrielle shut the door and turned the lock. Desiree helped Jesse drag Arthur's chair toward the door.

"You might as well let me go," he said.

The front door banged open. Desiree heard Benny prowling below. He would figure out where they were in no time.

She threw open one of the windows that faced the house next door. Crystalline pellets now scattered the sill, the rain mixing with hail into sleet. "Quick, the sheets." She took the end of the makeshift rope from Jesse and snaked it out the window. Jesse fed her the rest until one end neared the ground, and Gabrielle tied the other end around Arthur's bedpost.

Glass crunched and then something clunked up the stairs.

"He's on the walls." Gabrielle spread her hands to each side as if bracing herself between two surfaces.

The doorknob jiggled and then the door shuddered.

Desiree grabbed the jerry can, tossed it out the window and hoped it landed in better shape than the fire extinguisher. Then she clambered after it. The narrow opening squeezed her back and hips, but she made it through. Her shoes squeaked against the house's slippery side. Jesse came next, slid through easier, and scrambled after Desiree. She was about halfway down when Gabrielle started through the window.

Something banged behind her, and Arthur cried out. He'd probably been thrown to the floor.

Desiree hit the ground. "Get down here!"

Jesse landed beside Desiree. Gabrielle squeezed through the gap and started down the sheet, but she had trouble gripping with her bandaged hand. A white arm lashed out the window and yanked the makeshift rope.

"You have to jump!"

The ascending sheet dragged Gabrielle to the glass, where Benny's hand grabbed her hair. Her socks slid against the house, giving no perch to stop to fight him. At last, she let go of the sheet rope. Hair tore loose in Benny's fingers.

Desiree and Jesse cushioned the fall, but they couldn't keep Gabrielle's weight. Her leg hit the ground at an odd angle. Her teeth sank into her lower lip, muffling a pained shriek. There wasn't time to let her absorb the blow. Desiree had to hope the leg wasn't broken as she grabbed Gabrielle's arm and pulled her to standing. With her free hand, she grabbed the jerry can. It looked in better shape than Gabrielle sounded. Desiree took one arm around her neck, Jesse took the other, and between them they propped Gabrielle up and helped her limp one-legged between back yards. Her left leg buckled, forcing her to lean.

Sleet soaked their clothes all over again. They ducked into the shadow of the house next door. Benny had to be coming downstairs by now. Desiree reached around Gabrielle and unlatched the back gate. She didn't bother closing it after she and Jesse helped Gabrielle limp through.

"Desi?" It was the first time Gabrielle had called Desiree that. "If important people like the town council knew about him, why didn't they stop him?"

Desiree wasn't sure. "Maybe they couldn't find a way to stop him."

"I was afraid you'd say that," Gabrielle said.

"We just have to make it through the night. Like you said."

"Until next Halloween."

Desiree studied her face, barely visible through the icy rain.

"I have nowhere else to go. Grandma will come back on Monday, expecting me dead, and whether I am or not—look, if you make it out, never come back, okay? Never come back to Glade Street." Gabrielle pressed her good foot into the ground. "Leave me."

Jesse gaped. "What?"

"I'm dead weight. He'll be busy. It'll buy you both time. We couldn't move Sierra. Cut me loose."

"We didn't leave Sierra by choice."

"It's not Sierra's fault you were here," Gabrielle said. "It's mine."

How far up the cul-de-sac was this, 10 Glade, 11? Rows of pines hugged the back yards and water rushed beyond. There was no escape through there, especially with Gabrielle's leg, but could they hide? Desiree looked down at her clothes, her hand, and recalled her plan to blend with the night. It wouldn't work anymore. Benny was too smart, and she hated herself for letting it cross her mind.

She slipped from under Gabrielle's arm. "Having nowhere to go is better than being here. Every time he shows up, we run. Every time we run, he gets someone. Maybe we should stop running." It made an insane sort of sense. Her hand brushed Gabrielle's shoulder. "Don't let anything happen to Jesse."

Gabrielle cocked her head to one side, confused.

Desiree pressed her forehead to Jesse's, eyes closed and thinking of Sierra. Thinking how she had fallen apart, become the weakest of the group, and then Benny isolated her. Of how Gabrielle would follow in Sierra's footsteps if they didn't change their way. And then Jesse.

"Keep each other safe." Desiree tore off between houses, the jerry can sloshing beside her.

"Desi, don't!" Jesse shouted.

But Desiree couldn't answer. She was too busy singing "Jessie's Girl" and running fast as she could.

FOURTEEN: ARTHUR

Those little bitches.

Arthur tugged his arm loose from the fallen chair. Hitting the floor had sprained his right wrist, but messed up one of the girl's pathetic knots. That wasn't their fault. Boys learned outdoorsman skills like ropes; girls learned to take care of the home, same as their mothers. But what kinds of mothers did these girls have? Gabrielle's was dead and the other two, who could say? That was the problem.

He clawed out of the chair and sheets and then tore off his pajamas. Not easy to do with his wrist aching, soon to be swollen, but he needed to be outside. He was expected.

He didn't blame Benny for hurting him. Benny was single-minded. That's what made him so dependable, but even Benny needed help sometimes. Dressed in sweater and jeans, Arthur started down the stairs. He had only hit the second step when glass crunched under his bare sole.

Pint-sized cunts, all three of them.

He hoped Marian, Mable, and Judy were getting a good night's sleep in Atlantic City while he pulled glass out of his foot. Hadn't he warned Marian? She wondered if they couldn't arrange Halloween sleepovers elsewhere for Gabrielle until she moved away or aged out of Benny's predation. What was the harm in letting one kid stay?

To think Marian had almost made him feel sorry about it until he saw that car roll up to Judy's house.

One teenage girl wasn't too many on her own, but it was never only one. Even the shyest kids weren't alone these days, like the schools forced other students to befriend them. Let one kid onto Glade Street and she'd bring more. And more. Give it a year, and there would be a drug-filled, music-blasting party in their once-quiet neighborhood. And if that party happened on Halloween? Kids disappearing into Benny's guts here and there kept the neighborhood peaceful, but they couldn't allow an outright slaughter. Town council would never live it down.

Really, Arthur was saving lives. These kids had to die so that others wouldn't come.

He bandaged his foot and bound his wrist in cloth. Then he stuck on a pair of old snow boots that had been cramped into the corner of the bedroom closet and stomped downstairs.

That little freak had snuck up on him. Girls were supposed to dress like girls, but probably no one had ever told her that. She could give a hit; he'd see how she took one. He opened the inside door to the garage and found his thick raincoat, among other things. Things the girls fortunately hadn't found when they stole his lawnmower gasoline.

Sharp things. Blunt things.

When he was a kid, it wasn't like this, girls running rough, probably hiding piercings in their bellies and tattoos on their thighs. Boys used to be better, too. Everything was. Where were the youngsters with a passion for baseball? Well, how could they have any passion when there were no more heroes in the outfield? He missed the old teams and dime store soda parlors and riding around in the bed of his dad's pickup truck. Sinatra used to sing on the radio. Even the bad stuff made his heart ache for the familiar. War rations, bomb scares, Ed Sullivan on the television. Black and white, not like the fat, color TVs they had now.

These kids didn't know how good they had it and they squandered that prosperity on crap at every turn. Running with bad crowds, putting spikes on their coats, worshipping the Devil. What was a church organ to kids who listened to electric keyboards? Bunch of screeching and nonsense. And the garbage they filled their heads with at the cinema wasn't helping. Blood and guts and sex. They didn't make movies like *Singin' in the Rain* anymore.

And these girls didn't seem to care how they'd find a husband someday, trading their dresses for jeans and leather, spiking up their hair like godforsaken dinosaur spines. Of course they couldn't stick to their studies and stick to their own. Had these girls done that, only Gabrielle would've died tonight, no one else.

It wasn't his job to fix any of that. He was only one man. Still, he didn't want it in his neighborhood.

He could've seen better had that freak not broken his specs. When he stepped outside, ready to take on the night, he found Glade Street brighter than he'd left it, but at first he couldn't tell why. Had someone turned up all the lights where Greg and Prudence lived? No, this light was flickering and inconstant.

Someone had lit his neighbor's house on fire. He had a pretty good idea who it was.

There, down the sidewalk.

FIFTEEN: DESI'S GIRL

Seconds after darting out from between houses, Desiree regretted leaving the others. It was one thing to do the brave deed and another to be friendless and alone at the edge of the cul-de-sac. She was afraid she might spot Sierra's remains, but there was no sign of her. Images flashed of Benny breaking and sucking down bones, of unhinging his jaw like a snake to swallow a fleshy skeleton whole. Desiree pushed those thoughts away. She didn't want to know what had happened to the body. Her friend was gone.

On her own, and not really alone. Benny Rose lurked somewhere near. Doors stood everywhere, but no one who opened them would help her. Figures drifted into the street, bent and stiff, hidden beneath umbrellas and slickers. They noticed her now. While she watched, they wouldn't walk beyond the lampposts and driveways, but each time she turned away and looked back, she found they'd treaded a little closer. One step at a time, they formed a tighter net.

She had to make it count each time she looked away.

She changed the lyrics of her song to "Desi's Girl" and carried the jerry can to the house next to Arthur's. Fumes overpowered the rain's damp smell as gasoline spilled onto the doorstep and under the front door. The first match sputtered out. The second lit the door and spread dancing fire into the home.

Benny caught her eye. As she glanced at the wider cul-de-sac, freezing the neighbors again, she spotted his vague white shape between 5 Glade Street and 6 at the edge of the lamppost light. He saw her too, but wouldn't pursue yet. To chase might make him look silly, and a thing with a face like his refused to look silly.

His eyes shined until he sank back into the darkness between houses. They were still watching her even if she couldn't see them.

She moved on to 11 Glade. Here the door had rubber lining she wasn't sure would let gasoline through, so she tossed a rock at the picture window and poured gasoline over the sill. In moments, the living room was ablaze.

On the street, the residents stepped closer, their creased faces made ashen by cold and rain. Arthur's crap about witchcraft almost seemed real. The old folk looked like an ancient coven, tucked away in a quiet Vermont town where no one would interrupt their Sabbaths and spells.

"Any requests?" Desiree asked. It felt nice to sound cocky. That had to be why Sierra used to pretend at it. Probably felt even nicer to believe it, to not be terrified. "Something from when you were kids? What were the top hits of 1812?"

They were stern-faced, unflinching. Waiting for something to happen, not yet ready to make it happen themselves.

Where was Benny? He had probably doubled back along the cul-de-sac's entrance, through the pine trees, moving counterclockwise so he could surprise Desiree. That narrow stretch of Glade Street was a trap. Ducking into the pines risked zigzagging over rough terrain where Benny knew all the best paths. She had to keep an eye out. The street was getting louder and she wouldn't hear him coming. The sound of sleet now mixed with roaring fires.

At 12 Glade, her jerry can was running low. One house after this would do it, the most important house, and just in time, too. She was starting to tire. Singing gave way to humming as she chucked a match at 12 Glade and started toward 13.

When it burned, Gabrielle really would have nowhere. She'd have to find someplace else.

A firm hand grabbed Desiree's arm and spun her around, shaking the matchbook from her fingers. She was already shrieking, expecting teeth, but this hand was thick with pockmarked flesh, poking from the end of an old coat.

Arthur Donovan glowered over her. His neighbors slipped closer. "Enough," he growled.

Desiree tugged at his arm. She was like Sierra now, isolated. She reeled back the jerry can and swung, but it ricocheted harmless against his side and clattered on the sidewalk. She pulled out the scissors. His free arm swung overhead, where a damp strip of cloth bound his wrist. In his fingers, he clutched a hammer.

It crashed across Desiree's left bicep. She screamed again, louder. The scissors flew out of her fingers and splashed into the street.

"I said, enough!" Arthur let go of her arm and shoved her to the ground. One boot kicked her in the ribs. "Benny, she's here!"

Desiree cradled her arm. She hadn't heard a crack, but something felt out of place and burned beneath her skin.

The old folk became one with the darkness around her, cutting off her escape.

She groped at 12 Glade's fence and struggled to her feet. Arthur loomed with his hammer. Behind him, flames ate through his neighbors' houses, casting his twisting shadow across the sidewalk. The sleet was softening, too weak to put the fires out.

"I tried calling the police and fire department," Ms. Carmine said. "All I get is a message saying every operator's busy. Typical."

"They couldn't get through anyway," a man said, someone hidden behind the others. "Whole way in and out's still flooded." They started talking all at once, a dry cacophony of surly voices eager to out-shout the storm, fires, and each other.

"But maybe tomorrow."

"She set my house on fire. What does the HOA say about that?"

"We should try to collect the family photos, at least."

"For Mable's sake, yes."

"What do we do, Arthur?"

"Kill her, Artie."

The elderly circle went silent. Desiree eyed them for whoever made that last suggestion. Though she could see their ghostly faces, she couldn't tell them apart.

Arthur turned to them. "Benny has to do it, Prudence. If we do it, there's a body."

"But if it's only this one time," Prudence said, a graven-faced woman who hugged herself. A sullen man beside her held an umbrella over her hunched shoulders. "Look what she's done."

Desiree bared her teeth at them. "Because of you. You're killers." They weren't listening. It was as if they did not see her as a person.

Arthur glanced at the fire. The blaze made his face glow orange and softened the layer of icy droplets across his skin. He was already shivering. "If we kill her ourselves, it doesn't work."

Desiree lunged at him, her hand clawed, nails out and hungry for his face. He shoved her chest, and she dropped on her back again. Before she could get her bearings straight, the hammer slammed her right knee. Stinging pain shot down her leg.

"In the head, Artie," Prudence said. "She set our god-blessed house on fire."

Arthur turned on the crowd again. "Prudence, enough."

"Yeah, shut up, you ugly-ass hag!" Desiree shouted.

Arthur beat the hammer against the same knee as before. This time she heard a crunch before she screamed and rolled onto her belly to protect her miserable kneecap. The cul-de-sac's flooding soaked into her shirt and jacket. Rain pattered in puddles and drummed on nearby plastic. On the sidewalk, in arm's reach, lay the red jerry can of gasoline, close enough to empty that it didn't spill even though it was sideways.

"He won't do it if she's dead before he gets her," Arthur said. "That's his way."

"But he's not here," a man said.

"He's here. He can't be anywhere else." Arthur paced the sidewalk, looking around. "He's probably on the prowl for Gabby and the other one."

Desiree outstretched her good arm, grasped the handle of the jerry can, and tugged it close. Some of what gasoline remained had poured into the street. There wasn't much. She cupped her good hand into the nozzle.

A boot stamped the back of her injured leg and ground its heel. She screeched, tears in her eyes.

"What are you thinking? Pour it on my shoes? Light me up?" Arthur let off her leg and plucked up the soaked matchbook. "With what?" He chucked the wet cardboard at her face and leaned close. "This is what I'm talking about. They don't teach you kids anything real these days."

He leaned so close she felt his foggy breath through the sleet. So close she could slam her skull into his forehead and hurt them both. But she only wanted to hurt him.

Her good arm slammed her cupped hand into his face, splashing gasoline in his eyes.

He reeled back shrieking, one hand wiping furiously. The other swung his hammer, but it missed Desiree's head by inches. She grabbed his jeans and pulled herself up by his belt, his shirt. Her knee hated her, but there was no time to stop. He was right, she didn't learn anything real in school, knew nothing about how long gasoline might hurt him or how fast sleet would wash it out of his eyes. Pedal through the pain.

Her hand closed around the hammer's shaft. He pulled it, but she wouldn't let go, so she hung from his arm off the ground. Her left hand grabbed the hammer's head, arm hating her, right knee hating her, everything screaming. The old folk shouted from the street. Her good hand let go of the hammer and beat at Arthur's bandaged wrist. His fingers loosened.

The hammer popped free. She passed it from one hand to the other. He groped blindly after it, caught Desiree's ear, and tugged hard. Her good arm reeled back. She swung the hammer at his skull, at the purple patch where she'd struck him with the fire extinguisher. She struck him harder this time, crunching his temple into the socket below. He let go of her ear and staggered back, his face slack and stunned.

She swung the hammer again, now at the side of his head.

He collapsed sideways against the fence, one leg under him, the other sticking out. She didn't waste time with limbs. She wasn't like him, trying to keep her enemy alive for a cannibal's late night snack. Her next blow hit the side of his head, the same spot. The hammer sank deeper. He fell on his back, one knee poking up. His eyes were open and red.

Around them, the neighbors stopped shouting. Desiree felt them leaning in, poised to intervene. They wanted her dead. She couldn't make Arthur's mistake of dragging this out. Go big or go home. And hadn't the neighbors said the road was still flooded?

She could not go home.

She stumbled over Arthur's knee, fell across him, and righted herself on his chest. His arm lazily shoved at her. She lifted the hammer overhead and swung it crashing down on his scalp in a wet crack. He twitched beneath her, but didn't fight back. She raised the hammer again. Had he feared this moment when he waved at her in the early evening, thinking he knew how tonight would go? No, they were only teenage girls. What could they do? He couldn't have foreseen what teenage girls could become.

Teenage girls could be demons.

The hammer's head slammed through Arthur's skull, caving skin, tissue, and bones in a thunderous crunch. Blood slopped into his gray hair, down to the pavement, and slid off the sidewalk into the cul-de-sac's larger puddle, where sleet diluted the red. The elderly circle slipped back together as if afraid the touch of blood might curse them. They had never seen anything like this before, had they?

Neither had Desiree, but she wasn't going anywhere. She lifted the hammer, its head painted with gore, and swung it in their direction. "You're next!" she shouted. "You're all fucking next!"

They shuffled off the street. Some turned from her right away; others backpedaled until they were sure she wouldn't rush up behind them with Arthur's hammer. Back to their homes, or neighbors' homes if theirs were ablaze. The bottom floors were alight in the second and third houses Desiree had torched. At the first, fire had reached the upstairs and set the curtains alight.

She slid off Arthur's body and stood shakily, left leg strong, right leg folding under her weight. Switching the hammer to her other hand, she grasped the fence and pulled herself up. Red stains coated the white paint where Arthur's blood had splattered. Somehow that felt worse than what the hammer had done to his head. Desiree turned away. The fence helped her hobble along, but she didn't need to look at it.

The old folk were distant now, slinking past lampposts. A couple still watched across the cul-de-sac, maybe Prudence and her husband with nowhere to go. The rest hid indoors. They would go back to peeking from behind curtains where they felt safe.

The air grew chillier. Desiree needed to get closer to the fire or get indoors. Something wet ran through her hair and down her neck, but if it was Arthur's blood, it would soon be washed away. She kept along the fence.

Her injured arm tugged behind her. She stumbled back with it and spun around on one heel.

Benny's black eyes glowed with firelight.

She hadn't been this close to him before, and the moment crept across her eyes. His skin stretched taut as his jaw slid open. His wet lips, so thin they were almost non-existent, popped open. Raindrops slithered down his nose and curled around his spreading teeth. He tugged her bad arm, twisted it at the elbow, and plunged his mouth against her forearm. Teeth closed around skin and yanked back, stretching tissue from muscle. The pain was worse than anything Arthur had done. His hammer thudded on the sidewalk.

Desiree's mouth twisted open, screaming again. Without thinking, she yanked her injured arm toward her chest and clamped her teeth onto Benny. Blisters boiled across her lips. Her tongue was on fire. Bloodless flesh of his arm snapped away in her teeth and left tarry bone behind.

He wrenched off her, his face wrinkled in a sneer. Like he was offended.

Desiree spat the pale lump at the sidewalk and shambled between two fiery houses. The fence helped keep her upright despite her pulsing limbs. Finger-shaped white burns blemished her dark skin where blood seeped down her arm. Her lips, tongue, and gums—she would rather have felt nothing ever again than live with these burns. There was no blood in her mouth, only a charcoal taste. Benny didn't bleed. She couldn't say the same.

But he hadn't taken a chunk out of her.

Mud sucked at her shoes. To her right, the last house she'd set alight smoked from an open window. To her left, orange light shined through every crevice. Which way? Benny was strong. It would take nothing to grab her again, pin her in the mud and grass, and clamp his teeth into her neck.

She could practically feel him. She glanced back.

Benny wasn't following. He paced the sidewalk, feet splashing in puddles, looking to her and then to his arm where a chunk of wet white flesh was missing above the elbow. A predator prowled here, patient only in the sense that he hadn't struck yet, but brimming with furious indignation that anything bit back. The pressure in the air rippled as grass would around a pacing hyena, but even that analogy handed Benny too much dignity. Desiree couldn't picture a proper comparison. He was a sickly scavenger, so weak and diseased that he could only ever prey on children.

What was he waiting for?

She veered left into the back yard behind a burning house. She needed a cane or stick. The fence led her toward where pine trees crept onto the lawn, but they wouldn't keep her upright. Hiding would be better than running. Benny wasn't omniscient. He couldn't smell her out through the rain.

Could he?

Fingers grasped her ankle. She almost screamed before spotting Jesse's face in the ground.

"Down here!" she hissed, hands beckoning.

No time to think. Desiree sat shakily into the mud, and Jesse helped pull her into a hole in the ground.

SIXTEEN: THE GRAVE

The hole had ragged edges. Desiree thought it might collapse while she descended on her back through mud, but it held. Water had washed inside and eroded soil, uncovering hints of sheet metal underneath, a skeleton to the slanted tunnel.

She landed clumsily against Jesse at the pitch-black bottom. "Where?" Her voice came out in a grating croak. It hurt to speak.

"In the hole that Mr. Donovan told us about," Gabrielle's voice said, not far away. "Only one way in or out."

Story of this whole night. Desiree tried to answer, but her lips stung.

"We did what you told us," Jesse said. "I think this was the spirit of it."

Desiree splayed the palm of her usable arm against a grimy wall and slumped to the cold concrete floor. The space, whatever its size, filled with the *tap-tap-tap* of water dripping into puddles.

"We smelled the fire," Gabrielle said. "And we heard you scream."

"What did they do to you?" Jesse asked.

Desiree needed a drink. Or maybe a new throat. "Light?"

"Give it a minute, your eyes will adjust."

She forced herself to blink. Each time her eyes closed, she

didn't want to open them. If she slept, the pain in her arm, leg, and mouth might go away. She pictured this underground place staying pitch black forever, never gaining form, never becoming real. It was the easiest thing she'd ever imagined.

Flickering light poked down the tunnel, where outside a house burned bright. After a minute, Jesse's floating voice took on a kneeling silhouette in front of Desiree's face. A moment later, Gabrielle was a dim shape seated on the floor across the room. There was junk everywhere, all sorts of mysterious black contours.

Desiree's injured arm rested across her lap. She covered her mouth with the other hand and shook her head.

"You can't talk?" Jesse asked. "Why?"

"Hurts," Desiree croaked.

Jesse's fingertip touched Desiree's cheek and traced toward her blistered lips. Desiree shoved it away with a grunt.

"Sorry." Jesse stood. "We've been sitting in the dark, listening. I didn't barricade the entrance since it was all our light and we were hoping you'd come. Not in this shape, but you know." There was a squeak in her voice. "I didn't want you to be like Sierra."

Desiree swallowed. Even that hurt. Crying hurt, too, so she tried not to. She couldn't tell the others that she had run to buy them time, that she burned houses to get Benny's attention. It was supposed to stall and confuse him. They were things she would've done for Sierra if she could. Things that didn't work out anyway. There was no telling them how sorry she was to have blown it.

Jesse drifted into greater darkness, toward the back of the room. The ceiling sloped there, sagging so close to the floor that she had to crawl.

"I think this was part of Blackwood Mercy Hospital," she said. "There's a metal gurney, all rusted, and a cabinet with some old glass syringes, medical tape. Crazy, right? The hospital burned down over thirty years back."

Desiree listened to Gabrielle's breath between Jesse's sentences, the *tap-tap-tap*, metal scraping concrete. She thought of Arthur's analogy about mud and wet concrete and footprints, a supposed recipe for a ghost, or whatever Benny Rose had become.

"I think someone was trapped down here." Jesse crawled to one side and stuck her hand against an indiscernible wall. "There are little notches up and down, one after another. Someone was trying to dig their way out, but not doing too good a job."

Tap-tap-tap. Desiree wondered if Benny heard that tapping while he slept the year away, his belly full of children.

He had probably heard it while alive, but it wouldn't have sounded like water's drip. Probably debris instead. This was a basement. If Blackwood Mercy Hospital once burned overhead, its elevator might have gone first, and the stairway could've been blocked. When the building came down, who would've thought to look below? This place was used to people shuffling around in its darkness.

Jesse dragged her hand down the wall in a dry scrape. "I don't think Benny died in the fire." Her shoe plopped across a shallow puddle. "I think he starved."

"Is that why he's like this?" Gabrielle asked. "Could we feed him? Make him stop?"

We are feeding him, Desiree thought. She rubbed the blistered tooth marks on her arm and was glad to be in too much pain to say it aloud.

Something metal crashed against a wall. Jesse was digging. "There has to be something, right? Unfinished business, bones to give burial. That man, Mr. Donovan, said they didn't recover everyone who went missing."

Not right away, but that implied they had been recovered. If Benny was one of them, someone had eventually found this room, pulled him out, and taken care of his remains. The man was gone. The footprint in concrete remained.

But what about the others?

Desiree forced herself to crawl after Jesse into the deep darkness, her hand propped against the wall. If she found crutches, she'd count that as a miracle. Instead, her palm scraped the same patch of wall that Jesse was talking about and found the notches. Each was about two inches long, little deeper than a scratch. No one dug their way out of this place by etching lines in a row. Desiree started to count them. Four, five, six.

Glass crunched on the floor. "An old clock. And I think these are called forceps." The cabinet creaked open under Jesse's hand. "There has to be something."

No, there didn't, but she needed to believe there was. Eight, nine. Had there been water pooling when Benny was trapped, enough to drink that he stayed alive this long? Twelve, thirteen, fourteen. The notches stopped where the wall had eroded, but even if there were only this many, fourteen days without food and water? Impossible. He'd had water. And food.

What had Arthur said? Forty-one people recovered right away?

"This feels like a hacksaw," Jesse said. "Do you think this was the morgue? Did he eat people's bodies?"

Desiree leaned heavy against the wall. Understanding seeped into her and she was glad again to be made silent. Let Jesse and Gabrielle keep shuffling around in the dark. Let them never see what reared up in Desiree's imagination.

At the center of his bullshit, Arthur had been telling the truth. The people of Glade Street didn't summon Benny. He was already here, had been here since Blackwood Mercy Hospital burned down when he was trapped underneath.

And he wasn't trapped alone. Not adults, but five kids, down here for reasons unknown when the fire ripped through the upper floors. He wasn't a monster back then, was he?

There was no Cannibal King before the hospital burned.

Those cannibal crimes, the campfire tales, all stories with their events mixed up, articles from before and after the hospital burning remembered out of order and twisted into the fantastic.

The real Benny might have worked at the hospital the day it caught fire, someone trapped underground with five kids. Maybe it was an unused wing, forgotten during the recovery. Desiree could imagine Benny and the children cowering in pitch blackness, no light, no hope but patience. Enough air for a time. The underground might have been bigger then, the ceiling not sagging so badly.

Tap-tap-tap. Water must have spilled out of a burst pipe and puddled on the floor, where rainfall gathered now. They did not go thirsty. And food for Benny and five kids? They might have held out for a while, but in the end, they found a way. An awful, hard way, but a way.

Benny might have been merciful with the first and killed him outright with a chunk of debris. They ate together, ate him raw.

And maybe it was Desiree's morbidity after the night she'd had, but after the first, with less food per kid, it would've been smarter to cut pieces off someone still alive to make the supply last longer. One by one, cut apart, eaten, and died, eventually. And was Benny supposed to starve before a child? Not likely. They might have come after him in his sleep, even bit a few pieces off, but he got the better of them. He was the biggest, the only adult. And what had Gabrielle said? A mother bear would eat her cub to survive so she could have more cubs. An adult could always have more kids.

But adults seemed to forget that dead kids couldn't grow into new adults.

Desiree smelled copper in the air. Down in the dark, rendered silent, her imagination could flex its muscles. Did she smell her blood right now, or the children's blood from over thirty years ago? She couldn't say. It was all the same. Blood in the dark in the grave of Benny Rose.

Cradle of the Cannibal King.

"Nothing," she croaked.

Jesse stopped rummaging. "What are you saying?"

Desiree waved an arm across the room. "Nothing."

Jesse looked over the dark, hopeless shapes strewn throughout the underground. Her shoulders sagged. "But the silver bullet."

"There is no silver bullet." Saying an entire sentence was too much like nails shredding their way up Desiree's throat.

She grasped the gurney and shook it. Jesse grabbed the other side and dragged it against the wall where it halfway blocked the hole. The flickering light thinned. Desiree wanted to help, but her leg was a mess, her arm even worse. Gabrielle limped deeper into the room to rummage inside the medical cabinet.

"Do you think he's coming?" Jesse asked.

Desiree was certain. If he wasn't ready to follow her down soon and find everyone he'd been looking for, he would descend by morning when was ready to sleep.

She didn't think he'd wait that long. Likely he had passed the yard above, gone looking amid the pine trees, and then maybe Arthur's house, but he would come doubling back soon. She could see him against the fire, realizing his mistake, that he had missed his own grave, but that was okay. He was on his way. Not in a rush, because the girls weren't going anywhere, but coming at his own pace and coming with a smile.

A gangly shape distorted the firelight. They weren't ready.

What else did they have to block the way? Jesse scrambled across the floor, picking up and lobbing debris toward the gurney. The pieces were practically powder. Desiree pressed the shoe of her good leg against the gurney's underside, but it wasn't heavy and she had nothing to brace her back against. Soil dropped, first in pebbles, and then with a heavy, displaced thump.

A spidery shadow crawled face-first down the hole. The gap

left at the mouth was slender enough to give Benny trouble, but not to stop him. One pale arm reached over the gurney, grasping for Desiree's leg.

Jesse slid across the floor and jammed her shoulder against the frail barricade. If only they had something heavier. Metal clinked from behind. Desiree glanced over her shoulder, where grunting Gabrielle stood on her good leg and tried to tip over the medical cabinet.

Benny's hand latched on to the rusted underside of the gurney and yanked his upper half through the opening. His head appeared, teeth parted. Every nerve in Desiree's body shouted for her to scramble back, but her body hadn't been listening to her when she split from the girls before. Every time they ran, someone died. She wasn't running. She raised her good hand and swept her nails across Benny's face, scalding her fingertips.

He didn't care. His teeth sank into the soft flesh where Jesse's shoulder met her neck and squeezed out a scream. White fingers pawed at the gurney's underside, looking to grab another part of her.

Desiree grabbed first and yanked back. Her good leg braced the floor and shoved off toward the dark side of the underground. Jesse snagged, caught between Benny and Desiree, until her sweater and flesh in his teeth tore off her body. She fell on the floor beside Desiree, screaming and crying. One hand pressed at the raw strip where skin used to be.

The same place Benny first bit Sierra. Desiree couldn't let this happen again.

Benny swatted the gurney to one side and lingered in the mouth of the hole, chewing a piece of Jesse. Faint light brought his smile to life.

He's still having fun, Desiree thought.

She dragged herself back as best she could with only one decent arm and leg. Jesse crawled alongside her, past where Gabrielle fussed with the standing cabinet. The darkness swallowed them and made Benny all the brighter when Desiree looked back.

Shrieking, Gabrielle put her weight on her bad leg and slammed her shoulder against the cabinet. It tipped over and landed where the ceiling began to dip, between the girls and the hole.

There wasn't anywhere to run. Even if they could get around Benny, escaping the hole meant climbing, and Desiree couldn't do that without help. She couldn't even stand anymore. The ceiling pressed down on her and Jesse. Gabrielle followed, first hunching, and then crawling in a hobble on hands and one knee, the other leg dragging behind her.

Benny finished chewing the flesh from Jesse's shoulder and crept back into the room. He was in no hurry. This place was home. He crawled toward the fallen cabinet.

Still sobbing, Jesse grabbed the cabinet's edge and tugged it backward. Desiree grabbed the edge, too, but Jesse was the only one with four uninjured limbs. She was trying to pull the cabinet so deep into the room that it could jam between the floor and ceiling, leaving Benny nowhere to squeeze through. It screeched at every inch.

His arm snapped over the top, halting its progress. A raw patch darkened his white skin where blackened bones poked through. As they had aboveground when Desiree tore the flesh from his arm.

Maybe there was no silver bullet to kill him, but this place mattered. The man had died in this underground where the monster was born.

He'd been right here decades ago, eating kids. He'd been right here when they tried to eat him back. And how could anyone know who ate who in the end? Sure, Benny might've finished off the kids, or the remaining kids might have finished him and then starved before they would eat each other. Who could say? The room had to keep some secrets to itself.

Gabrielle made herself small as she could. Jesse sat frozen beside Desiree.

Benny dragged the cabinet back. It rotated, still screeching against the floor as he twisted it out of his way. He was strong, but the cabinet was clumsy, not shaped for dragging across concrete. When he finished, nothing would stand in his way.

Nowhere to go. Desiree was tired of that.

While his hands were busy, she scrambled across the floor, injured arm and leg screaming at her, and sank her teeth into the side of Benny's neck. Her body forgot the pain in her limbs. This was much worse, fire burning against her lips and gums.

Benny wrenched free. His skin stretched between his neck and her mouth until it snapped off, leaving another exposed wound underneath. He had that shocked look on his face again. Stunned, the way Arthur had looked when she first struck him with the hammer.

Devouring kids didn't make Benny special. He was just another old man on Glade Street. The difference between the man who hurt her and the man she could hurt was who swung the hammer.

She spat his skin on the floor and lunged again. He raised an arm to stop her, but her teeth dug into it and tore flesh away with a sound like tape yanked off a roll, revealing tarry bones. There was no blood, little tissue. He didn't work like any living thing in the world.

His face curled into a sneer and then his black maw opened. She threw up her bad arm as he lunged and let him clamp down where he first bit her outside the burning houses. Let him finish what he started, chewing from wrist to elbow. She dove for his neck again. Tears rained down her face. She hoped enough nerves would burn away that she could stop feeling his touch, but the pain wouldn't end.

He finished mangling her bad arm, reared back, and hissed, startling her. It was the first noise he'd made all night. He pounced while she was thrown off and knocked her on her back. She started to sit up, but his white hand slammed her chest. Her teeth couldn't reach his fingers.

His eyes glared down on her. She couldn't see them, but like his smile, she knew they were there. She scratched at his chest, kicked at his legs and genitals, but there was no feeling in him. His teeth snapped open and descended toward her face. He was going to start with her eyes and work his way down. Blood seeped across her blistering temple.

Someone plowed face-first into the side of his head, biting and tearing off an ear. Jesse gave a muffled shriek. She hadn't expected how much it hurt to touch him.

His mouth turned from Desiree, his free arm groping for Jesse.

Another shadow swept over Desiree and went for Benny's face. Gabrielle bit and screamed at once, her mouth full of pale, burning flesh. She didn't tear away strips, but kept chewing, face buried in his infernal skin.

Hot fluid poured onto Desiree's shoulder. Benny didn't bleed, but Gabrielle's lower jaw had hooked beneath his temple and burst one black eye. Her muffled scream faded, her throat burning too hot to make a sound.

Benny's hand loosened the pressure from Desiree's chest.

She shot up under him and clamped her teeth onto the underside of his neck. She couldn't see Jesse or Gabrielle anymore, only felt them moving around her, and Benny swatting and snapping as they bit him. She didn't need to know what they were doing. All that mattered was that she wasn't alone. He only had one mouth against three, biting him from all sides.

The closest they had to silver bullets were teeth.

Desiree pulled back hard as she could and the flesh in her teeth went with her. His throat tore open, a gaping hole between lower jaw and collarbone. Nothing he swallowed would make its way to that distended stomach. His white hands patted at ragged, pale flesh. His remaining eye widened. He looked like Gabrielle when Desiree first sat across from her in the lunchroom, when they cowered in the car trying to escape, and every other time she'd been scared tonight. Did he remember this feeling when he slept? Did he remember the children he'd eaten down here who came to eat him? Their tiny teeth. Their hunger, no different than his. Everyone who ended up in this underground wanted to live.

But Benny Rose was already dead.

Gabrielle fell quivering beside Desiree. She couldn't stop to help. If she stopped, Benny would become the predator again. She wouldn't hand him the hammer. "Get up!" she tried to scream. Some kind of sound came out before her teeth sank into Benny's lower jaw and tore the flesh upward, exposing his cheekbone.

He grasped at her face and his fingers scratched a trail of blisters down her cheek. He was trying to fuse her mouth shut, like he'd done to Paul. She ducked, his flesh still in her teeth. She didn't think about what it would do inside her, only swallowed and dove after him again. He tried to stand, but the ceiling was too close, the space cramped so that his height and reach meant nothing.

Jesse tore into his face, teeth cutting open his cheeks and nose. He snapped after one of her limbs, but catching her wouldn't stop the biting. Gabrielle crawled on her belly, chomped into his middle, and tore open his gut. They would die tearing him apart. Three more bodies for Benny's grave when the old folk came to bury their mess in the morning.

No, someone had to get out of here alive. They couldn't let it be Benny.

Desiree grabbed his head in both hands, every finger burning, and scraped her teeth under his socket, where she ripped out his remaining black eye. It came rough but gelatinous, a lump of fiery jelly hotter than any other part of him. She spat it on the floor.

He was getting softer, messier. She went for one of his arms; the other already hung limp. Half the pieces she spat out, half she swallowed. They didn't do her throat any good, but they were headed where they belonged. To let him go entirely undigested might mean handing him the hammer. She wouldn't chance it.

He tried crawling backward toward the light. She kept after him, hurting her hands every time she grabbed him. A barren patch revealed part of his ribs and sternum. Most of his face was gone. Jesse slid behind him and chewed down the back of his neck. Gabrielle was on all fours, still tearing at his abdomen.

After enough eating, he was no longer a threat. Soon, he stopped struggling altogether.

They didn't touch his lower half except to keep his legs from helping him out of the hole. He trembled, more bones than flesh, his maggot-white skin lying in tatters around him. He didn't hiss again. There was no throat, no tongue. The only sounds were his scuffling feet on the concrete, the girls' heavy breathing, and their snapping jaws.

Lastly, Desiree clenched her teeth around his lips. He wasn't smiling anymore. She made sure he never smiled again.

SEVENTEEN: DAY OF THE DEAD

Jesse crawled first from the hole. Blisters ran down her lips and jaw, and her tongue was a burned dead thing in her mouth. Blood crawled from the bite below her neck. One shoulder and wrist were ripped raw to the muscle. Shoes bracing the sides of the hole, her stronger arm reached inside and pulled Gabrielle to the surface.

Most of her face was scalded red except where her mouth had been charred black. One eye squeezed shut where Benny got her as good as she gave, and fluid seeped down her blistered cheek. Breath rasped in and out. She might have swallowed his eye. She fell to one side of the hole on her back while Jesse reached inside again and pulled Desiree onto the wet lawn.

The fires were dying down and sleet had turned to white flakes, the first snow of the season. That might have helped cool Desiree's wounds, but she couldn't feel much of anything. One forearm was a ragged suggestion of flesh around bone, and the upper arm was broken halfway between elbow and shoulder. Her leg was no worse than Arthur had left it, but it hurt like hell. Her mouth was a slit inside twisted burn tissue, her palms scorched. Her throat and lungs burned with every breath.

No one spoke. None of them could.

Gabrielle quivered on her back, remaining eye glazed over,

while Jesse crumpled to one side and curled into a fetal pose. Desiree fell on the lawn between them, one ankle dangling over the hole. Pieces of Benny Rose fought her stomach acid for dominance. Either they were burning her apart or they were being taken apart to become her cells.

If she was dying, if all of them were, at least they weren't dying down there.

Snowflakes fell on their faces, and morning ebbed into the gray sky. The sound of rushing water eased behind the trees. Soon they could cross out of Glade Street anywhere they liked if they found the strength. Desiree didn't think they would.

She wondered if her friends knew what was coming. Probably not. They hadn't been up here when Glade Street's residents called for the girls' execution. Even if they guessed, they couldn't picture it like Desiree. She wanted to sleep, let everything that was about to happen wash over her.

First there would be sirens. Red and blue flashing lights would forge the shriveling floodwater, at last returning to where it belonged below the banks of Lemon Fair River. The lights would cross the bridge, pull up Pontiac Drive, and make a left at the sign that said *Glade Street Retirement Community*. The police would only see that the neighborhood was established in 1963. They wouldn't know what graves it had been built upon.

They would pass Paul's car. There would be nothing left of Paul, same as there was nothing left of Sierra. One unlucky car would have to stop and inspect, but the rest would hurtle into the cul-de-sac. The old folk would have screamed bloody murder when they finally got through to Blackwood PD, and in this case, they were right. No sign of Sierra, Paul, or Adrian, but past the potholes and puddles, bloodthirsty Prudence would lead the police to Arthur's corpse.

They would comb the yards next. Desiree could almost hear their shoes sink into the earth, hear firemen blast the smoldering ruins she'd left for them. They had plenty of water after last night. It wouldn't take long to find the girls.

If they promised to let her sleep, she would bite the bullet, even a silver bullet, and take the blame for everything. Only, her hands were too numb to sign a confession.

Her fingers crept across wet grass toward Jesse's mud-caked thigh, pawed blindly, and found her hand. She answered in a gentle squeeze. At Desiree's other side, she found Gabrielle's bandaged hand, which was limp. Lucky her. She was asleep already, so soundly that her breath was silent. Desiree held her hand anyway.

She wanted to tell them things. They should know how brave they were, how much it mattered that they tore that thing apart with their teeth. She wanted Jesse to feel at peace over Sierra, having made sure no one else would die here. She wanted Gabrielle to look forward to next Halloween, whatever strange shape it took in Blackwood without Benny Rose, somewhere far from her horrid grandmother. She wanted them to know they were strong.

They should know that, far as she was concerned, they had never been more beautiful.

Sirens wailed in the distance. Soon they would be deafening. Desiree pressed the back of her head into the grass and mud and shut her eyes. Sirens be damned, she didn't have to think about them. She could picture anything she wanted.

Wasn't Glade Street already prettier now that Halloween was over? Didn't it smell fresher, as if aired out for the first time since Blackwood Mercy Hospital burned down thirty-four years ago? Not Glade Street alone, but the town. A diseased presence had slipped away.

Blackwood had no mall, no movie theater. Kids milled around town square on nice days and anywhere else they could on others. If they drove, they drove someplace else, because in Blackwood there was little to see and only the woods to hear.

The town's one glorious night each year was Halloween, because Blackwood had one thing that no other town had in the world.

Benny Rose, the Cannibal King, and all the stories that came with him.

But not anymore.

Glade Street's old folk shouted at police officers, telling them lies about what they had seen last night. Old folk who weren't going to like living here anymore. Old folk who didn't know what it felt like to be eaten. Desiree wanted them to learn.

She wanted them gone, the houses vanished, Glade Street returned to autumn's red and gold that it had not seen since before Blackwood Mercy Hospital was built. Kids would cross Lemon Fair River and come here to run loose, outside their parents' grasp. They would play hide-and-seek through the pine woods or tag in the wide open space. Sometimes they would just lie on the grass, like the girls right now, and stare at the clouds in the day and the stars at night.

And on Halloween, they would tell stories. Not about Benny Rose—he was old news. They would tell about new ghosts. Blackwood needed new ghosts. New things were rare.

Kids would tell about the Happy Halloween Fires that swallowed homes in big jack-o'-lantern grins. They would whisper about Mad Desi who stalked dark streets with nothing but a hammer and a hate-on.

And they would make up stories about the Silent Sisters who crept into old folk's homes and ate their flesh.

Those would be the most popular of all Blackwood's ghost stories. The more gruesome, the better. They were about all the awful things that monsters did to children, but in the end, the dead kids got their revenge.

With open mouths and merciless teeth.

ACKNOWLEDGMENTS

Short fiction is the foundation of my work. That might sound bizarre in a world that idolizes the novel above all other fiction writing, especially coming from a novelist, but when it comes to horror, the short story is the genre's truest sense of self. You don't sit around a campfire and listen to a novel being told for eight to fourteen hours.

You sit down and hear a ghost story. It lets out a cold breath on the back of your neck before you can prepare for it, and it's gone before you can look over your shoulder and see no one standing there.

Many of these stories are strange and personal. I'm grateful to my agent Lane Heymont and to Daniel Carpenter and everyone at Titan that these stories could be brought together here.

Several of them had other hands helping them earlier.

Thank you to Ken MacGregor for giving "Why We Keep Exploding" a home with other stories of silenced voices, and to Matt Blairstone and Alex Woodroe at Tenebrous Press for exploding its reach, also letting it be part of Tenebrous's wonderful contributions to the Trevor Project.

Everything Samantha Kolesnik touches turns to gold, and "Unkindly Girls" is no exception. It quickly became (and might still be) my most popular short story. Thank you for bringing out the worst in me, in the best way. And thank you to Ellen Datlow for bringing it back to print ahead of its appearance in this collection, spreading the bleakness on and on.

Thank you to Sara Tantlinger in giving "Without a Face" a place among stories by so many wonderful women in horror. Getting to be edited by her is a privilege I hope more authors get to know in the future.

"Last Leaf of an Ursine Tree" has a bizarre genesis, spawning from Ally Malinenko and I lamenting an *Anchorman* joke and then the same day being tapped by Christi Nogle and Willow Becker for a story about mothers. It wouldn't have come to be without that one-two punch, and I'm grateful to all three of you.

I cannot remember which song provided the misheard lyric that led to "Hopscotch for Keeps," but what I heard was, "I got a hopscotch kid I've trapped in a jar." After marrying it to a blacktop park I remember from childhood, John Brhel and Joe Sullivan gave it an incredible home with stories of other unsettling real-life places.

The now-defunct *Monsters Out of the Closet* podcast could not have been a better venue for "Autotomy" to make its debut. I hope someday the hosts bring it back.

"The Turning" traveled a tumultuous journey both in where it might appear and even what it might be called before landing in the caring hands of Vince A. Liaguno and Rena Mason. Thank you both for letting these were-dactyls fly.

And thank you to Eddie Generous for this book's longest story getting its first home. *Benny Rose the Cannibal King* was originally a novella, part of the Rewind or Die series from Unnerving Books, all wonderful throwbacks to VHS-style horror. I had struggled with the concept of Benny and his carnivorous persistence beforehand, but the alllure of 1980s-era horror broke the dam in my mind, and out flooded the story of the Blackwood girls facing a terror beyond death. It was my first book contract, back in 2019, and has remained a Halloween reread for many Benny fans. I hope the Cannibal King will continue to stalk pumpkin-filled nights from these pages, too.

The following originally appeared in the limited edition book *Of Night Tyrants and Terrors*, which collected *Benny Rose the Cannibal King* among other longer works of mine. Thank you to Paul Goblirsch for giving me a chance to reflect on it. That Afterword is here:

> "Nostalgia is dangerous. It lies to us, tells us to miss the worst times of our lives because of some innocuous, unrelated sensation of familiarity—the particular way a bedroom window creaked when closing, the burn of an old sandbox cover, the open emptiness of a childhood dream gone sour. For some people, that pain is precious. Especially on Glade Street, where the old ways are righteous and anything new and young is soiled.
>
> This is not exclusive to fictional places. Teenage girls get shit on for everything. Their music, their fashion, their hair, the way they talk, who they talk to, on and on. Society says they can do no right. Sometimes, it says they should die for it, and a common slasher trope says only the final girl can make it, especially if she's pure.
>
> I didn't want purity, and I didn't want a solitary final girl. I wanted final girls, a unit, together, who wouldn't abandon each other to carnivorous selection but would either die fighting for each other or become the carnivores and tear through the night.
>
> Sometimes the only silver bullet is a teenage girl who's had enough."

Years later, I stand by all of it. Maybe even more than I already did.

I'm grateful to my friends who've been there through all this and I'm lucky to know, and a special thanks to Cina and Ally for letting me use some of their words to introduce my own.

Thank you to all the readers and booksellers, the people who share their thoughts and share my characters' journeys. These stories don't come to life unless you read them. I'm grateful to you for doing so.

Lastly, thank you to my wife J, always at my side, no matter how many ghosts and monsters are lurking there too.

ABOUT THE AUTHOR

Hailey Piper is the Bram Stoker Award®-winning author of *Queen of Teeth*, *A Game in Yellow*, *All the Hearts You Eat*, *The Worm and His Kings*, *Unfortunate Elements of My Anatomy*, and other books of horror. She is also the author of over 100 short stories appearing in *The End of the World As We Know It: New Tales of Stephen King's The Stand*, *Weird Tales*, Shirley Jackson Award-winning anthology *The Hideous Book of Hidden Horrors*, and many other anthologies and publications. She lives with her wife in Maryland, where their occult rituals are secret.

Find Hailey at *www.haileypiper.com*.

PUBLICATION HISTORY

"Why We Keep Exploding" copyright © 2021. Originally published in *Stitched Lips: An Anthology of Horror by Silenced Voices* by Dragon's Roost Press, reprinted in *Your Body Is Not Your Body* by Tenebrous Press.

"Unkindly Girls" copyright © 2020. Originally published in *Worst Laid Plans: An Anthology of Vacation Horror* by Grindhouse Press, reprinted in *Fears: An Anthology of Psychological Terror* by Tachyon Publications.

"The Long Flesh of the Law" copyright © 2025. Original to *Teenage Girls Can Be Demons*.

"Thagomizer" copyright © 2025. Original to *Teenage Girls Can Be Demons*.

"Without a Face" copyright © 2020. Originally published in *Not All Monsters* by Strangehouse Books.

"Last Leaf of an Ursine Tree" copyright © 2022. Originally published in *Mother: Tales of Love and Terror* by Weird Little Worlds.

"Hopscotch for Keeps" copyright © 2020. Originally published in *Places We Fear to Tread* by Cemetery Gates Media.

"Magical Girls Child Crusader Squad" copyright © 2025. Original to *Teenage Girls Can Be Demons*.

"Autotomy" copyright © 2020. Originally produced on *Monsters Out of the Closet*, reprinted in *Shattered & Splintered* by AEA Press.

"The Turning" copyright © 2022. Originally published in *Other Terrors* by Houghton Mifflin Harcourt.

"We Who Hold the Median" copyright © 2021. Originally published as "The Median King" in *Diabolica Americana*.

"The Many Sins of Clara Greenstone" copyright © 2025. Original to *Teenage Girls Can Be Demons*.

"Benny Rose the Cannibal King" copyright © 2020. Originally published as a standalone novella, *Benny Rose the Cannibal King*, in the Rewind or Die series by Unnerving Books.

For more fantastic fiction, author events,
exclusive excerpts, competitions, limited editions and more

VISIT OUR WEBSITE
titanbooks.com

LIKE US ON FACEBOOK
facebook.com/titanbooks

FOLLOW US ON TWITTER AND INSTAGRAM
@TitanBooks

EMAIL US
readerfeedback@titanemail.com